Also by Molly McAdams

The Rebel Series

Lyric

Lock

The Redemption Series

Blackbird

Firefly

Nightshade

The Thatch Series

Letting Go

To The Stars

Show Me How

The Sharing You Series

Capturing Peace (novella)

Sharing You

The Forgiving Lies Series

Forgiving Lies

Deceiving Lies

Changing Everything (novella)

The From Ashes Series

From Ashes

Needing Her (novella)

The Taking Chances Series
Taking Chances
Stealing Harper (novella)
Trusting Liam

Stand-Alone Novels
I See You

Coming Soon
Brewed Series

A Rebel Novel

Limit

Molly McAdams
New York Times Bestselling Author

Copyright © 2019 Molly McAdams
Published by Jester Creations, LLC.
First Edition
All rights reserved. Except as permitted under the U.S. Copyright Act of 1976, no part of this publication may be reproduced, distributed, transmitted in any form or by any means, or stored in a database or retrieval system, without prior permission of the publisher.
Please protect this art form by not pirating.

Molly McAdams
www.mollysmcadams.com
Cover Design by RBA Designs
Photo by ©Regina Wamba
Editing by Ashley Williams, AW Editing
Custom Illustrations by DeepFriedFreckles

The characters and events in this book are fictitious. Names, characters, places, and plots are a product of the author's imagination. Any similarity to real persons, living or dead, is coincidental and not intended by the author.

Print ISBN: 9781950048991
eBook ISBN: 9781950048984

prologue

Zachary
ONE YEAR AGO

"Sutton?" I called out, a cruel grin on my face.

Silence met me.

And I loved it.

Craved it.

This empty feeling that filled the house and was laced with anticipation and the knowledge that my wife was somewhere in this house waiting for me to find her.

And that slight hint of fear that clung to the walls? That only made this all the sweeter.

Made my blood roar and my cock strain against my pants.

"Oh, Sutton . . ."

I climbed the stairs slowly, dragging out these minutes the way I knew she liked.

Taking the time to roll up my shirt sleeves and loosen

my tie as I hit the top step before turning to make my way down the hall to continue this game we played.

She ran, and I hunted.

She pretended to be afraid, and I found her.

I *always* found her. There was nowhere she could go where I would not follow.

Hunt her.

Stalk her.

Claim her.

Sutton had always been mine, and nothing or no one would take her from me. Including herself.

"Sutton." Taunting colored my tone as I strolled past the framed pictures and closed doors. My heart raced faster and faster as I drew closer to her, and I knew she felt it too.

The anticipation.

The thrill.

The way even the walls betrayed her, telling me exactly where she was.

I curled my fingers into a fist and hit it against the wall with a low *thump*, letting her know I was coming.

After another couple of feet, I hit the wall again.

And again.

And again.

I could practically see her shaking in fear.

The way she'd fight.

The way she'd beg me to stop.

The way she'd succumb.

Fuck.

My eyes rolled back and I fought the urge to grab my throbbing dick.

I passed the room she was in to tease her, to give her a moment's relief, to give her that split second of belief that she'd fooled me before I silently slipped into the room, through the bathroom, and up to the closet.

Step by taunting step.

Fear radiated through the wood.

Her frantic, panicked breaths crawled under the double doors.

I fucking loved it.

I dropped my forehead to one of the doors with a soft *thud*. My mouth curled up when I heard her low gasp.

There was no point in trying the handle, I knew, because I knew *her*.

It was all part of the game.

Always for the game.

Still, I gripped the handle and twisted, my feral smile widening when I felt the resistance from the lock.

Placing my hands on the barrier separating us, I said, "Sutton . . . open the door."

Seconds went by without movement from the other side.

Little tease.

"Open the door."

My chest heaved with a harsh, irritated breath when nearly a minute passed, and I slammed my hands against the surface. "Open the goddamn door, Sutton!"

One

Sutton
TWO MONTHS AGO

I blinked slowly.
 And then again.
The whole room spun. The women's tittering voices sounded far away and too loud all at the same time.

I was going to throw up.

I scooted my chair back, quicker and louder than I meant to. Then I had to sit for a few moments with my hands pressed to the table until I knew I wouldn't fall to the floor the moment I stood.

I didn't realize until I stood on unsteady knees that the room had gone quiet and every set of calculating and judgmental eyes had shifted to me.

"Excu—" I swallowed back the bile that rose and cleared my throat. "Please excuse me."

My stiletto-covered feet hadn't made it out of the

formal dining room before the guests' hushed voices filled the room.

Speculating. Assuming. Teasing.

Bitches.

I kept my shoulders back and my spine straight until I rounded the corner and was out of their sight, and then I grabbed my stomach and hurried toward the kitchen, praying the little I had forced down would remain where it was supposed to.

"Nadia," I called out as I pushed through the pristinely white swinging doors. "Nadia."

"Yes, Mrs. Larson?" she asked, her tone both worried and anxious. The latter wasn't for me.

It was for this day and the pressure that had been put on her and the rest of the staff.

Pressure my husband had put on them by putting it on me.

"You've been hiding away too long, feeling sorry for yourself because you have a headache, or some shit. We have appearances to keep up, Sutton. An image to maintain. Do your part."

Appearances.

My entire life had been about keeping up appearances—my marriage included.

Nadia's eyes widened when she got a good look at me. "Oh?"

With one hand, I clutched my stomach, with the other, I pressed the tips of my fingers to my forehead, which was beaded with cool sweat. "I feel faint and—" I staggered against another wave of nausea. "Sick. To my stomach. I need something."

Worry creased the corners of her eyes. For a few seconds, she simply stood there watching me. With a delicate clearing of her throat, she murmured, "Yes, Mrs. Larson. I'll find some sparkling water for—"

"Sparkling wat—what? No. I need . . . I need . . . God. Medicine. I need that medicine to make this stop."

"Go back to the luncheon, I'll bring you a water."

"I don't want water, Nadia." I was nearly shouting.

The catering staff instantly froze. Five heads tilted in our direction.

"I don't want water," I repeated on a wavering whisper. "This has been going on for too long. I need something to make it stop."

"*Sutton.*"

The tone was low.

Harsh.

Disapproving.

As it had been my entire life.

I turned to face my mother, who was standing just inside the kitchen, the doors closed tightly behind her.

I tried to stand tall. Tried to appear unaffected. But the room was spinning, and I just needed to get my hand on that bottle of pills.

My mother moved toward me until she and I were nearly nose to nose. "I don't know who you think you are, but you do not make a scene the way you just did at a luncheon—especially one you are hosting. And speaking of hosting, have you forgotten how? I am beyond disappointed in you, Sutton Jean—Sutton. *Sutton.*" She snatched my arm when I stumbled into the wall and lowered her voice even more. "What the hell is wrong with you? Have you been drinking? It isn't even noon."

I took a shaky step away when she tried to smell my breath. "Jesus, mother, I'm not you. I just . . ."

Just *what?*

My husband dismissed my worries or said I was being *dramatic again* whenever I mentioned what was happening.

My housekeeper continued to downplay it by saying I only needed water.

Telling my mother would only make this worse than it already was. She believed in never letting others know you were anything less than perfect. Staff knowing you didn't feel well was doing exactly that.

A show in front of a luncheon? That was just unacceptable.

I'd already seen multiple doctors this year. I had been told the same thing—I was stressed.

Whether or not I was, not one of those doctors had done anything more than tell me their diagnoses.

No vital checks. No tests. No prescriptions. No nothing.

The last one, however, had cornered me in a store last week and gave me a bottle of nausea medication.

She hadn't said a word or even made eye contact.

Just stepped up beside me, slipped it into my hand, and left.

"Here you go, Mrs. Larson," Nadia said, appearing beside me with a goblet of bubbling water. "Why don't we get you back to the luncheon?"

I reached for the goblet on impulse, my weak words contradicting my movements. "I don't want this, I need— I'll get it myself, it's fine."

I pushed past my mother and headed toward the cabinet where we kept our medicines, not realizing until I got there that Nadia was attempting to stop me while asking if she should send everyone home.

"Well, that's absurd, don't you dare do such a thing.

Sutton, pull yourself together and walk back into that room with me."

My mother was still talking, trying to make herself heard over Nadia, but I wasn't hearing either of them.

I was staring blankly at the medicine cabinet that was full of spices and oils.

I squeezed my eyes shut and shook my head before looking straight ahead. Nothing had changed.

"Where's the med—Nadia, what . . ." I took a step back and looked around the kitchen, confusion pulsing through me as I wondered if I was in the right place. One after another, I opened each cabinet, my frustration growing each time I slammed one shut.

Nothing.

Whirling around, I demanded, "Where is everything, Nadia?"

Her expression was set in determination as she stared at me.

"It's as though you were raised by savages," my mother continued without taking a breath. "I don't even know you anymore."

I shoved the water at her, not waiting to make sure she had hold of the glass before lifting a trembling hand to point at the cabinets.

"Tell me," I said to Nadia, my voice a mixture of confusion and frustration.

After nearly an eternity of neither of us giving and my mother ranting, Nadia nodded her head in concession. "Mr. Larson asked that all medications be removed from the house."

If I hadn't felt faint before, I would have then.

My knees buckled, but I managed to grab ahold of the

counter before I fell.

"He what?"

It was a breath.

A pained denial.

"Jesus, Mary, and Joseph, you have a dru—I can't even bring myself to say it. After all we did for you? Your father is going to have a heart attack. What will the members at the club say? Oh, for Christ's sake, I forgot about the women in the—"

"Mother." I turned my head slowly to set my glare on her. "Will you please, for once in your life, shut up?"

If it weren't for the situation, I might have taken that moment to soak in the horrified look on her face so I could memorize it.

But I couldn't.

All I could hear were Nadia's words on repeat.

"Nadia, I need those nausea pills," I whispered pleadingly.

Her brow furrowed. "Mrs. Larson . . ."

"I don't care what my husband said, I need those to get through these spells."

"What spells? Are you pregnant?" My mother covered her shocked gasp with a hand to her lips. "Why you waited so long after having Lexi, I'll never understand. But it is what it is, we'll have to do an announcement."

"Christ, Mother." I slanted something that felt like a glare in her direction before focusing on Nadia again. "Where's the prescription?"

"Prescription?" Nadia said, as though the word were foreign.

I nearly grabbed her when I shouted, "The prescription, Nadia. The one in that cabinet. Where did it go?"

Her head shook as if the movement were an afterthought. "Mrs. Larson, there were no prescriptions in the house."

I jerked back. "I put it there last week. I took one yesterday!"

Nadia's head continued to move in slow shakes of denial. "There were only the usual over-the-counter medicines."

"Then someone stole it."

Hurt flashed across Nadia's face. "Mr. Larson gave me the job, and I took care of it. If you are accusing someone, then you are accusing me, Mrs. Larson."

Never . . .

Nadia had helped raise me because her mom had kept my parents' house—still did. When Zachary and I had finished building this house, Nadia had moved in and had been here ever since.

I trusted her with my life . . . with Lexi's life. She could be holding the bottle of pills, and I still wouldn't believe it was her who had taken them.

"Of course, I don't think it was you," I whispered and reached for her hand. "I'm sorry for the insinuation. It's just that this nausea and vertigo are getting worse every day, and those pills were a godsend. Maybe I misplaced them."

Except I knew I hadn't.

And one other person *had* known about them.

He wouldn't.

He wouldn't.

But even as denial swam through my veins, there was a small voice in my head whispering that he *would*. Urging me to search the house.

Because I knew the monster Zachary could truly be. I knew the games he liked to play. Dismissing what was happening to me and then making me feel like I was going insane would be the least awful game yet.

The sickening feeling twisting my stomach worsened until I was sure I would lose it right there on the floor.

"I think this has been a very big day for you," Nadia said in a gentle voice. "Why don't you get some rest, and I'll see to it that your guests are taken care of for the rest of the luncheon?"

My mouth popped open to refuse, but the words that came out were the opposite of a refusal. "Yeah, okay."

"Out of the question," Mother snapped. "Bright eyes, bright smile, and walk back in there as if nothing has happened."

I simply stared at her for a few moments, wondering if she ever heard the words she said. Wondering if they were her mother's or if they were all a product of a life she'd wanted to create for herself.

A life she'd forced on me.

"Women are allowed to be imperfect, Mother." A defeated laugh fell past my lips. "If the women in that room can't understand that . . . well . . . well, they can go fuck themselves."

I turned around, wide-eyed, and walked quickly out of the kitchen and away from the formal dining room. The entire time, I half-expected my mother to follow me and reprimand me for my lack of manners first, and my language second. When she didn't, I was positive that hell had frozen over.

Once I was sure I was alone, I took a detour to the first place my mind had gone to: Zachary's den.

It wasn't that I couldn't go in there . . . it was just that I never did and he knew it.

Quietly, I let myself in and shut the door behind me, and then I started searching. I went through every plant, inside every book, and flipped every cushion as I made my way through his den. I even moved the paintings and degrees on the walls, checking for hidden safes.

There weren't any.

By the time I made it to his desk near the far wall, I was shaking.

I wasn't sure if it was more out of anticipation or the wave of sickness crashing over me, but I was sure my body was screaming at me.

Screaming to leave the den.

Screaming to tear through the drawers.

Because I knew I wasn't going to like what I found.

I frantically scanned the contents of the drawers, but they turned up nothing. I jerked open the massive cabinet door behind his desk, and the contents had me falling to my knees.

My trembling hand . . . my thunderous heart . . . my racing thoughts . . . they all halted.

Lining the shelf were little white pill bottles, stacked three high and at least a dozen wide. There was a small container with pink powder on the bottom, and a chart taped to the shelf directly in front of it that tracked how and when to increase from a half pill a day to three pills. The switch to three a day had happened a month and a half ago.

I reached for one of the bottles and jolted when the sound of the few remaining pills clambering around sounded like glass breaking in the strained silence.

I'd never heard of the pill, but something about the amount, something about them stashed in his office, pulled at my stomach. As though I *needed* to see this. As though it had everything to do with me.

I pulled out my phone and took a picture of everything and then quickly searched the name.

My heart sank when I read the description. Increase sexual recall . . . aims to balance chemicals in brain . . . increase sensitivity to stimulation . . . fainting, dizziness, and nausea . . ."

A gasp tore from my lungs, and the bottle slipped from my fingers as the last year flashed through my mind.

Zachary suddenly making my coffee and bringing it to me in bed every morning.

Always asking how my coffee was.

If I finished it.

The way I wanted him . . . craved him in a primal, unnatural way whenever he touched me—or even when I knew his touch was coming. Even when he came home in that chilling, terrifying mood that I hated.

"Viagra . . ."

He's been giving me the female Viagra.

I choked on a sob and scrambled to put everything back where I'd found it.

Anger and loathing and disgust ripped through me as I hurried from his den and up the stairs, shredding me until I felt bare and raw.

I staggered to a halt when I rounded the door into our bedroom and found Zachary holding a stack of clothes.

The man I was meant to love forever.

The man I was *told* to love.

The man I hated with every breath filling my lungs.

A dozen thoughts and accusations and demands crowded on my tongue, trying to be the first to break free.

An excited smile lit his face when he saw me standing there. "We have to hurry. Start packing for you and Lex. It's time."

I looked from him to where two of his suitcases were wide open on the bed, but I didn't move.

Time for what?

Where did the prescription go?

Why do you have those pills in your den?

How could you do this to me?

I hate you, I hate you, I fucking hate you.

That smile slipped away entirely when he realized I wasn't moving, but then it was back in place, pure charm and fabricated sympathies on his expression as he started toward me.

"I thought you wanted Vero back," he said softly, false concern dripping from him.

My friend's name speared me in place.

Everything else faded away as my chest wrenched with that familiar pain.

"Of course, I do."

"Then why are you standing there when I told you to pack?"

Hope swelled for the first time in so long that it made my dizziness intensify. "Did you find her?"

He closed the distance between us, pinning me to the wall, and placed his hands on either side of my head. "Who are you?"

I tried to push him back, but Zachary gripped my fingers in his and pressed my hand to the wall, returning to his position.

"Who are you, Sutton?"

"I'm your wife."

"That was what I thought, too, but I gave you an order, and wives don't disregard orders." Every word was said with ease. Every word oozed charisma he'd mastered so well.

He could bait anyone into believing anything with that face and that voice.

Hide the monster I knew lurked behind it all, waiting just for me.

He was terrifying and sinister and cruel, and he liked to play games that fueled my fears of when he would appear again.

"Everything we've prepared for was leading to this moment," he murmured. "So, if you want to help us get Vero back, pack for you and Alexis, and don't make me ask again."

My head moved in a subtle nod, and I flinched against the wall when he shifted closer, capturing my mouth with his and forcing a slow, lazy kiss.

My body betrayed me. My breasts ached even as my stomach twisted with unease and my heart hardened and filled with more hate than I knew I could possess.

Instead of relief at finally knowing why he could evoke any bodily reaction at all, I only felt disgust.

"Tell me you love me," he demanded, his lips still brushing against mine.

You're my every nightmare.

I wish I could be rid of you.

I hate you.

I swallowed my truths and whispered, "I love you."

Two

Sutton

Two months.

Two months since we'd packed up and started the Motel Hop, as Lexi had come to call it.

Since I'd come to the crippling realization that the *plan* Zachary and Jason had been working on to get Vero back involved so much more than I ever realized.

So much I never would've agreed to.

Two months since genuine fear for our lives had entered my heart.

I'd barely slept. Afraid that, at any moment, someone would find us in one of the seedy motels we'd been hiding in.

All things I'd been instructed by Zachary to tell our contact at ARCK. For once, at least, the emails to her had contained some truth.

Stretched versions interwoven in rehearsed lies, but truth nonetheless.

Except, the responses on her end had stopped days ago, which was the most terrifying of all.

At some point along the way, my life, the prepared lies, and what I knew about the so-called ARCK investigators had blurred.

I'd begun to believe Lexi and I were in danger. Our contact's concern had sounded so real that I'd guardedly and reluctantly started believing her words and promises . . .

Believing *her*.

I'd even begun fantasizing that they were our opportunity to get away from Zachary . . . to get away from the world I'd been meticulously sculpted for and trapped inside of for my entire life.

I'd somehow forgotten they were only posing as private investigators . . . as people who wanted to help save us. Their silence made the truth of who they truly were come screaming to the forefront of every thought.

Every breath felt strained.

Every minute felt haunted.

I'd been staring at the thick, black-out curtains for hours—maybe the entire night—afraid that, if I looked away for a second, someone would somehow appear there. I was on edge in a way I'd never been before.

"Are you gonna email your friends today?" Lexi asked from her own ratty motel bed, her voice soft and raspy from sleep.

My head was already shaking before the question finished leaving her lips. "Not today, sweet girl."

I'm afraid to.

I'm worried they'll be able to trace us if I do.
They'll find us.

"Maybe tomorrow?" There was the slightest bit of hope in her dubious voice.

She didn't know who the people of ARCK were or what they had done. I'd told her they were friends who were having their own Motel Hop adventure, updating me as they went, and had been so thankful when Lexi blindly accepted the lie. She even viewed the emails as a small sliver of excitement in our otherwise mundane days.

"Maybe tomorrow." I caught sight of the clock when I turned to face her and sighed. "You need to go back to sleep."

"I can't."

I tried to make my voice soothing and teasing when I said, "You have to. Princesses need beauty sleep, and I think it might be against Princess Rules to wake up before the sun."

There wasn't a giggle.

There wasn't a smile in the darkened room.

And it crushed my already splintered heart.

I knew she could feel my anxiety, no matter how much I tried to conceal it. I knew my sleepless nights were beginning to affect her. But there was nothing I could do.

"I don't want to sleep," Lexi said softly. "I don't feel right. I feel funny."

I was off my bed and by her side in an instant. My hand went to her forehead as I spoke. "What doesn't feel right?"

"My dreams."

My breath caught, and I slowly moved my hand to cradle her cheek before letting it fall altogether as I sat back on my heels.

"Do you want to tell me about them?"

"Just Daddy. But then he was gone, and it was dark, and I was scared."

"Oh, Lex." Her name was wrapped in a whisper. "You don't have to be scared because he's gone. He's—"

"I'm not."

The immediate, almost angry response stunned me into silence for a moment. "What do you mean?"

"I like when Daddy's gone."

God, I do too.

More than you will ever know.

Even thinking those words had a white-hot poker slicing through my gut.

I could practically feel Zachary's fingers closing around my neck. Feel his breath against my cheek as he grit out, *"Know your place, Sutton."*

"Why . . . why would you say that?"

For a beat, she just looked at her intertwined fingers, but when she spoke again, it was almost as if she were afraid of anyone other than me hearing. "He has a bad-man's smile."

I jerked back and searched her silhouette in the dark room. "Alexis, why—that is an awful thing to say about someone."

"It's hidden," she said. "It's behind his other smile. But I see it."

I was utterly speechless.

I wanted to demand she tell me what she meant, but all I could see was a door opening and Zachary standing in front of me with that cold, cruel smile because, once again, he had found me.

My stomach soured and sank.

I hated him.

I hated, hated, *hated* him for whatever he had done to instill this fear in our daughter.

The thought of Zachary ever doing to Lexi even a fraction of what he had done to me had me pushing to my feet to crawl onto her bed.

"Has Daddy ever hurt you?" My voice was strained as I tried to speak around the knot in my throat.

"No." Her answer was pure innocence and confusion as to why I would even ask. "Does he hurt you?"

Relief filled me so quickly I nearly choked on it.

Before I could answer, Lexi gripped my arm with both of hers as if it were a lifeline. "I'm scared. Like in my dreams. Do you feel it?" Her gaze locked on the curtains, and her eyes widened. "Someone's coming."

I stared at her in stunned horror as I processed her fear. Her words.

It was just a six-year-old's dreams and fears, except it was exactly what I'd been afraid of all this time.

I hadn't moved or uttered even a breath when someone turned the handle of our door before trying to push it open.

"*Sutton.*" It was low and full and boasted control.

I reached for Lexi, but she was already scrambling out from under the sheet and into my lap.

Gripping her face in my hands, I pressed my forehead to hers. "Get in the bathroom and lock the door. Don't make a sound and don't come out, no matter what you hear. Understood?"

I didn't give her time to respond, I just set her on the floor and pushed her in the direction of the bathroom.

Once she was locked inside it, I frantically searched for a weapon as the man at the door continued to speak.

Words I heard but couldn't comprehend as I tore through my suitcase.

Lamps in these places were bolted down. I had bad aim, so throwing the Bible they provided was out of the question.

That left my stilettos.

"I'm opening the door."

I scrambled to my feet and gripped my shoes, fear and rage pumping through my blood as I stared at the door, which was slowly opening.

I would do anything to protect the girl hiding in the bathroom.

I would kill for her.

I would die for her.

And I had a feeling I would do one of the two right then.

"Sutton, it's—"

I charged with stilettos aimed directly at the man. A cry ripped from my throat as I launched myself at him and began swinging.

"Jesus, what? Fuck—shit, it's Con—would you fucking *stop*?" he roared and shoved me away as though I weighed nothing.

When I took another step toward him and swung for his face, he stopped the attack with a firm grip around one of my wrists and then grabbed the other.

His chest moved in sharp jerks as he stared down at me.

In the pre-dawn morning, with only the overhead exterior lamp casting any light and giving him an eerie halo, he looked more intimidating than any man had the right to.

Like a furious, avenging angel.

The man was taller and broader than any I'd ever met.

Tattoos littered his arms and hands and creeped up under his collar. Muscles rippled as he held me away and prevented another attack against him. As he prepared to take me.

Steal me away from my daughter.

I would fight until my last breath before I let that happen.

"After what I went through to find you, *you're* gonna attack *me*?" he asked, his voice gruff.

I struggled to get out of his hold the moment the words *find you* left his lips.

When I couldn't budge, I flung the shoes at his face and then lifted my leg to knee him in the balls . . .

And, suddenly, found myself stumbling backward.

I had barely caught myself with a hand on the wall when he stepped into the room and shut the door behind him, already talking as he did. "Let's try this again without you flying at me with goddamn shoes."

Another step into the room, and I jumped at him, fingers curled into claws to tear at his face.

My scream ripped through the room and cut off when he stopped the attack by curling his large hands around my shoulders and setting me down in front of the bed as though I was nothing more than an annoying dog jumping at him.

"Did I get the wrong room?" The man glanced at the door. "Are you Sutton Larson, or not?"

I was so focused on my next attack that I didn't respond, which prompted a breath of a laugh from him.

"Yeah, helpful as ever. I'll take that as a yes," he rumbled as he released me and moved to turn the lights on.

I blinked rapidly against their harsh glow before finally narrowing my stare on the man.

He didn't make a move toward me.

He didn't look around for Lexi—and he *knew* about Lexi.

He just stood there, looking as exhausted as I felt. Raking his hand over his face and through his scruffy beard before gesturing to the door.

"Did you not hear a word I said?"

My head moved in subtle shakes as my mind raced, wondering why he wasn't trying to kidnap me. Wondering where the FBI agents—who had been watching Lexi and me—were. Wondering if I was dreaming, because this was already going so different from how I'd imagined it would.

"About being in the right room?" I finally asked.

"Jesus," he said on a breath. "*Before* I came in."

I hadn't.

I'd been looking for a weapon. A way to survive.

My silence was answer enough, judging by the way irritation leaked from him when he said, "Guess that explains the attack, which was terrible, by the way. If I were anyone else, you'd be fucked. But we'll get to that."

And with those last sentences, I was sure I'd gotten this all wrong.

Sure that I'd forgotten what all of the agents looked like during these past two months, and my fears had led me to attack one of them.

My mouth opened, but he continued before I could speak. "I'm Conor Kennedy. I'm one of the owners of ARCK."

Not wrong.

Oh God.

"Why are you here?" The question slipped out, full of accusation and loathing, before I could begin to filter myself. Before I could remember the plan or the part I was meant to play in it.

Surprise and confusion flitted across his face. "You've been asking us to come save you, if you remember."

"Yes, for a month, and no one ever came. So, I'm not sure why you'd bother now."

I was shouting, praying one of the agents outside, or in another motel room, or wherever they were supposed to be, would hear and come help Lexi and me.

Conor's mouth opened to respond, only to shut for a few moments. "Months." When I only stared at him, he clarified, "You've been asking for *months*."

Shit.

Zachary's emails.

Goddamn it.

"And you know why we couldn't come," he continued. "You weren't forthcoming. We had to make sure we could trust you and that we weren't walking into a trap."

"Does part of that trust include Einstein no longer responding to the emails she demanded I send, or you breaking into my room before dawn?"

His head bounced in quick, subtle nods. "Something happened to Einstein. By the time we were able to get into her computer, you'd stopped emailing. We didn't have a way of getting ahold of you."

"What happened?" I hated to admit that worry laced my words.

But that presumptuous girl had been the reason I'd started believing these people were who they portrayed themselves to be.

She was the reason I'd started to believe they were coming to save Lexi and me from . . . Jesus, *something*.

She was the one who'd made me believe ARCK was concerned for our safety. Even though it was a lie . . .

Their true purpose masked by false pretenses of help. My fabricated stories and real intent.

All of it.

Conor rubbed his neck, unease covered his face. "We'll get to that. For now, I need to get the two of you somewhere else."

Fear nearly consumed me, unfurling in my stomach at the unknowns that awaited outside.

Making my heart race at the thought of what would happen to my daughter if I didn't do as Conor said . . . and what would happen if I *did*.

My attention drifted to the door for a moment, but there wasn't any sign of Zachary or one of the men that were watching over us. "I want to know what happened and where we're going."

Conor was watching me, patience and understanding in his bright blue eyes. "I'll tell you what I know when we're somewhere else. For now, I need to get the two of you in another place."

"No, I want—"

"I know you're running from your husband," he said harshly.

My legs shook as I took a step back so that my legs were pressed to the bed. "What?"

"But, Sutton, he knows where you've been staying. Zachary knows where you *are*."

The members of ARCK weren't ever supposed to know I had a husband unless they refused to help. I was to stay vague in my story of having witnessed a crime and being afraid for my life as long as possible.

And I had.

The last-resort story hadn't left my lips for months, since the last time Zachary had forced me to rehearse it.

Conor couldn't know it unless . . .

Oh God, Zachary, what have you done?

An ink-like dread poisoned my veins.

I had a horrible feeling whatever had happened to Einstein had to do with Zachary because the last day I'd heard from Einstein was the last day I'd heard from him.

Worries and doubts crept in, and I held fast to the latter, because Zachary's path was never supposed to cross with ARCK's.

He and Jason had left to find Vero.

That was all . . . that was *all*.

"He has information no one should be able to get," Conor continued in a gentle and somewhat hesitant tone. "But we have to move *now* because I have a small chunk of time to move you to the next place. Get your daughter, and let's go."

Everything he'd just said screamed truth twisted with double meanings and lies.

I would know. I'd been talking to them in the same way for a month. And those double-meanings? They were exactly what I'd feared most.

He took a step toward me, arm extended. "Sutton, we have to—"

"Don't touch me!"

He rocked back and raised his hands. Shock and uncertainty pulsed from him as he studied me. "I won't touch you. But if your first instinct isn't to get far from your husband, I don't think you understand the danger you're in."

"I understand just fine," I said through gritted teeth. "And I'm not going anywhere with you."

A stunned laugh punched from his chest. His head shifted in the beginnings of a shake, but stilled.

Blue eyes went wide.

Body tensed.

Expression shifted.

"Hi . . ." It was all hesitation and unease and pacification, and when I looked to my right, I knew why.

My daughter was standing there, looking ready to take on the world, starting with the man in front of us.

"Alexis, no." I rushed to her and wrapped her up in my arms, moving her back toward the bathroom door. "I told you to stay in the bathroom. I *told* you."

She waited until I'd knelt in front of her to murmur, "I thought he was hurting you."

"No. No, baby, he wasn't." I ran my hands over her head and searched her worried eyes. "But even if someone was, staying in the bathroom keeps you safe. So, you need to stay here until I come get you, okay?"

She just stared without responding for a few moments.

When she spoke, she said, "He's scary."

My heart faltered before taking off in an uneven, ruthless pace. "Scary how? Does he have Daddy's smile?"

Lexi shook her head and then tried to peak out the door.

I didn't let her.

"Can't you see it?"

I shifted to look at the man in question as Lexi continued speaking quietly.

"Do you see his smile, Momma? It's like Prince Charming's."

The laugh that escaped my mouth was breathless and coated with as much confusion as I felt. I was more torn than ever between what I knew and what I had begun to believe was real during my conversations with Einstein.

With every minute, I felt myself being pulled in the opposite direction. Knowing Conor was there to harm us, only for his words and actions to bleed with concern that seemed so genuine.

Zachary had told me that someone from ARCK—or every member—would storm in and try to kidnap us when they arrived. I'd been told to expect that repeatedly until it was all I saw when I closed my eyes, making it impossible to sleep.

But that hadn't happened, and Conor hadn't tried to harm either of us. Not only that, my daughter thought this terrifying man had Prince Charming's smile even though I was positive he hadn't cracked a smile since breaking in.

I looked at Lexi, my head shaking in bewilderment. "You said he was scary."

"Giants are scary, Momma."

The corners of my lips twitched into a hint of a smile.

If only I could see the world and people the way she did.

Alexis didn't see his tattoos or his terrifying appearance or that he broke into our motel room. She saw his height and connected that with stories. She saw smiles that weren't there.

I pressed a kiss to her forehead. "Yeah, they are kinda scary."

"Do you think he'll scare the others?" she asked when I pulled away.

My brow creased as I took her in. There was worry in her own eyes, and her little shoulders were trembling.

"Lex . . . honey, what's wrong? What others?"

"It's like in my dreams," she said, her voice full of emotion. "Can't you feel it?"

"I thought—" I glanced to the side to make sure Conor hadn't moved before dropping my voice lower to ensure he wouldn't hear. "That was just the giant coming."

Her head shook in quick jerks. "It wasn't him. Someone bad is coming."

Three

Conor

I answered my phone without taking my eyes off where Sutton was crouched in the doorway to the bathroom, talking in hushed tones to her daughter.

"Yeah?"

"Phoenix had the black folder sorted and scanned into files. Sending you the zip."

At Einstein's direct tone, I looked at the empty desk beside me. "Shit, my laptop's in the truck."

"Find one now."

"Not everyone carries computers and tablets with them at all times," I reminded her as I caught sight of a laptop sitting on the shelf of the bedside table.

She scoffed. "Not everyone is as amazing as me either. You're welcome."

Once I grabbed the laptop, I moved back to the desk as I filled Einstein and Maverick in on the situation.

"I found the girls."

"Did you?" Einstein asked dryly.

"Why don't you sound surprised?"

"Because she already knew," Maverick answered before Einstein could come up with one of her smartass responses.

I didn't bother asking how.

She could have my phone bugged, for all I knew or cared.

"What I really wanna know is how she is," Einstein demanded.

I blew out a weighted breath. "She's, uh . . . she's something, all right."

Maverick choked on a laugh.

I could hear Einstein's smile in her next words. "That good, huh?"

I grunted something like a confirmation and cut a sharp look at Sutton. "We probably should've taken the hint when she wouldn't give us any information."

"Okay, sent. Tell me when you get it."

"I'm gonna need—" My eyes rolled when I turned on Sutton's laptop and it didn't prompt me for a password. Gritting my teeth, I said, "Gonna need to teach this girl about protecting herself."

"Thought that was your job." Einstein's tone was pure tease before it switched to impatience. "Jesus, are you on a dinosaur? Did you get it or not?"

"Give it a minute." As soon as I was in my email, I clicked Einstein's message and downloaded the zip file. "All right, it's downloading."

"This folder contained more than we ever could've

imagined," Maverick said, something akin to awe in his tone.

I rocked back from the desk and ran my hand over my head. "Before we get into that, I think I figured out why Zachary was going by Alex."

There was a pause before Einstein spoke. When she did, her voice was softer, hesitant. "Why's that?"

"Their daughter? Her name is Alexis." My head snapped to the side in time to see Sutton fly at me.

Eyes wild.

Jaw clenched.

Reaching for my phone and clawing at my arms.

"He didn't even try to hide who he was from me, and I still missed it," Einstein said as I held Sutton at arm's length.

"It was just another part of the game to him," Maverick said through the speaker.

"What Maverick said." I grunted when Sutton got in a hit to my throat. Forcing her away, I sent her a warning look but prepared for another attack. "I have to go. I have a hostile client and files to read."

As soon as I ended the call, she laid into me.

"Who were you talking to? You have no right to mention my daughter. And who the fuck are you to come in here, pretending to help us only to turn on us?"

Every demand was a whisper.

Every word was said with so much passion and hatred it felt as though she'd screamed them.

Every question was met with a step closer to me until she was nearly pressed against my chest and looking up at me.

I folded my arms, putting a barrier between us, and spoke in a pacifying tone. "Protecting you and your daughter will always come first for me until you no longer need me, and I will be the judge of when that time has come. Your lives come before mine. I will not turn on you. Understand?"

She narrowed her eyes into slits and held my stare.

"As for the call? That was Einstein. I was getting information and giving some. Considering this is what we do? It was a normal conversation. Nothing could be used if anyone was listening, which isn't likely to happen."

Apprehension filled her words. "I thought you said something happened to her."

"Yeah. Your husband did."

Her brow drew together slowly. Something like acceptance and worry flashed in her eyes. "I don't . . . I don't understand."

I unfolded my arm enough to drag my thumb across the screen of my phone and pull up the picture Einstein had sent all of us before we'd headed separate ways for this case. "This your husband?" I asked, turning the phone in Sutton's direction.

"Yes." The response was nothing more than an apprehensive breath.

"He drugged and kidnapped Einstein. Then he locked her in an underground bunker that was some sort of a fucked-up game designed to slowly kill her," I said, locking the screen of my phone and crossing my arms again. "Your daughter's name came up because he pretended to be a man named Alex."

Sutton backed up as I spoke, the blood quickly draining from her face. "No, he wouldn't. He isn't—"

Her mouth formed a tight line.

I watched her . . . studied the impact of my words and the denial that bled from her, and tucked it away to tell my team later.

Whatever she'd been about to say was clearly begging to be said.

But she didn't continue.

"He isn't what?" When she only looked at me, I asked, "A sociopath? A master manipulator?" A breath of a laugh rolled from my tongue. "One of our guys is a human lie detector, and he never once picked up on your husband lying. But Zachary admitted everything to Einstein when he was taking her. Probably because he was sure she wouldn't make it out alive. If we'd been a minute or two later, she wouldn't have."

Sutton's head was shaking in exaggerated, jerky movements. "No, you're lying. He—he's—he does." She choked on a sob and swung a hand toward the door. "But he wouldn't do something like that."

I took a step toward her, and she backed away. "I nearly lost a girl who means the world to me. I had to watch her limp body be brought out of that goddamn place. And when she finally came to?" I said on a growl. "I had to listen to what your sick fuck of a husband said and did to her. So, don't call me the liar."

Sutton's eyes screamed denial and pain.

Her lips trembled with emotion.

Her shoulders slumped, and her chest seemed to cave in with each ragged exhale. "Why are you here?" she finally asked, her voice thick.

"To save you. To protect you." I stepped back and

shrugged. "But if you don't trust me, this isn't going to work."

A hitched breath burst from her chest. "I'm not sure I trust anyone."

"Then this isn't going to work," I said simply and sat at the desk.

I needed to get the girls out of this motel and somewhere safe, but I needed them to go willingly.

If I were to pick them up and shove them into my truck, I wouldn't be doing myself any favors, and I needed all the damn favors I could get with this case. Especially with someone like Zachary out there.

And she was still so damn far from being willing.

I had just opened the main file from Einstein when Sutton reached for the computer. "This is my computer!"

I pushed her hands away each time she tried to snatch the laptop. "I needed one."

"You can't just go through my things."

Exasperation leaked from me when I turned on her. "I'm not going through it. I'm using it to go through files Einstein sent me. You also don't have a password on this."

Her cheeks flamed with heat, but she lifted her chin defiantly. "That doesn't give you the right."

"The minute you asked for our help, it did. As soon as we get you out of here, Einstein's going to go through everything she needs to in order to make sure no one can find you once we have you somewhere safe. At that point, you'll already be on your way to that location and won't have a say because we'll be wiping this computer."

If I hadn't been watching her so intently, I might not have noticed the slight widening of her eyes.

This girl and her damn red flags.

"You keep asking why I'm here, so why don't you tell me why I'm here, Sutton." When she just stared at me hesitantly, I said, "You asked for help but won't tell us anything we need to know. I get here, and you attack me and then fight me on everything I say."

Her stare drifted to the bathroom and held there for a few moments before falling to the floor.

"Why am I here, Sutton?"

Glassy eyes flashed to mine, pained and vulnerable. "I don't know anymore."

It wasn't an answer, but it was the most honest she'd been since I'd walked in.

I shifted in the seat to start going through the file, but I had only made it through the first page when Sutton asked, "What did he say?"

There wasn't a need to ask *who*.

I knew.

I lowered the screen of the laptop and turned to face her, but she was back to staring at the bathroom door again. Worry and confusion and fear warred on her face.

Scrubbing my hands over my face and through my beard, I loosed a sigh and thought of what to say—what to tell her.

"Einstein was there, she could tell you best," I finally said. "But we just got her back three days ago. It's going to take a long time for her to recover mentally, even for someone like Einstein."

At that, her mouth twitched into a faint smile, as though even Sutton had come to recognize Einstein's tenacity and ornery nature in their short conversations over the last few months.

"He got her to agree to a date. Drugged her. She started

to notice the effects and panicked, and that was when he first slipped—called her Sutton."

Her eyes widened and met mine.

"That was when it all started clicking for Einstein—who he really was. He told her that she should've left it alone. Should've left 'her' alone. Said you taking his daughter away from him was a game and claimed that you liked the 'slow chase.'"

Sutton walked unsteadily backward and fell roughly to the bed.

Her hands gripped the edge of it.

Her head lowered as her chest heaved.

"Do you want me to stop?"

"No." The word was soft, almost a plea. As if she were silently begging me to stop while asking me to continue.

I blew out a rough breath. "Uh, he said he liked giving you the illusion of safety before letting you know he was coming for you. And that this"—I waved a hand to indicate the motel room, her freedom—"was an illusion, and he'd come for you when you least expected. But if we helped you, then it was game over. Because as good as he is at finding people, we were better at hiding them, and that he never said you could leave."

I watched her disbelief and grief and anger for a while before I understood that she wasn't going to respond and that I needed to give her the only privacy we could afford in this tiny place. So, I turned, opened the laptop, and forced myself not to give in to the questions and thoughts bouncing around in my mind.

Sutton had made herself known as a massive red flag in my family, and she'd continued to hold true to that in the short time I'd been around her. Vague and argumentative and fearful of the people who wanted to help her.

Women who were gaslighted to no end often denied and defended. With a sociopath of a husband like Zachary, Sutton was a prime candidate to be one of those women. But there was a difference between an impulse to defend a man you'd been manipulated by and Sutton's genuine shock over everything I had said.

Especially when we'd thought that was the reason she was running.

I wanted to ask her again why I was there, ask her why she'd begged for our help, until I finally got the answer she'd avoided all this time.

But I had a job to do—we all did.

Einstein was doing what she did best, going through any and every system available to her, looking for Zachary through calls and texts, card transactions, traffic and housing camera systems.

Kieran and Jess were watching my back and looking for Zachary here on the ground.

My priority was simple, and yet the hardest of them all . . . earn Sutton and her daughter's trust and keep them safe.

The hard questions could be asked later.

Besides, if I were to demand those answers before she trusted me, I wouldn't get anything.

I scrolled through dozens of pages, opened another couple of files, scrolled through even more, and then let out a low whistle.

Families.

Illegal businesses.

Front businesses.

People linked to the families and a very basic list of crimes they've committed.

Dozens upon dozens of bank accounts, all of which had in-depth files of their own, and that was just the beginning.

"Fuck me," I said under my breath and then scrolled back to the top.

"What's wrong now?" Sutton asked warily from where she stood at the window.

At some point, she'd started moving around the room. Walking from the bed to the window to the bathroom to whisper through the door and back again. Her restlessness filled the room and made me feel more on edge than I already had.

"What does Tennessee Gentlemen mean to you?" I asked, then turned in the seat to look at her.

"Is it a whiskey?"

The corner of my mouth twitched up before I could hide it. "No . . . no, it isn't. Einstein was working on getting a black folder from an acquaintance of sorts before she was taken. Think of a black folder as all the information and dirt on any person or family who deals in illegal things."

I had a black folder. Every member of ARCK had one.

But Sutton didn't need to know that. She didn't trust us enough as it was.

"She was trying to figure out what could've scared you so badly that you would reach out to us. With . . . your . . ." I hesitated when Sutton deflated on her path back to the bed.

Shoulders fell. Chest caved. Eyes filled with something that strangely resembled guilt.

"Uh . . . with your location and the little you'd given us,

she had enough to go on for this folder. But everything your husband said solidified it. She and her boyfriend went to retrieve it while I was traveling here."

"She went to get it even after what happened to her?" she asked suspiciously.

If Sutton knew the women I worked with had been kidnapped, broken, tortured, and raped, only to stare death in the face with a smile for those they loved, she wouldn't bat an eye at Einstein having gone back to work two days after what she'd endured.

She'd probably ask for lessons, because coming at anyone with goddamn shoes wasn't going to cut it.

"Einstein was the only one who could get it," I said in way of a watered-down explanation. "There's also no way anyone can keep her from doing what she wants—doesn't matter what she's been through."

At Sutton's nod, I tipped my head toward the screen. "The Tennessee Gentlemen are a cartel. They have people working for them all over the state, but they're based here in Brentwood. Drug and weapons trafficking. Sex Clubs." I searched her face carefully as I spoke, finding only genuine surprise and horror on it. "It's made up of five families—"

"Don't say Larson."

"Larson."

"No," she said adamantly. "No. No, I would've known. Zachary isn't involved in things like that. He wouldn't—"

"Wouldn't kidnap and drug a girl? Try to kill her? All because she was trying to help you get away from him?" I lifted a brow when Sutton looked at me with sorrow and humiliation and anger. "Yeah, your husband isn't all that innocent. I think you already knew that, or you wouldn't be running." The words were laced with meaning and unspoken questions. A thinly veiled attempt to get her to reveal anything even though I knew it was too soon to push for answers.

But I couldn't seem to stop.

"But his brother and his parents," she offered hastily. "I know them . . . they wouldn't. They work in energy."

"There's an energy business listed as one of the fronts."

"I don't know what a front is," she snapped, her tone desperate.

"A cover business so incoming money isn't seen as suspicious. Also a way to launder dirty money in and out without the government being tipped off."

Her mouth had been opened to respond, but it slowly closed. After a few seconds, she moved toward the window again. "How do you know all this?"

Because I lived this.

This had been my life for so long with Holloway that none of this was shocking to me.

"It's my job to know these things."

She nodded, seeming to accept the answer and stole a glance out of the curtains.

"There a reason you're looking out there?"

She dropped the curtain but was slow to look in my direction again. "I've spent the past two months worrying someone was outside wherever we were, waiting for us. Just because you're in here, it doesn't mean someone isn't out there."

In that moment, I had other things to worry about, like a client who trusted her sociopathic husband more than me.

Besides, if anyone tried to come in, I'd take care of it.

Not that anyone would make it to the door before Kieran stopped and silenced them.

I cleared my throat and brought my attention back to the screen. "Other families in Tennessee Gentlemen include Woods, Vaughn, Thornton . . ." I looked up when a heavy exhale left her. "Sutton?"

"Why are you doing this?" she asked numbly.

"Which of those names mean something to you?"

Her jaw clenched tight.

"Why are you doing this?" she demanded, her tone harsh.

"You wanted to know what was going on," I reminded her. "This is what's going on."

"Whatever you're doing—whatever you're reading—it's bullshit. You're doing this to see what I'll do. See how I'll react. Is this another test?" she asked, her voice raising with each question. "Is this another one of your tests like with the emails and the phone call? Say things that will upset me and see how I respond?"

"Jesus Christ," I said on a groan and dragged my hands over my face.

"Well, is it?"

I let my arms fall and looked at her openly. "Look, I'm normally a pretty easy-going guy, but you're pushing me. I drove over eight hours to get here and then searched motels for three to find you. Once I did, you attacked me, and it's been a nonstop fight with you since because, for some goddamn reason, you're more suspicious of the guy trying to protect you than the one coming after you."

"What do you expect from me? I've been living like this for months. I can barely sleep. I'm terrified. But then you . . . *you,* one of the most terrifying men I have ever met, came in to 'save' us."

I nodded, not knowing how to respond to that.

Knowing I *shouldn't.*

If she knew the background that came with the appearance, she would know her fears were valid. And that would only make this more difficult.

"I'm not trying to upset you," I finally said. "This isn't a test, but you had to know those were necessary. You wouldn't give us any information we needed. You were secretive, and what you did tell us wasn't entirely true."

Sutton didn't respond with anything other than a slight hitch of her chest.

"And I expect you to give a little. Not much, but enough for me to be able to help you. Because that's all I want to do. Now, which of those names mean something to you?"

For a long time, she didn't answer.

When I was about to continue with the last name, she said, "All of them." She swallowed, the length of her throat shifting with the movement. "All of those families were at our wedding. They're at every party. I don't know the Thorntons very well, but I know the Woods and Vaughn families, and that—" She laughed uneasily. "That's complicated."

"Uncomplicate it for me."

Sutton's eyes found me again, indecision and anger rolling through them before they darted away. "I've never understood why the Vaughns were around. The wedding, I guess I understood because they know my parents . . . but, God, it was awkward. Everything else—all the Larson parties? It never made sense. Zachary said his family didn't know theirs, yet they were always there."

"Clearly, they know each other if they're all in on this. Tell me why the wedding was uncomfortable."

She blew out a slow breath, a soft laugh lingering at the end of it. "My daddy pushed me into dating both Zachary Larson and Garret Vaughn and told me I had to marry whichever one proposed first. I had no idea they knew each other until the Vaughns showed up at the wedding." She faced me and forced a smile. "It was tense between Garret and Zachary, to say the least."

My brows were drawn tight as she spoke. "Pushed you . . ."

"Business," she said, as if that explained it. "Both families donate heavily to my father's company. He needed to offer an incentive for them to continue, I guess."

I glanced at the screen, at the last family that made up the Tennessee Gentlemen, then looked to Sutton. "Was your maiden name Camp?"

Shock pulsed through her so forcefully I felt it slam into me.

"Why would you ask me that?" Her eyes darted to the computer and then back to me. "Why would you ask me that?"

I reached for the computer to turn the screen toward her, but Sutton was already off the bed and stepping away.

"No. No, no, no. No, *you're lying*."

"I'm sorry."

"You're wrong. I would've known. I would *know*," she screamed.

I didn't know what to say or do, so I did nothing.

Just sat there, watching as she drove her fingers into her hair, sank down onto the bed farthest from where I sat, and choked on a sob.

Every few moments, I heard her repeated, muted whispers. "You're lying, you're lying, I would've known."

I waited until her cries had calmed and then said, "I need you to uncomplicate the Woods family."

She whipped around, hatred pouring from her. "Why don't you uncomplicate it for me, *Conor*?"

I lifted my hands in a placating gesture. "I just need anything that might help—"

"Why don't you tell *me* what the name Woods means to you?" She stood from the bed and snapped, "What does the name Vero Woods mean to you?"

I stared at her in bewilderment before glancing at the screen to make sure that name wasn't on the page, even though I knew only surnames were on the displayed page.

"Christ, I don't know why I'm even trying with you."

A grunt punched from my lungs the moment I stood.

She tried to slam her hands into my chest again, but I gripped her wrists, hauled her close, and waited until her hate-filled eyes were on mine. "I have protected women for most of my life, but you are, by far, the most infuriating one I've met. I think it says something considering I just fucking met you."

"Glad to be the first one who fights."

My brow creased.

Confusion swam.

At that second, I felt her tense and pull me toward her in preparation to try to knee me again.

I roughly released before she had the chance and ground my jaw to stop from lashing out.

"We've dealt with women who were unsure. Women who changed their minds about a hundred times during the process. Women who were even so gaslighted by their husbands that they constantly struggled with leaving even though they knew—they fucking *knew* it was the only way they could stay alive. And it all came down to them being terrified to their cores. But you? Fucking hell," I bit out. "Why you ever asked for help, I'll never understand. Because you clearly don't want it."

"I want my friend back," she screamed.

I stilled at the unexpected response.

"Tell me what the name Vero Woods means to you. *Veronica* Woods."

"Nothing," I said slowly. "It means nothing."

A sad laugh fell from her lips. She nodded and swayed on her feet before walking on unsteady legs to the bed. "Of course it doesn't. Just as Sutton and Alexis Larson won't mean anything to you when you're done with us."

Once again, I just watched her. Stunned. Confused. Frustrated. Fucking exhausted out of my mind.

"Jason Woods is one of Zachary's closest friends. Vero Woods was his wife. She disappeared about a year ago." Her hazel eyes shifted to meet mine and flashed fire. "But you'd know all about that, now, wouldn't you?"

It took a couple seconds for her words to register past her anger and loathing, but when they did, I dropped back into the desk chair and pulled up the file on the Woods family.

There were five families in the Tennessee Gentlemen, but this cartel had gone on for generations, and there was a file for each core family. Inside each file, there was another file for each family member that explained who they were, any identifying information, everything about their life from birth through the present—including but not limited to schools and teachers and love interests and pets and cars.

But the main file gave the basics.

Name, dates, spouses, kids. Photos of the above.

When I finally reached Jason Woods's profile, shock and suspicion filled me.

The hell?

I fumbled for my phone and hurried to call Einstein. As soon as she answered, I told her to hold on and linked Kieran in on the call.

"I think I have something," I said when I had all four people on the phone.

Maverick with Einstein, and Jess with Kieran.

I glanced over my shoulder at where Sutton was staring me down and turned so I was facing her. "But it might mean we have a problem."

Surprise flitted across her face, but I didn't give her a chance to react.

I lowered the phone and put it on speaker so Sutton could hear. "Sutton's been hostile since I got here . . . I think I just found out why. She was completely unaware of the Tennessee Gentlemen and what they do, who they consist of, but she knows the families."

"I don't—" Jess hissed as Kieran tried to stop her. "I just don't understand."

"Don't understand what?" I asked.

Jess made a victorious sound. "I was just trying to figure out how someone could be hostile toward you."

Sutton's eyes widened. Her next words were so soft I nearly missed them. "Have you seen him?"

"Apparently, it comes easy for some people," I

murmured. "Anyway, when I said the last names of the people involved, she got upset."

"Obviously," Einstein said in that way she spoke. As if she couldn't understand how people didn't know all the things her genius mind knew.

"Woods was one of the ones that upset her the most. I asked what the names meant to her, and she came back with what Vero Woods meant to me." For a second, the only sound was the rapid tapping of keys, and it was obvious it infuriated Sutton. "Vero Woods was Jason's wife. Sutton said she disappeared a year ago and that I would know about that."

"Holy shit."

Kieran and Jess were demanding to know what had Einstein so taken aback, but I could hear Einstein filling Maverick in with hushed whispers.

"Guess you found her?" I asked in a low tone.

"I don't understand," Einstein said, those words sounding foreign coming from her. "There was nothing linking her to Tennessee or Jason Woods."

"Maybe they weren't married," I said, offering the only thing I'd been able to come up with in the short time since I'd seen the picture.

"Someone please fill us in," Jess said, clearly annoyed to be left out of the loop.

"Veronica Garza from last year. She's in the black folder as Veronica Woods."

"Wait, you think Jason and Vero weren't married?" Sutton's angry tone broke through the shocked voices filtering through my phone. "Of course, they were. They were married for years. I've seen her credit cards and drivers license before, they were in her name."

As trying as the woman in front of me was, I felt bad for her.

Not knowing what parts of her life were real or a lie would have been a lot for anyone to handle.

"Did you see them get married?" I asked gently.

"Well, no. They . . . they . . ." Sutton blinked slowly, trying to think.

"Not saying what did or didn't happen, Sutton," Einstein cut in, "but I can create an entire new life for someone—including identifications, college transcripts, work histories, and credit cards—in my sleep. With what the Tennessee Gentlemen do, and what your husband had to do in order to slip past us, it's entirely possible that Veronica wasn't married. Everything I ran on the girl we helped escape said she wasn't married or even had a boyfriend."

"Everything you ran also said she lived in North Carolina," Kieran added.

Sutton sucked in a quick breath. Her eyes swung to me. "Jason met her there. He was on a trip. They fell in love and eloped. It was a scandal because it all happened without anyone knowing, and Jason had been dating someone else before he went there. It died out as quickly as it happened when Richard Westcott had his wife forced out of their home so he could bring in his twenty-something-year-old pregnant girlfriend."

"Jesus," Jess said with a soft laugh.

I grabbed Sutton's attention and lowered my voice. "I'm gonna explain what happened after I finish this call, but I need to talk to them first." When she didn't move, I gave her a pointed look. "You can't be here for this part of the conversation."

Her jaw lifted. "And you want me to trust you."

I released an edgy laugh. "Fine. If you attack me again, I will lock you in this room and sit outside the door to make sure you can't leave unless it's with me. Don't think I won't."

Jess and Einstein were laughing so hard I could hear them even though I'd taken it off speaker.

Putting it back on so Sutton could hear, I said, "I need everything you have on Veronica's case, Einstein."

"Sending."

I kept my attention on Sutton when I said, "The reason we might have a problem—"

"Sutton knew we helped Veronica and her parents escape," Kieran said, his tone as lethal as ever.

"Exactly."

Sutton's body turned rigid and her mouth formed a thin line.

"Either you knew Veronica was escaping or she's had contact with you," Einstein said matter-of-factly. "Considering your hostility and what you said to Conor, I'm going to assume the first is unlikely. So, I'm going to put another *or* in there and leave it at that."

"Even if you've had contact with her, she would've told you that we couldn't relocate you to the same place as her. She also knows the risks of contacting anyone," I said firmly. "So, I'm taking out the second option."

"Agreed," Kieran mumbled. "Now is when you tell us how you knew."

Sutton didn't respond.

And from the few times she'd done this already, I knew she wouldn't.

"I'm gonna talk with Sutton," I said with a weighted sigh. "Will update later."

"You should've been gone a long time ago," Einstein said quickly.

"I'm aware." I ended the call and tossed it onto the desk next to the laptop.

No sooner had it stopped sliding than it was ringing again.

It was Einstein.

"I know how behind we are, Einstein," I said in way of answering.

"Kieran and Jess haven't seen any suspicious vehicles or people," she said distractedly. "I'm doing what I can from here while Mav goes through the files. Now, put the angry one on the phone."

I put it on speaker and held it out to Sutton. I didn't let her take it.

Sutton's eyes darted from the phone to me and back again. "Hello?"

"You really love throwing up those red flags, don't you?"

The corner of my mouth tipped up at Einstein's boldness.

Instead of a comeback, Sutton's shoulders hunched. "I heard what happened to you. And I-I'm so—" A strangled sound climbed up her throat. "I'm so sorry."

"Yeah. Well. It happens, I guess." Soft. Subdued. So unlike Einstein it was alien. I knew it would continue for some time, but I didn't like it. "But that's why I'm calling. I don't know what this new information about Veronica will mean for you and us or why you actually contacted us in the first place. Any other case, we'd probably pull Conor out of there. But after what happened, I know none of us would be able to live with ourselves if Zachary made it back to the two of you."

Sutton lifted her head to look at me.

Something I couldn't comprehend fought and raged inside her.

Questions sat heavily on my tongue, begging to be heard.

Why are you here?

Why did you contact us?

What are you running from if not your husband?

"And, Sutton, we no longer know where he is," Einstein said, shame coating her words. "He had disappeared by the time they found me. He could easily be in Brentwood, which is why you need to let Conor get you to another place until we're sure Zachary isn't following you. After that, we can relocate the two of you to a place he'll never be able to find you."

"Why did you send me the scariest man you had?"

I barked out a laugh that was quickly echoed by Maverick and Einstein.

"Take me off speaker." The laughter in Einstein's voice abruptly faded. "And hand over the phone, Conor. I know you're holding it."

I tapped off the speaker and gave Sutton the phone, but I still watched her intently as she studied me, listening to whatever the genius had to say.

Once she ended the call, she slowly gave the phone back to me, her eyes never leaving mine.

I could see a change in them, clear as day. That anger and hate had shifted to confusion and unknowns. It wasn't trust, but it gave me the opportunity I needed.

I curled the phone in my grasp and folded my arms over my chest. "I'm prepared to explain what I have to in order for you to believe me. But we need—" I swallowed back the words and paused for a moment. "It would be smarter and safer if I got us somewhere else first. Once we're there, I will explain what I know. If you have questions that I can't answer, I'll find the answers."

"Okay."

That small, surrendering word nearly knocked me over.

"Grab everything. We need to move as fast as we can." I looked around the room. "What can I help you with?"

Instead of moving in a frenzy like I needed her to, she just stood, watching me. "You're really here to save us?"

The oxygen escaped my lungs in a rush.

I wanted to ask what she thought I was doing here.

I wanted to know why she was so suspicious.

I wanted a glimpse into the mess of thoughts in her head.

I lifted my arms before letting them fall again. "Sutton . . . yeah."

She nodded as she turned for the bathroom. Just before she reached the door, she looked at me. "Where are you taking us?"

"Can't say. We'll continue a false trail while remaining in something similar."

"That won't work." Before I could ask her what the hell she was talking about, she knocked on the door and asked for her daughter to open it.

Alexis came out the same way she had before, glaring and looking at me the way her mother did. As if she didn't trust me and wanted to be rid of me.

Awesome.

"I need you to start grabbing our stuff from the bathroom. Do you think you can do that?"

Her daughter nodded and disappeared back into the small room, and Sutton turned to me.

"Zachary knows where we've been." She cleared her throat and glanced at me. "That's what you said. Right?"

"He does."

"Then he'll expect us to stay in a place like this. Even if we do a . . . a false trail, or whatever you called it. He won't expect me to go somewhere nice, because that's the kind of place I would *want* to be in. That's the kind of place I'm used to."

"And if you've been doing the unexpected, he'll expect you to continue to."

A shaky breath left her. "Right."

"Smart. All right, I'll have Einstein look for places while we pack."

"I also . . ." She worried her bottom lip as she glanced to the desk. "*If* he knows where we are, then I can't trust that computer. I don't want to take it."

I ran a hand through my beard as that suspicion swirled and grew and then nodded. "Go pack, I'll take care of it."

I had Einstein on the phone before Sutton had pulled out one of her suitcases.

"Well, you sure do like hearing my voice," she said when she answered.

For a second, my eyelids closed.

For a second, my free hand curled into a fist.

For a second, I let all that pain and sorrow tear at my chest before I shoved it away and focused on the job at hand.

"I need you to look for the nicest place around here," I

said quietly. "Somewhere a wife of the Tennessee Gentlemen would go. Get me a reservation and directions."

"Here I thought one of you would have a hard request for once," she murmured dully.

"And tell me how to destroy this computer's contents."

I could practically feel her excitement pouring from the phone before she spoke. "Well, at least I get to do something fun."

Four

Sutton

I looked around one of the most luxurious suites the resort had to offer.

Lexi and I had come here for girls' days and shopping trips. Zachary had brought me here for dates and weekend getaways.

I tried not to show the immense relief I felt being in a place like this.

I didn't want Conor to know that I felt so at ease, so at home here.

But I did, and I could tell Lexi did too.

One look at Conor, and I knew I didn't have him fooled. He'd been watching me intently, which seemed to be something he did often.

It was almost as unsettling as the way I found myself watching the terrifying man back. But for the life of me, I couldn't figure him out.

This avenging angel who was saving us . . . when I had been so sure he was there to harm us.

Absurdly tall and broad and, with each breath, looking as though he were bearing a weight I couldn't begin to imagine. Blond, unkempt hair and beard that matched the tattoos I kept getting glimpses of near the collar of his shirt and swirling down his muscled arms to his fingers.

But his blue eyes stood in contradiction.

Warm and kind, and, even when narrowed into the calculating glare he was giving me, there was something so gentle about them.

The man was devastatingly handsome in a dangerous way. Though, I was loath to admit it, even if only to myself.

"Do I want to know how you got us into this suite on such short notice?"

"Einstein," was all he said, as if that was all the explanation I would need. He let his attention shift around the room before resting on me again. "Guessing this is better?"

Of course it was.

It didn't smell like stale beer or have cockroaches in it.

Not to mention, I felt safer here than I ever had in the two months trapped in the motels and supposedly surrounded by FBI agents.

Men I hadn't seen a glimpse of when we'd gotten into Conor's truck or while driving here.

Conor had noticed the way my attention had constantly pulled toward the mirrors, saying, "If you're worried about being followed, I can assure you that we aren't."

Except, they had been there the first day we'd been forced into the motel by Zachary—all six of them. And every day following, one of them stopped by at exactly nine in the morning to give us food and let me know if they were moving us to another motel or not.

Zachary had even known about the time I'd run from the room to answer Einstein's phone call at the front desk. I'd been sure whoever was watching us had informed him.

It hadn't hit me until Conor said we weren't being followed that I'd never seen any of the agents except at nine every morning. The cars they transferred us in were never in the parking lots whenever I peeked out the windows, and it made me wonder if they'd ever been watching over us at all. Maybe Zachary had only made me think we were being protected and kept in place.

An *illusion*, as he'd told Einstein.

I hated that man with every fiber of my being.

My shoulders lifted in something that I hoped came across as a shrug when I finally replied, "Yeah, it's fine."

A disbelieving laugh fell from Conor's lips. "Right."

"I don't need a place like this to be *better*."

He took a step closer to me, which was really more like three, and let the corner of his mouth lift into a small smirk. "I don't know many people who could stay in those kinds of motels long and not run around in excitement once they get out. Especially someone who travels with five bags and bedazzled heels."

My mouth opened in horror, my hands rose in a vain attempt to swat away the words. "Those are diamond encrusted."

"Jesus. Thank you for proving my point."

"Excuse me for having money and using it," I said through clenched teeth. "I'll try not to flash it in front of the likes of you again. If this room is too uncomfortable for you, you're more than welcome to stay at the motel."

"The likes of me?" His brows lifted, and his smirk shifted into a full smile.

And that smile changed everything about the intimidating man in front of me.

Because it was boyish and bright with deep-set dimples peeking out through his scruffy beard.

It was beautiful.

Damn it, it really did look like Prince Charming's.

I jolted when I felt a small hand slip into mine, and it was then I realized how close Conor and I had gotten to each other.

I stepped back and cleared my throat . . . and then cleared it again when I still couldn't form the words. "I'm sorry, that was rude."

He shrugged. "It's what you think." Before I could respond, his stare fell to Lexi. "Bet you're hungry."

She didn't answer. I wasn't surprised.

She hardly spoke to anyone other than Nadia and me.

"Well, I don't know about you, but it takes a lot to keep me going, so let's order food." When Lexi didn't respond, Conor slowly nodded and then forced a smile at me. "She's definitely your daughter."

I pulled her closer and narrowed my eyes.

"I need coffee. A lot of it. And a shower." He took a step back and clapped his hands. "Einstein's already running security on the place, but I need to know that you won't do something stupid the moment I let you out of my sight."

"Like leave?"

His hardened stare told me everything.

That he heard the bite in my tone. That he saw my protective stance, slightly in front of Lexi. That he still didn't trust me, just as we didn't trust him.

"Yeah," he said after a moment. "Like that."

Conor was almost to the room when I relented with a sigh. "What do you want for breakfast?"

He stopped walking but hesitated before he turned. "Told you I'm a pretty easy-going guy, Sutton. Trust me, and I'll trust you. Work with me, and I'll help you in any way I can. Feed me, and I'll be happy."

"And if I do none of that?"

He glanced from Lexi to me and then shrugged. "I'll still be the guy protecting you."

"You promised me answers," I said in way of announcing I was in the suite's living room that evening.

Answers I desperately wanted.

I wanted to know the truth behind Vero. I wanted to know why she left and where she was. I wanted to know why I was lied to about her disappearance.

I wanted to know why Zachary had lied to me at all . . .

"I thought answers would be better given after your daughter was asleep. You could've told me earlier if I was mistaken." Conor glanced up from his computer when I didn't respond. "I also told you what I didn't know, I would research. I've been doing that."

I wrapped my arms across my stomach and walked hesitantly toward the couch he was on. When I spoke, my tone was gentler. "And are you done?"

A breathless laugh left him. "No way in hell."

He turned his laptop so I could see the screen and then minimized the page he'd been on, revealing files upon files.

Conor started scrolling through them, never stopping as

he spoke. "See all these different files? There is a general one, one for each family that has ever been a part of the Tennessee Gentlemen, as well as files for their payrolls, the bank accounts they have in different parts of the world, front companies, hidden companies, and trafficking. Anything you could ever think of, and anything you'd forget to think of, is in here. Each file is anywhere from a hundred pages to thousands."

"Jesus. How did—" Dread crept through me like a disease. "Is Alexis in there? Am I?"

He nodded solemnly and watched as I sank to the couch.

For long moments, I couldn't speak.

The lump in my throat grew as I wondered what could be in the file about us. Wondered what Zachary and his family could be into that there would be files on us at all.

"What does it say?"

"I don't know." Honesty dripped from his words, and he blew out a sigh before shifting the computer back to him. His hand moved to it, but after a second's hesitation, he dropped it and glanced at me. "I'm not investigating the two of you; I'm protecting you. If you want me to know every detail of your life, I'll let you tell me."

My exhale sounded strained. "Thank you."

"The rest of my team is also studying the files and looking at the crimes. However, I am learning everything I can about your husband and his family, as well as Garret Vaughn, Jason Woods, Veronica *Woods*, and Aaron Thornton."

I nodded, but the movement didn't seem like my own. I didn't feel attached to it. "Why them?"

Conor leaned back and folded his hands behind his

neck, showing a muscled chest and arms in a way that was wholly distracting and completely unnecessary.

I blinked quickly to tear my eyes from him and focused on the couch as he spoke.

"Seems the Tennessee Gentlemen were able to go unnoticed for so long because they don't do their own dirty work. Their illegal money went through so many different washers before it came back to them that it was nearly impossible to trace. But Zachary and the guys in your generation seem to have changed the rules and have been getting their hands really dirty for about a decade now."

This isn't real.
This isn't real.
This isn't real.

"I've never—" My breath hitched, and I reached for my throat. Despite my best intentions not to, I looked at him. "I've never seen anything. I've never heard anything. None of this sounds like something Zachary would do. Or Jason or Garret."

He offered me a sad smile. "I haven't even told you what they've done."

"But they have files. They have—*God*. How could I not have known that he was into anything?"

"It *is* called Tennessee Gentlemen, so we're guessing women don't know, but it's just a guess. That's only based on the facts that none of the wives have ever been linked to any of the businesses—illegal or otherwise."

"I should've known. Vero even knew . . ."

"I don't think she was meant to. Fuck, she didn't even want us knowing." He ran a hand over his beard, seeming to think about his next words carefully before saying, "We're assuming Veronica lied to us about who she was because she knew we would stumble onto all of this. We received a frantic email from her parents saying their daughter needed immediate help or she would be killed."

My heart wrenched so painfully that it stole my next breath.

I rubbed at my chest, trying to figure out where I'd gone wrong.

"Veronica arrived just after us that next morning, no car, no bag, nothing, and she was adamant that they needed to run as far as possible but wouldn't tell us why. Jess overheard her telling her mom about how she thought *he* had only been cheating on her, that she hadn't realized what all he was into. But when Jess asked, Veronica stayed silent. When Einstein searched, there was nothing that hinted at even a boyfriend."

"Wait . . . you put me through tests, questioned me endlessly, and held off coming here for weeks, but you helped Vero without any information at all?"

Not that I wasn't thankful.

If she had truly been in danger, I wanted her safe.

I just didn't understand the double standard.

"It isn't hard to get a sense for who needs our help and what type of help they need," he said smoothly. "Those who genuinely fear for their lives, we offer them new ones. Veronica and her parents were clearly afraid for her life, and her parents were fleeing with her, whether we helped them or not. They also lived about twenty minutes from us, so it was easy to get to them and actually see for ourselves. You, however, gave us nothing but red flags."

I wanted to laugh, only there was nothing funny about this at all.

Of course, I had. Everything had been a fabrication to lure ARCK in.

Every word had been from Zachary's mind. Lies piled on top of lies to fuel the ones he'd been feeding me.

"Your name, and all variations of it for anyone around your age, brought up nothing in any of Einstein's searches," Conor continued. "When you emailed, it was always at the exact same time and from different accounts, which you always deactivated directly after. Granted, you said you'd witnessed a crime, but that was weeks in. You said you were afraid for you and your daughter, but that was after you questioned *us* and had already set off a shit ton of warning bells with Einstein."

Everything Zachary had done, everything he'd been so sure was necessary to catch ARCK's interest, had only raised suspicion.

After a moment, I wondered if that had been his intent. If he'd known exactly what he had been doing all along.

If, instead of going to find Vero, he'd kept everyone perfectly in place.

Lexi and me trapped . . . scared.

The members of ARCK right where he wanted them so he could get Einstein.

One giant game, and I'd helped him execute it.

I felt sick.

"Right," I whispered, the word thick with my loathing and disgust.

"The only reason you get to know any of this is because we're hoping you can help link together something that might be missing. For some reason, you knew about Veronica and had a skewed understanding of it. If you know the truth, I'm hoping it'll help with our trust issues."

He lowered his voice so it was soft and gentle. "But this goes both ways. You need to let me in too, and there are obviously things you know that we don't."

"I don't know anything helpful," I said after a minute.

"You knew about Veronica," he shot back immediately.

My eyelids slowly slipped shut.

"How you knew and what you knew would be helpful."

When I finally opened my eyes, Conor was staring at me pleadingly. "But, apparently, everything I knew was false," I whispered.

"Sutton."

"I thought she was gone," I said quickly. "They made it seem as if she disappeared. *Jason* made it seem as if she'd disappeared."

"Then how did you know to contact us?"

I swallowed back the plan and the lies and how Zachary had pretended to be me, and struggled to search for any form of the truth I could give him . . . and found none. "Someone knew," I finally said. "Where I'm from, things like that don't stay quiet. Gossip moves quicker than wildfire."

Conor murmured a curse and pulled out his phone, sending off a quick text. "That changes things."

"What things?" For some inane reason, I was worried he was going to abandon us.

"We need to make sure she and her parents are okay. We also need to know *why* you're running." He studied me for a moment and then lifted a hand. "For the life of me, I can't figure it out. I can't figure you out. I'm not even sure you *are* running, Sutton."

He was right, of course. Not that I hadn't wanted to

leave Zachary for years, but leaving someone like him wasn't exactly simple.

Some relationships are arranged and kept for appearances.

Some marriages solidify family alliances or business relationships.

Mine was one of those.

It linked prominent families together. It fueled businesses.

Besides, if I'd left, I would've had nowhere to go. There would've been no security for Lexi, and I knew . . . God, I knew Zachary would've taken her from me even though he wanted nothing to do with her.

That didn't mean I hadn't fantasized of a life where I wasn't his wife. Where I wasn't his to control and shape and dictate. Where I didn't live in fear of the next time he would come home, wanting to play a game.

"I am running," I admitted softly.

I *hadn't* been, but I knew what it felt like to run from Zachary, to be chased by him. Even though my feet were firmly planted on the floor, I knew deep in my gut that I *was* running from him.

And by some insane turn of events, Conor and Einstein and the people at ARCK had given Lexi and me this opportunity we never would've had before.

"It's just that . . . the man you're telling me about is a different monster from the one I know."

"Both of them Zachary?" he asked in way of clarifying.

I dipped my head in a nod.

Conor blew out a slow breath, seeming to think while he did. "Okay . . . okay, all right. Do you know where he is —where he might be hiding?"

"I can't think of anywhere he'd go." I rubbed at my temple. "God, this doesn't seem real to me, that he would be hiding anywhere. He works, he comes home, he has drinks and plays poker with his friends—but you already know them, apparently. We go to functions and parties. His family has a house on the lake."

"Which lake?"

"Old Hickory."

Conor glanced at his laptop before shaking his head. "I probably haven't gotten to it yet."

"I don't understand how any of this could happen right in front of me without my noticing. Not just Zachary, but my father too. And Vero . . ." I shrugged helplessly and sagged against the cushions. "She was my best friend. She wasn't like the stuck-up debutant bitches I grew up with or the women we had brunches with to keep appearances—"

"She wasn't like you?"

My lips slowly parted in offense, but when I looked at Conor, he was fighting a smile.

"I guess I deserved that," I conceded. "No, Vero wasn't like me. She was . . . Vero was real. To know she went through this kills me. When she disappeared . . ."

I wasn't sure I could say the words because it had utterly wrecked me.

When I'd found out she had been taken from her home and sold in a sex ring, I'd grieved for weeks.

Only to find out today that it was a lie? To find out that my entire life was?

"Anyway," I said thickly and choked out a laugh. "What kind of friend was I if she couldn't even come to me when she thought Jason was sleeping around, or when she found out whatever else he was involved in?"

Conor didn't say anything, and I didn't want him to.

He just sat there for a minute, watchful as ever, before standing and bringing the laptop toward me.

"I gathered what I figured you would want to know and put it in one place. It starts with what little we had on Veronica. If you ever want to stop reading or need to take a break, I'll understand."

"Where are you going?"

He glanced over his shoulder and gave me another sad smile. "Just making a call."

I watched him leave the room before focusing on the screen.

Just seeing Vero's picture had my throat tightening and my eyes burning with unshed tears.

This day had been too much.

These months were too stressful and lacked far too much sleep.

I contemplated telling Conor I would wait to read the file until the morning when I felt more emotionally and mentally stable, but I knew I wouldn't be able to sleep if I didn't know what hid within these pages.

Conor was back before I made it to the third page, but he didn't sit on the couch and he didn't say anything. He just stood against the wall with his head tilted back and arms folded over his chest.

I considered the likelihood of him being able to sleep like that for a long moment before realizing that I was watching him again.

Blowing out a heavy breath, I returned my attention to the screen and continued reading about Veronica's life before she met Jason. Her parents' plea to ARCK, and the little information the ARCK team had gathered during their time with them.

Then the pages shifted to the Tennessee Gentlemen and turned into something straight out of a suspense novel.

One that wasn't my life . . . except it was, and I'd been too naïve to notice.

Murders. Weapons. Drugs. Payoffs. Sex clubs. And my husband.

My husband, my husband, my husband.

Zachary and his friends were everywhere. *My* friends were everywhere.

My father and father-in-law.

Other men I'd grown up knowing.

No matter how much I wanted to deny it, there was identifying information that made it impossible to refute.

There were pictures and bank statements and copies of letters and transcripts of phone calls.

When I thought about the man I knew my husband could be, I wondered if I should've known all along.

Sometime later, there was a knock on the door, and my blurred gaze shifted to Conor. He was completely unaffected by the idea of someone coming to the room this late at night.

When he came back, I realized why.

He was carrying a tray laden with ice cream and toppings, which he set on the couch next to me.

"I've heard it makes everything better."

I looked at him, shock and awe pulsing from me, but he was walking to his spot against the wall.

As soon as he reached it, he leaned back with his eyes closed and arms folded over his chest.

I glanced at the tray and stupidly felt like crying. My mother would be so disappointed.

Blinking away the tears before they could fully form, I asked, "Did you want any?"

He cracked open an eye and then let it close again. "Have a girl call me terrifying and then poor? That's nothing I need to recover from." His words were all tease and matched the smile slowly forming on his face.

Shame filled me and flamed at my cheeks. "I am sorry for that."

"Sorry you think it or sorry you said it?" The tease and smile were gone, and his stoic expression was back in place.

"Conor—"

"Eat. Read. I'll be here."

I tried to think of something that would've made up for my earlier words, but nothing would.

He was right.

I was sorry that I'd said what I had.

I was embarrassed that I'd acted like my mother. Embarrassed by the way I'd assumed and judged. But I still thought it, and he knew it.

The moment I picked up the bowl of ice cream from that terrifying man who, for some unfathomable reason, was still willing to protect us, I hated myself a little bit.

I crossed my legs, brought the bowl to my chest, and then turned my attention to the screen, which was where it stayed until the early hours of the morning when I finally fell asleep.

Heart full of pain.

Full of hate.

And broken.

Five

Zachary

"Sir?"

Garret looked toward the sound of one of his overcompensated nerds, brows lifted in question.

"Uh, no, sorry. Mr. Larson?"

I leaned forward and roughly set the tumbler of whiskey onto the table in front of me, slanting a glare in the direction of the man standing in the doorway. "Is there a reason you aren't glued to a chair?"

The man visibly paled and forced a swallow. "I'm sorry, I'm sorry, it's just that there's a call on the burner phone." He held up the phone in question, which was still lit with a call. "You-you left it. In the room. With us."

"Give it to me," I demanded, arm outstretched.

"I answered it," he continued.

"I can fucking see that, give it to me."

"I'm sorry. I'm sorry, Mr. Larson." He hurried to hand

me the phone. Before I could take it, he said, "I'm sorry for what you're about to hear."

Garret's chest shook with a harsh exhale. His attention snapped from the nerd to me and back again. "Is it Sutton?"

The nerd stepped slowly back, hands lifting at his sides. "I'm just—I'm sorry."

Garret stood, already seething, and kicked the table, sending my drink flying across the room so hard the glass shattered. "I told you. I fucking told you what would happen to her."

I didn't move or flinch, just held his murderous stare and pressed the phone to my ear. "What happened?"

There was a sigh on the other end of the line before one of my hired men said, "She's gone. Kid too."

"Gone *how*."

"Gone, gone. All their bags and everything."

"ARCK?"

"Most likely. Talked to a guy a couple rooms away, said he woke up to a woman yelling."

A slow grin stole across my face. "Then they're here."

"There's something else," he said cautiously. "The computer was still in the room, it was wiped clean. And, uh, her wedding ring, sir. It was on the bed."

The grin fell away.

The room around me faded.

My blood boiled as a dark rage slid through me like flash fire, but just as quickly, it disappeared and a laugh rumbled in my chest.

She knows.

She knows it's a game.

"Clever," I murmured. "Wait for my call." As soon as I

ended the call, I looked to the nerd, waiting anxiously in the doorway. "Clean up the glass and get me another drink. When you're done, get to the goddamn desk and find my wife."

Garret hadn't sat.

His breathing had only grown more erratic as he waited.

Once it was only us, I said, "*My* wife is fine. However, your concern for her gets more irritating by the day."

"One of us has to be. You offered up Sutton as bait for ARCK. After the shit you pulled with them, I wouldn't be surprised if we never see her again."

"She isn't bait, she's part of the plan. She's also mine to offer."

His eyes narrowed into slits. "We take care of our own problems. Vero was Jason's to deal with. But if you think ARCK is going to forget what the three of you did, you're fucking insane. They'll use Sutton to get theirs."

"She's fine, she'll be fine . . . and soon, every member of ARCK will truly understand why they shouldn't interfere with our affairs. But not if you try to save Sutton and fuck the entire thing, which is exactly why you have been where I could watch you this entire time."

He dragged his hands through his hair. "If something happens to her—"

"What?" The question was pure taunt and challenge. "What will you do?"

His hands lowered and a lazy smile pulled at his lips as he sat in the chair.

Calm. Calculating. The Garret I knew well.

And I had no doubts his thoughts matched my own.

"You and I both know you've had it coming for a long time," he finally said, words slow, smile growing wider by the second. "The day you took her from me, I started envisioning ways to kill you. The day you let her get hurt, I'll put you in the ground."

I just laughed.

This constant threatening of each other's lives would never grow old because I knew we both meant every damn word.

Just as I knew I would kill him long before he ever got the chance to kill me.

Six

Conor

I jerked awake, already reaching for where one of my guns lay under the couch.

My movements halted as soon as I glanced and met Lexi's hazel eyes. Narrowed into the same squint her mom had favored that first day. But behind that attitude was excitement and curiosity similar to a certain genius I knew.

"Lexi," I said gruffly. "Told you that you've gotta stop doing that."

In the three days since I'd found them in the motel, she hadn't said a word to me, and today didn't seem to be the day that would change.

If she didn't have her mom's attitude, I would've found these mornings a lot creepier.

I sat up and rubbed my hands over my face and then dropped my forearms to my knees before lowering my head so it was level with hers. "All right, let's do this. I bet you breakfast that you'll break first." A small laugh crept up my throat. "See what I did there?"

Nothing.

Stone-fucking-wall.

"I bet Beck could've made you laugh. You probably would've liked him." I slanted my head to the side but didn't break eye contact. "Although, he looked scarier than I do, if you can believe it."

Nothing.

"As big as me, but he wasn't nearly as pretty." I almost winked, but I stopped before I could and let out a low whistle. "Oh, you almost got me there. Anyway, there wasn't a part of the guy that wasn't covered in tattoos, except his head. And he had this beard that—" My fingers scuffed over my jaw.

Curled into my beard.

Beck had kept his meticulously wild and untamed. Part of the Beck charm.

Whereas mine had always been neatly trimmed.

I'd stopped taking care of it after he was murdered.

I didn't know when mine crossed over the line of being more like Beck's than my own.

Something tugged and clawed at my chest, but I choked it back.

I forced out something that sounded like a laugh. "But he was funny. The funniest and most loyal guy anyone ever knew."

Nothing, but at least she was no longer glaring.

I blinked and sat back. "You won, kid. Guess I'm buying."

She won every day.

Wouldn't have mattered. The room was under fake

names and a card linked back to one of my accounts that had nothing to do with ARCK, so I would've paid anyway. But it was the only time Lexi spent any real time near me.

"Who?"

My head snapped up at Sutton's voice.

I tried not to, but I couldn't stop the way my eyes raked over her body as she walked across the living room to the couch.

Barely there shorts and a threadbare cotton shirt that looked expensive as fuck and like it was made that way. The satin robe she was slipping on would do nothing to hide it, because she always left it open.

She'd worn something similar every damn morning.

And it'd gotten harder and harder not to watch her.

Not to sneak glances.

I was on the verge of calling my team and telling them I was done. That someone needed to relieve me and give me a different job on this case because I no longer had a clear head—could no longer think straight.

"What?"

Sutton's lips curled into a brief smile. "Who were you talking about? To Lexi," she clarified when I only stared at her. "Were you trying to sell her on you?"

"Oh, no. No, it was Beck. My older brother."

Her brows slowly lifted as she lowered herself to the couch. "I didn't know you had a brother."

"Keyword being *had*."

"Oh." Unease and sorrow flashed across her face. "I'm sorry."

"Me too." I forced a smile when Lexi dropped the room service menu next to me. Handing it back to her, I said, "Why don't you order today?

She just stared at me as if I'd said the dumbest thing in the world and then went to sit next to Sutton.

Jesus Christ.

"I've got it," Sutton murmured. "Did you want anything in particular?"

I shook my head as I pushed from the couch. "Food is food."

I went to the second, smaller room that belonged to me, not that I had actually slept in it since I needed to be close to the girls if anything happened, and rushed through my shower so I could get back to them.

So I would know they were safe.

But as I was wrapping the towel around my waist, I looked at myself in the mirror and paused, not knowing when the last time was that I'd done that.

My hair wasn't long, but it was longer than I normally wore it.

My beard was definitely closing in on Beck territory.

And it fucking hurt because I looked just like him. Seeing even a glimpse of Beck made me remember everything.

All the good and the bad and the really fucking bad and the best I thought our life could ever get before it all went to hell.

A life away from the mob was what he'd wanted. A *normal* life.

I wondered if he'd be happy with the company Kieran and I had built.

I wondered if he'd be happy with this life or if he'd be itching for something else, something even further from the mob.

I wondered if he'd be proud. Because, fuck, that was all I'd ever wanted, to make him proud.

I slapped at the wall, shutting off the light, and went into the room to dress, all the while listening to the muted voices in the other room.

Sutton hadn't said a word for an entire day after she'd read the notes on Veronica and the Tennessee Gentlemen. I'd been worried that I'd made a mistake and that the small, hostile, dialogue we'd had would vanish completely or that Lexi's suspicion of me would grow because of it.

Neither had happened.

Lexi? I'd crack her one day.

And Sutton had started talking again yesterday, just little conversations here and there. Never touching on Veronica or the Tennessee Gentlemen, only staying superficial, and I hadn't pushed it because I knew she would open up when she was ready.

I could see it in the way she looked at me and the small smiles she gave and how she seemed more at ease around me.

She was getting comfortable with me. The trust would come.

I finished shrugging into my shirt and snatched up the gift for Lexi as I left the room.

As soon as I opened the door, Lexi fell silent.

I'd stopped taking offense to it on the first day. Right about the time Sutton told me I wasn't allowed to call her by her real name again.

"Hey, Lexi," I called out as I rounded the corner into the living room. "Some friends of mine stopped by last night, and they brought something for you."

I dropped down in front of her and bit back a smile at the pure suspicion in her eyes.

"My friends and I all had pretty interesting childhoods. Most of them weren't normal, like running around and playing with friends whenever we wanted. And my friend wanted to remind me that as hard as it is for adults to be stuck in hotel rooms, it's harder for a kid. So, she brought this for you." I handed her the tablet already loaded with a ton of games.

"Oh," Sutton said, uneasily. "Uh, wow. Lex, thank Conor and then take that into the bedroom, okay?"

I lifted a hand, knowing Lexi probably wouldn't attempt to thank me anyway. "It wasn't from me."

"Then take it into the bedroom."

I looked to Sutton, wondering at the bite in her tone as Lexi passed me.

As soon as Lexi disappeared into the other room, Sutton was off the couch and whirling on me. "What exactly do you think you're doing?"

I had no fucking clue.

I just stood there because I didn't know how to respond.

"You don't just give a kid a tablet, Conor, especially a kid who isn't yours and who you've only known a few days."

A laugh left me. Dark, edgy, uncomfortable, and embarrassed. "Uh—"

"And if you do, you ask the parent first. You don't just give it to the kid."

"Right. Got it. I, uh. Shit." I ran a hand through my hair and shrugged as I tried to figure out what to say. "I'm sorry. I didn't realize."

"How do you not realize? That's common sense."

I swallowed back the immediate reaction, the one that would hint at my life, and said, "The only kids I've been around since I was one are currently babies. So, no, it isn't." I gestured to the closed door. "I *am* sorry. Jess thought Lexi might want it. She loaded it with educational games and—"

"Are you kidding?" Shock covered Sutton's face. Her hands lifted in the air before falling, as though she didn't know what else to do with me. She turned and took a couple of steps away before storming in my direction. "You brought a whore here when my daughter and I were in the other room? She bought my daughter a present?"

I ground my jaw to keep from lashing out.

If Sutton only knew how right she was.

If she only knew that Jess was a better woman than Sutton ever would be.

"Jess," I said through gritted teeth, "*Jessica* is Kieran's *wife*. The three of us founded ARCK. *They* came here last night to give me an update. And, yes, she thought she was being helpful by buying the six-year-old who's been cooped up in motels and hotels for over two months a tablet. She even had Einstein help her lock it so no one could trace it and so Lexi can't accidentally enable anything so that it can be traced."

I waved a hand at where Sutton stood, her cheeks burning red with anger.

"Who the fuck are you to talk to people the way you do? To judge them. To assume what you do." I took a step closer and lowered my voice. "You honestly think that I'd have *anyone*, especially a whore, up here when I'm working a job? When that job is to protect two lives." I held up a hand when her lips parted. "Don't answer. Because I know what you'll say, and I already know the truth." I slowly walked backward toward the kitchen. "But you made your point. Don't give gifts without consulting parents first. Noted."

I left her there, staring at me with a horrified look.

Dropping into one of the chairs at the kitchen table, I placed my elbows on the cool surface and raked my hands through my hair until I was sure I was calm.

Calm . . .

I'd always been the calm one.

I'd been the one who went with the flow.

Life turned upside down? Roll with it.

Pulled into mob? Roll with it.

Brother murdered in front of me? Fucking roll with it.

It was what I did; it was how I survived.

Until this job.

And the fucked-up thing? Even though Sutton sure as hell was pushing, I wasn't even sure she was the one pushing me over the edge. But she was there, so she was getting the full brunt of my frustration.

If I were being honest with myself, it was this life.

It was losing people again and again.

It was not knowing if I'd ever see them again when they walked away from me.

Nearly losing Einstein had been a tipping point I hadn't seen coming.

"My mother."

My hands dropped to the table, and I lifted my head to look at Sutton.

She was standing opposite me, wringing her hands together and worrying her bottom lip.

"What?"

"You asked who I am—I'm my mother." She easily fell into one of the chairs, her attention on the windows as she spoke. "My mother is the most judgmental and rudest woman I've ever met. I'm embarrassed when she opens her mouth, horrified by some of the things she says, and growing up, I vowed to never be her."

"I—fuck," I said on a ragged breath.

"Don't try to take it back, I know it's what you think." She winked as her lips curled into a smile, but they quickly fell. "It's also true. And to think, I used to pride myself in being her greatest disappointment."

"That can't be true."

A startled laugh escaped her mouth. When she spoke, her tone was light and held a hint of a tease. "I don't know if I should be offended by that."

It took me a second to realize what she would be offended by—how my words could've been taken. "No, that —shit, I didn't mean it in that way. I meant you're her daughter. You can't be a disappointment to her."

"Oh, but I am." A mixture of old pains and defiance filled her eyes. "She never missed an opportunity to let me know that I fell short of the perfection she expected—even at my wedding."

Something about my expression made her smile.

"It's just how she is. She's all about appearance and status and being better, or having more, than every person in the room with her. She planned my entire life out so I would succeed, which would make her look good. Her goal was for me to end up on a path that continued the cycle. And it killed her that I was always straying from it—that I wanted to at all."

I tried to imagine Sutton living anything other than the life I knew her to have, and I couldn't. For how obviously it horrified her that she played the part her mom wanted her to, she played it damn well.

"What *did* you want?"

Longing crept across her features before she could force it away. Her cheeks stained pink as she forced out a flippant breath. "It was nothing—really. Just a way to rebel against my mother's perfect world of debutante balls and pageants."

Bullshit.

Sutton had to be the worst liar I'd ever come across.

I drummed my fingers on the table and gave a shrug like it didn't matter to me either way. "I don't know what a debutante ball is, but I know a little something about rebellions." The corner of my mouth pulled into a smirk at the inside joke Sutton would never understand. "Why don't you tell me about it."

She took a deep breath, as if she was about to, only to exhale just as quickly and curl in on herself. "It's stupid. You'd laugh."

"You don't know that."

She gave me a doubtful look. "Zachary did when I told him," she whispered, full of resentment and shame. "Laughed and walked away, and that was the end of the discussion."

"Yeah, I'm not him," I said in a low tone. "Try me."

Hesitation warred on her face before she finally said, "I wanted to do hair." She sat, maybe waiting for me to react a certain way, and when I didn't, she shrugged. "I didn't have dreams of being a singer or an actress like my friends did, or even becoming the first female president. I just wanted to do hair."

"Why didn't you?"

Her brows lifted in amusement. "I don't think my mother realized it was something I loved. When I graduated high school and told my parents that I wanted to go to cosmetology school, they didn't even acknowledge that I'd said anything. Didn't even bother laughing," she said sadly. "Just went back to eating dinner."

My parents had died when I was young, but I was sure they would have pushed Beck and me into doing whatever we wanted to.

Well . . . maybe not joining the mob.

"So what'd you do?" I asked when she didn't continue.

"I continued on my mother's path." Her eyes flicked up to meet mine. "I had been set to go to their alma mater since before I even cared about college. I was supposed to join the sorority my mother had been in and major in whatever they chose. I didn't care. And I did go. I even rushed . . ."

I felt my mouth pulling into a smile in response to the one on her face.

"But I took the allowance my parents were giving me and went to cosmetology school part time. During the summer, I switched to full time and even took a course at the college so I could give my parents a reason for not coming home. But then they came for family weekend my sophomore year and had lunch with the dean, who's a friend of theirs."

She lifted her slender shoulders in a shrug, and for the first time, it didn't seem like she was brushing off something huge. It looked like she was defeated.

"He told them that I was in danger of failing most of my classes. Probably had something to do with the fact that I never switched back to part time when summer ended. And that my heart was clearly in one school and not the other.

"When my parents confronted me, I simply said, 'I told you that I wanted to go to cosmetology school.' They were so mad and humiliated that they pulled me from both and took me home that day—sent for my things later. That drive home was when my father told me that, since I had decided college wasn't important, then it was time to continue with the next step in my life. He told me that both Garret Vaughn and Zachary Larson had been showing interest in me and I had to choose one."

"That's when you started dating them?"

She nodded. "The morning of my first date with Garret, I grabbed the scissors from the kitchen, cut my hair off, and then went into the dining room where my parents were eating and dropped it on the table. My mother actually screamed as though I'd dropped a dead animal in front of her. She was furious. She asked how I was supposed to convince either of the boys to marry me looking like a *used-up junkie*."

I couldn't stop the laugh that slipped out. Partly at her mom's reaction and partly in pride of Sutton's actions.

"To be fair, it was pretty awful since I'd just grabbed the length of my hair and started cutting. I had to get it fixed that afternoon."

"You should've left it."

A bright smile covered her face. "I did, in a way." One of her hands lifted to play with the ends of her hair where it almost brushed her shoulders. "My hair had always been so long, so I've left it this short ever since as a reminder of what they took from me. Plus, my mother hates it this length."

"I don't." The confession was out before I could begin to filter myself, and I cleared my throat. "I never said you were your mom, by the way."

"No. No, you didn't. But I think I am, and it terrifies me as much as it angers me to know that." She dropped her head into one of her hands and released a sigh. "Funny, how you think of yourself when you're in one setting surrounded by certain people . . . and then how you really see yourself when you're removed from it."

"What, and put with the likes of me?" It was a playful taunt, and her eyes brightened and smiled even though her expression never changed.

After a couple of minutes, she finally said, "With someone normal." Her hand fell to the table, and she leaned across as she lowered her voice. "I would be embarrassed if someone like you were to ever come around one of my parents' parties or one of mine."

My head jerked back. A huff punched from my chest. "Wow. All right then."

"Not embarrassed that you were there," she hurried to say. "Embarrassed of what you would see. What you would hear. What people might say about you just because you don't come from what *they* see as proper bloodlines. I'd be horrified by them."

Sutton's eyes took on a faraway look. She swallowed slowly, the delicate movement wholly capturing my attention.

"I've been thinking about that a lot . . . I wonder if Vero felt like she didn't belong because she was different. She was such a light among awful people. I wonder if that was why she didn't feel like she could tell me what was going on. Maybe I was just another one of those women in that world she never really felt a part of? And after what just happened, I'm wondering if I ever said anything horrible to her without realizing it."

"She was your best friend?" When Sutton made a confirming sound in her throat, I shook my head. "Then it wouldn't have mattered. I've said things to Kieran. He and Beck said and did things to each other. It never changed that bond."

Sutton was nodding, but there was a sudden sadness on her face and in her eyes that was different from before. "What happened to your brother?"

He was shot.

Pushing Kieran out of the way to save him.

I could see it as clearly as when it had happened a year ago.

My head moved in small jerks. "Yeah, we aren't gonna go there right now."

"Of course, I'm sorry. That was rude of me to ask." She looked to the table and ran her slender fingers through her hair. "There is something else I was wondering. About the ones who showed up last night."

I didn't say anything, I just waited expectantly. Because Sutton was fidgeting, and I had a feeling she wasn't waiting for me to tell her to continue.

"First of all, I'm sorry for what I said about the girl. That was . . . also rude. It was a nice thought, what she did for Lexi." Her eyes darted between the table and me a few times before holding mine. "I'm wondering why they are here instead of in North Carolina."

"They've been here the whole time. They drove up a couple of hours behind me. They're my eyes outside, and they're the ones leaving the false trail."

"And you didn't think I would need to know that?"

"No," I said immediately. "I'm keeping you and Lexi safe in here. I'll keep you safe during transport. They take care of what happens outside the resort. They're also on the ground looking for your husband because, until we know where he is, we can't risk relocating you permanently."

She thought on my words for a moment. "I thought Einstein was doing all that?"

"Einstein does things none of us can, but it's all hacking into systems and looking for people that way. Combine her with Kieran and Jess, and we always find whoever we need."

"She couldn't find me."

I smiled tightly. The need to defend Einstein rose, but I pushed it down. "No, and that's the issue we're facing because Zachary has Garret."

Sutton's brow furrowed. She pushed back in her seat until she was sitting straight and stiff. "I don't understand. They don't speak. God, as far as I know, they hate each other."

"But they're useful to each other," I said. "Garret's family is in tech, right?"

"Well, yes, but what does that have to do with Zachary or anything that's going on?"

"When Einstein searched you, you didn't exist. At all. When you mentioned your daughter in the emails, she searched for children who had missed school, dropped school, anything she could think of—but there was nothing. According to records, the two of you don't exist in any form."

"But we do, I'm right here. Lexi's in that . . . file. That folder . . . the black folder thing. We were in there."

I leaned back and folded my arms over my chest. "The man who gathered the information for that folder knew about the tech company and the illegal businesses, so he would've had the mind to hack systems. When Einstein erases or creates people, she keeps records locked deep, which is common for people who do what she does. Whoever does the creating and erasing for Tennessee Gentlemen must do it too, and that's where your information probably came from."

"But what does that have to do with what's happening now?" she asked after a few stunned seconds. "And what does that have to do with Garret?"

"You and Lexi were erased. Veronica Woods was created, and her file came from Garret's company's server. If I looked at yours, I bet it would say the same. Which means either Garret or one of his employees is the equivalent of our Einstein, and is the person who helped Zachary with all the shit that happened to Einstein since hacking is how they got to her. Both Zachary and Garret disappeared without a trace on the same day, so someone is very carefully covering their tracks."

"Jesus." She started wringing her hands again, and it was then I realized what she was actually doing.

She was playing with her ring finger.

With the empty space where I had clearly seen a ring the morning I'd found them at the motel.

"Your ring."

Her hands stilled. Her body visibly stiffened. Her eyes widened as she stared at me. "What?"

"Your ring." I nodded toward her hands. "You were still wearing it when I found you. I haven't seen you wear it since."

"I, uh, I lost it. I'm not sure where. I noticed it after we'd already unpacked here."

I wasn't Dare, the human lie detector, but I was pretty goddamn sure that was a lie.

"Yeah? Need me to look for it?"

Her head was shaking in quick jerks that were setting off every warning bell. "No. No, I have. Everywhere. It's probably for the best, though, right?"

When she started to stand, I lunged across the table and grabbed her wrist, ignoring the way she jumped and the fear in her eyes.

"You're lying. Trust me, and I'll trust you. Lie to me? That trust is gonna be damn near impossible to rebuild."

"I didn't want it," she cried out. "I didn't want something that tied me to him. That signified I belong to him, so I left it in the motel."

I loosened my hold when tears filled her eyes and slipped down her cheeks.

"I know what kind of man he is, and I know how he can be. Trust me, I know." She choked on a sob and pressed her hand to her chest. "But even still, I didn't know he was capable of what he'd done."

She crumpled in on herself, her back heaving, her sobs tearing at me.

I released my hold on her wrist, but I couldn't seem to pull my hand back.

It was resting on top of hers, engulfing hers, and I knew I needed to move it.

Knew this was wrong.

But taking my hand away wasn't an option.

"I think Lexi knew," she murmured after a while.

She was resting her cheek on the table and had an arm curled protectively around her head.

The other hand was still under mine.

She hadn't tried to move it.

"What do you mean?"

She lifted her head enough so that her chin was on her arm and her red-rimmed eyes were staring at something just past me. "About Zachary. She said he had a bad-man's smile. I thought I had kept her from it all. I thought . . ."

"Thought what?"

Her stare flicked to me, shame covering her face in those seconds before there was a quick knock on the door.

"Room service."

Sutton quickly sat back, blinking away whatever she'd been about to say, and pulled her hand out from under mine to brush away the lingering wetness on her cheeks.

I tried not to notice . . .

The loss. The feeling of wrongness. The way my body craved to reach for her hand again.

A growl built deep in my chest as I pushed from the table and headed for the door.

Agitation and need pounded through my veins.

A need I couldn't afford.

Wrong time. Wrong place. Wrong girl.

Story of my fucking life.

Seven

Sutton

"You cold?" Conor asked from where he was sitting against one of the walls, staring at his laptop.

"Me?" I glanced from Lexi to Conor, only to find him watching me. "No."

He shut his computer and tilted his head, his eyes moving to my hands. "You've been pacing in tight circles, rubbing your arms and wringing your hands."

I clenched my hands into fists against my stomach, refusing to acknowledge that he was right. "I'm fine. I—" The words jumbled in my throat, making it impossible to speak.

When Conor's eyebrows lifted in question, a short, airy laugh tumbled from my mouth, and before I realized it, I was moving, pacing again.

He set his computer on the floor and headed toward

me, his voice low so it wouldn't carry to Lexi. "Either you're cold or there's something wrong. Tell me."

My shoulders caved with a defeated sigh when he placed his hand on my elbow, keeping me there and facing him.

I wouldn't acknowledge that I swayed toward him.

Or that the heat from his hand warmed me and comforted me.

I wouldn't acknowledge that his voice moved through me in a way that resonated and lingered.

"There's something I wanted to ask you," I whispered and then hurried to wet my lips. "Or, well, something I was hoping you would help me with. But I'm not sure if it's even a good idea, and you'll probably laugh at me."

"Try me."

I nearly backed out and made up a half dozen other things to ask before finally saying, "I was wondering if you would help me learn how to defend myself."

Surprise covered his features as he released me.

"See? It's stupid."

"It isn't," he argued quickly. "It's smart to know how. But tell me why you want to know."

"Let's play a game, Sutton."

My palms swept up my arms again as I tried to ward off the soul-deep chill. "Because I've never been able to," I confessed, shame dripping from my words. "And my attempt with you was pathetic. I don't want to be in that position again."

"No attempt to protect yourself is pathetic, but there are things you should know, especially when coming at a man over a foot taller than you." He dipped his head close as he passed me, causing chills to race over my skin, and whispered, "Like don't."

"Wait"—I turned to follow him—"what do you mean *don't*?"

His mouth was stretched into a breathtaking smile when he glanced over his shoulder at me. "You'll see."

Twenty minutes later, all the oxygen punched from my lungs.

I stumbled back and started falling just as Conor grabbed my arm to stop me.

His light eyes searched my face as he steadied me, his fingers somehow both firm and gentle. "You okay?"

I wasn't sure which was worse—the odd pain of having the breath knocked out of me or the humiliation of having Conor stop me mid-run so effortlessly.

"Ow." I lifted a hand to my chest and rubbed at the Conor-sized ache.

I was kicking myself for ever thinking this was a good idea and seconds away from giving up on the entire thing.

"Aren't you supposed to be going easy on me?"

"No," he replied. "Tell me if you're okay."

I rubbed at the pain for another second before dropping my hand. "Well, I'm starting to think it isn't fair that I can't get past your freakishly long arms."

His chest jerked with a silent laugh as he released me. "Doesn't matter if it's fair. It's *real*. And if this *were* real, I would've already knocked you unconscious and kidnapped you about fifteen times."

Odd how he was teasing me about the very thing I'd feared he would do.

If he only knew . . .

The corners of his mouth twitched when I got back into place. "Let's go."

I considered his relaxed stance for all of a half second before running at him.

He sidestepped me and tapped my shoulder as I passed, making me stumble a few feet before finding my balance.

"Okay, this isn't working," I said, throwing my hands into the air.

"It isn't working because you keep charging me. When are you ever going to charge someone?"

I glared at him. "I charged you that first day."

"And it didn't work," he said gently, not that I needed the reminder. "You give up?"

"Jesus, yes." Exhaustion and gratitude wove through my words.

"Then come here."

I studied his expression for a moment before warily moving to stand in front of him.

I regretted ever asking for his help.

I was annoyed with how fast he was for how absurdly tall he was.

I was embarrassed that I couldn't even get close enough to touch him.

And I hated that I couldn't stop looking at him.

The way his bright eyes seemed to dance. The way his smile seemed to change his face completely. The way his muscles rippled at the slightest movement.

God, don't get me started on his laugh.

Rich. Full. Free in a way that made me long to hear it again.

The way he was fighting a smile when I reached him let

me know my thoughts had to be written across my face. Blood rushed to my cheeks as I worried over which ones he was seeing.

"Before we started, I told you not to come at a man my size. Now you see why," he said in a low tone. "If your attacker comes at you, don't charge. Do what you can to hide, even if they've already seen you. Because, if you charge, they're ready for you and know what you're about to do. If you hide, you have a chance of finding something to defend yourself with and making them come to you."

"Oh, Sutton . . ."

"Let's play a game."

I forced the sinister words from my mind and tried to ignore the ice-cold fingers gripping my spine. "Okay," I said with a jerky nod. "What do I need to find?"

"Anything sharp to stab them with. You can even use your damn heels if you don't see anything else."

"I knew those were a good choice," I murmured, but he just continued with a soft laugh.

"Anything long that you can wrap around their neck. Because these?" He tapped on my hands, and my breath caught when he trailed his fingers along my palms, leaving heat in their wake. "They wouldn't be able to do much around my neck other than annoy me for the second or two it takes me to remove them."

"Okay."

"Once you get the hiding part down, we'll talk about where to aim." He took a few steps back and nodded. "Let's go."

My mouth opened in protest. "I thought we were done."

"With your way. You needed to get it out of your

system." He rolled his neck and set those eyes on me. "Go."

I turned and started for the kitchen, but I had only made it two steps before Conor gripped my arm and spun me back so that we were chest to chest. "Got you."

Was it horrible that, for a second, I forgot what we were doing?

How was it possible the fear that had plagued me for years was completely absent in this situation? It should be crippling me.

All I could focus on was how close his mouth was and the way his body felt, so big and hard against my much smaller frame.

I blinked away the thoughts and tugged against his hold. "You have to let me get away first."

"Let you?" That damn Prince-Charming smile was back, teasing me with those boyish dimples as he released me and prepared to go again. "You have a lot to learn."

Eight

Sutton
ONE MONTH AGO

I bit nervously on my bottom lip as I scanned the email I had memorized from one of ARCK's members. A reply to me that had been sent nearly a month ago, except I'd never sent an original email in the first place.

Another reason to be so damn frustrated with Zachary.

Another reason to hate him.

If it hadn't been enough to find out that he'd been drugging me for over a year, to realize how the plans for rescuing Vero had shifted only an hour later had me ready to scream and fight and do something I'd wanted to for so, so long.

Except I'd been too stunned to say anything at all. Too stunned to move.

Not that I would've been able to get far.

When Zachary told me to pack, I'd thought he and Jason had found Vero without ever needing to put our original plan into action—for me to email her captors with our fabricated story. To lure them back to Brentwood in hopes of trapping and arresting them to find out where Vero was.

I'd thought he had planned for Lexi and me to stay with my parents while they went to find my friend.

As a safety measure.

As a way to keep an eye on me while he was gone, a way to control me.

Only to realize I'd had it so, so wrong when Zachary dropped us off at a motel and introduced us to the six FBI agents working this case who were to watch over us while he and Jason were gone.

To keep us in place.

Before he left, he'd taken my phone and wallet and left us with a laptop, telling me as long as I had it, he could find me. He gave me one instruction: Read everything.

The six men were also given one instruction: Don't let the girls leave.

Once I'd stopped silently seething and had gotten Lexi as settled as I could, trying vainly to make her believe we were having an adventure, I'd read *everything*, as Zachary had called it.

It was nothing more than a letter and a short email conversation, explaining what he couldn't to my face because he was a coward.

He wrote that he and Jason were still going to find Vero and that the plan was the same, only with minor tweaking. Minor being, our daughter and I were to stay in a seedy motel, waiting for human traffickers to *come for us*. I was told to remember the story we'd been working on, to practice it, and that it was to remain a last resort to buy them time.

He reminded me incessantly how smart these people were and how I needed to be convincing. He never mentioned Lexi. He never apologized for roping her into this—he never apologized at all.

At the top of the email conversation he'd saved for me, he wrote: "Read this, know it, believe it. Remember, they lie to make you wonder. They lie to gain your trust. You need to do the same so we can find Vero. Wait for my word, I'll feed you the lines."

The emails had been between me and one of the ARCK members, except it was the first I was seeing it.

One where Zachary, who was posing as me, started the process of luring the members of ARCK to Brentwood by asking for their help. In return, the member asked questions and details about my life, which Zachary hardly gave up.

From the signature in the emails, the member went by Einstein.

I wasn't sure if I was impressed by the member's confidence or annoyed by it.

Knowing who these ARCK people really were and what they did, I was firmly siding on annoyed.

Just as I was annoyed with the last response.

We help those who genuinely need it.

Upon investigation, we've found there is no Sutton Larson in existence.

I'm not sure how you found out about us, whoever you are, but please do not contact us again unless you truly have need for us.

I didn't understand it.

How could there not be any record of me?

Or was this part of their lying to make me wonder? If it was, I was fairly certain they had succeeded, because that one line hadn't left my mind in the last month while I'd waited, as Zachary had ordered, for his word.

I began tapping out the response I'd been instructed to send this morning, and then because I couldn't help myself, I snuck in the question I'd been dying to ask.

Please. We do need help. Genuine help, as you call it.

I'm afraid. Afraid for my daughter's life and my own.

I don't understand what you mean. Existence? I am Sutton Larson. Sutton Larson is me.

I'll find a way to get you a copy of my ID if that will prove it to you. But we need help. We need to get away, and I don't know if I can do that by myself.

I'm afraid they're watching us closely . . . if you understand what I mean.

That was why it took so long for me to reach out to you again.

We will be here as long as we can wait.

If you don't come for us, I'll write to you when I can. Please don't contact me. Just come.

I attached the address of the disgusting motel we were in and then hurried to send off the message when the clock read two minutes before noon. Once the email went through, I deactivated the email account and shut down the computer, just as Zachary instructed me to do.

I nervously glanced over to where my daughter sat on her bed watching me, and forced a smile. "All done."

She nodded, the movement nothing more than a slight bobbing of her head. "How long are we going to be here?"

Emotion clogged my throat as I searched for the answer that would make her happy.

Make her smile again.

But I didn't have one.

"I don't know, baby," I replied honestly. "As long as it takes."

A sliver of unease tightened around my heart and stole my next breath because, for the first time, I truly dreaded what would happen at the end of all this.

Nine

Sutton

I sank down onto the chaise next to Lexi, and she sighed. "What's wrong, sweet girl?"

She pursed her lips but didn't look up from the tablet. "So now we're doing the Suite Hop?"

I glanced around the new suite, which was nearly identical to the one we had been in yesterday, only with a slightly flipped layout, and held back an echoing sigh. "Better than the Motel Hop."

When I'd woken this morning, Conor had explained that it would be easier to stay in the same location and switch rooms since it was so vast.

I'd agreed, only because we were already here.

Plus, I loved this resort.

We'd moved to a new suite on a new floor under a new name, making sure the room we were leaving was still booked for another day in case anyone was watching the comings and goings other than Einstein.

Once we were settled, Conor had made himself scarce—as seemed to be his new normal. Apart from when he'd taught me how to defend myself, he'd been slowly distancing himself from me since breakfast the day before.

Physically.

Mentally.

Emotionally.

By last night, he was harsh and agitated, and that was when he spoke to me at all.

Lexi giggled but didn't respond for a few moments as she chose the correct word on her tablet. "When do we get to go home?"

After making sure Conor was nowhere around, I asked, "You want to go home? With Daddy?"

I didn't have to wait for her response to know the answer.

A darkness passed over her face.

Her tiny body tensed.

"I don't like that house, Momma."

Considering that was my dream house and I'd carefully picked out everything I wanted in it, I tried not to take offense since this was a six-year-old. "Oh yeah? Wanna tell me why?"

Lexi looked at me before tucking her chin against her chest. "It has a bad smile like Daddy."

I tried to laugh to cover the way chills crept over my body. "Houses have smiles?"

"If you look real hard, you'll see it."

"Okay." I rubbed my hand over her arm, as if that would help put warmth into my own body. "You know, I don't understand smiles. You said Mr. Conor had Prince Charming's smile, but you still seem pretty unsure of him."

Her cheeks blazed red, and somehow, impossibly, she tucked her chin even lower.

"Oh, I see. So that's why we don't talk to him?" My lips slowly curled up. I dug my fingers into her side and relished in the laugh that burst from her. "The giant isn't so scary anymore?"

Instead of a response, I got a slight jerk of her shoulders.

"We aren't giving Momma the silent treatment." I snuggled down so I was at her level and grabbed the tablet from her hands. "If you don't want to go to our house, tell me where you want to go."

Her wide, hazel eyes blinked up at me. "The house in my dreams."

"Why don't you tell me all about it?"

I laid there, my heart full and a smile on my lips as she launched into an extremely detailed description of a house she'd dreamed up.

My eyelids felt heavy when I stepped out of the humid bathroom that night. My body still had not fully caught up after those months of barely sleeping in the motels, and I was ready to crawl into bed and sleep for days.

But where I expected to see my daughter, the bed was empty.

The room was dark.

There wasn't a sound coming from the suite.

I hurried for the door, Lexi's name on my lips, but as

soon as I had it opened, a sigh of relief left me. Because she was there . . . sitting on the living room couch.

Tablet on her lap.

I kind of hated that thing. I was also thankful for it.

I was sure it made the days go by faster for her, and it helped her learn while we were locked away.

Sitting on the floor next to her, Conor was staring at something on his laptop, most likely still reading the files.

My heart took off at a thunderous pace as I studied him.

I told myself to look away, to look anywhere else but at him, but it was impossible. Just as it was becoming harder and harder to stay away from him when he was near.

I cleared my throat and prayed that the light coming from the kitchen area wasn't enough to betray the blood heating my cheeks.

Conor pushed to his feet and snatched his laptop from the floor. "Dinner's in the kitchen."

My mouth was open to thank him for ordering food, for watching over us . . . to ask him what I had done to make him act this way so suddenly, but he was already gone.

I jerked when the door to his room shut.

It could've just been me, but it felt like he'd slammed it.

"I think that means he likes you," Lexi said, and I dragged my attention away from the closed door to where she was sitting.

"Wha—no. He doesn't . . . no, absolutely not. That would be completely inappropriate, and he knows that." I headed toward the kitchen to see what Conor had ordered, but only got a few steps before stopping and asking, "Why do you say that?"

She rolled her eyes in a *duh, Mom* way. "You told me Kai liked me because he wouldn't talk to me and pulled my ponytail. Mr. Conor doesn't talk to you anymore and slams his door, so that means he likes you."

"Okay, first, you're supposed to be in bed." I stared at her until she smiled bashfully. "Second, as I said, it would be completely inappropriate on so many levels. He's helping us. We're clients of his."

Technically.

Sort of.

No one else needed to know the true details of that, including Lexi.

"Most importantly, I'm married to your father."

Lexi didn't respond, she only watched me until I finally headed to the kitchen.

But I didn't pull my dinner from the microwave.

I just stood there, berating myself for the improper thoughts and feelings I'd let develop.

"I know Daddy scares you too."

I jolted at Lexi's soft voice.

"Jesus, Alexis." I pressed my hand to my chest and tried to restart my heart. Not realizing for a moment what exactly she had said. "Wait . . . what?"

"I know he scares you too."

"Why would you—" I hesitated because she wasn't wrong.

And this sassy child saw so much more than she ever should have. Much more than I'd ever realized.

"What do you mean, Lex?"

"You never let me have sleepovers, but you let me sleep at friend's houses or Mimi's house, like, a lot."

I reached for the counter and gripped it tightly, praying it would keep me standing.

"When we're at the house, you're happy and you talk to

me. But not if Daddy's home. Your smile goes away and you stop talking and you send me to find Nadia or to my room."

"I love your father, Alexis." The words were a strained whisper and tasted like the worst kind of lie.

She studied me for a while, her face pinched in concentration. "Can you be scared of someone and love them at the same time?"

No.

No.

No, tell her no.

But I felt my head dipping down in a shaky nod.

"Then don't be married anymore." Lexi shrugged as if it could be so easy.

"It isn't that simple." It was more complicated than I could even begin to comprehend.

Her body sagged in defeat. "But we don't have to see him again, right, Momma?"

That look.

That question.

It gutted me. What kind of a mother was I?

How had I missed so many signs? How had I missed *this*?

"Why didn't you ever tell me that you were scared?"

Lexi's chin wavered, and when she spoke again, the words were soft as a breath. "To keep the bad smile hidden."

I bent down and wrapped her up, lifting her into my arms and squeezing her close to me. "Oh, Lex, I'm sorry. I'm so, so sorry." I walked her over to the living room and sat with her still in my arms. "I'll never make you go back to that house. You'll never see him again. We'll go find a new house and start over."

"The house from my dreams?"

I leaned back and gave her a shaky smile. "I'll do my best."

How had this happened?

How had we come to this?

How had this all become *real*?

Ten

Conor

Awareness flashed across my skin.

Familiar and warning all at once.

I finished pulling on my boxer briefs, my head tilted to the side as I listened for any sounds that shouldn't be there.

A scream rang out just as I reached for my sweats.

Lexi.

I didn't even take the time to grab my gun, I bolted from the bedroom as my name tore from the girls I'd sworn to protect.

Sutton slammed into me with Lexi tucked close to her side and panic covering her face as she shouted things too fast for me to understand.

But just as quickly as I started pushing them behind me, I stopped.

"Are you fucking kidding?" I asked through gritted teeth.

My heart was racing.

Adrenaline was coursing through my veins.

Jess raised her hands in mock-surrender, but her smile widened. "Nice color on you, Conor."

Kieran's head snapped in her direction before he slanted a cold glare at me. "Look in that area again, and I'm killing him."

She just sighed and rolled her eyes. "Get over yourself. It's all he has on. It's hard not to notice."

"Did neither of you think it was a good idea to warn me you were coming?" My grip tightened on Sutton for a second before I realized I was still holding her close to my chest, shielding her from our visitors.

I didn't let myself think about how good she felt there.

I didn't let myself wonder why she wasn't trying to get away from my touch.

I hurried to release her and then faced Kieran and Jess, who were talking quietly.

"*Again*, why wasn't I warned?" The question was pure growl and grit.

"Is too," Jess hissed at her husband before sending me a wry grin. "It seemed to us that you needed to talk, but in our defense, we thought you would be within sight of the door when we showed up."

"Yeah. Talk. On the phone." I raked my hands over my face, groaning as I did. "Stay here, I'm gonna grab clothes." Turning to the girls, I said, "You should probably go to your room for—"

"No," Kieran rumbled.

That was it.

One word.

But it stopped me the same way it always had.

It wouldn't matter how long we were out of the mob or how long we were partners in a company, Kieran would always be the assassin and underboss I took orders from.

He tilted his head toward the girls standing behind me. "We need to talk to Sutton too."

I nodded. "All right. But I need to talk to the two of you in my room before that happens."

At his affirming grunt, I turned to Sutton and Lexi.

Lexi was huddled close to her mom's side, eyes narrowed at the couple behind me.

Sutton was standing straight and tall, looking as though nothing could touch her, but I could see the slight tremble continuously moving through her body.

"You okay?"

Her eyes darted to mine before dropping to the floor and then bouncing back again. When she spoke, her voice was soft and laced with unease. "Who are they?"

"Kieran and his wife, Jess. I told you about them. We started and own ARCK together."

Her chin lowered slightly, as though she were acknowledging my words before her head moved in sharp jerks. "Conor, they were just there. I never even heard the door open. How did they *get* the door open?"

I reached for her arm without thinking and gripped her gently, soothingly. "I know. That's—"

"And you weren't there."

A choking noise sounded in my throat.

The hatred and accusation in her tone hit me, feeling as though someone had kicked my legs out at the knees.

"I don't know why you're avoiding me like a pariah, but you should've been there."

"Sutton, I'm sorry."

She just ripped her arm from my grasp and hurried Lexi away.

"Son of a bitch."

"Is *way* too," Jess mumbled to her husband.

I slanted a glare in their direction. "Thanks for that."

I charged into the room and roughly pulled on a pair of sleep pants and a shirt, when I turned, I wasn't surprised to find both of them directly behind me.

Silent as the fucking night.

They could get into anywhere, even places that seemed impossible, which explained their sudden appearance in the suite.

And I loved them like family, but in that moment, I kinda wanted to take a swing at Kieran.

From the way he was testing the weight of one of his blades, he knew it and was waiting.

"Your text was alarming," he said in that lethal tone of his.

"Unlike you," Jess corrected.

"Does that explain the surprise visit?" I asked on a sneer. "Again, I needed a phone call. Not a show of what you can do that would scare the shit out of them."

"We're here," Kieran grunted. "So explain."

Instead of launching into the reason behind my earlier message, I just stared at Kieran's unapologetic expression for a few more seconds before blowing out a rough breath and shoving past them to shut my door.

Once I was facing them, I said, "I want someone else to be in charge of relocating the Larsons."

Jess looked stunned, but Kieran was as impassive as ever.

He and Lexi should have a stare down.

"And why would that be?" Jess asked, drawing out each word.

"Because I can't."

Plain and simple.

"You can," Kieran argued. "We've all done our share, but you're the best at this part of the job. People like you, people trust you. Eventually, the Larsons will too."

"No, you don't understand. I *can't* be the one who does this." I drove my hands through my hair and left them there. "I can't trust myself to be alert. To do the job the way it needs to be done. To think rationally. Put me somewhere else."

Jess's mouth curled into a wicked grin. She pushed Kieran with her elbow. "Told you."

Kieran just stared at me for a long while, indecision playing in his piercing eyes. "I'm sorry, man. There's nothing we can do. You know it as well as we do."

"No, I don't."

"Jess and I are needed on the ground so we can look for these guys. Einstein's too close to this case to bring her to Tennessee. And we can't bring Maverick, Diggs, or Dare here, none of them know the steps we go through."

"Besides, Dare has a family to think of and Maverick needs to take care of Einstein," Jess added.

Something somewhere inside me still pulled at that.

I wondered if it always would.

"You know," Jess began, her voice softer than before, "you're probably the best person for this job simply because of the situation."

Kieran murmured her name in a low warning.

She lifted her hands in the air and rolled her eyes. "Just saying. No one would keep her safer."

With a threatening look in my direction, Kieran said, "No falling for clients."

"I know."

"Conor—"

"I said I fucking know, man."

Kieran's expression slowly fell as he stared at me.

I knew it wasn't shock from what I'd said or my desperation and frustration. I was sure he'd heard worse from me over the years.

"What?"

After a few seconds, he swung his attention to his wife. But when he spoke, his gruff words were for me. "Look just like Beck."

Jess nodded. "You sound a little like him right now too."

"Jesus fuck," I said in my best Beck voice.

A startled laugh burst from Jess. Her dark, wild eyes turned glassy as her head shook. "Not even close."

I rubbed at the aching in my chest and shrugged. "I tried."

Kieran wove his hand through Jess's hair and pulled her close so he could whisper something in her ear. After a second, she pressed a kiss to his chest and then slipped out of my room.

I strained to hear, but there were no screams. No sounds of muffled voices.

"I need you to tell me," Kieran said, snapping my attention back to the room. He was standing there with his arms folded across his chest, blade peeking out from under one arm, staring at the floor.

"What?"

"Is it the way she looks, or is it something else . . . what is it that's distracting you?"

A ragged breath escaped me, fast and hard. I stepped back until I hit the bed and then roughly sat. "I don't know. I'm trying not to think about it because I know I can't and shouldn't for—fuck, so many reasons."

"Tell me the first one that comes to mind."

"She's married."

"Not."

My eyelids slowly closed, and I lowered my head. Because I *knew* that.

"I know," I said softly. "She doesn't though."

"First reason that comes to mind," Kieran demanded again.

"I'm in charge of protecting them."

"First reason that comes to mind."

I lifted my arms out to the sides and huffed. "The fuck do you want me to say?"

Kieran didn't respond. He just stared at me pointedly.

My lips formed a hard line as Kieran and the room faded away, and I was taken back to a day that haunted my thoughts.

"I blame her," I finally said.

"For Einstein," he assumed.

I swallowed thickly and jerked my head in something that might have resembled a nod. "If Sutton hadn't looked into us, Zachary wouldn't have found out. He wouldn't have become obsessed with keeping her, and he wouldn't have done what he did to Einstein."

"It's a risk we all take. Einstein knew that when she joined the company. And, shit, it's less of a risk than we usually take."

But she hadn't been breathing.

She was in Death's arms.

We almost lost her.

A defeated laugh climbed up my throat when Kieran breathed a curse, because I knew he'd figured it out.

"How long have you loved Einstein?"

I thought back to that first day and admitted, "Since about the minute she walked into ARCK and told us that, since we were no longer mortal enemies, we might as well become best friends."

Kieran took slow steps until he was pressed to the wall and let his arms fall to his sides. After a second, he started rolling the blade along his knuckles as he stared blankly ahead.

That ever-present murderous expression more threatening than ever.

"You had a chance," he said after a while.

I had stared at Einstein where she paced a few feet from me.

I hadn't even known she was going to be in the office today, and then there she was, grabbing my hand and hauling me into the back room and closing the door behind us.

Something I had thought of doing more times than I probably should have, but with this, with the way she was pacing and whispering to herself, every fantasy I'd ever had with her was the last thing on my mind.

With a deep breath, she turned to me and said, "I want you to kiss me."

Shock tore through me the instant I realized those words had actually left her lips.

"I want you to kiss me, and I want you to take me back to your place and-and-and I want you to sleep with me. I want you to have sex with me."

I choked on my next breath as a dozen responses tried to climb up my throat.

This was everything I wanted, and everything she wasn't.

I could see her. I could see her pain and how uncomfortable she was.

I could feel my heart racing and my blood heating at the thought of finally having a taste of the girl who I was sure would remain nothing more than a dream for the rest of my life. I could feel my body begging me to say yes.

But I knew her.

As much as I wanted the woman in front of me, she would never choose me. Not like this.

If I was sleeping, this was the worst fucking dream, and I was so goddamn confused.

I nodded and tried to remember what I was on the cusp of agreeing to when I was pretty fucking positive I was supposed to say no.

But I had already started walking toward her and imagining what it would be like to lose myself in her. What she would feel like. What she would taste like.

Turn around.

Turn around.

Turn around.

And then my hand was in her hair, and I wasn't sure why I'd ever thought I could turn her down.

It was in that exact moment that she tensed and brought me crashing back to Earth.

I knew it was more than not going through with this for her sake. It was that I wouldn't be able to survive the heartbreak of Einstein. She had always belonged to one man, and no matter what was happening with them then, she would always belong to him.

Leaning forward, I pressed my lips to her forehead and then forced myself away from her.

It was the single best second of my life.

"There's your kiss," I murmured gruffly. "I'm not taking you back to my place. And I'm not sleeping with you."

The following second was agony.

Her body sagged with relief. She blinked quickly, as though she were trying to take in her surroundings, and then glared at me. "Why does everyone keep rejecting me?"

A stunned laugh burst from my chest.

And, just like that, I had my confirmation that I wouldn't survive Einstein.

I could barely catch my breath.

I wanted to hit whoever everyone *was.*

I wanted to know why she'd put me through this at all when we both knew it was never what she wanted.

"Don't know who the rest of everyone is," I said uneasily, "but I'm guessing it might have something to do with the blow to our pride we would suffer."

Her wide, curious eyes studied me. "Not following."

I forced a smile and tried to hide the pain in my tone when I answered, "When you scream Maverick's name instead of ours when we're inside you."

Her face flushed and paled all at once.

Her breathing deepened.

"You're beautiful, Einstein." They were words I'd been holding back for a year. "Anyone would be lucky to take you home, but we all know you don't want anyone but him to."

Her stare drifted to the floor as she took a step away.

She looked horrified.

She looked like she was in pain.

She looked like she was trying to figure out a way to hide from the world.

"Tell me why you're doing this," I begged as she turned for the door.

"Because I don't want him. I can't," she had said so softly I nearly missed it.

"Einstein—"

"I have work to do."

She had been out of the room before I could get an answer out of her.

But I still hadn't been able to get that look of panic and pain out of my head. So, like a fucking idiot, I told Maverick about the entire damn thing.

In part, to see if he would tell me what had happened between the two, which I never found out. In part, to make him hurt a little if he had hurt her, which I accomplished.

Mostly, because I knew Einstein was suffocating without him, and I'd had a front row seat to the entire thing.

Her bliss and her pain and their recent in-my-face reunion.

"No," I finally said to Kieran. "I never had a chance with her." A breathless laugh left me. "Must be a Kennedy thing. Loving girls who don't belong to us."

Kieran didn't find that funny, considering he was married to the girl Beck had loved.

He blew out a slow breath. "Back to Sutton."

"What about her?"

"We have rules in place for a reason."

"I'm aware. I helped build those rules," I reminded him.

"Sutton's a special case." He glanced at the door. "Has she told you why she was running from Zachary?"

"Everything she's told me, I've already told you."

"Jess and I are here to find out once and for all, and how she knew about Vero. There's a possibility she might not need reloca—"

"She does," I said adamantly. "You know she does. Even if we didn't know what Zachary was capable of, she's also running from a cartel."

He stared at the floor with a grim look on his face. "Then you need to decide what she means, and what she *will* mean."

"I'm not . . . I don't think I'm following."

"It isn't a Kennedy thing, it's our world, Conor. Lily felt stuck with me and couldn't be with Dare. Beck loved Jessica, and she and I weren't supposed to be together because of who she was working for. Libby, Jesus, that was a clusterfuck. And Einstein—" He gave me a guarded look but slowly continued. "Einstein was trapped in a relationship with a psychopath while wanting to be with Maverick."

"You have a point?"

"You never missed a post on Holloway for a girl. The first I ever hear of you loving someone is Einstein, and when she gave you the green light, you turned her down because you knew it was what she needed. And now you want to be pulled from a case because of a woman."

I wasn't sure if he was scolding me or still making his point.

I was also pretty damn sure this was the longest I'd ever heard Kieran talk.

"If she's interesting for a night, then push that shit back and do your fucking job. If she's under your skin and in your head in a forever kinda way?" He lifted his shoulders in a ghost of a shrug. "We have enough trying to prevent us from living. I won't be what stands in your way from this."

I lifted my arms out to my sides. "I don't want there to be a *this*."

A cruel grin covered his face. "I wanted to kill Jessica when I met her. Look how that turned out."

I pushed from the bed and took a few steps toward him so my voice wouldn't carry when I said, "I don't want anything from her. I can't. I look at her and I see what happened to Einstein."

"That isn't all you see, or this wouldn't be an issue."

Fuck if he wasn't right.

The problem was that I hardly saw that anymore.

The problem was that I'd hated her before I ever met her, and that hate had turned into something I wasn't prepared for. Wants and needs that had grown faster and more intense in these few days than my feelings ever had over the course of a year with Einstein.

This conversation stood proof of that.

"Kieran—"

"Don't let anything happen then," he said simply. "But if you do, know that there is no going back from this. She's it, or she isn't." He headed for the door, but just before he grabbed the handle, he looked at me. "Consider the consequences if she is, Conor."

I studied the sadness etched deep in his eyes for a moment before asking, "What am I missing?"

"If she's it, there's no keeping Sutton and Lexi with you. You get relocated with them."

I staggered back a step before steadying myself.

Before I was able to catch my breath from the blow he'd dealt, Kieran had slipped from my room and shut the door behind him.

Eleven

Sutton

I slipped my arm out from underneath Lexi's sleeping form and tiptoed to the door.

The entire way there, I considered not answering it.

Part of me was still angry with Conor for allowing people to get inside the suite. For not being there when it happened. Though, the longer I'd laid in the room, the more I'd been able to see the situation for what it was.

I knew it wasn't his fault for not being there—he couldn't be next to us every second of the day, and it wasn't fair of me to expect that.

Really, I was frustrated at him for being so cold lately and itching to beg him to tell me what I had done.

To know what had changed between us.

To see him smile again.

That damn Prince Charming smile hidden within that intimidating, tattooed, avenging angel.

I think that was the worst of it all. Because it was dangerous to want to see him. To *want* to know what had changed between us when there wasn't anything between us to begin with. When nothing could ever be there.

"Jesus, you're a mess," I whispered as I reached for the handle on the door.

Conor was waiting on the other side, mouth set in a scowl, eyes distant.

Perfect.

A soft sigh pushed past my lips as I slipped out of the room and closed the door behind me. At the moment it clicked, I looked past Conor and saw the two people standing behind him.

My muscles tensed.

My blood ran cold.

Lexi had told me they had confusing smiles. Part-bad, part-good.

The girl talked in precious, six-year-old nonsense, but she had yet to be wrong.

"Conor, I don't trust them." The words were so soft that I wasn't sure if Conor could hear them, and he was directly in front of me.

But the man across the room was the one who smiled in response.

Slow.

Chilling.

I grabbed the handle and was rocking back a step when Conor twisted his head and finally looked at me. "If you don't trust them, then you don't trust me."

I snuck a quick glance at the two waiting. "But they—" I hurried to clamp my mouth shut, knowing I was about to go on another rant that was sure to make my mother proud and horrify me.

"I would lay my life down for those two, and they would do the same for me, or any stranger, in a heartbeat." With that, Conor walked away.

Shame filled me just as it did when I had let Conor know all the things I thought about him. Then again, he probably knew exactly what I was thinking about the people.

The girl was dressed in tight-fitting clothes that—*no*. No. Not going down that path.

Because then I would still be thinking it.

She was pretty. Beautiful even. There, I could focus on the positives.

Actually, she was so pretty that it was incredibly intimidating. I suddenly felt self-conscious in my pajamas and no makeup.

I forced a smile and tried not to fidget as I walked to where they were waiting in the living room.

"I'm Jess," the girl said with a wicked smile as she extended her hand.

I shook it awkwardly. "Sutton."

Her smile grew. "I know. How's Lexi doing with the tablet?"

"Oh, um, good. Thank you for that."

"We brought coloring books and crayons." Her smile softened as she inclined her head. "They're in the kitchen."

"She'll love them. Thank you, that's very kind."

"We need answers," the man next to her said.

I knew Conor had said his name before, more than once probably, but for the life of me, I couldn't think of it.

Jess smacked his chest. "Don't mind him. He's grumpy and scary and all those fun things, but he's really here because your safety is our priority." She stepped closer and gave me a saucy wink. "However, he isn't so good at the whole talking thing. You've been warned."

She moved past me, practically dancing, and fell to the couch with a giggle.

I watched the man follow and sit beside her before I headed to one of the chairs. As soon as I was seated, Conor went to stand against the wall.

"We're sorry for scaring you before," the man said. "We expected Conor to be there. It's also habit to let ourselves in."

"You aren't the only one to get scared," Jess said with a grin.

"Still not okay in this situation," Conor added.

"Anyway," Jess continued. "Kieran and I are here because we need answers that you haven't exactly been forthcoming with."

Oh no.

"You never did say why you and Lexi were running or why you needed to be relocated." Jess's eyes flashed to Kieran. "You also didn't know about Zachary's secret life, so that makes us wonder what exactly happened. What crime you saw."

Oh no, oh no, oh no.

Oh God.

My heart stuttered.

My palms began to sweat.

The story swam around and around in my mind, but when I opened my mouth, the words wouldn't come.

I looked to Conor, but he was staring straight ahead, features hard and unreadable.

"I know Daddy scares you too."

"Can you be scared of someone and love them at the same time?"

"We were scared."

Silence stretched for so long I thought I might go insane.

Finally, Jess cleared her throat. "We know, Sutton. But of what? What did you see?"

The only thing I could think to tell them—the only truth—I didn't know how.

It was something I had stupidly been about to confess to Conor yesterday before breakfast had shown up. Thinking back, I was glad I hadn't when the rest of the morning seemed to change everything between us.

One moment, he'd been helping and teaching and teasing me.

The next, it was hardened features and gruff tones and a coldness that radiated from him.

With another glance at Conor to confirm he hadn't moved, I looked at Jess and Kieran. "I'm sorry, but I don't feel comfortable telling you."

"Jesus," Conor whispered.

"It's personal," I said, my tone pleading and full of anger at the same time.

After a moment, he turned to me. "I know it is. *We* know it is. But this was why there were tests, Sutton. This was why we struggled to trust you, because all you do is evade. Now we're here, trying to help, and you still won't give."

"Then why are you here?" I prayed no one could hear the hurt in my voice.

"Good fucking question."

"Conor," Jess said, her tone full of warning, but he didn't stop.

"We've had people who needed help getting out of an abusive house and we've had people who needed to vanish." He pushed from the wall and took slow steps toward me but stopped a few feet away. "None of us doubts that the second option is what you need, but we had the information on *why* before you did. For fuck's sake, Sutton, you were more concerned with finding Veronica than getting away from Zachary when I found you."

I hated that I was trembling.

Trembling from the guilt over all the lies and half-truths.

From the ache that had built from his distance.

And because this angry version of him *should* have fit him but didn't and somehow made me want him more.

"I know you're afraid of him, I know. I've heard you. But relocating someone isn't something people just decide to do for fun. It's because they're in real danger. It's because that's the *only* option they have. If what you wanted was to find Veronica, tell us. If something happened with Zachary, fucking tell us. It doesn't change what he *has* done or that we know you need to get away from him."

It was there on my tongue, begging to be said.

All of it, ready to spill at their feet.

But every time I tried to open my mouth, I couldn't seem to. My throat felt thick. My tongue felt heavy with lies and unknowns and worries.

My eyes began burning, and I realized why my throat

felt thick . . . why my chest felt weighed down with disappointment and hurt.

I forced a shaky smile at Conor. "Einstein lied."

I pushed from the chair and walked stiffly to my room.

None of them tried to stop me, and I wouldn't have let them.

I hurried through the room and silently shut the bathroom door behind me so I wouldn't wake Lexi.

Once I was alone, I struggled over the idea that one day I might have to tell them the truth and what the repercussions of that would be.

Struggled with why I was so upset by the change in Conor.

I couldn't figure out why it even mattered.

He was no one and meant nothing. He needed to mean nothing.

I lifted my head to look in the mirror and tried to figure out how life had landed us here. How a man had gotten so deeply under my skin in less than a week. Why I had fit against his body so perfectly, and why it had felt so good to be pressed against him earlier.

Large, firm, protective—

My brows pinched together as I remembered that moment. The way he'd grabbed for us and pulled us close, ready to shield us from the danger.

The way he hadn't let me go.

It didn't fit with his coldness the past two days or his anger tonight.

"It doesn't matter," I quickly ran my hands over my face. "It doesn't matter, it doesn't matter." With a determined sigh, I took one more look in the mirror and then left the bathroom.

I had just started slipping into bed when I heard a hesitant knock on the bedroom door.

Like last time, I considered letting it go unanswered.

But, like an idiot, I found myself stepping out of the bed and moving toward the door. Reprimanding myself the entire way there.

It wasn't Conor.

And from the look on Jess's face, my disappointment was noticeable.

She tilted her head back. "I made the guys leave."

My heart skipped a beat. "Forever?"

A secret smile lit up her face. "Just long enough for us to talk." Holding up a hand in the air, she said, "I promise not to force you to tell me anything you don't want to."

I glanced at Lexi, who was still out cold, and then followed Jess into the living room.

Once we were seated, she began. "I've never seen him like that. It was like watching Beck—" She hesitated and then made a face. "Um, Beck was . . ."

"Conor's brother."

Surprise lit in her eyes. "Right. Beck was, well, passionate, I guess you could say." A soft laugh tumbled from her lips. "And by passionate, I mean, he let you know what he thought and felt with all his emotions. But he was the best."

"I heard something like that."

Her eyes narrowed in wonder. "I'm surprised Conor mentioned him."

"Uh, well, he didn't. Not to me anyway," I hurried to clarify and then realized that was only more confusing. "I walked in when he was telling Lexi about him."

Jess nodded in understanding, and once again, that

secret smile crept across her face. "Conor has always been calm and gentle. Seeing him mad is always such a shock because it rarely happens, but when it does, it's over as fast as it began. Kieran claims it didn't start until Beck died."

"You don't need to defend a stranger to me."

"I could tell it hurt you."

My mouth opened to deny it, but Jess raised a brow and effectively shut down any lie I might have given her.

"What did you mean by *Einstein lied*?"

I pressed the tips of my fingers to my temple. I felt like an idiot for having said anything at all, for letting him get to me that much.

"The first day, Conor was talking to her, trying to convince me it was okay to go with him," I began. "Einstein told him to give me the phone and take it off speaker. She said that Conor was the heart of ARCK and the best man for the job. That he was the biggest, but he was also the kindest. She said that if any of the others had come, they would've started grabbing our stuff and shoving us into their car. And she knew Conor wouldn't."

And he hadn't.

He'd been angry, but so had I.

And in all that, he'd never pushed me. An act that would've confirmed everything I'd been told about him. About them.

"She was right," Jess said with a light laugh. "Kieran and I wouldn't have given you an option. We would've just hauled you right out of there."

After meeting them, I wasn't surprised by that.

"Everything she said about Conor was just as true."

"It didn't look that way tonight, or these last days," I

finally admitted. "He's so angry with me, and it came out of nowhere. Even that first day when I attacked him and was constantly fighting him or insulting him, he wasn't like this. Frustrated, sure, but I don't blame him for that. But this? He's . . . he's cold."

Jess studied me for a long while before saying, "Don't take it personally. He's working through some very difficult things and has been through a lot. Not that you haven't."

A huff escaped me. "How can I not take it personally? He hasn't changed the way he acts around my daughter."

"I can't answer that," she said with a lift of a shoulder. "He's being a jerk, but those boys usually are when they're figuring things out. I would know."

"Must just be a universal guy thing," I mumbled under my breath, but Jess still let out a laugh.

It was throaty, wild, and a little crazy, and it fit her so perfectly.

But as soon as it began, it ended, and a solemn look took over her features. "I'll agree to that," she said numbly and then looked at me. "You said it was personal, and I understand not wanting to go there with strangers. Trust me, I do. But can I ask you one thing?"

My nod was hesitant, and I regretted it as soon as it happened.

"Considering what we do for women, and what you *didn't* know . . ." Her darks eyes had been searching mine but fell just before she asked, "Was he abusing you sexually? Or physically, emotionally, mentally . . . anything."

I heard the question, but I had a feeling she was really only asking the first part.

A soft laugh sounded in my throat, even though this

was not at all funny and her question had been entirely inappropriate.

I hadn't been abused.

He was my husband. I was his wife. What happened in our house was for us to figure out and wasn't supposed to leave our walls.

Then again, I wasn't supposed to leave *him*.

"No. But I somehow still felt violated," I admitted as rows of pills and pink powder floated through my mind. Another laugh, this one louder and a little frantic. I rubbed my head, pushing out away memories. "That sounds so stupid."

Honesty and sorrow bled from her when she said, "No, it doesn't."

I jolted when the door to the suite opened, my body relaxed and my heart took off like a thousand butterflies when Conor rounded the corner into the living room.

Kieran followed close behind and went straight to Jess. He dropped a kiss on her lips before heading to the kitchen, but Conor slowed as he neared us.

He cleared his throat, but his voice was still low and gruff when he said, "Didn't think you'd be out here."

"I can leave." I moved to stand, but he shook his head.

"No," he said quickly. "This is for you."

He carefully handed me a white bag, but as soon as it was in my hands, he walked past me to join Kieran in the other room.

I opened the bag and felt my stomach flip and mouth pull into a smile at the container of frozen yogurt waiting at the bottom.

On the clear lid, written in bold permanent ink, was: "I'M SORRY."

I glanced to the guys, who were already whispering something that looked tense, then to Jess.

Once again, she was wearing that secretive smile.

She lifted a hand and snapped her fingers. "Over as fast as it began."

Twelve

Zachary
ELEVEN MONTHS AGO

I nodded when Garret Vaughn stepped into my office and ended the call I was on.

When three others followed him in, I quickly looked them over, sized them up, assessed the threat, and almost laughed because they were the biggest nerds I'd ever seen.

"Larson," Garret said gruffly, extending his hand to shake mine.

I grunted something in response and gestured to the chairs and couches filling the room. "Before we begin—"

"They're silent," Garret said with a wry smirk. "Completely. They don't know how to talk because they like the way money feels too damn much." He glanced at the men weighed down with equipment. "They're my best."

I dipped my head. It was the only thanks he would ever get from me, no matter what happened from here on out.

Once we were sitting, I loosed a sigh and said, "It's bad."

"I figured as much when I saw your name on my phone."

I rubbed at my jaw to stop from punching the ever-present smirk off his face.

A dark laugh slipped out at the thought of him on his knees, pleading for his life. The image of his blood staining my carpet would fuel my dreams for years to come.

One day.

Every man had goals, after all.

"As I said," I continued, "it's bad. You hear about Jason Woods and his wife?"

"Only that she left."

I leaned in closer. "She *fled*. He'd gone to the club one night and had been in a viewing room with two women. Looked up in time to see Vero running away."

He hissed through his teeth and smacked his hand on the arm of the chair. "Goddamn it, how did she get in there?"

"Gets worse. By the time he made it home, she wasn't there. He thinks she left straight from the club because she left all her stuff, including the files full of information on him that she'd been gathering. Some right, some wrong. It all started with her thinking Jason was cheating on her."

"Well, she wasn't wrong," he said grimly. "He should have known better than to fuck other women and then go home to his wife smelling like them."

The corner of my mouth tipped up.

I wasn't going to agree or disagree. Any response I gave, Garret would only dissect it and use it against me. The way he did with everything.

"She thought he was into illegal things, thought he had men working for him. Drugs, money laundering, embezzlement, prostitution. Even thought Thornton might be in on it and that they'd killed people to silence them." I grunted in acknowledgment when Garret's eyes closed on a mumbled curse. "But she thought he was going to a strip club at night."

"There was no mistaking that place for a strip club once she got in."

I let out a grim laugh.

If that wasn't the goddamn truth.

The sex club the Woods family owned was far from a strip club. Only those with pockets deeper than the goddamn ocean were members, and it thrived. Hidden *just* enough to keep it off the radar, bougie as fuck, and filled with every fantasy any man or woman could ever think of.

Woods's wife had money to get in, but the bouncers should've known to never let her near the doors. The one from that night was already in the ground.

None of our wives were allowed to even know about it, never mind actually be allowed inside.

They were showered with money and anything they could ever want, they didn't need to know how it all came to be.

Traffickers and murderers didn't remain off government, cartel, or mafia radars for generations by telling their women the ins and outs of business. The moment one found out, word would spread, and the Tennessee Gentlemen would be hunted until there was nothing and no one left.

"So, what are we gonna do about Vero?" Garret finally asked. "She needs to be kept silent."

"And that's the problem . . ." I leaned back in the chair and spread my arms wide. "She made it to her parents' in North Carolina and then vanished."

"Vanished," he said dully.

I waved a hand through the air. "Gone. No trace of her parents. No trace of Vero—real or otherwise."

"Real—" His brows lifted in recognition when I gave him a knowing look. "*Oh*."

"Yeah. *Oh*. Forget about that one?"

"For a minute, yeah." He scrubbed a hand across his jaw, nodding as he did. "Well, it's hard to find ghosts, but it isn't impossible."

A slow grin spread across my face. "I can make it easier." When Garret only stared back expectantly, I said, "Woods still has Vero's messages linked to his computer, and she was talking to her parents on the way. Her mom sent some message saying, 'This is them. They'll be here when you arrive,' and there was a link to ARCK Private Investigation attached. Woods and I have been looking into them. Small company made up of four people in an even smaller town in North Carolina. They *are* private investigators, but they have a hidden contact page for those who are afraid for their lives. It says they can help you start over."

"That isn't how it works. You don't interfere in TenGen matters."

"They'll figure that out soon enough." At his questioning look, I said, "We need to find out everything we can about the people in this firm and where they sent Woods's wife. Then we need to show them what it feels like when someone takes and hides something that doesn't belong to them."

"Why are you heading this?" Hesitation crept through

his tone. "Why not Woods?"

"Because he came to me, like everyone always does," I said pointedly, which only seemed to spark his anger. "When we decided to take matters into our own hands, we said we'd have each other's backs if shit ever went south to keep it from getting back to the older generations. That's what I'm doing."

"And what, you're gonna collect on him when the time is right?"

I shrugged. "Every favor needs to be repaid."

A feral smile inched across his face. "Then expect me to come collecting for *this*."

"She's already my wife, Vaughn. Can't have her now."

His smile only deepened. "For now."

"I'll bury you alive if you attempt to take her."

"Back?" The word ripped from him on a growl. His breaths were uneven when he said, "Take her back, is that what you mean? You fucking stole her from me."

"I told you, every favor needs to be repaid." The corner of my mouth twitched up. "Does your little girlfriend know you'll always compare her to someone else . . . obsess over someone else?"

Rage and wrath clashed in his eyes before they snapped away.

He barked out a command, and the three nerds came scrambling over. With a cold look in my direction, he said, "Tell them what you need so we can be done."

It was the only response I would get.

I knew Garret Vaughn would always love Sutton. But he couldn't have her . . . no one could.

I pulled up ARCK Private Investigation's hidden contact form while waiting for the coffee to finish brewing.

Hidden because these pieces of shit didn't want just anyone stumbling onto their site—then again, I wasn't just anyone.

Their true site boasted of their services and who they were . . . veiled stories of who they were, as I had come to find out since that day Garret Vaughn and his band of nerds had first stepped into my office eight months ago. But this page was nothing more than a white text box and a few perfectly scripted words to lure someone in.

Someone like Vero.

Someone like my wife, if she were ever to start thinking for herself. But she was too compliant and obedient to, so there was no one better suited for this.

> *If you are a victim of domestic violence, you don't deserve this. There are people who are ready to help you.*
> *If you're afraid for your life in any situation, you don't have to be.*
> *We can get you out of your situations and help you start over.*

Bullshit.

I glanced at my even shorter message and attached the fake account I'd created for Sutton in the email section before hitting submit.

> Is this real? Can you help?

A cold smile pulled at my mouth as I slipped the phone into my pocket and fingered the small container in there.

Once the coffee was ready, I glanced around the kitchen before pulling out the container and dumping its powdery contents into the mug.

Within seconds, it had dissolved into the black liquid and its taste was masked by the creamer. Once again, it was as if nothing had ever been there, and my beautiful wife would never be the wiser.

And she thought I was the idiot.

That I wouldn't figure out what she was doing by withholding her body from me until certain times of the month to prevent from getting pregnant.

I'd figured it out long ago, it had just taken me a while to decide on a game that fit her offense. A game where she slowly began wanting me more and more until she couldn't help herself when I came for her, until she was insane with need, seemed appropriate enough.

And this past year *had* been slow . . . but goddamn if it hadn't been worth it.

In the beginning, she threw out excuse after excuse to avoid me.

The last month or two? One touch from me had her writhing.

Soon, I'd have that bitch begging.

I headed upstairs and let a weighted breath ease from

my lungs when I sat on the bed near Sutton's feet.

She moaned in response and reached for her head. "Whatever this is . . . it's getting worse." Her face pinched, showing her discomfort as she pushed herself to sitting. "I need to see another doctor. Someone has to know what's going on."

Oh, but they won't. I pay them too much to.

I forced back a smirk and held out her coffee. "Maybe this will help for now."

As soon as the mug was in her hands and she'd taken the first sip, I released another heavy sigh.

"What's going on?" she asked weakly. "You're distracted and stressed lately. I've never seen you like this."

I scrubbed my hands over my face and pushed from the bed.

After pacing around the room a few times, I stopped near the end of the bed so I was facing her and folded my arms over my chest.

My expression was a mixture of agony and worry and hesitation.

A perfect mixture.

One I'd been practicing for this exact moment.

"It's Vero . . ."

Sutton sat up so suddenly that she winced and then swayed. "Is she back?"

My head moved minutely, and I cleared my throat, pretending as if I were choking back emotions I wasn't sure I even possessed.

"Zachary." It was a breath filled with dread.

I could feel the corners of my lips curling up in a victorious smirk behind my façade.

"She never left," I finally said. After another few

seconds, I risked a glance at her. "We thought she left —*Jason* thought she left him. He kept trying to call Vero, her parents, her friends, anyone who might know where she went. No one had seen her. And then a neighbor came forward saying they heard screaming coming from the house the night Vero . . . was taken."

Her eyes widened in confusion. "What?"

"Jason checked the camera system. A van full of people pulled up right after Vero came home. They got her before she could even reach the front door and dragged her into the van. One of them followed behind in her car."

Tears were slipping down Sutton's face, but her head was shaking and denial shown in her eyes. "No. No, that can't—*no*. Who would kidnap her? What do they want?"

"It's worse than that," I said warily and gripped at the back of my neck. "These people . . . they're a group from North Carolina posing as a private investigating firm. They're really part of a human trafficking ring. They take a handful of girls from an area and then move on."

Her mouth fell open in silent horror.

"That means they're still on the hunt."

"How—" Her hand dropped to her stomach and squeezed. "How do you know this?"

"Jason's been working with the FBI since that neighbor came forward."

"This . . . this just can't be real. It can't." Her head snapped up. "We have to get her back. How do we get her back?"

I couldn't fight the smile that time.

So naïve.

So trusting.

"We have a plan."

Thirteen

Sutton

I woke with a start.
 Heart racing.
Sweat clinging to my body.
Fear gripping my spine.
But instead of the dark room I'd been in, there was a bright, open area. Instead of the hard floor I'd been on, there were cushions supporting me. Instead of the door I'd been staring at, there was the most precious face in the world.

Wide hazel eyes were locked on me, worrying in a way no six-year-old should.

"Were your dreams really scary, or were they only a little scary this time?" she asked, her voice soft as a whisper.

"No, no. It was nothing," I said through the adrenaline

tightening my throat. "Nothing, sweet girl. Good morning."

I sat up and looked around the living room of the suite, at the muted television, and the blanket draped over me.

My mind raced as I tried to figure out why I was there, tried to remember going to bed. I couldn't remember anything past talking with Jess and Kieran about where Zachary could be hiding.

For hours, they'd asked about the lake house and his normal routine. All the while, Conor had sat nearby, regret and indecision bleeding from him.

I quickly covered myself with the blanket when Conor rounded the corner into my line of sight, even though I was no less dressed than I had been the night before.

"Morning. Ordered food a few minutes ago." His rough voice no longer held that coldness from the past two days, but the warmth was still missing.

I brushed at my wild hair and prayed I didn't look like a train wreck. "Thank you. Conor, wh—" He turned those bright blue eyes on me, making me forget what I was going to say.

Kind.

Gentle.

Everything they were supposed to be, but it didn't feel like enough.

They weren't dipping over my body before quickly darting away like they had those first few days.

They were simply watching, waiting for me to continue.

That should have been a good thing. He was helping us . . . protecting us. I may not have started out as one, but I had turned into his client. So, he shouldn't look, and I shouldn't want him to.

Except I *did*.

I wanted the lingering glances and teasing words.

I wanted the way he always seemed to find an excuse to brush past me when he spoke to me, making me shiver and crave more of his touch.

I wanted to know that he felt this connection that was as undeniable as it was irrational.

I blinked quickly, breaking the contact and pulling myself out of my absurd thoughts. "I'm sorry. I, uh . . . I was wondering about why I was here?"

"You mean why you slept out here?" When I nodded, he said, "Well, I considered moving you. But then I thought you might wake up and attack me, and who knows what you attack like when you're asleep. You might have managed to get a good hit in."

I risked a glance at him, but he was looking at his computer screen. The corner of his mouth was tipped up, and that small smile felt incredibly significant.

"Well, thank you." I eased myself off the couch and grabbed the blanket I'd been covered with. "At least it finally got you to sleep in a bed. I'm sure that was nice after nearly a week on couches."

If I hadn't been studying that perfectly imperfect smile, I wouldn't have noticed the moment it shifted, became forced.

After a second, he made a confirming sound in his throat.

That was it.

A step forward. A step backward.

Perfect.

The man was infuriating.

I went to the bedroom to change and get ready for

another day of sitting in the suite, and it wasn't until Lexi came bounding in that I realized I hadn't thought twice about leaving her out there with him.

Each morning, I'd find her in the living room, having stare-downs with Conor. And despite my unwanted feelings that wouldn't seem to stop surfacing for him, there had always been that underlying fear whenever I saw Lexi with him.

Fear that came from months and months of Zachary feeding me lies. Months of expecting something wholly different when it came to any ARCK member. Fear that I had felt was confirmed when Conor broke into the motel that morning.

But, somehow, I'd come to expect him there, had come to be comforted by his presence, had come to know that we *were* safe as long as he was there.

That Lexi was safe.

"Did you brush your hair?" Lexi asked, immediately inspecting my head.

I self-consciously touched my hair. It had been as wild as I'd feared and nearly impossible to tame. "Yes . . ."

"It was really poofy when you woke up."

I dropped my hand to my side and narrowed my eyes. "Don't be rude, it comes from an ugly heart."

My eyes widened in horror as soon as the words left my mouth.

Oh dear God, I am *turning into my mother.*

As a kid, I'd always hated whenever she would say that to me. It made me think there was something wrong with my heart.

As I got older, I heard the hypocrisy in her words and

began hating who she was as a person. How she thought. How she spoke to people and of them.

Turns out, I was no better than she was.

I crouched in front of Lexi and grabbed her shoulders. "I shouldn't have said that. It *is* true, in a way. It really is." *Damn you, Mother.* "But I know you weren't being rude, you were just teasing me in a silly way, not in a mean way. So, I'm sorry for saying that."

Lexi was staring at me as if she didn't know why we were even talking about this. "Okay."

"I just want to be sure that, in the future, you won't point out things about other people. Even though my hair was probably funny and it didn't hurt my feelings, your words could hurt someone else's feelings."

"Like when you hurt Mr. Conor's?"

Being kicked in the stomach would have hurt less than that innocent question. "Yes. Exactly. I need to work on that. Not only with saying it but also with thinking it."

Lexi placed her hands on my cheeks and forced me to look at her. "It's okay, Momma. I think he'll forgive you."

"Thanks, sweet girl."

I snuck a kiss to her nose and smiled when she laughed and skipped away. Before she reached the door, she stopped and turned, dropping her voice to a loud whisper. "When I woke up this morning and went looking for you, Mr. Conor was sitting at the door."

My head tilted. "Oh?"

"He was still sleeping."

The air escaped my lungs in a rush when I realized what she was saying, what that meant. The man hadn't slept in a bed or on a couch last night. He'd slept on the floor. That, in and of itself, stirred even more unwanted emotions inside me.

I nodded and offered Lexi a brittle smile.

Once I'd gathered myself, I followed her out of the room and into the kitchen where Conor was setting out the food he'd ordered.

Breakfast was a quiet affair since Lexi still wasn't speaking to Conor or around him.

I was fairly certain Conor preferred not to say anything to me, and I didn't know what to say to him. I was upset that he didn't take the opportunity to sleep on a bed when I'd been begging him to sleep on the one in his room. I was irritated that he didn't just wake me, and I was kicking myself for being so selfish that I took the only bed he obviously felt comfortable using.

By the time it was over and the plates were cleared away, all I could think of was talking to him about it, but I was afraid I would explode on him the second I opened my mouth.

After Lexi was set up with the crayons and coloring books Jess had brought, I wandered back over to the kitchen table where Conor had set up his laptop.

As soon as I sat, he said, "You're the first only child female in any of the core families."

I blinked, trying to reorganize my thoughts, completely taken off guard. "Excuse me?"

He flipped his laptop around to me, revealing a massive family tree. "It's becoming clearer that this is men only, so we were only looking at the men with the five core last names. But I recognized one of the men on the payroll in the drug ring as one of Jason's uncles by marriage, not blood. With thousands of people on the payroll, it isn't unreasonable to think that the men brought in by marriage might be on it too. I've been building this to see who's related by marriage, how they are, and to see who is in on it. So far, every man has been."

It was overwhelming to see generations of five families splitting off and growing, and to know that every man on that page was—or had been—involved with illegal things.

"You're the first only child female in any of the original families," he repeated.

"What does that mean?"

"Your dad was an only child too," he said with a sigh. "The Camp name is going to die out of the Tennessee Gentlemen."

I was so focused on the names that I didn't register what he was saying at first. I'd been nodding, though, for who knew how long.

Shock pulsed through me when my childhood flashed before my eyes in a split second. "Oh my God."

In the next, fights and fears and realizations ripped through my mind.

"What?" Conor was out of his seat and sinking into the one next to me, leaning over to look at the screen and then me. "Sutton, what?"

"My parents. Za—Oh Jesus." I shook away the memories and dropped my head into my hands.

Conor must have realized that I needed time, because his chair shifted back and, eventually, that calm patience he exuded reached me.

"It's my life, it *was* my life, and it was supposed to be normal." I looked up and found him watching me. "How do you come in and say something—say *one* god damn thing—

and change everything I knew?" A weak laugh tumbled from my lips. "Or make it make sense . . ."

His eyebrows slowly lifted, but he didn't push.

Just waited.

"My parents, they—God, they fought constantly when I was young. Younger than Lexi, but I remember it clearly. Every time, it was because my dad wanted my mom to have another kid. When I got older, I remember thinking about how weird that was. I was in middle school when I overheard him threaten to divorce her if she *couldn't* have another."

He actually looked appalled by that, but I waved his horror away.

"Don't feel too bad for her. Remember, she's an awful person." I dropped my stare to the table and traced patterns with the tips of my fingers as I continued. "Eventually, those fights stopped and they stayed married. I heard our housekeeper telling her husband that my dad was the reason they couldn't have more children."

"Asshole."

My lips twitched into a smile because he wasn't wrong. "Lexi's an only child."

"Zachary has a brother to carry on the name."

I risked a glance in his direction. "I don't think that mattered to him. He was so mad when we found out we were having a girl that he didn't speak to me for days. Then, just a week after Lexi was born, he told me we needed to start trying for a boy as soon as possible. Demanded it, actually."

Conor was silent, but it wasn't a contemplative quiet.

It was tense. Furious.

Uncomfortable.

I swallowed thickly and shifted in my chair. "I was so overwhelmed and emotional, I wasn't sure if I wanted another baby at all. I'd had a plan. Get married and get pregnant two years later, maybe have another baby two and a half years after that. We'd only been married a couple of months before realizing we were pregnant with Lexi. I hadn't been ready, and I wasn't prepared to be pregnant for *years* following our marriage. When I said no, he went days without speaking to me again."

I dropped my arms to my waist and curled them around myself, trying to keep the trembling away.

"There's something I want to tell you."

But I also don't because it shouldn't be anyone's business other than Zachary's and mine.

Because it's you . . .

That couldn't be an excuse. It shouldn't even be a factor.

"I didn't feel comfortable saying it last night, and I won't apologize for that. I don't know Jess and Kieran, and this is . . ."

"Personal," he murmured.

I nodded, the movement faint. "Before I tell you, I have a question."

"Anything." It was immediate, open, and full of some emotion I wanted to explore and refused to acknowledge.

"The drug trafficking within Tennessee Gentlemen, is that only illegal drugs, or is it pharmaceuticals as well?"

Conor was silent so long that I finally looked at him again. There was a question in his eyes, as though he were trying to figure out where I was going with this before I could tell him.

With a subtle nod, he said, "Both."

"Zachary had these mood swings where he would punish me by not talking to me. And he did this thing that—well, the more it happened, the more I was sure that I didn't want another child with him because I hated having anything that tied me to him at all. So, I made sure we never had sex at a time when I could get pregnant."

"Birth control?"

A tremor rolled down my spine.

That hadn't been an option. I couldn't force myself to say the words . . . they were too humiliating.

"He really wanted another baby," I said instead.

I might as well have shouted the truth with the way Conor's mouth formed a tight line and his eyes darkened with anger.

"Around the time Vero disappeared, I, uh, I started wanting him." Mortification slid through my veins. I hurried to get out the rest, knowing it would only get harder to say. "In a way that wasn't normal for me. Over the last year, it only grew. Even when I was afraid of him, my body still craved him. The day—" I almost choked on the truth as I swallowed it. "The day Lexi and I packed up and left, I found a cabinet in his den. It was stocked full of female Viagra, and there was a chart of how to go from a half pill a day to three a day."

Conor's eyes had widened with shock, but his hands were formed into fists.

"I had withdrawals from it the first week we were in the motel. I didn't even know that was a thing with something like that."

It took a minute before Conor's absentminded nodding stopped. "What did you mean by *even when I was afraid of him*?"

And just like that, I was back in a closet.

Just as I had been in my nightmares before I'd been able to wake myself this morning.

"You told me something the first day that Zachary had said to Einstein. About me running, and the slow chase . . ."

I finally focused on the kitchen and Conor again. He looked ready to burn down the world if it meant finding and stopping Zachary.

"He calls it a game. *Our* game. Only it was never a game for me."

Fourteen

Conor

I was vibrating with barely restrained rage by the time Sutton finished telling me what Zachary had done.

The drugs.

The fucked-up game he played, not that I should have been surprised. We found out with Einstein that he liked to play games. Thank God his version of games with Sutton didn't have death as an outcome, but still . . . these versions . . .

Fuck.

Not only did I have to listen to the shit he'd done to her but I also had to picture her accepting it, even *wanting* it at the end because of the goddamn drugs. The way she described it—even as tame as her descriptions had been—had been more than I could handle.

Each hour in her presence seemed to put me at greater

risk of doing something stupid. Something I couldn't afford.

And, yet, there I was.

Wanting to punch a man because he'd touched her.

Wanting to slowly kill him because he'd hurt her.

Wanting *her*.

I scrubbed my hands over my face and stood, needing to get away from her before I made the biggest mistake of my life.

I slid my phone from my pocket and took a step toward my room. "I have a call to make."

She sat forward, panic flashing in her eyes. "Don't—"

"I'm not," I quickly assured her. "I won't. I need to talk to them about the situation, but not what you told me."

My eyes automatically shifted toward the empty living room and the girls' closed bedroom door.

"What's Lexi doing?"

Sutton loosed an exhausted sigh and turned, though she couldn't see anything other than the wall at her back. "Coloring in the bedroom."

The suite was suddenly too silent.

My heart too loud.

Unless Lexi was asleep, their bedroom door was always open if she was in there alone.

I didn't strain to listen for signs of a silent girl drawing.

I didn't remain where I was.

Because everything in me told me this was wrong.

"Lexi?" I called out as I hurried across the suite. As soon as I reached the door, I grabbed the handle and knocked as I opened. "Lexi."

The room was dark, as was the bathroom.

The coloring book and crayons were on the floor.

When I turned, Sutton was halfway across the living room with her arms still curled around her body, her brows pulled together tight in confusion.

"Lexi, now is the time to respond to me," I yelled, turning in a circle.

"Alexis Raine." Sutton's tone was stern, but there was no escaping the fear woven in.

I had my phone at my ear and was storming across the suite to where Sutton was running and yelling for her daughter.

"Get here, get Jess in the room with Sutton." My voice dropped, and I held Sutton's shattered stare. "Lexi's gone."

"What do you mean she's gone—what do you—*Lexi!*"

I ended the call and caught Sutton just before she could take off again. "Do not leave this suite. Do not open the door. Not for anyone other than me, Kieran, or Jess. Understood?"

Fat tears rolled down her cheeks. Her trembling hands drove into her hair. "Where's my daugh—oh God, oh God."

"Sutton, tell me you understand!"

Her face crumpled as she nodded.

I raced out of the room and down the hall to the stairs, calling Einstein as I went.

"Favorite gentle giant, what can—"

"Stop," I shouted as I jumped half the flight and hit the landing. "Lexi. Lexi's gone. Check the cameras."

She hissed a curse, and then there was nothing as I tore down the stairs, looking for any sign of her.

If she had been taken, they wouldn't have used the elevator.

If she had been taken, I would never forgive myself.

"I hate to be the one to ask," Einstein said distractedly, "but how the fuck did a girl disappear?"

"Cameras, Einstein."

"Fair question."

I burst out the door and looked around at the massive resort that was crawling with people going in and out of the different shops and restaurants lining the main floor.

And that was just inside.

I started jogging, searching faces as I did. "Sutton was telling me details about Zachary. We were on the far side of the suite, Lexi was coloring in the room near the door."

Jesus Christ, there was so much water in here, and I had no fucking clue if the girl could swim.

Indoor pools, waterfalls, and it all seemed as big of a threat as the possibility of someone taking her.

"Good news, she left the room by herself. No one got in there without you seeing them." Einstein hesitated and then made a muffled noise. "She *ran* out of the room."

I stopped in the middle of a cluster of restaurants and turned, searching faces and the water surrounding me, trying to think like a girl I didn't know.

"It doesn't make sense," I ground out. "Everything was fine with her."

As far as I fucking knew.

I dragged my free hand through my hair and let out a growl. "Can you see where she went after?"

"Already on that. Waiting on elevators."

I glanced at the stores and then ran in their direction, praying like hell she had stayed inside and gone to one of these.

I was already pushing past people to get into the first

store when Einstein said, "She got off on the ground floor, waiting to see where she goes. Hold on, Kieran's calling."

A second and third store, and I was struggling to breathe. I had one job, and I'd failed in the worst way.

My head was so clouded that I was seconds from going to the front desk, finding a PA system, and demanding security help look for her.

Considering I was supposed to be keeping her hidden, I knew I couldn't. Rationally, I knew that.

But I was so goddamn close to caving.

"She went right," Einstein suddenly said.

I hurried out of the store I was in and ran to a place where I could see the elevators, nearly knocking over a man as I did. "Shit. Shit, sorry."

I kept the elevators in my sight as I started going to my left, Lexi's right, which led toward all the restaurants.

"No. No, that's all restaurants. She wouldn't have gone that way."

"Okay, but she did."

"We just fucking ate, Einstein."

"There's only so fast I can follow her when I have to constantly switch cameras." That distracted tone she got when she was working on something was heavy with irritation. "Not saying she stopped at any of them, but she went that way."

My head was shaking as she spoke. My legs were already taking me the other way. I looked ahead and had to struggle to stay standing when it felt like my knees were knocked out.

On the opposite side of the atrium, Lexi was slipping out of a shop.

"I found her." It was a relieved breath wrapped in guilt and pain.

And then I was running, straining against every instinct to yell the girl's name.

I didn't remember the people I ran into or pushed past. I didn't remember the obstacles littering the path to get to her. I just ran straight to her.

It was the longest run of my life.

I dropped to the ground and caught her around her shoulders just before she entered another store.

Her tiny body jolted, but she relaxed as soon as she saw me.

Her face was red, and her eyes were puffy.

I wanted to yell at her for leaving.

I wanted to demand to know why she had.

I wanted to beg her to finally talk to me and tell me what was wrong.

Before I could get a word out, she threw herself against my chest and sobbed.

My chest ached in a way I couldn't explain. I wanted to tear my heart out because it ached for her. I wanted to protect her from whatever had hurt her. I wanted to make sure she never cried again.

I was also pretty goddamn sure that hug was better than any word Lexi could've ever said to me.

My phone, which was still clenched in my hand, rang. I lifted it and then answered the call when I saw Kieran's name on the screen.

"I found her."

"All right, I'll head back to the room. The two of you need to get back. Now."

I didn't respond. Just ended the call and leaned back to

look at Lexi. "We need to get back in the room, but we'll talk about this in there, all right?"

Her head was moving in huge, stubborn shakes as I spoke. "I don't want to. No one cares about me anyway."

There was that feeling again.

Tore my heart out. Crushed it and set it on fire.

She believed what she was saying, and to have her first words to me be so utterly devastating?

Damn.

I leaned my head close to hers and lowered my voice. "What are you talking about? For such a smart girl, that's the craziest thing I've ever heard."

Her lips quivered and her eyes, which were so much like her mom's, filled with tears. "I heard Momma talking to you." She sniffed quickly. "Heard her say Daddy was mad about me. That she didn't want me."

My mind raced as I tried to figure out what she was talking about, and then it hit me.

Zachary wanting a boy.

"No. No, Lexi, no. That isn't—" *Fuck*.

I dragged a hand over my face and fought with myself.

I could feel the need to get us out of the open like my next breaths depended on it, but there was also this damn voice telling me that Lexi needed me *right* there listening to her.

"Your mom wanted you," I said slowly, making sure she heard and understood me. "I don't know her well, but what I know for sure is that you are the most important part of her life. If she didn't want you, she wouldn't have looked like her entire world had been ripped away when you disappeared just now."

Lexi's body jerked with a new round of sobs. "But I heard her, I did."

"We were talking about something that's a little hard to explain. Something that has nothing to do with your mom not wanting you." I dropped my head lower until I caught her stare. "I swear to you."

"You promise, promise?"

"Promise, promise." I gave her a pointed look. "Now, you did something really dangerous, so we need to get back to the room and get you to your mom."

She slammed against my chest again and wrapped her arms around my neck. "I'm sorry, Mr. Conor."

"I know, Lex." I stood with her still in my arms and started toward the elevators.

As soon as we were in the room, I released her and watched her run into a crying Sutton's arms.

Kieran and Jess were there, both standing away so that I barely noticed them, both wearing looks that had me biting back a curse.

I left the girls in the living room and passed my friends on the way to my room. I didn't hear them enter or shut my door, but sure enough, when I turned, the door was closed and they were both standing against it.

"Tell me how she got away." Kieran's demand was soft, lethal, but it held a hint of worry. As though he were afraid that I was about to confirm something.

When I relayed what I had told Einstein, Kieran only lifted a skeptical brow.

"Okay, obviously that was the wrong answer. Why don't you tell me what you think was happening?"

He glanced at Jess. "With what we talked about last night—"

My bitter laugh was enough to stop him. "So, what, you think I was too busy fucking a client to notice that her daughter slipped away?"

"Conor, we just need to know," Jess said with a sigh.

"The fact that you keep trying to give me the opportunity to tell you something else is pissing me off." I tried to relax my hands, which had curled into tight fists, but the adrenaline from almost losing Lexi and their unwillingness to trust my words was pumping through me too hard. "I told you what happened, if you don't believe it, then we have bigger problems."

They were silent for a while before Kieran said, "I told you I wouldn't stand in the way. But if it's—"

"Get out."

"If it's putting people at risk," he said, his raised tone harsher than I'd ever heard it.

"I said get the fuck out," I seethed. When they didn't move, I stepped closer and lowered my voice so I wouldn't be heard outside the room. "I told you to take me off this case, if you forgot. To jog your memory, you said no. What happened today has *nothing* to do with what we discussed last night." I snuck a glance at Jess. "This is all pretty comical considering I remember a time when a girl got in the way of *your* jo—"

Kieran was directly in front of me with a knife pressed to my throat before I realized he'd moved.

I swallowed, the action pressing the blade harder to my skin. "Job."

My eyes shifted to Jess, who was staring at us with a mixture of sadness and horror.

I only felt the first.

I knew the fucked-up ins and outs of Kieran. Knew he'd

been trained to be an assassin from the day he could walk. Knew he had more control over knives and blades than most people did over their body. Knew he had a demon in him that craved the kill.

Just as I knew he was the only person I'd trust to have my back.

To have him pull a knife on me? It hurt.

I gripped his arm and pushed it away, knowing he'd let me because he was already fighting the instinct to kill. "Apparently, I hit a nerve."

His chest jerked with ragged breaths when he stumbled back, looking more ashamed than I would have thought him capable of. "Different. It was different for us."

My mouth opened to deny it, but a laugh came out instead as I sank down onto the bed and rested my elbows on my knees. "You're right. It was. You were actually fucking Jess."

I didn't remind them of the other differences because that would only hurt Jess. And I'd pushed Kieran enough for one day.

"If what you say was happening was truly what happened, then okay. I'm sorry for doubting you," Jess said as she walked over and sat on the floor in front of me. "What did she tell you?"

A hesitant sound formed in my chest. After the bullshit of the last few minutes, this wasn't about to go over well. "I was actually getting up to call you when I realized Lexi was gone. I told Sutton I wouldn't tell you the information she'd given me."

"Conor," Kieran said on a groan.

"What I *can* tell you is all you need to know right now." I gave him a pleading look. "Trust me on this."

His only response was that hard, threatening stare.

"Zachary played games with her, but they weren't fatal like with Einstein. What he did to her? Still enough to make anyone want to get far, far from their husband. Jess, I think it's something you should talk to her about. If she tells you, you'll understand why."

"Pretty sure I already do," she murmured, but she still gave me a confirming nod.

My attention shifted to the door, as though I could see the woman somewhere on the other side of it. "Like I said, it's enough for any woman to want to get far away from her husband and press charges, but it isn't enough for a relocation."

Jess looked to Kieran, but he didn't take his eyes from me.

"What are you thinking?" he finally asked.

"However word got around about us helping Veronica, Sutton didn't know any of the specifics behind it. I think . . . shit, I don't know," I ground out.

Everything was just speculation because she still had yet to come right out and say exactly why she and Lexi had contacted us. I was starting to wonder if she ever would.

"She wanted to get away from Zachary. She needed to," I continued. "I think she knew we could make Veronica disappear, so she wanted us to make her and Lexi disappear, and maybe put them together. She went for an extreme, not realizing what she was asking for, or that there are people out there who genuinely need this."

"Only to find out who Zachary truly is, that she's in the middle of a cartel, and relocating her really is necessary," Jess mumbled.

"Right."

"But she hasn't trusted us from the beginning," Kieran said. "She's still withholding information—like what *crime* she supposedly saw, why she was scared, and why they were surrounded by people."

"I know."

"We need to know these things."

"I can't force her to tell me. None of us can." I loosed a slow breath and said, "She knows we didn't have information from Veronica . . . that we helped them without any reasoning."

Kieran mumbled a curse.

"She opens up when she wants to, and I have to let her."

Kieran grunted, the sound both irritated and mocking. "Last night you—"

"Jesus, last night," I breathed. It was rough and raw and full of regret.

Last night I'd been reeling from the ultimatum Kieran had dealt.

Refusing to allow a client to get into my head and under my skin.

Telling myself over and over again that Sutton was the reason for Einstein nearly dying, trying to build up that hate again, trying to make *her* hate me.

I'd barely lasted five minutes. As soon as Sutton's eyes had gone all glassy, I'd nearly broken.

When she'd stood and walked away, I'd lasted until her bedroom door clicked shut before I was going after her.

Jess had stopped me with disappointed words and a cold glare, and forced me and Kieran out of the suite.

"I wasn't thinking clearly," I said. "I could've ruined what little trust I've built with her, and you know it. When she's ready to tell me something we should know, she will."

"We don't have time to wait for her to trust you," Kieran rumbled. "It's been months of trying to get any information from her, and now we need to find people."

"Maybe she was afraid," I said, voicing an idea I'd been thinking over since that first night with Sutton.

"Of?" Kieran prompted.

"Us," I said simply. "She didn't trust us before, she was hostile when I found her, and she's been slow to trust me. I've been thinking about how she asked for our help and questioned us a lot, but if she only knew that we were involved in Veronica's *disappearance* and hadn't known why Veronica would need us? We were a risk she was taking . . . we were an unknown."

Kieran sighed after a moment. "Fair."

Jess was staring so intently at the floor, as though she were forcing herself not to look anywhere else, that unease gathered in the pit of my stomach.

"What, Jess?"

She angled her head toward Kieran, away from me, and licked her lips nervously.

I wasn't sure I'd ever seen Jess nervous in the time I'd known her.

"Jess," I prompted louder.

"There's an *or* we aren't discussing," she said on a rush. "It's something Einstein mentioned."

From the way Kieran was studying her, he was in the dark as much as I was.

"Jessica," he said softly, a plea and demand all at once.

"Einstein's systems started getting hacked not long after we moved Veronica. We *thought* it was because Sutton had been looking into us that whole year, and Zachary somehow found out. And that could still be the case. She could have been looking because she knew about our involvement with Veronica, and that was what started the chain of events," she rambled, quick to backtrack on the speculation.

"*Jessica.*"

She shared a wordless conversation with Kieran before glancing at me. With a stuttered exhale, she said, "The *or* is that Sutton's emails about wanting to be relocated could have been part of Zachary's game, and we've walked right into another trap."

I didn't respond because I had a feeling that my immediate response wouldn't have been met well, all things considered.

So instead, I waited.

Kieran said, "I want to know what you think."

"I'm not expecting you to believe me, so I don't have a response."

His eyes darkened with frustration. "Sutton's shock when she learned about the Tennessee Gentlemen, you think it was genuine?"

"Absolutely."

"Is there anything she's confessed to you, other than this morning?"

I thought over the last five days. "Not confess so much as put together pieces in a way where she can't help but say it. Like I've shocked and stunned her so badly the words just come out." I waved a hand toward him. "But everything I know, you know."

"Except for this morning."

"It doesn't help or harm the case. It gives her a legitimate reason to want to get away from him," I argued. "But she hates him for what he did to her, and she feels betrayed by everyone around her. That betrayal grows with each new thing I reveal. So, if you're asking me, I think she would've fessed up if this were one of Zachary's games."

"Agreed," Kieran said on an exhale and then walked forward, extending a hand to help Jess off the floor. "No more disappearances."

I ground my jaw to keep from responding in a way that wouldn't help anything.

"When are you moving next?"

"Tomorrow."

"Make it today. Get with Einstein on the times." His tone left no room for question, so I simply dipped my head in a nod. "And, Conor . . ." He waited until my narrowed stare was focused on him before saying, "Sutton needs to give us something more than she did last night. We've been everywhere listed in the files. There's still no trace of Zachary or Garret. Remind her that, until we have eyes on him, she's stuck here."

"Understood."

Fifteen

Sutton

I watched Lexi coloring at the kitchen table of our new suite that evening, arms wrapped tightly around myself to ward off the bone-deep chill I hadn't been able to shake since Conor had realized she was gone this morning.

Gone.

And all because of me.

I kept replaying the conversation in my head, trying to think of how it must have sounded to her. My heart cracked a little more each time I did.

I kept wondering how we hadn't known. How we hadn't heard her leave. Even after Conor tested it and we both realized we wouldn't hear the door close unless someone slammed it, I still couldn't wrap my mind around how Lexi had slipped out unnoticed.

Because that meant someone could've come in and grabbed her unnoticed.

A full-body tremor ripped through me, stealing my breath.

"Cold?"

I looked up when Conor appeared beside me.

"Um, I don't . . ." It was all I could get out.

Because I couldn't figure out if I was. I felt it down to my soul, but I was sure it had nothing to do with the temperature in the room.

My attention drifted back to Lexi for a minute before the thoughts that had been begging to be freed all day finally started slipping out. "We keep switching rooms, but what if whoever's helping Zachary hacks the cameras? They'll see which room we go to."

"Einstein has fake camera feeds that play three times a day, at random times. They're long enough for us to move rooms, which is why we have to wait to move, when we do."

I nodded, but the movement was jerky. Because his answer didn't help with the rest of the thoughts clustering together on my tongue.

"I hadn't thought about it before," I said, my voice soft as a breath, "but I thought of something earlier, and now I can't stop thinking about it."

The tips of his fingers grazed my arm when I didn't continue, and I both cherished and hated the way my skin warmed with his touch. The way my body ached for more.

An ache so pure and genuine after a year of tainted cravings that I felt as if I might go insane before this war inside me ended.

There were so many unknowns and suspicions and doubts wrapped up in the man next to me, but I was legally bound to another, so how could I still want Conor so fiercely?

Alarm rang in his tender voice. "Sutton, what is it?"

"When Lexi disappeared, you made me stay here."

"To pro—"

"You made me stay, Conor." I stepped deeper into the living room and held his confused stare. "That's my daughter, my world, and she was gone. Every instinct told me to find her, and then I had you in my head telling me to stay, and I listened because, what if she came back and we were both gone?"

"You don't understand."

"Then you had Jess come here," I continued, not caring that he was trying to explain away something I'd already expected him to. "That was when it hit me. She was here to make sure I didn't leave. And I wondered . . ." A soft, almost frantic sounding laugh left my lips. "What if you and Jess and Kieran are only doing to Zachary what he did to all of you. And Lexi and I are your Einstein, and I've been blindly taking you at your word?"

"Sutton, no."

"That was why I couldn't leave to find Lexi, because you couldn't risk losing me too."

"No—fuck," he growled and drove his hands through his hair before he reached for me, bringing me close and dropping his voice. "Of course, I couldn't risk losing you. I can't risk losing either of you because it's my job to keep you *safe*. To keep you away from a goddamn monster."

"And how do I know that you aren't the monster?"

He released me as though I'd burned him. His chest moved with rough jerks as he stared at me with a mixture of pain and resentment.

"How do I know you aren't the one lying? How do I know that you *helped* Vero and didn't hurt her? My entire life has been a lie, why should I believe you?" I asked through gritted teeth. "You called Zachary a master manipulator, but what if that's you?"

Of everything I'd said, the last hurt the most.

He flinched as if it had been a physical blow.

Anger flashed across his face.

For long seconds, he stood there with a far-off look. And then those bright eyes captured me and he closed the distance between us with one large step, bringing our bodies flush together.

I swayed when his lips met my ear, but all thoughts of the way it felt to have him against me fled the moment he spoke.

Rough.

Filled with anger and pain.

And meant to hurt.

"If you want to be manipulated, then leave. Go back to the bastard who drugged you for a year."

We didn't speak until long after Lexi had gone to sleep.

We didn't see each other either.

I knew where he was, of course. As soon as he had said those words, he'd pushed past me and gone to the door. Lexi had even bounded over there to leave crayons and a page from her coloring book with him.

I didn't know what he did with them or what he said to her, but she was all smiles when she came skipping back into the living room.

My body had ached to go to him, to talk to him. I knew if I did, I would find him leaning against the door, arms folded over his chest, head ever so slightly tipped back.

The picture of power and strength and ease.

And utterly handsome.

Which was why, as I closed the door to our bedroom, I told myself a dozen times to go back into the room and try to sleep or to stop in the living room. To do anything other than continue down the path I was on.

Tonight, it felt dangerous.

I rounded the corner to the hall leading to the door, and sure enough, there he stood under the glow of a dim light.

Power.

Strength.

Ease.

Devastating.

His guarded eyes followed me as I approached and then went back to looking straight ahead once I was resting against the wall adjacent to him.

"Conor, I'm . . ."

"It's what you think," he murmured when I hesitated.

My eyelids slipped shut, and a pained breath wheezed from me.

Deny it. Deny, deny.

If I were home, talking with any of the people I normally surrounded myself with, it would have been exactly what I would've done.

I could easily be caught talking trash and then brushing it away with a few exaggerated, kiss-assing sentences, both parties knowing all along that I was completely full of shit.

Fake.

Fake smiles. Fake emotions. Fake words.

That was all we were. All *I* had been . . . until a giant of a man broke into my motel room and started calling me out on every flaw.

"I don't know what I think anymore," I finally admitted. "You came in and turned my world upside down, taking away everything I ever knew. When I really focus on the specifics, I wonder why I believe a complete stranger over the people I've known my entire life—especially when it could just as easily go the other way."

"Understandable."

I looked into his solemn expression, searching for the hurt that I'd seen earlier, but it wasn't there.

"But what you said . . ." He shifted to face me. "It doesn't make sense. You came to us, and we were trying to help you before Zachary ever came to town or took Einstein."

My lips parted, a denial on my tongue, before I remembered . . . before I caught the slip I couldn't afford to make.

"We were already so far into the case with you when that went down. Jess and I were panicking because we had lost our communication with you. Only to find out after we got Einstein back that you were connected to all of it. So why would we be doing what Zachary did to Einstein with *you*?"

Oh . . . "When you put it that way, I guess you wouldn't."

"And why would you be standing here with me if you truly believed it?"

Because I can't stay away from you.

Because there's something about your soul that I crave.

I swallowed thickly and lifted a shoulder. "Probably

because I never really could believe it. But I think a part of me wants to."

"Would it be easier if it were true?"

Yes . . . and, no.

Then I wouldn't feel so disgusted with myself.

I wouldn't be the only one—

I forced back the thought.

"I think it would destroy me if it were," I admitted softly, breathlessly, the words meaning so much more than I ever should have admitted aloud.

He dragged his hands over his face and groaned into them. When they fell limply to his sides, he slid down the door until he was sitting with his arms resting on bent knees.

Oh Jesus.

My heart was racing, and my cheeks were burning with embarrassed heat.

I wanted to leave, and I wanted to stay. I wanted to take back what I said as badly as I wanted to reach out and touch him, to have that contact with him.

But I was terrified that, if I did any one of those things, I would push him into that cold, distant Conor.

I rocked to the side, and at the last moment, I dropped to a crouch beside him.

As he had been when I'd first joined him, he was staring straight ahead, and for the life of me, I couldn't think of anything to say. But standing back up and leaving was no longer an option.

"So . . . only you and Jess were panicking?" I tried to make it come out teasing, but my internal panic was evident in the jagged words.

The corner of his mouth twitched into a smirk. "Kieran doesn't panic."

My head moved in quick bounces. "I guess I can see that."

"Sutton," he murmured so softly, and my shoulders caved with the rejection I already felt coming.

A rejection that shouldn't have been necessary because I shouldn't have allowed myself to feel anything at all.

"Don't, please." I pressed my hands to my knees and started pushing myself back up. My mouth was open, ready to beg him to forget anything I had said, when he snatched my wrist and pulled me toward him.

I stumbled before righting myself, this time closer than we had been before.

My breaths were embarrassingly uneven, and I didn't care.

Because he was staring at me in a way that I wanted to capture so I could remember this look and this feeling for the rest of my life.

"What you think of us, of me, it isn't true. There's still something you should know."

His words should've had panic and suspicion rising, but I found myself holding my breath, waiting to hear his voice again.

"When we finally got Einstein back and she told us everything about Zachary, I hated you."

Shock pulsed through me so forcefully that I wrenched back. "What?"

"The way I saw it, you looking into us started a domino effect that led to Einstein almost dying. I blamed you for it, hated you for it. Then after nearly twelve hours of driving here and looking for you, you were hostile and ungrateful, and it made me resent you more."

So many things I hadn't realized before that moment clicked into place with a few sentences. I felt like an idiot for not seeing it before.

Embarrassment filled me as I thought over everything I had already said and done and possibly even hinted at.

I shifted to sit on the floor and tried to put as much distance as possible between Conor and I without making it obvious. "Why did you come then?"

"A case is still a case, no matter my feelings on it."

And he hated me.

Not only that . . . "Einstein." I forced myself to meet his curious stare. "I don't know how I haven't heard it until tonight. I mean . . . I don't know how many times I've heard you talk to her or say her name."

Conor's expression shifted into some form of dread.

"She means something to you."

His silence was answer enough.

Such an idiot.

It doesn't matter. It can't *matter. I'm still married. I'm his client—he hates me.*

Then why did it bother me?

I forced a smile. "So, what's the story there?"

"There isn't one," he said honestly. "I knew the day I met her that she belonged to someone in a forever kind of way. You don't fuck with that."

"But you love her."

His head moved in the slightest of nods, and his eyes unfocused. "I did." With a broken inhale, he turned those piercing eyes on me. "I thought you should know where my head was when I came to Tennessee . . . you know, since we're in the habit of saying what we think."

I cleared my throat, my forced smile tighter than ever. "Well, at least I know. Even if you hadn't before, I'm sure I would've earned your hate by now."

"Hated," he corrected. "Unjustly."

My heart skipped a beat before taking off at a torturous pace.

"So, you don't have any doubts about what *I* think . . . I think you're spoiled and judgmental and your attitude pushes me in a way nothing ever has. I think you're passionate and loyal and so goddamn charismatic, and all of it combined is fucking addicting." His stare dipped over me before shifting straight ahead. "But if you don't go to your room, I'm gonna do something I can't come back from."

I wasn't sure I could breathe, let alone move.

I also wasn't sure I wanted to.

"Sutton, I need you to go." The warmth and need in his voice said the opposite.

I pulled my bottom lip between my teeth as I fought with what I knew I should do and what we both clearly wanted—what *couldn't* happen.

I dragged in a sharp inhale when he reached out and gently pulled my lip free before smoothing it over with his thumb.

"Go." It was a rough, dark plea that I felt all the way to my core.

Curling my hand around his, I slowly pulled it away from my face and shifted to my feet again.

Before I stood, I confessed, "I was wrong about you in

every way. You are kind and caring and everything I could only ever wish to be."

With each step away from him, I hoped he would stop me.

But that hope died a little more the closer I got to my room.

I could feel my disappointment and want echoed back at me from him. Still, I didn't allow myself to turn. If I did, I would do exactly what Conor had said.

Something I couldn't come back from.

Sixteen

Conor

"You have to let me do something," Sutton yelled in exasperation the next day.

Lexi giggled.

I just watched as Sutton paced in a tight circle.

For most of the thirty minutes we'd been working on defense, she had been pacing, irritated that I hadn't let her get a hit in.

Once she was facing me with that frustrated and determined look in her eyes, I stretched out my arms. "That isn't going to help you. You should know this by now. If I let you get away with things now, then you'll expect it to go right if the real thing happens."

"But it will make me feel better," she grumbled.

"You done trying your way?"

Her face fell. "That whole . . . this whole time you've

only been letting me—" Her mouth opened and shut a few times before a frustrated huff left her.

"Are you going to charge someone again?"

"Not after what I went through the other day."

I gave her a pointed look. "And I'm betting you won't try any of the things you've been doing today."

Her eyes narrowed in a way that held none of her normal attitude and was fucking adorable.

"Come here."

She held her glare for a few moments before relenting with a sigh and trudging over. I closed some of the distance she'd left between us, and immediately felt the charge in the air, just as I noticed the shift in her expression.

The way her eyes darted to where Lexi was sitting, watching us.

The way her cheeks stained pink.

The want and confusion and rejection that splashed across her face before she could hide it.

She cleared her throat when I grabbed one of her hands in mine.

"I'm sure you've heard things before. Hitting stomachs. Stomping on feet. Punching noses." I didn't miss the way she flinched at that last one. "I'll hit you back if you knee me in the balls, but I doubt you'll get a shot in since you always give yourself away."

She blinked quickly and looked from our joined hands to me. "I do not."

"How do you think I pushed you away both times you tried?"

Her mouth stayed open as her eyes drifted away, remembering that first day. "Because you're unusually good at this?"

My chest moved with a silent laugh as I pulled her hand higher up. "Forget most of the things you've heard. A hit to the groin, yeah, that'll stop a guy. But if he's determined to get you, that'll only slow him down for about a second. Everything else I mentioned is only going to piss him off because he already has so much adrenaline pumping through him for it to faze him. Got it?"

Her slender neck moved with her forced swallow. "Then how am I supposed to fight?"

I tightened my grip on her hand. "With this. And this." I brushed my thumb against her bottom lip and wondered if she noticed the way I lingered there. Unable to move on.

"My lips?" she asked breathlessly.

Yeah, she noticed.

I was also pretty damn sure she could bring me to my knees with those lips.

"Your mouth. Your teeth. That's the easy one, so we'll do it first. If you can't get away from someone's hold, bite. Don't bite to hurt, bite to tear. Understand?"

"Oh, that's disgusting."

"It can also save your life."

"Got it." She was nodding, but all the blood had drained from her face. "Be a zombie."

"Now, your hands." I grabbed the other and lifted it so they were at eye level with her, and then tapped her thumbs. "You can dig out eyes."

"Christ, why?" Her hands fell, and she rocked back a step. "Why are these all so gross?"

I pulled her back by her hands and lifted them to where they had been, but I didn't release her. "Because the chances of someone as small as you choking out someone as big as me are slim. The chances of you outrunning me? Sutton, you won't."

I hated that I'd put the shuttered look in her eyes. There was no doubt her mind had gone to Zachary. But even if she'd grown up in *my* world, being chased and captured was what she needed to worry about most.

"If you ever find yourself in a situation where you need to defend yourself, you have to expect that you'll be caught. And when you are, there are things you can do. These are the last resorts if you can't get away."

Her head moved in a faint nod.

I turned her around and pulled her into my arms.

I didn't miss her soft gasp or the chills that raced up her arms or the electricity buzzing between us, but I knew I had to ignore it.

"If you're back to chest, you want to turn. There's only so much you can do like this, and even if you get out of a hold, the attacker can grab you again." Wrapping my arms around her chest, I forced myself to breathe and tried like hell not to think of the way she felt.

Tipping her head back and kissing her wasn't an option.

Telling her I regretted asking her to leave last night would only make this worse.

"She's it, or she isn't."

"Broaden your stance and brace yourself so I can't buckle your knees," I finally said, long after I'd started holding her, and nudged her legs further apart. "If you end up like this and don't think you can move, use the attacker's hands. Snap their thumbs or use the nerves in their wrists. It makes them lose control of their hands, and their grip will loosen so you can turn in their arms."

Taking her hand in mine, I showed her how to use the pressure point in my wrist.

With each second, her breaths grew heavier and my head got closer to her skin until my nose was skimming the side of her neck.

Once she got the hang of it, I whispered, "This is where you turn."

A stuttered breath punched from her chest. "Right."

As soon as she did, I locked my arms around her back, keeping her close.

I told myself not to notice the way her breasts pressed against me with each of her rough breaths.

It was the sweetest agony I'd ever endured.

"Keep your arms up," I said, my voice strained. "Make sure they don't get pinned at your sides or between you and the attacker. Then they're free to do, or help you do, any of the gross things. Or start punching."

Her hands fell to my chest along with her expression. "I thought you said to forget about punching."

I released my hold on her to grab her hand and then formed it into a fist before loosening it into an open palm. Each time showing her before doing both again. "If you're going to hit, know where to hit. Go for the throat, try to break the trachea."

"So, all I have to do is turn around and punch you in the throat?"

A deep laugh burst from my chest. "You can try."

I turned her so her back was against me and wrapped my arms tight around her.

Flashes of her underneath me and against a wall assaulted me as I curled my hands around her slender wrists.

A groan rumbled in my chest at her soft gasp, at the way she pushed back harder.

I was stuck in hell and pressed against heaven.

Dropping my mouth to her ear, I silently cursed everything standing between us when she shivered. "Let's go."

Seventeen

Sutton
FIVE YEARS AGO

My brow furrowed when I glanced at the nursery room window as I pulled up the driveway.

It was habit to look at that window.

The room it looked into had turned into my favorite in the house, and it was filled with tears and love and more joy than I'd ever known was possible. That room made this home.

But the light should've been off at this time of night unless Lexi was fighting sleep or fussing because she was growing.

But, if that were the case, I was sure Zachary would've called.

He always got so angry when she woke late at night, which was why I couldn't believe he'd given me an entire night out with my girlfriends without calling to complain or asking a hundred questions.

Then again, after nearly a year of either being locked up in the house or going everywhere with a newborn, I so deserved this.

I hurried into the house from the garage, eager to see my Lexi if she was up and having trouble tonight, but I came to an abrupt stop when I rounded the corner of the hall leading into the large entryway and found Zachary standing at the foot of the stairs.

Tall and broad and commanding, and as if he'd been waiting for me.

"H-hi." My eyes flitted to the top of the stairs, to the silence up there, and then back to him. "I thought—"

A chill crept over me, sliding down my spine like an alarming caress.

Before that moment, I hadn't really looked at Zachary. But once I did, I couldn't stop.

His smile was cruel and cold, and his eyes had this darkness about them that made him look deranged.

He looked like a monster.

"Zachary?" I took a hesitant step back, but my soul reached for the staircase, for the room up it and all the way down the hall.

"Let's play a game."

"I don't—I don't want to. I'm tired. I want to check on Lexi and then go to bed." When there wasn't a response of any kind, I risked a step in his direction. And then another.

Each step had that chill spreading and increasing, but something in me told me I needed to get past him.

The moment I made it to his side, his arm shot out and wrapped around my waist.

Firm, possessive, and almost painful. "Zach—" I tripped

and fell out of one of my stilettos as he hauled me against his chest.

His mouth went to my neck, and his other hand went to my breast.

Kneading and gripping until I was crying out in pain.

"Zachary, *stop*."

"Let's play a game."

"I said no." I drove my elbow into his stomach and shoved, but he hardly budged. "What is wrong with you tonight?"

His teeth raked across my neck so roughly it made the room spin and my stomach churn.

Before I could attempt to push him away again, he said, "Let's play a game called *Where's the Baby*."

Time slowed.

Panic engulfed me, threatening to take me under.

Whoever he was, the man holding me was not my husband.

I swung my attention to him. My plea was nearly inaudible. "Zachary, where is Lexi?"

That smile grew, brightening his monstrous eyes.

I turned for the stairs, already screaming her name as he yanked me back.

Zachary's hand was on my face, his fingers digging into my cheeks. Seconds disguised as an eternity passed as he studied me, his erection pressing firmly against my stomach. "Run, Sutton. I can't wait to find you."

The second he shoved me away, I turned, running and screaming and kicking off my remaining shoe as I went.

The stairs felt never ending. Each step creating three more above it, taunting me. And once I reached the top, the hardwood felt as if it were made of quicksand.

I'd barely made it three steps before Zachary's voice rang out from the foyer.

"*Sutton.*"

One word.

My name.

In a voice I knew but had never heard. A voice as wicked as it was threatening.

My body betrayed me as I reacted to that sinister tone and fell to my hands and knees. Shaking and shaking with failing limbs and muscles.

The ominous pressure clinging to the walls made it nearly impossible to breathe.

I crawled a few steps before finally regaining the strength in my legs and pushing to my feet. Then I ran for Lexi's room.

I nearly cried in relief when I reached it, but the victory was short-lived because the room was empty.

"*Lexi!*"

I turned in circles, looking everywhere, before tearing out of that room and heading for the room across the hall.

Nothing.

The bathroom. The linen closet.

Nothing. Nothing.

"Oh, Sutton." Closer. Near the top of the stairs.

My legs trembled and threatened to give again, but I remained standing as I ran for our bedroom.

I slid through the doorway as Zachary reached one of the last steps.

My frantic search turned crippling when our room showed no signs of Lexi, and I moved to the bathroom. There was still the main floor of the house, but I would have to go past—

I jerked when there was a loud *thud* against one of the walls.

"Oh, Sutton . . ."

I turned and nearly jumped when there was another loud *thud* against the wall.

This one farther from me but closer to the bedroom door.

I shakily retreated until I was pressed to the vanity, tears pouring down my cheeks, and dropped to a low crouch as I listened to him hit the wall farther and farther away—and yet, closer and closer.

There was something sinister in the knocking.

As if he were taunting me with the fact that, no matter how slowly he followed me, he was going to catch up with me.

A sob ripped from me when he entered my line of sight in the bedroom. "Where's Lexi, where's Lexi, where's my baby?"

"Found you."

"Where's my daughter?" I screamed.

Nothing.

Nothing more than that slow walk that had me fearing for my life.

I screamed and swung at him when he grabbed me, lifting me and dragging me out of the bathroom. Incoherent pleas for our daughter and for him to stop tore from my lungs as he shoved me onto the bed.

Even as he tore at my shirt and roughly removed my shorts, my screams never ceased, and I never stopped trying to get away from him.

Hitting.

Clawing.

Kicking.

That frightening look on his face only seemed to grow, as though my fight were exciting him even more.

Until I punched him in the nose.

Blood pooled.

His eyes narrowed with a nauseating mixture of want and bloodlust.

"Tell me where my daughter is," I begged.

Zachary's head tilted, as if he couldn't understand why I was asking. "At your parents'."

My mind raced. "Is she . . . is she safe? Is she okay?"

"Why wouldn't she be?"

Relief filled and overwhelmed me so swiftly that I forgot everything else for that brief moment.

Brief.

Then there was pain, and that damn face was staring down at me like he was enjoying that he'd just stolen my breath. That he was hurting me.

"Stop, stop, stop," I cried out and tried to shove him away. "Za—*that hurts.*"

I tried to scramble away, but he only yanked me closer.

I tried to claw at his arm, but he only restrained me.

I tried to kick him, but he only slid his hand around my neck, squeezing and squeezing and squeezing.

My body tried to rebel against what he was doing, and that only made him go harder.

Stop, I tried to mouth.

"You want nothing because I give you everything," he said in a perfectly clear voice. "You always talk about *taking care of* your husband and *giving* for your husband." Lowering his face to mine, he pressed a deceptively soft kiss to my parted lips. "This is how you take care of me."

The hand around my throat disappeared.

My next inhale sounded like a scream.

"Zachary p-please. It's too—"

He hushed me and brushed a finger over my lips. "Know your place, Sutton."

Tears fell relentlessly as he used me over and over again until he left me alone on the bed. Aching. Bruised. Bleeding.

Long after he was gone, my eyes were still squeezed tight, my lips faintly moving. *Please, God, let me disappear. Please, God, let me disappear.*

Eighteen

Conor

My eyelids opened to a darkened room.

My arms were folded tightly over my chest.

My breathing was slow, and my heartbeat soft, so I should have been able to hear what had woken me . . . but there was nothing.

Nothing was out of place. There were no feelings creeping through the suite, hinting that something was about to go so fucking wrong.

There was a tugging deep in my gut, telling me I needed to stay awake.

I pushed to sitting and ran a hand over my face before looking around the room as I reached for my gun. I turned the safety off and chambered a round as I stood. Held it down by my side as I went around the suite, checking the door and my room before heading toward the girls' room.

But I never got that cold feeling that usually crept over me when something was wrong—or about to go wrong.

I racked the slide, palmed the unused round, and was putting the safety back on just before I heard it.

"Momma?" Lexi's groggy voice was loud enough that it stopped me mid-step.

I rocked back, waiting.

"Momma. *Momma!*"

I barreled through the door of their room and took in what was happening, my hand on the slide and finger on the safety again.

But as soon as I had both of them in my sights—once I was sure there wasn't a threat—I dropped my arm and pressed the gun tight to my side to keep it from Lexi's view as I hurried to her.

She was kneeling on the bed next to Sutton, shaking her shoulder and trying to wake her.

And Sutton? Sutton was tense and trembling and whispering what sounded like pleas. Her chest was jerking with rapid, forceful breaths, and her face was pinched, as if she were in pain.

I touched Lexi's shoulder and then reached past her to wrap my hand around one of Sutton's tightly clenched fists.

My mouth was opened to say her name when her gasp tore through the room and her eyes flew open.

And in those few seconds, terror and anguish were etched there before she was able to focus on us.

"You're okay," I said softly. "It was a dream."

Her eyes darted from me to Lexi, nodding as she did. "I'm fine. I'm fine."

Lexi bent closer to her mom. "Were your dreams really scary or only a little scary this time?"

"They were nothing," Sutton said, her voice shaky and weak. "It was nothing."

Her hands finally unclenched below mine and then she was pushing up so she was sitting.

A frantic-sounding laugh left her. "I didn't realize we were having a late-night party. I would've been ready if I'd known."

Lexi turned to me and climbed to her feet on the bed so she could whisper in my ear, "Momma has bad dreams. A lot. But she never says so."

"Alexis," Sutton hissed, reaching for her daughter and pulling her back to the bed. "That isn't something you tell people, understand?"

Lexi's head lowered in embarrassment. "I understand."

"I'm really sorry you came in here. You shouldn't have—"

"Sutton." I waited until she finally looked at me, the first time she'd met my stare since waking, and shook my head. "That's what I'm here for."

She gave me a look. "You're here to protect us."

"Lexi sounded scared. And you—" I snuck a glance at Lexi and then swallowed what I'd been about to say. "It's what I'm here for."

Her mouth curled into a grateful smile, but it wasn't enough to hide the humiliation that still covered her features.

I ran a hand over Lexi's head and left without another word. Sutton was so damn proud, and I could tell my being there was making it harder for her to keep it together.

I dropped to the couch and put my gun back in its spot underneath, but I knew if I laid down or closed my eyes, all

I would see was the pain and the fear and her strained, labored breaths.

A groan built in my chest as I stood again and began pacing the length of the living room.

Over and over as I wondered what it was that Sutton saw in her sleep.

As my mind went wild with possibilities.

As my need to find and put an end to the man who called himself her husband grew.

To make it worse, she didn't realize what he'd been doing was abusive.

Or she refused to acknowledge it.

Brainwashed. She was brainwashed by the worst kind of man, and I wanted to erase everything he'd ever put in her head.

I looked up when the door to their room clicked open in the otherwise silent suite.

Sutton's eyes sought out mine as she gently closed the door behind her before walking toward me.

Unsure.

Slow.

But moving forward, nonetheless.

She stopped a few feet away, rubbing her arms as if she were cold.

"Everything okay?"

"Of course, I just couldn't go back to sleep." Her head listed to the side. "I didn't want to wake Lexi again."

I watched the way her body jerked every few seconds, interrupting the constant trembling, and then I walked over to the couch to pick up the blanket I'd been using earlier.

When I turned, she was a handful of feet away and moving closer, once again slow and unsure.

As though she were testing the boundaries, seeing what I was going to do. Where I was going to draw our line in the sand this time.

I just closed the distance and draped the blanket around her, holding it tightly together in front of her longer than necessary before finally stepping back toward the couch.

Once she was sitting near me, I asked, "How often does it happen?"

Her forehead creased. "Being cold?"

She knew that wasn't what I was asking, just as we both knew that chill had nothing to do with the temperature.

With a subtle shake, I said, "The dreams."

"Oh." A shield, made of little more than a faint shrug and a dismissive laugh flew up around her. "It was really nothing. I told you."

"Sutton."

Her brows lifted and a fake smile pulled at her lips, but her eyes didn't meet mine.

I leaned forward and pressed my hand under her chin until she looked at me. "You're a bad fucking liar."

Her jaw tightened against me—stubborn and prideful.

After a few seconds, she released a weighted breath and admitted, "Once a week, sometimes twice. More since we started living in the motels."

I dropped my hand and folded my arms across my chest so I wouldn't reach out for her again. "Tell me."

She looked like she would argue, but just as quickly, she sighed and leaned against the couch, pulling the blanket tighter around her. "It's the same thing every time. Well, more or less. It's being chased."

"By him?"

She nodded through a full-body shiver. "It's never the

thought or the feeling, it's a memory. Tonight was from the first time it happened, right before Lexi turned one."

She didn't go into detail, and I didn't need her to.

She'd told me enough that I could already imagine what she was seeing.

I would listen, God knew I would listen to whatever she would tell me. But when Sutton finally accepted what had been happening to her for all these years, she would need someone who would understand what she'd been through.

"There's something you should know so you don't feel ganged up on or betrayed by me when it happens."

I felt her tense even though there was at least a foot separating us.

"When Jess was here, I asked her to talk to you. I didn't give her specifics," I hurried to add. "I didn't tell them anything. But Jess seemed to already understand. And, Sutton, I think you *need* to talk to someone like Jess about this."

"Why? I don't . . . I *told* you that I didn't feel comfortable, and I won't. What makes you think she is who I need to talk to anyway?"

"I didn't tell her your story. I'm not going to tell you hers."

A blanket-covered shrug and a dismissive laugh. "It doesn't matter, I'm not talking with her or anyone else about it. It isn't anyone's business, and it isn't a big deal."

"Sutton, stop." One of my hands betrayed me by reaching out for her before I was able to force it to my side. "Everyone has shields, and yours are becoming more obvious with each day. You do it to make something huge seem like nothing. You do it to brush things away and come out looking unharmed. And I can tell by that horrified look on your face that your mom probably does it too."

"Oh Christ."

The corner of my mouth twitched into a smile. "You aren't hard to figure out, Sutton." I leaned closer and lowered my voice. "But I know that if I were to tell you exactly how fucked-up those *games* were . . . how gaslighted you've been . . . you wouldn't hear me. You need someone who has been there."

"It's private, Conor. What happens in a home is meant to stay in the home."

"You told *me*."

Her mouth opened, but nothing came out. After a moment, a jagged exhale left her. "That's . . . it's—"

Different.

The unspoken word hung in the air between us as if she'd shouted it.

"I'm not asking you to go public with it. But you were told to allow and accept something until you believed it was normal, something that never should've happened. And, right now, only your subconscious seems to understand what you don't or *won't*."

Minutes came and went, and the silence between us only grew.

Indecision warred on Sutton's face until she finally let her head fall onto the couch with a soft bounce.

Her eyes shifted to mine, but her expression was so impassive that I couldn't tell what she was thinking.

"I can't remember the last time I had a normal dream or nightmare," I admitted, shattering the silence. "It's like you, I see parts of my life played out instead."

"Good or bad?"

"Usually the latter. Beck . . . I see Beck a lot." I forced out a rough breath and looked up into her curious stare. "He was murdered right in front of me."

"Oh God. Conor . . ."

"Kieran was shot once, and then Beck pushed him out of the way. Took the rest."

I'd stood there, torn, because Kieran had been yelling for me to go save Jess. Not realizing what had happened to his best friend and my brother—that he had been dying on the grass. And I'd known there was nothing I could do to save him.

I would've given anything in that moment to take his place.

"I'm . . . I'm so sorry." One of Sutton's hands slipped into mine as if it belonged there. "Was this on a case? What happened to the person who shot them?"

I considered what to tell her.

For asking so much truth from her, I knew it was hypocritical to withhold so much of my own.

But my truth was a dark life that she was just learning existed. That she was just beginning to fear. The last thing I needed was for her to be afraid of me.

"Uh, no. No, it wasn't. And he was killed."

Savagely, by Kieran.

Seconds after Beck was shot. Minutes before I emptied an entire magazine into the Holloway boss. And hours before we permanently shut down the Holloway Gang. A decade-long dream of Kieran and Beck's that Beck didn't live to see.

Sutton seemed to accept my vague response because, after a moment, she whispered, "You really miss him."

My chest moved with a pained huff. "Yeah. Yeah, we

were close. Our parents died when I was eleven. We didn't have anywhere to go, and Beck was afraid we'd get split up if we went into the system, so we lived on the streets for a couple of years until we were found by—" I choked back Mickey, the Holloway boss's, name. "Well, Kieran was one of them. They took us in, and we were with them until the day Beck died just over a year ago."

"That's why you trust him so much," she said, as if finally understanding something.

"Kieran?" I dipped my head. "I know how he looks. I know how Jess looks too," I said with a soft laugh. "Kieran never looks anything less than ready to kill the next person who walks in front of him, and Jess looks wild and a little crazy, but they have their reasons. Just as I do, just as *you* do. But they're the best. No one I'd rather have on my side."

"If I've learned anything this week, it's how deceiving looks can be. And if you're telling me they're the best, then I have no doubts it's true." Her lips curved into a thoughtful smile. "Jess said something similar about you. So did Einstein. You all must mean a lot to each other."

"Yeah, it's a weird family that shouldn't work for so many reasons. But it does."

A soft laugh sounded in her throat. "I don't know what it's like to have friends like that. To have anyone like that, really."

"Sutton . . ."

Another one of her shields formed around her. "Sorry, that was . . . I'm sorry. Anyway—"

"*Sutton.*"

"What did you do?" she asked before I could continue.

"Before ARCK. You, Beck, Kieran, and whoever else took you in?"

We were in the Irish-American mob.

Our boss was a sick fuck who I was happy to put into the ground.

Beck sold drugs for him. I counted and ran and did all sorts of shit until the time came where I had to keep his daughter safe from our rival gang. Kieran was—and still is—one of the most feared assassins in the country.

"I protected women."

Sutton's brows lifted in surprise. "So, the same thing?"

My head moved in a slow denial.

The surprise faded to wonder and curiosity. "Why do I feel like there's so much that you aren't telling me?"

"You wouldn't be this close to me if you knew."

Her stare fell to my lips. When she spoke, her confession was so soft that I wasn't sure she meant to say it aloud. "I'm not sure anything could make me want to be farther than I am now."

A groan rumbled in my chest. "Sutton . . ."

Those wide eyes slowly shifted to mine. "Yes?"

"Fuck." I dragged a hand over my face and tried to remember every reason I needed her to leave.

"She's it, or she isn't."

I couldn't think past that first one with her face so close to mine.

It would be so easy to lean in. To pull her to me.

To press my mouth to hers. To taste her.

To hear her sigh my name . . .

Fuck.

"I think you should go . . ." The words were strained and rough, and I wasn't sure how I managed to say them at all when I was imagining all the ways to make her stay. "You should try to get some sleep."

She quickly blinked, as if my words had brought her out of a daze, and jerked back.

Embarrassment flooded her face. Her lips parted, but no words left them.

I sat there, locked in indecision.

Wanting to take it back. Wanting to keep her there.

Knowing she needed to leave and that it was dangerous to even entertain those thoughts and wants and fucking *needs*.

The second her foot touched the floor, I grabbed her arm, hauled her back to the couch, and brought her mouth down onto mine.

Her reaction was instant.

Her body shifted so she was in my lap and relaxed against me. Her hands moved to drag through my beard and then weave into my hair. Her lips parted, and a whimper climbed up her throat when I teased her tongue with my own.

Fucking ecstasy.

I dragged my hands down the curves of her body, gripping the top of those damn sleep shorts that had been taunting me for days and groaning when she rocked forward over my hardening dick.

I moved across her jaw and down her throat in slow kisses and teasing bites, listening to her moans and her hitched breaths as I did.

Making sure I wasn't pushing her too far.

Knowing we needed to stop and not giving a fuck.

I grabbed her hands and gently pulled them from where they'd been locked in my hair to behind her back. Taking both her wrists in one hand, I slowly pulled until she was slightly arched, keeping my eyes on hers as I did.

Heat.

Need.

Trust.

"If you want to stop, we stop. No questions."

She rocked against me in response, a whimper escaping her parted lips.

Using my free hand, I pressed the tips of my fingers to her stomach and slowly dragged her shirt up. Inch by inch, waiting for her to put a stop to this, waiting for any sign that this was too much.

As soon as the shirt was over her breasts, Sutton leaned forward, only to be stopped by the grip I had on her wrists.

A sound of frustration built in her chest. Passion burned in her eyes. "Let me kiss you."

The corner of my mouth curled up.

I slowly pulled down on her arms again until she was arched more than before, her breasts fully exposed to me.

Full. Fucking perfect.

I leaned forward and captured one of her nipples in my mouth and groaned when she shivered against me.

"Conor, please." The tips of her fingers curled against my hand, pressing tight as she pushed down on my lap and rocked harder than before. "Oh, God, please."

Sliding my hand into both of hers, I pulled down farther still and dragged my mouth from her breast in a line down her stomach.

Without warning, I released my hold on her, wrapped an arm around her hips, pressed the other hand to her back, and stood.

Her shocked laugh ripped through the room as she

struggled to wrap her arms and legs around me, and then her mouth was on mine and she was sighing against the kiss.

I paused to close the door softly behind us and then took those last steps to the bed, and gently laid her in the middle of it.

With one last kiss, I pushed back to search her face.

Bright. Excited. Free.

So damn beautiful.

"Tell me where your head is," I begged.

Her eyes skated over my face before meeting mine again. "Wondering why there was ever a part of my life that didn't consist of you." She shifted up to press her lips to mine. Soft. Teasing.

I captured her mouth then, telling her everything in that kiss that I couldn't say with words.

That I was afraid we were going to hurt each other.

That allowing ourselves to do this was only going to make our fallout so much worse.

Because there was no doubt in my head that there was going to be fallout.

I had been sure I wouldn't be able to handle the heartbreak that came with Einstein. But this? There wasn't any coming back from it. I should've known that, the second I fell for anyone at all, there wouldn't be.

Especially if it was for a woman I was already so set on hating . . . and couldn't.

I pushed away when she started tugging my shirt up my body, finished tearing it off, and then let it fall to the floor.

My blood pounded at the raw need and desire that crossed her face.

I slowly removed her shirt and those tiny fucking

shorts, watching and memorizing as I revealed more and more of her until she was completely bare.

Dipping down, I pressed a kiss to her mouth and then brushed my thumb across the same place. "You're fucking beautiful."

Sutton blinked up at me, completely taken aback, but I was already climbing off the bed and gripping her legs, pulling her closer to the edge so she was nearly hanging off.

Surprise crossed her face, and I couldn't help the grin that tugged at my mouth at the way her eyes widened when I went to my knees.

I took my time spreading her and teasing her with my thumb until she was shaking and her breaths were coming in sharp jerks. Then I leaned forward and licked her from entrance to clit.

Her sharp inhale filled the room, and she arched away from the bed. I did it again, and she slammed back down. Again, and her fingers twisted into my hair and pulled tight.

And *again*—my name left her lips on a needy sigh.

Sweetest fucking sound.

I pressed two fingers into her, pumping her slowly as I devoured her until she was a trembling, panting mess, arching away and pulling me closer.

"Conor—oh God, oh God."

Her fingers tightened in my hair as she fell apart against me. Her hushed, pleasured cry made something deep inside me roar.

With a need to claim her.

To make her come again.

To make this last forever.

I continued moving my fingers in and out of her until her shaking was nothing more than little tremors, and then I slowly made my way up her body, leaving a trail of kisses as I did.

Once I was on the bed, I wrapped an arm under her and hauled her limp body closer to the center, my smile wide as I took in her satisfied expression.

After one last kiss to the base of her throat, I started rolling to the side when she stopped me with a hand on either side of my face. Then she was pulling me toward her and pressing her mouth to mine, moaning against the kiss and teasing me with smallest flick of her tongue.

"Please."

I shifted only enough to look into her pleading eyes. At the desire there. At the fear.

Only, this fear I knew. I had seen this. She was afraid of what I would say. Of where I would draw that line.

She sucked in a shuddering breath and released my face. Her hands quickly trailed down my body and gripped the top of my pants.

We can't.

"Sutton—"

"Please."

We *shouldn't* for reasons I couldn't remember.

"Sutton . . ."

But I was already so far gone . . .

"Fuck." The word was nothing more than a growl in my throat before I was kissing her and she was pushing my pants down and gripping my length in her hand. "Fuck."

"She's it, or she isn't."

"She's it, or she isn't."

"She's it . . ."

The words faded away when Sutton curled her legs around my hips and guided me to her entrance, stroking me as she did.

I wanted to take her. Claim her.

But I took my time sliding in, inch by inch, savoring her gasps as she stretched around me.

Nothing had ever felt so damn good.

And then I was moving.

Slow. Controlled. Each thrust more powerful than the last. Each one forcing a whimper from her lips.

I dipped down and passed a soft, teasing kiss across her mouth, keeping in time with the rocking of my hips. Loving the way she arched to meet me. The way she moaned into my mouth. The way her entire body responded when I dragged my teeth over her bottom lip and bit down before releasing it.

Pushing up on the bed, I curled my hands into the comforter and drove into her harder and harder still, never taking my eyes away from hers as I pushed us both toward the edge.

Her fingers dug into my shoulders as she lost herself, exploding around me. Her mouth opened on a silent moan. Each shockwave that passed through her felt like my own, gripping my cock and bringing me closer and closer to the end that felt more like a beginning.

I pushed in once . . . twice . . . and then curled an arm underneath her, holding her close and savoring every part of this as I moved inside her.

The way she felt against me.

The way her lips parted the harder my movements became.

The way her fingers slid into my hair again and gripped tight when I finally found my release inside her.

The way she was studying me in fascination when I opened my eyes.

So far gone.

I gently curled my hand around her chin and brushed my thumb across her swollen lips. "Jesus, Sutton, what are you doing to me?"

Nineteen

Zachary
TWO MONTHS AGO

I paced back and forth, arms folded over my chest, eyes on the floor as I tried to tell myself it was enough.

But I had to be sure.

I stopped and stared at Sutton, who was sitting on the bed and watching me with tired eyes. "Again."

Her shoulders sagged and full lips fell open in protest.

"Sutton, I need you to know this as if it's real. I need you to *see* it in your mind."

"But I know it, I do."

"If you could just cry."

Her head was already shaking. "I can't. You know I can't fake crying."

I ground my teeth and spoke slowly so she'd hear every word. "They're unlike anyone you've encountered. They'll ask again and again even though they already know everything and they *will* know if you're lying." I dropped to the floor in front of her and raced my hands up her thighs. "Let's go over it one more time, all right?"

"What does it matter if this is only to be used as a last resort?"

"Because, if it comes down to it, that means we're failing and this will be the most important story you ever tell."

After a few seconds, she nodded warily.

I stood, took a few steps back, and demanded, "Show me that it happened."

"Lexi and I were playing out back. Zachary wasn't supposed to be home, so it surprised me when I heard his voice coming from the guesthouse."

"*Show me, Sutton!*"

"Lexi was already headed that way, but she stopped just outside the window," she continued, her body trembled and her voice wavered. "She just froze. She looked so scared. So, I hurried over there and saw these men inside. One was on his knees, and Zachary was in front of him with a gun aimed at his head."

My mouth curled into a slow smile.

Perfect.

Twenty

Sutton

I woke in Conor's bed alone.

Traces of heat still lingered in the empty space beside me, but there wasn't a sign of him in the room or adjoining bathroom.

And it didn't bother me.

Last night had been the first night he'd actually slept in a bed, and his residual body heat told me he hadn't been gone for long.

My mouth pulled into a smile as last night played out before me in flashes.

Searching lips. Learning hands. Whispered words and pleasured cries. Highs I'd never experienced before.

Conor loved the same way he did everything else—affectionately . . . powerfully. Shows of strength woven in gentle touches and brushes of his lips.

It was intoxicating.

Addicting.

Hard and soft, as if he'd known exactly when I needed more and how to drive me insane with barely there teases.

He'd called me beautiful . . . and it had been so honest and raw and powerful that it'd felt as if the words had branded on my soul.

I'd wanted to hear those words my entire life. When Conor whispered them, I was thankful I hadn't before that moment.

They wouldn't have meant as much.

They wouldn't have meant *everything*.

I sat up when I heard Conor's deep, muffled voice, which was quickly followed by the even softer voice of my daughter, and then hurried from the bed.

Once I shrugged into my clothes, I started for the door but paused when I reached it.

I didn't know how I was going to explain to Lexi where I'd slept. I didn't know how to deal with this in front of my six-year-old when Conor and I hadn't even talked about it, and I was mar—

"Oh God." I pressed a hand to my churning stomach and let my forehead drop to the door as guilt spread through me like a sickness.

I was the worst kind of person, and I didn't know how to sort through my warring thoughts and emotions.

Last night had been the best of my life, and until a minute ago, I'd wanted it to happen again. I wanted Conor's gentle soul and no-bullshit attitude. I wanted his warm personality and easy smile.

But that didn't change the fact that I was married. It didn't matter if Zachary fueled and filled my nightmares or that I never wanted to see him again.

He was still my husband.

How did I let this happen?

I swallowed back the guilt and sadness and stepped away from the door so I could open it, my head so conflicted that I forgot what I was walking into until I looked up and saw Conor and Lexi having their morning stare-down.

My heart skipped a beat before taking off in a wild, beautiful rhythm.

Conor's eyes flicked in my direction, heat and raw desire filling them as he watched me walk through the suite.

It stole my breath.

The entire thing.

The way he connected with my daughter in a way Zachary never could—*refused* to.

The way he made my body come alive with one look, even from across the room.

The way it felt wrong not to go to him.

I hadn't just *let* this happen. I'd been powerless to stop it.

I paused behind Lexi and tilted her head back so I could press a kiss to her forehead. "Morning, sweet girl."

Her eyes danced, and her giggle warmed my soul as she hurried to focus on Conor again. "That doesn't count, Mr. Conor. Momma made me stop looking."

"I'll let it slide. But next time, you owe me breakfast."

I used the opportunity to slip away to our room, but I couldn't stop from sneaking glances at them as I did.

His animated expressions and the way he spoke to her.

Her eyes, which were narrowed, and her smile, which was stretched to the max because she clearly adored him.

It was all so perfect in a surreal way.

This was the perfection my mother should've strived for. Should've wanted *me* to strive for.

My steps faltered, and I hurried to push that thought away. This was all too much to be thinking about with a man I hardly knew. Especially when . . .

My fingers automatically sought out my naked ring finger as that guilt swirled within me, thick and suffocating.

I took my time in the shower, trying to sort through my dizzying emotions, and dressed in my remaining clean clothes in a daze.

After setting out something for Lexi to wear, I gathered the rest of our things in the hotel's laundry service bags and left them by the door of our room before going out to face the source of my torment.

Lexi came bounding over to wrap her arms firmly around my hips, nearly knocking me over in the process. "Did you fall asleep without the dreams?"

My hand stilled where I'd been running my fingers through her hair. "What?"

"Mr. Conor said you had trouble going to sleep after your dreams last night and you thought you were going to wake me up. That's why you went to the other room."

"Did he?" I lifted my head to find him watching me with a guarded expression that didn't ease even when I sent him a thankful smile. "He's right. And yes, I did sleep."

"Without dreams?"

"Without dreams," I said softly. "I put your clothes on the bed. Why don't you go change? You can leave these clothes in one of the bags by the door, okay?"

She ran off without a word, but I didn't have time to worry about what to say to Conor or what to do with the need racing through my body to just be near him. Because, as soon as the door shut behind Lexi, Conor was stalking toward me with a look of frustration.

"Bags?" The word was nearly a growl as it ripped from his throat.

"Yeah, we don't have any clean clothes."

His head jerked. "What?"

"We don't have clean clothes. The resort has a laundry service."

I hadn't realized how tense he was until he let his body relax.

I took a step closer and reached out to take his hand in mine. "What did you think I was talking about?"

He rubbed the back of his neck and studied me for a second before nodding to my bedroom. "You were in there a long time. When you came out, it was clear as day what you were thinking. Feeling. And I fucking get it, Sutton. I do . . . but then you said *bags*. Even if last night hadn't happened, that would still be cause for alarm because clients can't up and leave."

"Is that all you see me as?" I asked carefully, preparing myself for his response. "Just a client?"

He wrapped our joined hands behind my back and pulled me against him. Then curled his long fingers against my neck, gently cradling so he could brush his thumb across my lip in that way I was quickly falling in love with.

"Nothing changes why we are in this situation. And because we're in it, last night never should have happened. It also never would've happened if you were *just* a client."

It was the right and wrong thing to say.

I had no doubts that Conor spoke with absolute truth, just as I had no doubts that he had never done this before. It wasn't only that he didn't seem like the type of guy, it was all the times he'd tried to stop it from happening. It was the connection between us that was more than carnal need.

In his answer, he drove home the reasoning for my torment.

I maneuvered out of his hold and started for my bedroom, struggling to control the burning in my eyes and tightening in my throat before I made it there.

But I didn't make it there.

I hadn't made it halfway before Conor started after me, quickly eating up the distance and pulling me into the kitchen, his mouth at my ear. "I wasn't trying to upset you."

"We're in this situation because of my husband," I said as soon as he turned me so I was facing him, my voice soft and strained. "My *husband*, Conor. I'm *married*."

The worry covering his face melted into a hardened mask as he released me.

"There are so many conflicting feelings inside me that I can't think straight. I'm still legally bound to him despite what he's done and the situation. And how do I explain it to Lexi when that's her dad, even though—Jesus." I loosed a ragged breath. "Even though he scares her."

I gripped my stomach and stepped back until I was pressed to the counter.

"Sutton," Conor murmured, his nervousness and worry clear on his face. "There's something—"

"I feel like the worst kind of human," I continued, speaking over him. "And I'm not sure why, or if I even should. Then there's you—" I looked over when the door to my room opened and Lexi came skipping out.

"I brushed my teeth, and I brushed my hair."

"Good," I said with a tense smile. "Hey, I need to finish talking to Mr. Conor. How about you go decide what you want for breakfast? You can turn on the television too."

Her eyes widened with excitement. "Yeah!"

Conor lunged for her and snatched her into his arms before she could take a step.

Lexi's amused scream was cut short by his hand clamping over her mouth.

Paralyzing fear slammed into my body as I watched the entire thing unfold in a second, unsure of what to do.

I wanted to grab Lexi from Conor and pull her against me, but his eyes were unfocused and his head was tilted to the side as if he were listening for something.

The possibilities of what could be coming were making it hard to breathe.

He moved toward me, keeping his steps silent and Lexi facing away from the entrance to the kitchen as he did.

Once they were beside me, he lowered her to her feet and waited until my arms were wrapped around her before quickly going back the way he'd come. His hand went to the back of his pants before he suddenly relaxed and called out, "Warning."

A wild, feminine laugh came from the front of the suite, making Lexi and me jump.

Conor twisted and relaxed against the counter a few feet away from where we stood. With an irritated look in my direction, he said, "Close your eyes."

Lexi slapped her hands over her face without hesitation, but I stood there, still frozen.

I wasn't sure what my expression looked like, but Conor's softened.

"Close your eyes," he said again, his tone coaxing.

With a jagged exhale, I did.

"Do you feel that?"

I felt Lexi's arms leave her face and stretch forward. "What are we feeling, Mr. Conor?"

"Not with your hands. Just listen and *feel*."

I wasn't sure I could feel anything other than the fierce pounding of my heart. The pressure on my chest. The way my body felt all kinds of wrong after that adrenaline spike.

"You see how it's hard to breathe?"

I almost cracked an eye open and asked if he could hear my thoughts.

Lexi giggled when she asked, "Because Momma's squishing me?"

Conor made an amused sound. "Do you feel heavy and on edge?"

Even though Lexi was claiming that she felt as light as a feather, I did feel heavy and on edge, so I opened my eyes.

And standing near Conor were Kieran and Jess.

Conor's eyes were locked on mine as he slanted his head to the side and said, "Kieran."

"Yes, I know. Good morning."

"No, it's Kieran," Conor corrected. "What you're feeling."

Lexi must have finally opened her eyes, because Jess did a little wave in her direction and Kieran dipped his head.

"What do you mean?" I asked, keeping my tight hold on Lexi. I knew we weren't in danger, but I couldn't shake that feeling and needed her close until I did.

"When you're in danger, when someone's coming for

you, you feel it," Conor explained. "It's dark and paralyzing and cold. If you aren't expecting these two, you'll feel that. You'll also feel *them*. Jess is wild energy, but it's subtle. I still don't notice she's there until she's right next to me."

Jess mock-bowed.

"There's a pressure that comes with Kieran. Makes it hard to breathe. Makes your body heavy and shaky in a way that's closer to the after-effects of a panic attack than fear."

I forced a smile. "That's pleasant."

The corners of Kieran's mouth twitched into a smile.

"You don't notice it if you know he's there," Jess said with a secretive smile. "But what our boy here is saying, is that he's been around us long enough to know when we're coming even though we forget to knock most of the time."

"All the time," Conor corrected.

She rolled her eyes, but her expression was all playful teasing. "Anyway, continuing on. If you're ever in a situation that you hopefully won't be in." Jess's eyes darted to my daughter for a quick second. It was enough to tell me that she wouldn't go into detail in front of Lex. "Remember what you just felt . . . and pray for it."

I nodded. "Understood."

Conor stepped forward and dropped to a crouch so he was eye to eye with Lexi. "Jess is here to talk to your mom. I know you don't know him, but can Kieran hang out with us?"

She watched Kieran for a while before stepping from my hold to whisper loudly in Conor's ear. "Does he color too?"

"Of course," Conor said at the same time Kieran said, "Absolutely not."

Conor's mouth twisted into a broad smirk when he

stood and turned to face his friend. "Looks like you're about to color."

"Please take photographic evidence and send it to Einstein so we'll have it forever," Jess said with a little clap as Kieran turned and stalked off toward my room. She tossed Conor her phone before he left. "Just in case he steals yours."

I watched them go, trying to evaluate how I felt about Lexi being alone with those men. Both I hardly knew, one I barely trusted. When Conor turned and offered me a reassuring smile before leaving the door cracked behind him, my apprehension settled.

It was as if he'd known I would be worried because Kieran was such an unknown.

"Couch?" Jess asked, even though she was already walking that way.

I followed, knowing why she was here and wanting nothing to do with the conversation.

My brows rose when I rounded the corner into the living room and saw the coffee table littered with bags, cups of coffee, and food containers.

I hadn't even heard them set anything down on their way in.

Jess swiped a cup as she passed and practically danced her way to the couch.

How she did that without looking ridiculous, I would never know.

She gestured to one of the other remaining cups. "Grab one and sit."

I picked up a cup and toyed with the lid. "I know why you're here," I said as I sat opposite her.

"I can see that. I can also see you don't want me here."

"It isn't—no, that is not—Christ."

A soft, melodic laugh sounded before she took a long sip of her coffee. "I meant for the conversation," she murmured against the cup.

"Oh." I swallowed thickly and forced my hand into my lap so I would stop fidgeting with the lid. "It isn't you."

"It's that I'm not someone you trust, which is fine." She lifted her free hand toward the bedroom that held the boys and my world before placing it against her chest. "I understand. But in understanding that, I have to tell you that I already have an idea of what you aren't telling me. I don't know specifics, but I have an idea."

My head was shaking before she finished speaking. "You don't."

"Okay." Her tone was soft, but there was the subtlest hint of skepticism.

"You *don't*. I told you that he didn't abuse me—in any sense. I wanted—" I choked on the lie before it could escape.

Because I hadn't wanted him.

I'd *never* wanted him, even long before the games began.

Jess was silent for a minute before saying, "Okay, maybe he didn't. But you also told me that you felt violated, so I was hoping you would explain that to me."

An hour later, I'd somehow told her the entire thing.

From the very first game until I found the pills, leaving out anything that had to do with Zachary and Jason's plan to get Vero back, contacting ARCK, or how I'd really ended up here.

Jess had stayed silent throughout the entire thing,

listening intently. The only reason I knew she was paying attention at all was the deep sadness that started seeping from her when I talked about the years that should have been kept behind the walls of my home.

Throughout it all, I told myself to stop, but it was like ridding myself of a disease.

Once I began the process, I couldn't stop.

"Sutton, I hear you, I do. But that—everything you told me—*was* abuse. Mental, physical, sexual . . ."

"No. No, it wasn't."

"It was. The games . . . if you had enjoyed what he was doing, you wouldn't have run from him. You wouldn't have nightmares about it. You wouldn't be shaking while telling me about it."

"You don't—you don't understand. It's just something he wanted to do. I was fine with it."

A startled huff escaped her. "Did he tell you that you were fine with it?"

My mouth formed a thin line . . . because he had.

So many times.

"There's kinky, and then there's what he was doing. You told him to stop. You told him he was hurting you. He told you to shut up and *play your part*, Sutton. That's disgusting." She sat forward and reached for my hand. "If Kieran did any of those things, he would find himself in a grave."

Anyone else, I would take the words as nothing more than a hypothetical statement.

With Jess, I kind of wondered if she would put Kieran there herself.

"But it wasn't always like that. There were times that it wasn't."

"Yeah, but did you want those times to happen? Did

you enjoy it?" she asked, her tone gentle, hesitant. When I only stared at her in silence, stunned that she would ask something so bold, she gave a little shrug. "You mentioned that you held off, made sure you didn't have sex at times. That isn't normal for someone who *wants* to be physical with their partner."

"I didn't want another baby," I whispered, partially in embarrassment, partially in caution in the chance Lexi could hear me.

"That isn't what I asked."

I gaped at her for a few seconds. "What does it matter if I wanted it or enjoyed it? There are obligations I had as his wife; I was filling them."

Her eyes widened, but instead of responding, she said, "I'm not attacking you. I just want us to talk so I can help you understand what was happening. I know once you finally see it all for what it was, it's going to hurt, but you need to."

"No, *you* need to understand that what you're trying to say happened didn't. You're trying to take seven years of my life and change it into something that is just—God," I cried out.

At some point, I'd stood.

At some point, I'd begun yelling.

But Jess just sat there, calmly watching me, pain and worry filling her dark, dark eyes.

My body shook as that soul-deep chill worked through me, and I turned to start pacing so I could warm myself up.

One of the times I was facing her, I stopped and gripped my arms to try to calm the trembling. "There are things that happen between a husband and a wife that are for them to figure out, things that are not meant to leave the walls of their house. It is the wife's job to make sure that her husband is satisfied at *any* cost. That's what I was doing."

"Who told you that?"

"My mother," I yelled. "Jesus, why am I even talking about this with you? I don't even know you."

Jess looked horrified. "You *should* want to make the man you love happy. You *should* want to make your partner happy. But not at any cost. Not at the cost of your happiness. Not when it comes with the price of him physically hurting you and raping you and telling you to allow it because it is your job. Telling you that you enjoy it until you believe him." She paused when a sob wrenched from me, her eyes studying me for a few moments. "He had to drug you to even make you *want* to have sex with him."

"I know," I snapped and dropped my head into my hands as every fear and every resentment and every hatred came rushing up to overwhelm me.

Jess was silent as I cried, only reaching out to place a hand on my knee when I collapsed onto the couch again.

"I went to my mother after the first game." I finally lowered my hands to look at Jess. "I was scared and distraught and ready to leave Zachary. I told her what had happened, or, at least, I tried to. She stopped me before I could finish and told me snap out of it. Asked if he was my husband and then told me to stop being ungrateful and to go home. To remember everything he gave me. She said, as wives, we had to sacrifice ourselves to our husband's needs. As I was leaving, she told me to remember that couples without problems are what people want to see. That the ins and outs of a marriage are to remain within the walls of a home. And that marital problems should be forgotten before they begin."

"She sounds as bad as Zachary."

A soggy laugh climbed my throat. "She isn't pleasant, but she made it seem normal. Like it was to be expected in a marriage. So, I tried to tell myself it was. I told myself it hadn't been as bad as it seemed or that I could handle it because, most of the time, Zachary was so charming. But then it happened again and again, and every time, all I wanted was to get away—to disappear. It was why I ran and hid . . . it's instinctive to hide from that kind of evil. But I was told that I wanted it and enjoyed it, and it was easier to survive it if I closed my eyes and made myself believe that it was normal. If, when it was over, I made myself believe that I was doing what I was supposed to as his wife."

"None of that was normal."

"I know." My eyelids slipped closed. "I've known." I swallowed through the shame threatening to choke me. "But I didn't know how else to survive him and what was happening."

Jess gripped my hand in hers and squeezed tight. "You *did*, and that's what matters."

"I don't know if I love him," I admitted softly.

"That's understandable."

"No," I said quickly and opened my eyes to focus on her. "I don't know if I ever did. My father made me date two men and told me whoever proposed first was the one I had to marry. I knew both of them, but I didn't know them well. I hadn't had any interest in dating them before, and the circumstances surrounding my father's command made me want to date them less."

"What kind of screwed-up place did you grow up in?"

My chest moved with a silent laugh. "Somewhere I thought was normal until a week ago. Funny how much can change in such little time." I shook my head, as if that could clear it from the onslaught of this week. "When Zachary proposed, my mother asked if I loved him, and I said of course not. She asked again, and I laughed. Then she asked again, and I realized the only answer to her question was *yes*. She asked me every day until the wedding. My answer always had to be yes."

I reached for my naked ring finger and exhaled shakily.

"But, like I said, he's incredibly charming, and like everything else, I told myself the lie enough times that I started to believe it."

"I've heard that about him."

My eyes flashed to hers, and for a second, I couldn't understand the anger there. "Einstein," I finally whispered.

Her mouth twitched into an oddly beautiful mixture of a smile and a frown.

"I'm sorry for what happened."

She waved my words away. "You didn't know what he was going to do."

Except I had, in a way.

Say it. Say it . . . just say it.

She'll understand, she has to.

But if she doesn't . . .

"Uh, but Zachary, there were things he did and said almost immediately after our marriage that were . . . off, I guess, and then the games started a couple of years in. So, if I ever had truly loved him, or had started to, it died that first night. Not that it would've made a difference. Then, for the last year, I'd been so confused because whenever he touched me, or whenever there was the possibility of it, I wanted his touch in a way that made me almost sick in my soul. All I kept thinking was, how could I be afraid of someone and hate them and *want* them in that way?"

"It wasn't real," Jess said gently.

"I know that now. I knew when I found the pills, but it doesn't change the disgust I felt and still feel with myself."

After a moment, Jess said, "I want to tell you that you shouldn't feel disgusted—and you shouldn't. It was nothing you did. I know that feeling, though, and I know it takes time to work through." Her mouth stretched into a meaningful smile. "Time and *maybe* the one man in the world who can chase your demons away."

My cheeks blazed with heat when I realized her meaning.

It had only happened last night, and I doubted Conor had said anything to them about it, but he *had* been up before me and I'd taken so long getting ready . . .

"I so knew it," she whispered. "I knew it, I knew it. There's so much tangible tension between the two of you, I knew you liked him too."

"He told you he liked me?"

"He asked to be removed from the case because of it." Jess must have seen the way her news sent a punch to my chest because she hurried to add, "Obviously, that didn't happen since he's still here."

I wanted to know when he'd asked to leave and what else he had said to them, but I knew gaining answers would only muddle things that were already so complicated.

"There are things you need to know, though. Conor is the bright spot in our world. He's happy and kind and there for anyone when they need him. Yet, for how caring he is, he protects his heart. He never reveals his interests. Ever. Which means he doesn't need someone to fuck and move on from." She leaned forward, her face slipping into something wicked and slightly unhinged. "So, let me be the one to tell you that, if you hurt that man, I will kill you before anyone else can."

Once again, I had the strangest feeling she wasn't being hypothetical.

I swallowed thickly and nodded before shaking my head. "It doesn't matter, I can't . . . *we* can't. I want to—God knows I do. There's something about him that calls to me in a way I've never experienced. But as much as I want to answer that call, we can't. I'm still married to Zachary."

A breath of a laugh crept from Jess. "Not."

"What do you mean *not*?"

"You aren't married. You never were." Her expression fell for a moment before her eyebrows lifted in surprise. "Did you not know that?"

No.

No, no, no . . .

She's lying.

But no matter how many times my mind screamed denials, I couldn't forget the way the words had easily fallen from her lips, as if she'd been unconsciously correcting my mistake.

A mistake she clearly thought I should've recognized.

My chest heaved with harsh, ragged breaths as I tried to hear her words and understand their meaning.

My mind just kept rejecting them.

Because that would mean . . . what the hell did that mean?

"What do you mean?" I said through clenched teeth, not realizing that I'd yelled or that I was standing again until she was there with me, trying to calm me.

"Take a breath."

I was.

I was taking too many too fast.

"Slow breath," she said gently but firmly.

My head was shaking, and I was backing away from her and stumbling over the coffee table.

I didn't even feel the impact when I fell to the floor.

It felt like those last months with Zachary all over again—as if I were going insane.

I *was* married. I knew I was.

I had a ring—*had*. I'd had a ring.

There had been a wedding, and a church and a priest and a damn reception. My mother had been awful and had continuously told me I was the only imperfect thing there.

But in just a few sentences, I was wondering if it had all been another lie.

In one conversation, I felt like I couldn't trust anything I'd known.

In one week, my entire life had changed.

"Sutton, it's okay. Just breathe," Jess said as she crouched next to me.

"Don't touch me," I screamed and jerked my arm from her hold. "I spent seven years with that goddamn monster because he was my *husband*, so tell me what the fuck you mean."

Kieran was suddenly in the room with us seconds before Conor came charging in after him.

"I thought she knew they weren't married," Jess whispered to the guys. "I didn't realize."

My gaze swung to Conor, a plea for him to tell me they weren't really tilting my world on its side again, but he was staring at me cautiously.

"You knew," I choked out. "You knew, and you didn't tell me? You knew I was *disgusted* with myself for being tied to him. You knew I hated that I was still bound to that man in any way . . . and you didn't tell me?"

Nothing.

Conor simply continued to watch me as I yelled at him. Only moving when I struggled to stand from the floor.

I swatted at his hand. "Don't you dare touch me. You *knew*."

From the way his jaw ticked, he heard the double meaning in my words.

Not only did he know that I was sick over my lingering, legally binding connection to Zachary, he'd known I was torn up with guilt over what we had done *because* I was still married. Even if to a man I hated.

I pushed past him and whirled on the three of them when Jess called my name. "I'm done. I'm done having you all rip the floor out from under me. I'm done having my world twisted into something I don't even recognize with each new bomb you drop." A frantic, breathless laugh bubbled up my throat, and I reached for my head. "I feel like I'm going crazy because I don't know what actually happened, what's real, what to believe."

I stumbled to the side and hurried for the bedroom, slamming and locking the door behind me.

A cry ripped from me when I saw Lexi sitting on the middle of the bed, hands pressed tightly to her ears as she sang to herself.

Crayons and papers and coloring books littered the bed,

but I just climbed on top of them and pulled her hands down.

Her wide, hazel eyes opened. "Mr. Conor told me to sing so I could only hear myself, but I could still hear you yelling. I didn't know if it was because you were mad or sad or scared."

"I'm sorry," I whispered. "I wish you hadn't heard anything at all."

"Are you okay?"

I nodded and shifted so we were lying on the bed facing each other, her hands held protectively in my own. "I will be."

The lie had never felt so thick on my tongue.

Twenty-One

Conor

Sutton hadn't said a word to me for the rest of the day. I'd seen her.

She'd come out of the room with Lexi and their bags of laundry around lunchtime. Not that she'd eaten anything.

Other than calling to have someone come get their clothes, she'd been silent. Sticking close to Lexi and staring off to the side or out the windows.

It had been like the day after she'd read the files all over again.

I hadn't pushed—I knew better than to try. I also knew this was probably for the better. To end it before it could begin, only it *had* begun.

And every time I stole a glance at her, last night was all I could see.

Her wrapped in my arms. Her bright eyes and satisfied smile. How it looked when she was free of any of the weight that had been pressing down on her. The way she'd whispered my name and fit against me—around me.

"She's it, or she isn't."

I knew . . . I knew that, no matter how much my heart rebelled against the thought, I had to make sure she *wasn't*.

Because there was already too much mistrust and pain between us, and it was only bound to get worse.

A groan built in my chest, and I dragged my hands over my face just as my phone rang.

I glanced at the screen, confusion tugged at me before fear filled my veins when I saw Maverick's name on the screen. "What happened?" I said in way of a greeting.

"Wanted to make sure you were awake."

I looked around the darkened suite. "Am I not allowed to sleep?"

The second a knock sounded on the door, I was off the couch, my body tense. I started to ask Maverick if he'd had anything to do with it, but the call dropped.

I grabbed my gun from the coffee table and hurried to the door, listening for anything that could give me a hint as to what waited on the other side.

"The fuck," I mumbled when I heard a familiar voice complaining in the hall. I didn't even bother looking out of the peephole. Just unlocked the door and threw it open to reveal Maverick, his identical twin Diggs, and . . . "Einstein. The hell are you doing in Tennessee?"

She huffed and pushed past the twins and me to get into the suite. "I like how you all keep asking me this like you could keep me away."

"Clearly, we can't," Maverick said in a tone that let me know he didn't agree with her being here either.

"Oh, *oh*," Diggs called out as he walked in, flipping on

lights as he went. "If this is what all your cases are like, sign me up for the next one."

"It isn't."

"I've told him that three times already," Einstein said with a roll of her eyes as she set her bags down and then looked pointedly at the guys. "Get the rest while I find us a room."

"How long did you pack for if there's more?"

"Weapons," Einstein and Maverick answered at the same time.

I nodded in understanding.

Diggs sighed dramatically. "I'm dying of starvation."

"You just ate two burgers," Einstein argued, already pulling out her laptop.

Maverick shoved Diggs toward the door and then pulled Einstein close, pressing his forehead to hers and whispering shit I kind of wished I couldn't hear.

Still bothered me to see them together.

Still hurt.

But it wasn't nearly as bad as it had been. The girl locked away in the suite was the reason for that.

When the door slammed shut behind the guys, I stalked over to where Einstein was setting her computer on the coffee table. "You shouldn't be here."

"You keep saying that like maybe it will sting a little less the next time you do." Her lips were twisted in a smirk, her fingers flying over the keys, her eyes fixated on the screen.

"I'm serious."

"Oh no, Conor's serious."

I dropped onto the couch next to her. "*Einstein.*"

She looked away from the screen, her tone both

mocking and amused. "*Conor.*"

"After what happened to you, you shouldn't be anywhere near where Zachary is."

Her expression fell as something haunting filled her eyes, but she didn't respond.

"You aren't ready for this. You aren't ready if you see him. And if *he* sees *you*? Einstein, he *knows* you. He's seen Maverick and Diggs. None of you should've come. It risks too much."

I looked up when I heard a door open and shut, and cursed the way my body and heart and mind reacted the instant I saw her standing there.

Barely there shorts.

Threadbare shirt.

Fucking beautiful.

Instead of acknowledging Sutton, Einstein whispered, "We've never had a case like this. We've never had it mean something to us too. This is personal. The twins were giving Kieran and Jess a week to find Zachary and Garret. That week came and went, and I couldn't keep them away any longer. There was no way Maverick was coming without me."

I pulled my attention away from Sutton to say, "He should've known to keep you away."

Einstein smirked. "He tried. When has that ever worked for any of you?"

"This is dangerous."

A cold kind of ruthlessness settled over her features. "He got me once. He'll never get the opportunity again."

I stood, let out a frustrated sigh, and took a step in Sutton's direction. Her brows were pulled low as her stare bounced between Einstein and me, as though she were trying to piece something together.

"Sutton, this is Einstein."

Her expression shifted slowly until she was watching Einstein blankly. As if her mind was already so overwhelmed with everything else that she needed time to process what I'd said.

"Done," Einstein said and then came to stand beside me. "Well, I would say it's good to meet you, but that feels wrong in this situation. I'm glad to see you alive."

Sutton's head just moved in some combination of a nod and shake for a moment. "Yeah. Yes, I should say the same to you. I'm sorry. When I heard what happened . . ."

"It's okay. We don't have to talk about that."

I wasn't looking at Einstein, but I could hear the subtle change in her voice. She was trying to seem unaffected by what had happened when it was still too soon for her to be anything but.

"Sorry for the late-night intrusion, and if we woke you," she said, changing the subject. "There was a lot of slamming and groaning."

Sutton's sharp stare flashed to me. Pain, hurt, and betrayal swirled in her eyes.

"He's kind of uncontrollable when he's hungry," Einstein continued, "really, all the time."

"She's talking about Diggs," I said quickly, reaching for Sutton even though she was too far away.

She still took half a step back.

"Diggs," I said again. "He's one of the twins. That's who Einstein's talking about."

"Yeah, who else would I be talking about?" Einstein asked.

"Me." That one word held so much meaning, all of which went right over Einstein's head.

She couldn't see Sutton's hurt.

She couldn't hear how I was trying to protect Sutton.

She was the smartest person I knew, but she didn't see relationship cues until they smacked her in the face.

Einstein's shoulders bunched up. "You aren't the one we have to take care of like a gremlin."

"Sutton doesn't know that," I reminded her. "She also doesn't know the twins are here."

"Well, she should be inside my head." She blew out a slow breath and faced Sutton again. "So, the twins are here . . . *literally*," she added when there was a knock on the door.

When Einstein turned to let them in, I reached for Sutton again and then tried to contain my own hurt when she took another step away.

I had to remember this was necessary.

It was for the best.

"They just showed up," I explained. "I didn't know they were coming."

"Your friends seem to do that." Her voice was all bitter indifference, but I could hear the pain behind it. Knew it was just a front to protect herself.

"We've never had a case like this."

Sutton's eyes followed Einstein until she must have gone out of sight.

When her stare fell to the floor, her entire body seemed to crumple. "I can't . . . I can't do this." She started to turn and ignored when I called her name, but stilled when Diggs entered, already yelling.

"Oh, *oh* . . . oh," he said smoothly. "Hello, sweetheart."

I slowly looked over my shoulder, my eyes already set in a glare.

"I wouldn't have kept you waiting had I'd known you were what we were coming for." His mouth twitched into a cocky smirk. "What do you say we find a room and I introduce myself?"

I felt the way Sutton shifted closer to me, even though Diggs was still halfway across the suite.

"That's Diggs," I said through gritted teeth.

Maverick smacked his brother over the back of the head as he passed him and hissed, "Control yourself." He stopped a foot from me and nodded to Sutton. "Maverick, that's Diggs. I'm gonna apologize now for anything he says to you. He's been like this our entire lives and will never change. It's worse when he's hungry, which he currently is. But I promise, he's harmless."

Diggs was holding his arms out wide when Maverick walked back toward Einstein. "Love blockers. All of you."

"He is harmless," I said to Sutton, even though I still wanted to punch Diggs for setting his sights on her for even a second. "He'd hit on a tree if he was hungry enough."

Diggs's smile widened, still aimed at Sutton. "I'll show you what I've got in common with a tree."

A couch pillow smacked against the side of his head before I could take a step toward him. "Fucking eat something," Maverick said from where he was pressed close to Einstein's side.

Sutton let me pull her behind me when Diggs sauntered into the kitchen, winking at her as he passed. Once he was out of sight, she moved away from me again.

"What?" Diggs shouted. "There's no food in this kitchen."

"My daughter is asleep," Sutton snapped in a harsh whisper. "Would you please stop yelling?"

Diggs came out of the kitchen slower than he'd gone into it, confusion splashed across his face. "We have a baby mini in here?"

"Oh my God," Maverick said on a groan. "Dude, how many times did we tell you that she had a little girl?"

"Yeah, I don't think I was paying attention."

Sutton came to my side and lowered her voice. "Are they staying here?"

"In the resort, not with us." I curled my hands into fists and crossed my arms over my chest so I wouldn't be tempted to do something stupid.

Like reach for her again.

"That was what Einstein was doing when you came out here," I said. "Finding a room for them."

"Well, when—"

"Conor, you left without packing the essentials," Maverick called out from where he'd moved to the floor, and opened a large bag full of weapons. "What do you want or need?"

An uneven breath punched from Sutton's lungs. "Oh God."

"No—fuck, man. Can we not do this right now?"

Maverick's eyes darted from me to Sutton and then back again. The questions on his face were clear as fucking day, but I refused to answer when Sutton was beside me.

He wondered if Sutton knew who we really were, what we did.

If she knew what we planned to do when we found Zachary.

And, if the answers were no, if *I* was going to be the one to tell her.

"Why does he have that bag, and when are they leaving?" Sutton asked, her words strained.

"I have a fake feed ready to go," Einstein said in response without looking up from her laptop. "But we need to talk with Conor first, and it's easier to do in person since we're here now. It also might be better if you aren't in here."

"Einstein," I said in a low, warning tone.

"I have a feeling this isn't the kind of conversation you'd want others around to hear." Her stare slowly lifted from the screen to pierce me with an accusing look.

Fuck, if I didn't know with that one look that she'd found out about Sutton and me.

And I didn't know how to respond or feel about it.

We'd already imploded on the first day.

I nodded and looked to Sutton. "She might be right."

When Sutton opened her mouth to argue, I gave her a small shake of my head.

"I'll explain what I can in the morning."

"What you can," she said with a forced smile. "Which will be nothing."

"Sutton." I reached for her arm, and felt my body exhale in relief when I finally had her in my grasp. "You don't understand."

"You're right, I don't." Her chin trembled even though she tried to steel her jaw. "I don't understand anything that's happening in my life anymore. But you can't expect me not to worry about all these people who keep showing up. It isn't just me they're coming around, it's my daughter."

"I know, and I'm sorry it keeps happening this way, but I didn't know they were coming."

"Why is that?" she asked, desperation weaving through her tone. "If you're supposed to work together and be this *family*, why do they keep surprising you like this?"

I debated what to tell her for only a second before going with the truth. "After the first day on a job, we only talk when we have to, and when we do, we keep it to things that aren't identifying. Kieran and Jess show up without letting me know, *they* showed up without letting me know, because none of us trusts anything that Zachary could get into." I gestured to the living room with my free arm. "But you can trust them."

"Trust them, trust Kieran and Jess. Trust *you*," she said through clenched teeth, reminding me of how much I'd already hurt her. "I can't even trust my own life, and you want me to blindly trust people who show up with massive duffle bags full of guns. Why are they even here?"

"'Cause I'm a motherfucking bloodhound, baby," Diggs said with a clap. "And I've got hunting to do."

Sutton stared at him in bewilderment before turning for the bedroom.

"Everything," I promised, pulling her back to me. "I'll tell you *everything* in the morning."

A disbelieving laugh fell from her lips before she slipped from my grasp and left.

"Speaking of identifying," Einstein said once the bedroom door was closed. "I just got a message from Kieran. I let him know, without exactly letting him know, that we're here. Do you want to know what he said?"

"At this point, there's a lot he could've told you."

"Women ask for our help for a reason, Conor," she said, skipping whatever Kieran had said. "Not for you to take advantage of their emotional states and vulnerability and sleep with them."

Maverick sent me a wary look.

He wasn't surprised.

He'd known.

He could see.

Diggs just snorted before choking on a cough when Einstein shot him a glare.

"It isn't like that."

"It doesn't matter what you think it's like, you don't know what's going on in her head," she argued. "Some women need emotional and physical comfort in these situations, and they shouldn't be getting it from you. Jesus, Conor, they aren't even my rules—they're *yours*. I shouldn't be the one enforcing them. What the hell were you thinking?"

I ground my jaw to keep the words gathering on my tongue from slipping free.

"You aren't gonna say anything?"

I was struggling not to come back at her with something I knew would be painful.

My head moved in subtle shakes as I said, "I told you that it isn't like that, and it isn't. That's all you need to know."

"No, all we need to know is that you're going to end this. Immediately."

"Einstein, you know me, you know this *isn't* me. So, if I've put myself in this position, then you know it's because she means something."

"But *she* can't. She's a client—one whose sort-of-not-really husband is a manipulative sociopath. We don't even know if we can trust her."

"Avery," Maverick whispered her real name on a sigh.

She kept right on going. "Conor, I adore you. I do. I want you to find someone. Someone who isn't a client or in this fragile state and will regret whatever you do later."

"You have no fucking room to talk," I said, the words slow, my voice already filled with the pain I knew she was about to feel. "For you to tell me that I'm taking advantage of her in this situation means Maverick was taking advantage of you when you were with Johnny and after he died."

Maverick let out a low curse. His head fell against the side of the couch, and he reached back to grip Einstein's leg.

Whatever Einstein had been about to say died in her throat.

She just stared at me with those wide eyes, her mouth hanging open as if I'd slayed her.

And I wanted to take it back.

"I'm sorry. God, I'm sorry, but you have to see the similarities. I needed you to stop and think. Realize who you're talking to, who I am." I pressed a hand to my chest. "I'm not some guy who takes advantage of women. You know that. If you stop and think, you fucking know that."

Her eyes slipped shut on a slow blink.

"What's happening is difficult and jumbled and a fucking mess, but trust me to know not to take advantage of *any* woman. Trust me to know what is on the line by crossing this one."

"Okay," she finally said.

"Does she know?" Maverick asked, turning to look at me.

I let out an exhausted breath and went to sit on one of the chairs in the living room. "Which part?"

"What the plan is when we find Zachary?" Ruthless vengeance filled his eyes. "Why we're here."

"She will tomorrow."

"And how do you think she'll take that?" Einstein asked, her focus already on her screen again.

"Not sure. There's a lot we have to talk about. She just found out this morning that they were never married and feels a little betrayed because I didn't tell her."

Einstein glanced at Maverick before shooting me a look. "Considering your situation, I don't know why you didn't."

I dragged my hands over my face and bent forward to rest my forearms on my legs. "Reasons I'll have to explain to her when she lets me."

"Right. Has she given any locations on where Zachary and Garret might be?" Maverick asked, leaning forward to, once again, open the bag of weapons.

"I don't want any," I said before he could offer again. "I have a gun in my room, another on me, and extra magazines placed around the suite. "I'd take you up on it if Sutton's daughter weren't in here with me, but she is, and she's six."

"Understood."

"As for locations, I've asked. Kieran and Jess have asked." My shoulders moved in a brief shrug. "Anywhere she can think of has been checked already. She doesn't seem to know a lot about him since she spent so much time trying to avoid him."

He nodded, accepting the answer almost as if he'd been

expecting it. "Einstein pulled blueprints of the resort. Diggs and I are studying them in case shit comes to a head here. It's a fucking nightmare, but..."

"He would be coming to us," I assumed.

"Exactly."

"The problem with this place is that there's so many damn people. If Zachary's men are here, Kieran and Jess wouldn't know."

"I've been doing facial recognition every day and running it against people we have in the files," Einstein said. "And, you're right, it's a problem. We're near their town and in a major city where a lot of their illegal dealings happen. That means most of their contacts live around here. And people come and go from the resort daily because of the golf course and spa and blah, blah, blah—including people in the files. I went back nearly a month before you brought the girls here, and this place is always littered with people on their payroll."

"Do we leave—fuck, no. Never mind." I let out a slow breath and bit back a laugh when Diggs snored himself awake.

"Did we get food?" he asked before he was even fully conscious.

"No," Maverick murmured and then asked me, "Why can't you leave?"

"We're vulnerable if we do. It was enough of a risk moving them here, it isn't worth it to be out in the open again when we don't know where Zachary is, not when he has an entire cartel and thousands of people on their payroll who could be watching."

Diggs snorted. "We have... us."

"Speaking of," Maverick said and then searched through a side pocket on the weapon's duffel.

I snatched the balled-up black fabric from the air when he tossed it at me and felt my blood run cold.

"We all decided, and Dare made it official," Einstein said, sitting back and smiling at me. "You're one of us."

"Um." A breathless laugh crept up my throat as I unrolled the black bandana. "Yeah, I, uh . . . I'm kind of staring at my nightmare."

The three of them laughed, but Einstein's faded almost as quickly as it began.

Because she knew what I was seeing when I looked at that bandana.

It wasn't just a decade of dreading when our rival gang would show, hidden in shadows and behind black bandanas. It was that night Johnny had nearly killed me while wearing one of these. It was watching Dare aim a gun at Lily, the girl I'd been charged with protecting for years, and killing Johnny instead.

His best friend.

But I knew what this meant. It was what Kieran, Dare, and Beck had been working toward for so long—a truce between us.

It was what Einstein had been doing by stitching our families together after Kieran and I had dissolved the Holloway Gang—creating one family.

It also meant we were putting a foot back into the life we'd sworn to leave.

Kieran and I had known it was inevitable when the mob had continuously pulled us back in after we'd all attempted to break away from that world.

Holding this bandana meant Dare had accepted it as well.

"We have a couple for Kieran and Jess too," Einstein said softly. "After everything that's happened the last couple months, there's no point in continuing to deny what we are or that we're in it together."

"Means a lot." I smiled my thanks. "But there's no way in hell you're gonna get us to call ourselves Borellos."

Diggs and Maverick laughed.

Einstein only smiled. "Borellos or not, you're officially Rebels."

Twenty-Two

Sutton

My steps faltered when I left the bedroom the next morning.

It was still early, the sun hadn't even risen, but Conor was there, putting coffees and bags onto the kitchen counter. Ones that looked similar to what Jess and Kieran had brought the day before.

He cleared his throat as he straightened. "I was gonna come wake you."

His words from last night played in my mind again and again, filling me and leaving me more confused than ever.

I'd stayed pressed against the bedroom door last night, trying to choke back the overwhelming feelings from the day—God, the week—and trying to understand why it had hurt so damn bad to see Conor with Einstein. When he'd sided with her and asked me to leave.

It wasn't as though I wanted to be in the room with people I didn't know. I'd wanted answers from Conor.

And that was when I heard them . . . him and Einstein fighting about me.

"If I've put myself in this position, then you know it's because she means something."

Out of everything that had happened yesterday, that was the one thing I tried to hold tight to during the night. Everything else still felt like too much to sort through and deal with, and for some asinine reason, clinging to what he'd said helped me to keep the image of Conor and Einstein out of my head.

Walking out to see him talking with another woman who was beautiful in a wild, alluring kind of way that I could never compete with was shocking enough.

To find out who she was?

It didn't matter that he had told me that she belonged to someone else, all I could think in that moment was what she had meant to him.

Still, he'd fought for me.

I grabbed the sides of my robe and wrapped them around myself, giving my hands something to do. "Were you . . ."

"Thought it would be better if we talked before Lexi woke up."

I sucked in a stuttered breath and nodded, not knowing if I was ready for this but sure I wanted every answer he could give me.

He handed me one of the coffees and asked, "Why are you up so early?"

"Couldn't sleep." It was short and vague, but at least it was partially true.

"Me either. Jess dropped off food on her way to see Einstein."

My brows lifted as I brought the cup to my lips. I made some sort of confirming sound in my throat as I passed by him to sit in the living room.

"That isn't fair, and you know it," he said once he was seated near me.

"What?"

"That look you kept giving me last night, the one you just gave me. Like her being here is a betrayal."

I swallowed past the knot in my throat and pulled my knees to my chest.

"You know nothing ever happened with her. You already know there is no story to tell."

"I know," I said quickly, preventing him from continuing. "I know, and I know that it isn't fair because you've had to listen to the stories I've told you. But I . . ." A defeated breath broke from me.

"You what?"

"I've heard the way you say her name," I whispered, laying my heart bare. "She means something to you, and when I walked out and saw the two of you right there? Jesus, it hurt in a way that didn't make sense. This sickening jealousy spread through me, making me feel so stupid because I hardly know you and don't have a claim on you at all."

His bright eyes darkened with something intimate and raw. "You don't?"

My shoulders sagged, because God knew I wanted to.

"Yesterday, I kept telling myself the distance you'd put between us was good," he said roughly. "It was what we needed because we'd crossed a line we shouldn't have. And then I'd see you, and whatever distance was between us would feel like too much. It killed me to know I was the reason it was there and the reason you weren't looking at me."

"Why didn't you tell me about Zachary?" I asked, the question no more than a murmur.

"The times it came up, there was always something in the way. Trust, you already finding out too much at once, us being interrupted." His head slanted in a faint shake. "When you were panicking yesterday morning, I tried. I started to. Then Lexi came out of the room and Kieran and Jess showed . . ."

"You should have told me that first day."

"The file I gave you to read," he began carefully. "If you would've looked at it closely, you would've known."

I stopped mid-sip. "What?"

"It's how we found out. Your marriage certificate, did you see it?"

I remembered going through the file, scrolling right past the certificate. "Yeah?"

"It wasn't signed," he said gently, as if trying to make me understand something.

"What do you mean? I remember when Zachary and I went and signed . . ." The words died as Conor shook his head.

"It wasn't signed by an officiant. No marriage certificates in the last couple of generations of the Tennessee Gentlemen have been signed. And none of them are registered with the state. From the labels on the scans, they were all hidden deep in the cartel's attorneys' files."

I stared blankly ahead before asking, "What? *Why*, what does that mean?"

"We only have assumptions. If something happens, none of the women have any claim to money or businesses. Divorce is becoming more common. They're trying to protect themselves. Smart for them, considering they've remained unknown all these years."

My entire body caved as the reality hit me.

"I know it's a lot."

"That's an understatement." I thought for a second before asking, "Are my parents married?"

"Your dad's generation is the first to do this."

"My dad used to threaten my mom with divorce," I said, reminding him of our conversation from days ago.

"I'm guessing your mom doesn't know that she isn't legally married. If your dad ever left her, he would have likely faked the divorce and she would have found herself with little to nothing without ever learning the truth."

"This is all so surreal," I whispered.

"Even if this wasn't something they did, you and Zachary would technically no longer be married since he had you erased. You and Lexi don't even exist."

"How does that work . . . when you take us wherever we're going?"

When this was over.

When I have to say goodbye to you forever.

Conor studied me, looking as if he were going to say something only to change his mind so many times before he said, "Einstein. She'll make new identities, background stories, everything you need."

I wondered for a second what those identities and background stories would consist of before realizing I didn't want to know. There were more important things I needed to talk to him about.

"You said you would tell me everything."

He nodded, sat back, and tapped his thumb on the lid of his cup a few times before clearing his throat. "The other night, I told you that you wouldn't be so close to me if you knew what I wasn't telling you about my life."

My heart raced as I waited for him to continue.

Judging by the hesitation in his tone and worry etched in his eyes, I wasn't sure if I wanted him to anymore.

"It's because I'm not that different from Zachary."

No. No, that was something I couldn't believe. There wasn't an ounce of Zachary in the man in front of me, I was sure of it.

When he didn't offer anything else, I asked, "In what way?"

"I was in the Irish-American mob from the time I was thirteen. Kieran? He's an assassin."

If I hadn't been positive I was sitting on the couch, I would've thought I was falling to the floor.

There wasn't—no.

I saw him . . . I *saw* Conor and his tattoos and his unimaginably tall, muscled body. But he was good to his core. He wasn't a criminal. He couldn't be in the mob. God, how was this a thing? How was this even real life?

This was in movies and—

Hands gripped and squeezed my heart, stealing my next breath as the rest of what he'd said finally registered.

"You let an assassin near my daughter?"

"Sutton, wait."

"Conor, you brought an assassin around my daughter." I screamed the words. At least, it felt as if I did.

But they came out hoarse and strained and with hardly any weight behind them.

"Kieran was trained to be one from before his first birthday. He didn't have a choice. He also hates that side of himself and uses his skills to do this," he said, gesturing to me. "To save people. This is what he and Jess want to do."

I gaped at him before repeating, "An assassin."

"Yeah, one who's on your side. Same as Maverick."

I stilled, caught off guard. "What do you mean?"

"Maverick's an assassin too."

"No, he—" I blinked, trying to match the information being thrown at me with the people who had popped into my life over the last week. "But he looked like a person."

"And I don't?" Conor lifted his shoulders. "Diggs is a tracker. Einstein was their hacker. They're mafia. We come from rival gangs that go back generations."

"But . . . you're friends. You work together." I lifted a hand, trying to take back what I'd said and stop him from responding at the same time. "How is this even a conversation we're having? This can't be real."

"You grew up in a cartel and never knew." When I just gave him a hopeless look, he said, "None of us wanted that life anymore. The Borellos disbanded first, and the day Beck died, Kieran and I disbanded ours."

"You can do that?"

"It's complicated. But, yeah."

I had a feeling I didn't want to know the specifics of what made it complicated. "So, you're no longer in the mob?"

He shifted back and ran his hands over his beard before raking them through his hair. "Also complicated. It's hard to ever fully get out because people know who you are. Some shit happened a couple of months ago, and then Einstein was taken, so we've all had to acknowledge that old enemies will never let us be out. If anything comes at us now, we'll be ready as one family."

"That's why you want me to trust them," I assumed. "Because you're all in the same, what, gang?"

"No. I want you to trust them because *I* trust all of them with my life. I've seen what they'll do to protect and find each other. And with most of us in this to protect you and Lexi, the others will too."

I dropped my stare to my legs and tried to wrap my head around everything, thankful that Conor didn't push me to talk about it. That he left me with my thoughts.

"I don't understand," I said a while later. "I've read about the Tennessee Gentlemen and what they do. And you all come from mobs, but you own a private investigating company that specializes in helping women in bad situations? That doesn't sound right to me. Everything I've seen in movies fits with the Tennessee Gentlemen. Drugs, weapons, crime in general."

"All of that was us," he said cautiously. "I told you about Dare the other day, he's the human lie detector. He became the boss of the Borellos when he was just a teenager. Turned the entire thing around and started pulling them out of every illegal thing he could so he could shut it down. Kieran and Beck worked with him to take down our boss because he was a sick bastard who was into the worst kinds of things. We all wanted different lives, but like I said, there's no escaping it."

"Do you wish you could?"

His eyes drifted for a while. "The things I wanted to escape, we did. The rest, what we still face at times? It's part of my life. It would be nice if the people I cared about didn't get taken."

My mouth pulled into a frown. "Right."

"Sutton, you should know . . . the twins, Einstein, why they're here." He shifted uncomfortably, amplifying my own worry. "Kieran's never not found someone. The fact that he hasn't found Zachary yet is bad, and Maverick's getting anxious."

"Why?"

Conor stared at a spot on the floor for a second before lifting his head and looking at me with resolve. "Because Zachary's still alive."

A stunned breath left my lungs when I realized he was serious. "I'm sorry?"

"After what he did to Einstein, none of us would've let him live. That he turned out to be your husband made it complicated because there was more danger for you and it created a conflict, but none of us are going to forget what he did to her." He looked me dead in the eyes. "And I can't forget what he did to you."

"You . . ." I shook my head, trying to figure out how these words could actually be leaving my tongue. "You're going to kill Zachary?"

"As soon as he's found."

My mind was slow to catch up and demand clarification. "Wait, would *you*?"

"In a heartbeat." There wasn't an ounce of hesitation. Those few words rang with honesty and a sort of knowledge that had a brick settling in my stomach.

"Have you—"

"Don't ask that," he said on a breath.

An answer in and of itself.

It suddenly felt hard to breathe as I pictured the man

before me, the one who had worshipped and loved me the other night, in that life . . . killing someone.

"That's everything," he said gruffly as he stood.

"Where are you going?"

He lifted his hands slightly at his sides, coffee cup in hand. "Giving you space. Time." He had only gone a couple steps when he turned to face me. "No matter what, I will protect you and Lexi with my life."

My heart both swelled and ached. "I know."

If there was anything I was sure of, it was that.

The sun was finally starting to rise when I pushed from the couch in search of Conor.

He hadn't left me that long ago, and I wasn't sure that I'd thought through anything at all. There was just so much information . . . so many lies and secrets that I could barely concentrate.

Couldn't begin to wrap my mind around the type of life this man had lived.

I found him standing against the door, just as I knew I would, and came to a stop right in front of him.

"I have a question." When he dipped his head, I said, "You told me that before ARCK, you protected women. Why did you lie when I already knew you were keeping things from me?"

"I didn't. That was my job for the last . . . fuck, five years in the mob. I was the protector." His head slanted, but those piercing eyes never left me as he attempted to gauge my every reaction. "Our boss's kids had been taken out, one by one, and only his daughter had survived. We faked her death, but there was still a chance people would find out she was alive, so my job was to protect her."

"Did you and she . . ."

"No." A rough laugh sounded in his chest. "She'd been with Kieran her entire life. Ended up falling in love with Dare, the guy determined to kill her. They're married and have a kid."

Unreal.

This was all so utterly unreal.

"And before those five years?"

After a minute, he said, "If you really want to know, I'll tell you."

"I'm not sure I do," I said softly. "I'm not sure I can handle anything else. I can't—" I pressed my fingers to my temple and let out a shaky breath. "I can hardly think. I feel like my head is going to explode because there's just so much happening, and it keeps happening."

"Clear it."

A sharp huff escaped my throat as my hands fell away. "You say that as if it's simple."

He pushed from the door and started to take a step toward me, but he stopped just shy of touching me. "May I?"

"What?" My chest hitched as every thought and want and need came rushing back, just as strongly as before.

Nothing of what he had said had changed that, and a part of me was relieved.

It meant it was honest and real.

Another part was so weighed down with thoughts and emotions that I couldn't imagine being with him in that way at this moment.

"I've had to clear my head a lot throughout my life. I work out when I need to. I also used to fight with Beck. Fighting's how he kept us fed when we lived on the streets," he explained when he saw the confusion I felt playing out on my face. He jerked his head in the direction of the living room. "So, if you still trust me to be near you, to touch you, let's go."

My shoulders sagged as the barely hidden pain in his voice tore at my chest. "I wouldn't be standing here if I didn't."

We'd been going so long that the sun had fully risen and I'd lost count of how many times we'd started over.

How many times I'd managed to break free from Conor's hold.

How many times he'd told me where to hit and how.

How many times I'd punched his palms, over and over again.

And it felt so damn good to hit something, to get that anger and that pain out, that an agonizing breath broke from me when he wrapped his arms around me and told me to go again.

Conor's grip on me tightened, pulling me closer against his chest. "Sutton—"

"I hate him," I said through clenched teeth. "I hate him for everything he did. For the way he hurt me and used me and filled me with fear that never left."

I twisted my hands, trying to find a weakness in Conor's grip.

When he realized what I was doing, his arms tightened and his mouth met my ear. "Keep going."

"After everything he did, I want to see him being

lowered into a grave," I seethed and struggled against his hold as my throat tightened with emotion. "I should feel like a horrible person for saying that and thinking it, but I don't. I want him to know the fear he made me feel. I want him to feel the pain I felt. And I want him to pay for it so he can't do it to anyone else ever again."

I got a hold of Conor's thumb and pulled back until I had one hand free and then worked on the other hand, blinking against the wetness gathering in my eyes that was making it too blurry to see.

"I hate my mother for always telling me I wasn't good enough. For making me think that what Zachary was doing to me was normal." Tears streamed down my face at an unforgiving pace as my body released every pent-up thought. "And I hate that Zachary turned my dream house into a goddamn nightmare. That he made me feel trapped there."

The moment I felt Conor's hold loosen, I jerked my other hand free, turned, and immediately swung for his neck.

He blocked the strike.

And the next.

And the next.

He gripped my fist in his hand, refusing to let go, and then did the same with the other when I threw my next punch.

"Keep going," he said softly, never releasing his hold on my hands.

My head dropped to hang between my shoulders. My body jerked with my sob.

"I hate that you were in the mob," I said softly. "I hate that everyone you're surrounded by was too and that my daughter is near them. But I feel as if I know you better than maybe I even know myself." A sad laugh fell from my lips. "In this week, I've come to know more about you than I ever knew about Zachary in the seven years we were married. I've come to trust you more."

I used his hold on me to pull myself up and tried to look at him through my tears.

"I never let Lexi be alone with him. If I had known everything yesterday, I would still watch you and Kieran take her into the room and know that she was safe. That I didn't need to worry as long as you were with her."

Conor's body seemed to sag with relief. "Keep going."

"I don't know what it says about me that I still want you more than my next breath, but . . . I do."

He released my hands and slowly wove his into my hair.

His mouth passed across my forehead before he was pulling me against him, holding me as if I were precious and fragile.

"Clear?" he asked after a minute.

A shuddering breath worked through my body, and as the last bit of air pushed from my lungs, I realized how free I felt. Emotionally drained, but free. "Clear."

Twenty-three

Zachary

I sucked in a sharp breath through my teeth when I ended the call and forced the smile that had become permanently feral this past week.

"There's obviously something you want to say, so say it."

Garret remained silent, so I turned my glare on him, only to find him smirking like the bastard he was.

Slamming the burner phone down, I leaned forward and dropped my voice to a growl. "Told you to fucking say it."

He shrugged as though he didn't have a worry in the world. As though a bullet in the head wasn't a real possibility in the coming minutes if he didn't stop with the goddamn smirking.

"Find it funny," he finally said when my hand began twitching.

"Your mocking tone and slow-to-reveal thoughts have

reached a limit. And, fuck, if I haven't waited a long damn time for you to push me to this point."

That smirk only widened.

Not a hint of fear.

He should fear me.

"Find it funny that your plan ended with Sutton holed up with another man."

I dropped back into my chair with an amused huff, all homicidal thoughts slipping away. "If you're implying something, I'd love for you to just come out and say it."

"I know better than anyone how well Sutton can juggle two men."

A genuine smile tugged at my mouth for the first time this week.

This game, I could play.

"If you're trying to make me jealous, you won't succeed. Because no matter what you think happened back then, she *always* belonged to me." I waved toward the computers and screens set up in the room and shrugged. "As for what's happening now? Maybe in a world where she ended up with you, there would be worries of her being unfaithful. But this isn't that world, and she's mine."

That smirk died, and his jaw ticked under the pressure he was putting on it.

"Sutton knows her place. She knows her role in this . . . and she's playing it well."

Twenty-Four

Conor

I kept my eyes trained on Sutton's as she carried the clean laundry past where Lexi and I were coloring on the floor.

"Yours is on your bed," she said with a shy smile, her eyes dancing and saying a dozen other things, all of which I was begging to know.

It wasn't until just before she reached their bedroom that she finally looked straight ahead and slipped out of sight.

"You need more purple."

I tore my attention away from the room and focused on Lexi, who was looking at my picture. "Purple? What's wrong with what I have?"

She rolled her eyes. "There's no purple."

I flicked her forehead before reaching for the purple crayon. "Don't roll your eyes."

"Momma does it."

Didn't I know it. It seemed to come naturally for her. The action was also just so *Sutton*.

Lexi was different—she was made of everything pure and good in the world. Someone as sweet and adorable as she was shouldn't already be rolling her eyes.

"Your mom is an adult," I said, trying to think of anything that made sense. Pulling the adult card made sense. "When you're an adult, you can roll your eyes all you want."

"'Kay," she murmured.

I dropped the crayon and held my arms out, showing off the masterpiece blob I'd drawn. "Done."

Lexi looked at my picture and gave it a nod of approval before sliding her paper on top of mine and pointing at the semi-stick figure people clumped together in the middle. "That's me and that's Momma and that's you."

My fucking heart.

It felt like it was exploding and aching and swelling all at once.

I swallowed, trying to push past the knot suddenly taking up residence in my throat, and nodded.

"That's great, Lex—" A strangled laugh left me as I took a closer look at the picture. "Why do I have a crown?"

And why the hell was my entire face a smile?

"Because you're Prince Charming," she said as if I should have known.

A fuller laugh built in my chest. I hooked an arm around Lexi's neck and pulled her close. "*I'm* Prince Charming?"

First time in my life I'd ever been called anything close to that.

Pretty sure she was the only one who ever would see me that way. I fucking loved it.

She gave me a *duh* look and reached for my face. "You have Prince Charming's smile. I see it when you don't smile, but it's really a lot better when you do."

I was sure that, in that moment, nothing could've stopped my smile.

But it fell.

Slowly. Surely.

Because I realized Sutton wasn't the only one who had come to mean something to me in such a short time. This little girl had burrowed herself so deeply into my heart I had a feeling there was no removing her.

To try would destroy me.

I'd fucked up . . . crossed so many lines.

My job was to help people. To keep them safe.

To fall for a client was a hard limit.

I'd done that. I was so far past that.

Because these days—meals with the girls, coffee with Sutton, and coloring with Lexi—I wanted them for the rest of my life.

I wanted to be the one who protected them from anything and everything. I wanted to tell Lexi not to roll her eyes. I wanted to fight with Sutton and wait for her to come to me so we could talk it out. I wanted *everything*.

I didn't know how to have it, though.

I wasn't sure I could.

"Thanks, Lex," I said in a gruff voice and then looked to see what she was adding to the picture.

A shadow of a person directly behind us.

"Who's that?"

"It's Daddy," she whispered. "Do you see his bad-man's smile?"

She hadn't drawn a mouth on the shadowed person at all yet.

I released her and watched intently as she continued to draw. "Why do you think he has a bad-man's smile?"

"Because I've seen it," she said simply. "It's always there. But I saw it that day for real, for real. And it is way worse when it is really there."

"What day?"

Her crayon paused and her voice dropped to a low, fear-filled hush. "When he killed that man."

My blood slowed, grew cold. I wanted to demand to know details. To know every-damn-thing, but I was trying to figure out the best way to go about this when I was talking to a six-year-old.

"Lexi, what do you mean he killed a man? What man?"

Her shoulders bunched up. "He was in front of Daddy. Like this." She rose to her knees and placed her hands behind her head, her wide eyes darted to me for a second before she dropped back to the floor and went back to coloring.

"Can you tell me what happened?"

Lexi's hand stopped again, but her eyes remained on the paper for a moment. When she finally looked to me, true fear covered her face. "If I say it, his bad-man's smile will come back."

"Did he tell you that?"

Her head moved in slow, faint shakes. "That was what he told the man."

I was torn between wanting to hunt down the man who had put this fear in his daughter's eyes and wanting to be there to listen to Lexi—to get a story we'd all been waiting for. "Lexi, I'll never let him near you."

When she moved this time, she dropped the crayon and scooted closer to me so she could whisper in my ear. "Daddy said the man told on him. And then he went *bang. Bang. Bang.* I don't want him to know I told."

Shit.

I wrapped my arms tight around her and hugged her close. "He won't. I'll make sure of it."

"You promise, promise?"

"Promise, promise." I set her down and bent to be closer to her eye level. "Thank you for telling me. That was very brave. I have to talk to your mom now, though."

Fear fell over Lexi's face in a second. "You can't. The bad smile will come. It's coming in my dreams. And Momma's so, so scared of Daddy."

"Lexi, listen," I began, my voice firm. "I'm here. I will *be* here. If someone comes, I'll stop them from getting to you. But I *have* to talk to your mom about this, and I can't do that until you say you understand."

Her mouth trembled before forming into a hard line. She lifted her chin in a way that looked so much like Sutton and nodded. "I understand."

"You're so brave." I pressed my forehead to hers and then pushed to my feet. "Stay here. Draw me a picture of the house from your dreams, okay?"

She was nodding and lying on her stomach, already reaching for a new piece of paper before I ever turned away.

Then I was stalking across the suite, headed for the girls' room.

Sutton slammed into me as she came running from the room.

I grabbed and steadied her, already hissing under my breath, "When were you gonna tell me that Lexi saw Zachary kill someone?"

She jerked in my hold, her face paled.

"I've been asking and asking—"

"What?" she whispered, horror coating the word. "What do you—*what*?"

"I've given you so many goddamn opportunities to tell me what happened. Why you really ran . . . and there was never anything that hinted at *this*."

"What do—I don't—she didn't."

"She just fucking told me, Sutton. I don't need a lot of experience with six year olds to know that fear was real."

Sutton looked to where Lexi was in the living room.

It wasn't until she called out her name that I realized she was shaking in my arms.

Her body trembling uncontrollably as she pulled away and hurried to Lexi.

"Lexi, baby, what did you tell Mr. Conor?"

Lexi looked from Sutton to me as she stood, her face scrunching with worry. "I told . . . I told him about the bad-man's smile. About when I saw it for real."

"When did you see it?" Sutton asked, her panic barely leashed.

When Lexi told the story this time around, it was said on a rush and between cries. "When Daddy killed the man. He said he told on him. I knew that if I told on him, then his bad smile would find me."

Sutton's shoulders were shuddering with her rough breaths.

She looked as if she'd seen a ghost.

"When was this, I need to know when this was," she pleaded.

"At the party." Lexi was still crying and hurried to wipe her face. "The party I was supposed to stay away from. I was playing outside even though Nadia told me not to. I heard Daddy talking in the guesthouse, so I went to see why he was there. Because that wasn't where the party was."

Sutton stood from her crouch, her fisted hand shaking as she lifted it to her head.

She stepped toward me, her hushed whispers frenzied and nearly inaudible. "He knows. Conor, he knows. Zachary knows that she saw him."

"How do you know?"

"Just trust me," she cried out before dropping to her knees and pulling Lexi into a tight embrace.

One of her hands covered her mouth and the other fisted against Lexi's back. I was no longer sure where her shaking ended and Lexi's began.

When I crouched behind Lexi, I could barely hear Sutton's muted, "I'm sorry, I'm sorry, I'm sorry."

Her panicked eyes met mine as she held out the fisted hand toward me.

I reached for it, unsure of what she was doing, and felt my heart begin to race when she dropped something into my open palm.

A half-crumpled piece of paper and a wedding ring.

With Sutton's fear and how she'd been bolting from the room, I had no doubts in my mind the ring was hers.

The one she'd left back at the motel.

When I opened the paper, my blood ran cold.

Let's play a game.

I was on my feet and running to their room, my phone already to my ear.

"Get us a new room; we need to move," I ordered as soon as Einstein answered.

"That doesn't sound good." Within seconds, the sound of her tapping away on her laptop filled the other end of the line.

"Jesus." My chest heaved as I pulled note after note off the hangers that had come back with the girls' clothes.

All of them had the same message as the one in my hand.

"Einstein," I said, silently begging her to move faster as I rushed through their room, grabbing their bags and suitcases and shoving everything I could see into them.

"There's nothing," she said quickly, frustration leaking through her tone. "It's Memorial Day weekend, there are high school proms, college graduations. The place is packed."

"Fuck." I dragged a hand through my hair. "How did you get a room?"

"You'll see when you get here, I guess. How long do you need?"

"Five minutes."

"Then it'll start exactly five minutes after we hang up." She ended the call as soon as she finished talking.

I started a timer on my phone and then finished throwing the clothes into the bags.

Once I was done, I forced myself to appear calm when I felt anything but, and walked into the living room.

I wanted to rush. I wanted to grab the girls and run.

I wanted to fucking kill someone.

I dropped to a crouch in front of Lexi and let my mouth slip into a grin. "Suite Hop, you ready?"

"Again?"

"This one will be the most fun of them all," I said and held up my hand for a high five. As soon as she smacked it, I jerked my head in the direction of their room. "Grab anything I missed and pack it up, okay?"

Her eyes brightened, a smile threatened at the edges of her mouth. "Okay!"

Once she ran into the room, I pulled Sutton into my arms and crushed my mouth to hers, swallowing her surprised gasp and trying to erase all her worries and fears.

Sliding a hand up, I curled it around her cheek and waited until those captivating eyes were on me. "It's going to be okay."

Her face crumpled with worry. "How did he find us?"

"We'll figure that out later. Right now, all we should focus on is getting the two of you somewhere else. Got it?"

She nodded as a few tears slipped free.

"We have a couple of minutes before we move. I threw most of your stuff into your bags already. Keep Lexi calm and her mind off everything else."

I released her and rocked back, but she lifted onto her toes and pressed her mouth to mine. Her fingers slid into my hair as if we had all the time in the world for this kiss.

Damn it, if it didn't feel like we did for those seconds.

A repressed cry sounded in her chest when she pulled

away and started for their room, wiping beneath her eyes as she did.

I ran around the suite, gathering my gun and extra magazines and packing and trying to get in the right frame of mind.

I knew I had to be ready for anything that might be waiting for us in those halls, but I also wanted to appear calm and unaffected for Lexi. It felt impossible to do both.

I met the girls near the door just as my alarm went off and forced a quick smile. "Let's go."

I let Sutton know where we were going so she wouldn't be blindsided when we got to the new room, and wondered how this was going to work with all of us in an enclosed space.

I didn't have to wonder long.

Maverick opened the door to their suite as we walked up to it—the biggest damn suite of the entire resort.

Over twice the size of the ones we'd been staying in, which had been huge.

Lexi pressed close to Sutton's side as she took in the three strangers. Wary and untrusting, exactly like her mom.

"*This* is how we got a room," Einstein said with a cheeky grin.

"Because, why not?" I said with a laugh that felt forced.

Fear and adrenaline were still coursing through my veins, making me feel on edge.

"Well, it came in handy today, so you're welcome."

"And it's fucking epic," Diggs shouted as he rounded a corner, sandwich in hand. "Oh, *oh*—oh, dude. Is this the baby mini?" He sauntered up to where we were and held out a fist to Lexi.

She didn't respond in any way.

He held the hand in the air and looked around like he couldn't understand what had happened. "I got burned by a baby mini. The hell's up with that?"

"Jesus, he's never gonna let this go," Maverick mumbled under his breath and then gave me a look. "Where do you want to talk?"

Before I could answer, Diggs dropped to a crouch. "Diggs," he said, pressing his hand to his chest before gesturing to Lexi. "Baby Mini. Here's how it is, I'm the coolest one here, and you're gonna find that out real quick. I make a mean sandwich and will sneak you all the snacks. I also build forts like you've never seen. But you're gonna break my damn heart if you burn me at hello."

Lexi giggled, and then, from where she was hiding behind Sutton, whispered, "I love forts."

I felt Sutton's shock reflected on my own face.

It took Lexi days before she said anything to me and she still wouldn't speak to Kieran or Jess.

Diggs took a massive bite of his sandwich and grinned. "Hell yeah, Baby Mini. I knew we would be best friends. Let's go get you some food."

Sutton reached for Lexi when she took off after Diggs without a second thought, but I pulled her to my side to whisper in her ear, "He's like a golden retriever. She'll be fine. And you know your daughter better than anyone . . . she wouldn't have followed him if he weren't okay."

She released a shuddering breath, her head bouncing in something that resembled a nod.

I dug my hand into my pocket and pulled out the papers and ring, extending them toward Einstein and Maverick as

I said, "These were with the girls' laundry when it was brought back."

As soon as Einstein saw the typed words on the notes, her entire body lurched, and she stumbled back.

I took a step toward her.

Maverick reached for her but stopped when she waved him off.

"Okay," Einstein said in a weak, shaky voice. "Okay, I'll check cameras."

Once she was gone, I looked to Maverick. "She shouldn't have come."

He rubbed the back of his neck as his mouth twitched into a grimace. "I know, but there was no keeping her home. She was determined."

I knew that too.

I cleared my throat when Maverick gathered everything from my palm. "The ring. That's Sutton's, I think." I shot her a questioning glance.

Her eyes were shut, and her face was the same ghostly white it had been before. "It's mine."

Wrapping my arm around her waist, I pulled her close again, trying to pour my strength and peace into her as I told Maverick, "She'd left it in the motel I found her in."

His eyes darted between us before settling on her. "You're sure you didn't lose it here?"

"No, I took it off and left it on the bed as we were leaving. I didn't want the reminder."

Maverick nodded and then gave me a meaningful look. "Then someone who works for him knows you're here, because neither Zachary nor Garret haven't set foot on the property. Everyone who was here when you arrived is now gone. Einstein has monitored every check-in. Diggs and I searched every possible hiding place in the resort. That doesn't mean we won't find him."

He handed me the notes and ring and then reached for some of the bags. "There're three rooms. Sutton, how—"

"She'll be with Lexi," I answered before he could finish.

"Then you can take Diggs's room," he told me with a smirk. "He's been planning this fort since we got in here last night. He won't be sleeping anywhere else."

Once we were following Maverick through the two-floor suite, Sutton lifted her head to ask, "Is he being serious?"

"I've never seen one, but I've heard stories. Their forts are legendary."

Twenty-Five

Conor

The day passed in a blur of watching camera feeds—both the hotel's and different houses of some of the Tennessee Gentlemen—helping the twins build the fort, and spoiling the shit out of Lexi.

The girl was eating it up.

The twins and Einstein had made her a cape and a paper crown, claiming she was a superhero princess. When Jess stopped by, she braided her Rebel bandana into Lexi's hair.

Not that Lexi responded to any of them other than Diggs.

Sutton about fell over when Lexi came running up and announced that she was a Rebel.

Diggs had been the source of her laughter, her horse, and personal chef. I was trying not to let it get to me that he was clearly Lexi's favorite. Guess I should have expected it since he would always be a kid at heart.

But having her run up to me with the brightest smile to show me each new thing?

It'd made the frustrations of not getting anywhere with the ring or notes ease.

It'd made the fears of knowing that Zachary knew where the girls were melt away a little.

It was the first day since getting Sutton and Lexi that I felt good. Normal even. As if this were just another day back in Wake Forest with the friends that made up my family.

From the girls' laughs and smiles, I knew it was the same for them.

Sutton let out a contented sigh and rested her head against the couch. Her eyes shifted, taking in the massive fort we were in. "This is incredible."

It took up the entire two-story living and sitting area, even extending to cover parts of the stairs that led to the top bedroom. When I asked where they had gotten all the sheets, Diggs just grinned mischievously while Maverick pointed at him.

The floor was littered with pillows and blankets, the couches and chairs were all arranged around the room, with a sofa bed dead center—where Lexi was.

There was also way more food than we'd ever be able to eat.

"Lexi loves it," she continued, a soft smile playing on her lips.

"Think she loved today."

That same contented sigh hummed in her throat. "They

made it so special for her. She's going to crash soon and sleep so well."

"A bunch of mobsters. Who knew?" The words were pure tease and earned me an eye roll, but that smile was still tugging at her mouth.

I ran a hand over my beard and glanced at Lexi.

She was already on her stomach with her head on her arms, trying to stay awake to watch the movie.

"What are your thoughts on leaving Lexi in here?" I chanced a look at Sutton in time to see her confusion shift into something else.

Something needy and filled with desire.

But then she blinked. "Without one of us? I don't know. They've been so great with her, but I don't know them well enough to leave her with them."

"Not the whole night. And if you say no, not at all," I assured her. "But there's something I hoped you would do for me."

Her brows lifted, her confusion back and mixing with her curiosity.

"I asked Jess to pick up some things for me a few days ago, and I've been holding on to them." Pain tugged at my chest, but I pushed past it. "My brother was scruffy in this precise way. Looked ragged as fuck, but he worked hard for it. I always told him he looked like he was still homeless, and he called me the pretty-boy lumberjack. When he died, I stopped trimming my beard and cutting my hair. It wasn't a conscious decision; it just happened. Didn't realize until this week how much I look like him, and I wonder if I was doing it so I'd have a connection to him."

Sutton shifted forward and slid her hand into mine. "Conor, I'm so sorry."

"It happens. In our life—in that life—it happened a lot." I swallowed thickly and said, "But it's been over a year, I've got to let that go. And I want you to do it."

It took a few seconds before her eyes widened in understanding. "Wait, what? You want me to cut your hair?" I'd barely nodded before she began shaking her head. "Conor, I haven't cut hair in eight years. I didn't even graduate. What if I mess up?"

I silenced her with a brush of my thumb across her lips. "Say no, and that will be the end of it. But I trust you, and I want you to."

She looked at me helplessly for a few seconds before dropping her head against my chest.

Her back shook with a rough exhale, and then her hands were on my face and she was pulling me down to press her mouth against mine. Her fingers curled against my beard, gently tugging and trailing across as if she were trying to commit the feel of it to memory.

I smiled against the kiss and pulled back to look at her. "It isn't going away. It'll just be shorter."

Her eyes followed where the tips of her fingers were still playing before darting up to mine. "I've just kind of grown attached to it."

I grabbed her hand and pressed a kiss to her palm. "Kind of grown attached to you."

Through the light of the television, I could see the darkening of her cheeks. The woman really was beautiful when I made her blush.

"I've never done anything to deserve a man the likes of you."

Hushed.

Exposed.

And so fucking backward.

I pulled her closer and whispered, "You're wrong."

I brushed my lips across hers once . . . twice . . . until she was reaching up and pressing her mouth firmly to mine. Opening for me when I teased her lips and whimpering when our tongues met.

Short, passionate, and filled with something I was afraid to define.

All too soon, it was over.

Because even though the dark gave us some cover, Lexi was still in the room, and we'd been careful not to even touch when she was around.

I stared into Sutton's eyes, which were swirling with that unspoken, forbidden emotion for a few more seconds, prolonging the moment before looking across the room to where Lexi lay.

Diggs was draping a blanket over her.

"Think Lex is asleep." Thick, gruff, strained . . . and all I could manage.

Sutton pulled from my arms and turned, a smile tugging at her lips when she saw Diggs tucking the thick material around her.

"Guess he's harmless," she murmured. With a quick inhale, she shifted to press her head to my neck. "I'm honored you want me to help with something that means so much to you, and I will. Let me check on Lexi first and make sure her guard dog will stay."

A soft laugh escaped me as I watched her make her way through the pillows and blankets over to Lexi's makeshift bed.

And there it was again—that feeling from earlier. As if my heart were exploding and knitting together all at once.

When she bent to give her daughter a kiss, a thought rushed up so swift and so unbidden that I nearly choked on it.

Mine.

I tried to shove it down.

Tried to remember every complicated aspect of our situation. Why I couldn't—*shouldn't*—entertain thoughts like that.

But it felt as real as the oxygen filling my lungs.

Those girls were mine.

I stood, dragging my hands over my face and mentally cursing myself for ever getting in this position.

For letting myself fall.

For whatever reason, women who I couldn't touch or have or *keep* were put in my life.

With a sharp exhale, I dropped my arms and looked across to the woman I had, without a doubt, fallen for as she spoke quietly to Diggs.

Arms folded protectively around herself, as if she still had lingering doubts about him—about all of them.

From the way Diggs was sitting with arms raised in surrender, looking like the whole world might not be a joke after all, I had no doubt Sutton was warning him what she would do if he let anything happen to her daughter.

When Sutton took a step away, Diggs extended a fist toward her.

At the last second, she bumped it before making her way back to me. Her chin was lifted, but she looked completely unsure of herself.

"He won't be leaving her side."

No, no he wouldn't.

My chest hitched with a silent laugh as I led her to the

room I'd hijacked from Diggs, grabbing a kitchen chair as we went. "He can find a way to turn anything and any situation into a joke, but I think you might've actually scared him."

"He should be," she whispered with a soft smile. "I have diamond-encrusted heels, and I know how to use them now."

My next laugh was louder, fuller.

Once we were in the bathroom, I situated the chair in front of one of the sinks and reached for my phone, nodding at the bag in the corner as I did. "Everything's in there."

I didn't realize how quiet and still Sutton had gone until I'd found a picture from before Beck died.

She had set out the contents of the bag on the counter and was trailing the tips of her fingers over them in reverence.

"Did she get the right stuff?"

The corner of her mouth twitched. Her head moved in the faintest nod. "I never thought I'd touch shears again." Her entire body seemed to cave as she turned to me. "I'm sorry, I'm sorry, this isn't about me. I can't imagine what it means for you to do this because I can't imagine a connection like that."

I caught her chin between my fingers and passed a quick kiss across her lips to stop her rambling.

"I *can't* imagine what this will mean for you," she murmured. "But you don't know what it means for you to do this for me. For you not to laugh in my face. For you to encourage it instead of destroy it."

Always.

I'll always encourage anything you want to do.

I struggled to force away the treacherous thoughts that rose so effortlessly.

Sutton's eyes danced as she turned to look at the counter. "Even though I probably don't remember how to do this anymore, let alone hold the shears." She reached for one and gave me a wry smile. "Diggs should definitely be scared now."

"He should." Amusement crept through my tone. "And I'm sure it'll come back naturally." Sliding my phone across the counter, I said, "That's how I used to keep it."

Her breath caught as she reached for the phone. "Goodness."

"What?"

"Those dimples." She shot me a quick look, eyes and smile bright. Cheeks *so* fucking red. She reached for my face, her fingers trailing through my beard. "I know you have them, I mean . . . they're impossible to miss, even with all this. But they're so much more pronounced when your beard is shorter."

"Yeah." I cleared my throat. "They're impossible to hide."

"Why would you want to?"

They'd made me a target in the mob from day one—because I didn't look like I belonged. Because I was young and hadn't grown up in that life. Because I wasn't hardened from the inside like Beck had been.

I had to work harder and faster, be tougher and stronger, than the rest to prove my worth. To get out from in front of the boss's crosshairs.

All the while, Beck and Kieran had tried to protect me by keeping me in jobs away from the most danger. They hadn't realized how much danger doing that put me in.

Beck got to sell on the streets while I was used as a drug-and-weapons runner. While I was forced to figure out how to dress wounds and save the lives of other members who had been shot or stabbed. While I got thrown into a darkened basement in kill-or-be-killed fights if I *didn't* save them, or simply because Mickey felt like being a bastard.

I never knew until I made it out if the man I was fighting was some random person they picked up, someone who owed the gang, or a fellow member.

Beck gave me shit when he saw bruises or cuts for taking fighting lessons from someone else.

That was what he and Kieran were told, all they knew, and they were too wrapped up in their jobs to ever think otherwise. To ever suspect that the members who disappeared were anything other than casualties of our life.

And our boss had loved every second. Loved that he had held my life in his hands for years until the day came when I could've easily ended *his*. All because he'd picked up two kids.

One who was angry and hardened from the inside out, as if he'd been born for the mob. Another who was tall and lanky as fuck, with dimples taking up most his face.

"They don't fit," I said simply.

"What, with your tattoos and your massive size?" she teased. She ran a finger down my cheek, tracing where it would be if I had been smiling. "I think they fit you perfectly. You're still plenty scary, trust me."

"Scary enough to have Prince Charming's smile?"

Sutton's eyes widened, and a grin tugged at her perfect lips. "How did you know about that?"

"Lexi told me."

She hummed a small noise. "She said that the morning

you broke into the motel room. You hadn't even smiled yet." After lifting onto her toes to press her mouth to mine in a swift kiss, she dropped down and turned to the counter. "And then I saw you smile."

I studied the way she pulled her bottom lip between her teeth.

"Prince Charming?"

"Oh yeah." She flicked her eyes in my direction. "Wrapped up in a terrifying, terrifying man."

I spun her and tugged her against me before slowly lifting her onto the counter. "So, it's just the smile then?"

The words were all tease and dripped with need.

The space between us came alive.

Her chest lifted and fell in exaggerated movements as her head slowly shook.

Her legs curled around my hips.

Her hands pushed under my shirt, lifting as she felt every defined ridge.

"It's everything," she said breathlessly. "It's the way you look at me. It's the way you aren't afraid to put me in my place. It's the way you talk to my daughter, and the way she adores you. It's this feeling like I'll never get enough of you."

Her hands trailed back down, one of them toying with the top of my pants before she was curling the other around my neck and kissing me. Teasing me with her tongue in a way that about drove me insane.

When she spoke, each word had her lips brushing against mine. "And every part of you is so utterly beautiful it takes my breath away. The good, the terrifying, your heart—"

I captured her mouth, swallowing her words and her moan as I dipped my hand inside her tiny shorts.

A growl rumbled in my chest when I found her already wet for me.

The instant my fingers brushed over her clit, she trembled.

I bit down on that full lip she loved to torment me with so much as I pushed two fingers into her deeply.

Her responding gasp washed through me, making my blood heat.

Every beat of my pounding heart was roaring its claim.

Mine, mine, mine.

I brushed my thumb over the lip I'd just bit at the same moment I put pressure against her clit. My mouth tugging into a grin when my name raked up her throat.

Seconds.

It'd been seconds, and she was already quivering.

Already clenching tight around my fingers.

Already arching from the counter and sucking in uneven breaths.

I pressed my forehead to hers and demanded in a low tone, "Open your eyes."

Her response was instant. Heavy-lidded and filled with lust and locked onto mine.

"Let go."

"Conor, please."

My lips twisted into a smile, and I leaned forward so they were a breath from hers. "Let go," I whispered again and curled my fingers inside her.

She shattered.

Crying out and shuddering against me as I pushed her

higher, never once letting up until her body sagged against the mirror.

I pulled my fingers out slowly, relishing in the way she jerked against me when I brushed against her sensitive clit again and again before removing my hand.

She reached for me, using my shirt to pull me closer, and then her mouth was on my neck and she was reaching for my pants.

I gripped her wrists, stopping her when it was the last fucking thing I wanted to do.

I wanted to rip off her shorts and fuck her until she screamed my name . . . but I would want more and more and more.

I waited until she looked at me, an unspoken question lingering in her eyes, before I said, "If I have you again, I won't be able to let you go. Think about what that means for you and Lexi. What it means for *me*."

Instead of the fear or hesitation or uncertainty I expected, there was only longing.

And it made this so much harder.

I gripped her tighter and tried to remember what I was saying. Why I was saying it. Why I wasn't picking her up and taking her to the bed.

"Think," I pleaded through clenched teeth. "And after you do, know that the next time I fuck you, I'm not letting you sleep until you're spent. Trembling. Aching. Throat raw from screaming my name."

"Oh God." Her body shook and cheeks filled with heat, but those eyes . . . they still churned with want and need.

I buried my face against her neck, breathing her in and telling myself this was right.

Pretending I hadn't said *the next time* as though we both already knew it was inevitable.

Pressing my lips to her soft skin, I whispered, "Think."

I helped her from the counter and held her in my arms for a while before releasing her and stepping back.

I was about to tell her we didn't have to continue with our original plans when she bent to pick up something off the floor.

My phone.

I hadn't even heard it get knocked off the counter.

She held it out, her head tilted back to study me. "Is this Beck?"

The pain was there, but I felt the smile that stretched across my face as I looked at the picture now showing on my phone.

He was sitting next to Lily, busting up laughing.

"Yeah. Yeah, that is." I gestured to the picture. "That was his best friend, Lily, the girl I was charged with protecting for those years."

Surprise coated Sutton's expression when she glanced at me. "Kieran's ex?" When I nodded, she went back to looking at the picture. "I can't . . . Jess looks made for him. I can't see this girl with someone like Kieran. Or any of you, really."

A sharp laugh forced from my lungs. "Don't underestimate her, she's tough. Lily was the princess of the mob. She went from dating an assassin to dating the rival boss. Twice, she faced the guy who almost killed me and came out alive."

That got me her undivided attention. From the alarm seeping from her, I knew Johnny wasn't something I had told her about yet.

"Someone almost killed you?"

I couldn't count the number of times I'd fought for my life because of Mickey or the mob in general. Yet, out of them all, Johnny was the only one who nearly succeeded.

I shrugged and offered her a smile. "He didn't."

Her eyelids fluttered shut as she released a slow breath.

After a moment, she nodded and looked at the picture again. "I can see the resemblance in you and Beck, but I think you're right. It's mostly the hair. You look so different when it's short."

"Different how?"

Sutton fought a smile and failed, forcing one from me. "It's you. It's so obviously you. But the length in this," she said, tugging at my beard, "changes everything. Two completely different men."

"And which guy do you prefer?"

She pulled her bottom lip between her teeth as she tugged me toward her.

Before our mouths touched, she asked, "Am I allowed to say both?"

I kissed her slowly, thoroughly, until she was relaxing into me and sighing against the kiss. "That doesn't help us now."

When she leaned away, that full, bottom lip was between her teeth again.

I pulled it out and smoothed it over with my thumb. "Drives me crazy when you do that."

The words were low and husky, and the way she responded to them and my touch didn't help remind me why we were in here instead of the bedroom.

Her tongue darted out to wet her lip, barely touching

the tip of my thumb and forcing a groan from me. "Fuck, Sutton."

I gripped the counter behind her so I wouldn't pull her closer. Wouldn't turn her around and bend her over. Wouldn't do any number of the stupid things filling my head.

I managed to push myself away and took a few steps back, putting distance between us that felt necessary and useless.

Her head bounced in a faint nod. "Um, both. Really . . . both." She tried to smile, but it didn't reach her eyes like it had before. "And even if I cut it, I could always ask you to grow it out again for me."

She realized what she said a few seconds later, what her words implied. Her stare fell to the floor, but not before I caught the deep sadness pulsing through her eyes.

Dangerous.

All of this.

After clearing her throat, she glanced up. "Can I wash your hair?"

A weighted breath escaped me at the question that didn't fit with the tension filling the large bathroom.

Nothing we'd planned to do or had talked about seemed important anymore. Because we had an expiration date.

One I thought we could outlive.

One we both obviously wanted to.

One that was staring us in the face, mocking us for thinking we could survive it.

"Yeah," I said softly. "Tell me what to do."

She nodded to the chair behind me, which was still in front of the sink. "Just sit."

I did as she said, turning the chair to sit in it sideways so I could lean my head back.

Sutton moved around the bathroom for a minute, gathering towels and shampoo before coming over to turn on the water.

Once it was the temperature she wanted it, she wrapped a towel around my shoulders and placed another rolled-up one behind my neck.

She looked calm in a way I hadn't seen her before as she bent over to wet my hair and wash it. Dragging her fingers through and massaging, releasing every tension and worry and frustration that had been building over the past weeks.

If I hadn't been so focused on her face, her hands would've put me to sleep.

By the time she was towel-drying my hair, she was smiling. Soft and free.

She grabbed my phone and brought it back to me. "Could I see that picture of you one more time?"

I turned the chair so I was facing the counter and pulled up the picture she asked for. But when she placed the phone down again, the picture of Beck and Lily was filling the screen.

Through the reflection, I watched as she slowly ran her fingers through my hair, playing with it for a few seconds before grabbing one of the combs and shears.

I gripped her wrist, halting her movement, and waited until her eyes met mine in the mirror. "Thank you."

Her body relaxed and that sadness crept back into her eyes as she nodded. "No matter what your hair looked like, you and Beck would always look different."

My stare drifted to the phone.

I wanted to turn it off.

But I had a feeling she'd left it up there for me, and I didn't want to tarnish the gesture that was supposed to be thoughtful.

"Yeah, we aren't identical."

"No." A frown briefly pulled at her lips before she shook it off. "He looks sad in that picture."

"He's laughing."

Her eyes briefly met mine in the mirror, and that one look told me she was afraid she was saying the wrong thing.

That she was afraid she'd hurt me.

But she still whispered, "His eyes look sad."

Lexi must have gotten her intuition from her mom—with her comments about smiles and seeing them without them being there—because what Sutton saw wasn't in that picture, except it had *been* there.

Present. Every day. Our heavy life weighing Beck down, slowly defeating him.

Beck was happiest with Lily. But even at his happiest, even laughing with her, that darkness had remained around him, pressing down on him.

"Endlessly," I said. "That's a hard life, and Beck had a lot more put on him than I did. Working with the enemy to take down our boss. Trying to protect me even though he knew he couldn't. Seeing the girl he loved every day for a decade and knowing she hated him because of what he did."

A pained sound crept up Sutton's throat. "That is sad."

"It's Jess . . . the girl."

She paused with her hands in my hair, her eyes wide. "Kieran's Jess?"

"Yeah. It's a long story."

Her brows lifted. "We have time."

"Why don't you tell me one?"

Shock blasted from her, and for a second, she just stood there. "I don't have any that are happy really."

My laugh was hard and sharp. "And mine are?"

"They're exciting." She shrugged. "It all sounds so unreal, like a movie. And you have a family of people who love you and who seem to have fun, even in the worst situations. Mine are all stories of avoiding my mother and Zachary and trying to have Lexi anywhere but at the house with him."

"Your mom is pretty fucking bad."

Sutton gave me a look saying I didn't know the half of it. "Tell me something."

Every story I could think of involved someone dying.

When there weren't rivalries or people being taken, we lived normal lives. But, then again, Sutton hadn't had a normal life either. "I'll give you a story if you tell me something from your life. Anything."

A laugh tumbled from her lips, like she couldn't understand anything I would want to know. "All right."

"Diggs is a bloodhound. He can smell and track things that people shouldn't be able to. There's a war between him and Einstein that's been going on since long before I knew them, and it revolves around scones."

"Scones," Sutton repeated in a dull tone.

"Mini blueberry ones, Einstein's favorite. They get stashed in our office so Diggs can't find them. One day, he found out she kept them there and came rushing in when we were having a meeting. He tried to grab the box and ended up slamming into Einstein's desk, knocking it over.

Shattered three computers that had unsaved data on the case we'd been working on."

"No." Sutton's mouth was wide with shock. "Over *scones?*"

"Guy loves food. You've seen how much he eats." My chest moved with a silent laugh at Sutton's knowing expression. "Einstein lost it and tackled him, yelling at him. Which would have seemed reasonable since we lost data, and her entire world is computers and hacking. Except she wasn't yelling at him about the computers, she was demanding he drop the scones."

"This is a serious war," Sutton whispered.

"Clearly."

"Now I know never to eat a scone in front of him." She went back to cutting my hair with a sigh. "I don't have anything nearly that fun. Oh, I did punch the runner-up at a pageant in the face once."

I didn't think I could smile any wider. "She try to take your tiara?"

"I found out right before we went on stage to get crowned that she'd been sleeping with my boyfriend. I waited until after the ceremony, I have class, after all," she said with a wry grin. "Then I told her she could have him. I didn't want a boy who lowered his standards to second-best because he couldn't get into my pants. She called me a frigid virgin, so I took off my crown and punched her."

A loud laugh burst from me, filled with surprise and pride.

"Class. Right." I shot Sutton a wink through the mirror. "Tell me more."

And she did.

She told me stories about sabotages in the pageant

world and the drama between debutants, but she never once touched anything that had to do with Zachary or after their fake wedding.

The smile that tugged at her mouth as she talked and worked was faint, but it was fucking stunning.

When she'd finished with my hair and tilted my head back, her words died on her tongue. Slowly, she set the clippers down to pull her fingers through my beard, watching fixatedly as she did.

My voice was rough when I asked, "Do you want me to keep it?"

"Would you if I asked you to?"

In a heartbeat.

I'd keep the damn scruffy beard. I'd grow it back out for you. I'd alter my entire life to keep you in it.

So far gone.

So deep in dangerous territory.

"Of course."

She studied me before pulling me slightly closer, the action hesitant before she closed the rest of the distance and pressed her mouth to mine.

The kiss was hard and short and had a lingering taste of her pain from the unknown.

Sutton didn't say anything when she pulled away. She wouldn't even meet my eyes.

She just picked the clippers up and turned them on, answering my question with that action alone.

Twenty-Six

Sutton

I took a step back when I finished, my eyes bouncing over this new Conor who looked so similar, and yet, so incredibly different from the one I'd come to know.

So handsome that it hurt to look at him.

Or maybe that was the tension pressing down around us, the unknown questions resting in the air.

"If I have you again, I won't be able to let you go. Think about what that means for you and Lexi. What it means for me.*"*

I carefully took the towel from around Conor's shoulders as he stood and turned for the mirror.

His words and his shuttered expressions played through my mind again and again as I cleaned up.

How any time there was a mention of us past this case, unease bled from him and he shut down.

Confirming what I'd feared when he had first said those words.

"Sutton."

I looked up, trying not to let it show how much it affected me when he just said my name, and lifted my eyebrows in question.

"It's perfect."

The honesty in his voice filled my soul.

I would never be able to repay him for this, for what he'd done for me.

I hated that the night felt beautiful and passionate and *tainted* all at the same time.

I couldn't understand how we'd gone from him bringing me to a body-numbing high to a kiss that lacked any warmth or response from him.

And it made it hard to breathe.

Because I knew what he was doing.

He was preparing me for a goodbye that he'd seen all along.

One I thought wasn't coming when we'd both willingly fallen into this.

Conor crouched in front of me, stopping my hands. "Look at me."

I braced my heart and my jaw when I sat back.

"Thank you for this," he said slowly in that low, low tone that seemed to move right through me. "You did an amazing job."

"Thank *you*. I really do hope you like it."

His eyes searched mine, his mouth opened, and I knew whatever he was going to say I wasn't ready for.

Not with the roller coaster we'd already been on in the last hour alone.

"Can you check on Lexi?" I asked before he had the chance to speak.

He cleared his throat and nodded. "Let me help you first."

"No, I'd really rather you check on Lexi."

He hesitated for a minute, a war clearly waging within him before he pushed from the floor and left.

As soon as I heard the bedroom door open and shut behind him, I sank back onto my heels and struggled to take a full breath. Tried not to make sense of what he was doing.

I knew I couldn't and trying to would only make this harder.

By the time he came back, I had finished cleaning up the mess.

He didn't say anything, just leaned against the wall and folded his arms over his chest.

"Lexi?"

"Still asleep. Diggs is too. Maverick and Einstein are in the kitchen working." From his gruff tone, it was clear he didn't plan to let this go without saying his peace.

I didn't want to hear it.

I wasn't ready for it.

"You said Maverick and Diggs were here to find Zachary, but they've been in the suite all day."

Conor rubbed a hand over his jaw as an aggravated smile tugged at his mouth.

He knew what I was doing . . . I didn't care.

"They have reasons that I'm not getting into with you."

"Why?"

"Because this is not what we should be talking about right now," he said, his tone at once pleading and frustrated. "It isn't what *you* want to be talking about."

"I don't want to talk about anything else with you."

"Sutton—"

"No, don't." I held up a hand, begging him not to continue. "You can't do what you've been doing to me all night and then talk to me like *I'm* the one causing this distance. You put it there, I'm dealing with it."

His head jerked back. "Distance?"

A disbelieving laugh punched from my lungs. "Everything I said was the wrong thing tonight. Every time I opened my mouth, you shut down and put a step between us. That last kiss? It felt like I was begging you to respond, and there was nothing."

Conor looked dumbfounded.

"You want me to think about what this would mean for Lexi and me?" I pressed a hand to my chest. "You said it like I *had* to think. Like I hadn't already thought about it all. I thought that was what we both did after we slept together. Weighed the risks and decided that they didn't matter."

Just like that, his entire expression shifted. Shuttered. Shut down.

Pain spread through my chest, both cold as ice and hot as fire, stealing my next breath.

"You want me to think about what this would mean for you?" The question was barely above a breath. "Apparently, I don't know what it would mean for you, because you sounded unsure. It sounded like you were trying to convince me to stop and think—*for you*."

"Jesus, do you have any idea how wrong you are?" He tossed his arms in my direction, pleading with me in that single action. "Yes, Sutton, I want you to think. I want you to think about what being with me means. Wanting to be with me and deciding to stay with me are entirely different.

I want you to think, because I already don't know how I'm supposed to let you go, and if I let myself have you again, I won't be able to."

"Then you should've thought of that before tonight . . . or *today*." I pressed a hand to my aching chest. "You should've thought of that before pulling me deeper and deeper in."

"I have been."

It would've been easier if he'd yelled the words.

But the agonized whisper ripped through me, shredding me in the process.

"Every time I look at you, I try to remind myself that I'll lose you. Every time I touch you, I think of ways to prevent it, and every time you say something that involves us after this case, it eats me alive because I want that more than I've ever wanted anything. And that scares the shit out of me because my gut instinct is to do anything to make an *after* happen. But I have a family I can't abandon, and I can't keep you."

"I don't—*what*? Then why would you say you wouldn't be able to let me go?"

"Because I won't," he said, his voice twisted in torment. "The only way to stay with you is to be relocated with you, and that's something I can't do. So, I would try to keep you in a world we both know you don't want Lexi or yourself in, a world you aren't safe in. We both know how that ends."

My chest pitched with uneven breaths.

"That's it? That's our only outcome?"

His eyelids slowly closed, his head slanted in the faintest denial, but his mouth stayed firmly shut.

"If you'd already counted us out, you should never have

played with my heart. You should never have made me fall for you and want something with you only to rip it away."

"I don't know how to count us out. I know the ending, I see it, and I can still see what we could be if that ending didn't happen. Sutton, I want to give you everything. I want to give Lexi the fucking world. But you aren't mine to keep."

"That isn't for you to say," I cried out. "It isn't for you to decide what our ending is when you submerse us in your life and show me what it could be like. It isn't for you to tell me that I wouldn't fight to be with you. That I am not yours." I turned to grip the counter, my head hanging so he wouldn't see the embarrassment that went with my confession.

"Being mine means pulling you into a world darker than you were ever in and having your eyes open the entire time. Being mine means you and Lexi will be in the open and still visible to the Tennessee Gentlemen." When he spoke again, his voice was closer and wrapped in a plea. *"Think."*

I knew I couldn't begin to understand the warning in that single word.

I also knew I'd never been in as much danger as I had been these last weeks, just as I'd never been safer.

"I need us to be safe, Conor. I need to know *Lexi* is safe." I shifted my head to look at him. "I haven't had that comfort since Zachary hid her from me five years ago. But I do when she's with you. My decision was made when you told me about your past, about your life, and I still chose you. I took everything I knew into consideration when I made my choice. My daughter and I have never been safer or happier than we are when we're with you." A sad laugh forced from my chest as I let my head fall again. "I thought you'd already decided not to let me go. Clearly, I was wrong."

"Wrong? I—damn it, Sutton." He released a slow breath, his alluring presence of peace and strength pressing closer around me as he stepped forward. "You say that like I don't want you. Like it isn't slowly killing me to keep myself from you for even a second. Like my blood doesn't hum with the need to make you mine forever."

My eyelids shut with a weighted exhale when his body pressed against mine.

A large hand slid slowly around my waist, gripping my stomach possessively. His forehead dropped to my head, and his mouth skimmed the shell of my ear.

"Sutton, I won't let you go."

A warning.

A plea.

His pains and his fears and his wants in a few words that moved through my veins and filled my soul.

"Then don't."

No sooner had the words left my lips than I was turned and his mouth was crashing down onto mine.

Our kiss was all-consuming.

Every brush of his lips and stroke of his tongue was a claim. Every revered grip on my body was a vow that left a trail of lingering heat.

Nothing had ever felt like this. Too much and not nearly enough.

As if each touch was another brand on my heart.

As if I needed him to breathe.

My fingers trailed through his hair as he lifted me onto

the edge of the counter, my head tilting back as he made a slow descent down my neck.

A whimper escaped me when he hitched my knees around his waist and stepped closer, giving me the slightest tease of pressure where I was aching for him.

"Yeah, sorry . . ."

I scrambled back, choking on the shocked cry when I opened my eyes to find Jess in the bathroom with us.

"This can't wait," she continued with an unapologetic shrug.

Conor's body seemed to expand to cover mine, his back heaving with his exaggerated breaths.

He didn't turn to look at Jess. But I knew from the coldness in his eyes and the bite in his words that he was using the mirror to stare her down.

"Better be a damn good reason."

"I said it couldn't wait." She looked at her nails before dropping her hand. "Besides, I was expecting to walk in on something different since I was told you were in here getting your hair cut." Her mouth split into a wide grin. "Which looks amazing."

"Jess," Conor growled.

"Fine," she mumbled with an eye roll. "But we need you now."

As soon as she left, Conor let out a slow breath and looked at me, hesitation warring on his features. "I have to go."

"I heard."

"Tell me that you know I don't want to."

A faint smile tugged at the corner of my mouth.

I dragged my hands over his beard and pulled him closer to kiss him slowly, thoroughly.

"I think we're finally on the same page," I whispered against his lips.

He stole another quick kiss before helping me off the counter and stepping away.

At the last second before he reached the door, he rocked back and ate up the distance between us. Curling an arm around my waist, he tugged me close and dropped his mouth to my ear.

I was blushing and aching and had an appeal for him to stay on the tip of my tongue when he left.

His hushed words of making good on his earlier promise and what he planned to do to me lingered behind while I cleaned the shears and clippers with a lazy smile.

That smile and warmth gave way to a sickening and cold fear when I left the bathroom and saw Conor's bag on the dresser in the bedroom.

Next to it were the crumpled papers and my ring.

LET'S PLAY A GAME.
LET'S PLAY A GAME.
LET'S PLAY A GAME.

Over and over and over again.

"How did you find us?" I breathed, as if Zachary would be standing behind me and about to answer.

The way I couldn't stop shaking and the chills that flashed across my skin made it feel as if he might be.

I wrapped my arms around my body and turned, wanting to get away from the sight of anything that had to do with him when a thought slammed into me so forcefully I thought I might be sick.

Those notes had been on every one of my and Lexi's clothes, my ring had been tied to the belt of my robe.

Conor's clothes had gone out and come back with ours.

I ran across the room and hurried to open his bag, my trembling hands making it difficult to work a simple zipper.

I thought through today, through the packing and the outfits. Conor had changed since we'd moved suites—I was positive he'd changed clothes this evening.

But when I finally got into his bag, all the cleaned laundry was still in a haphazard lump from when he'd rushed through packing, still in their bag and untouched.

"Please no, please no, please no," I breathed as I ripped the bag off and hurried through item after item of clothing.

Nothing.

Not a single sign of Zachary having left anything for Conor to find.

I was so dizzy with relief that I wasn't sure what relieved me more.

If it was because there weren't any more notes or because he wasn't targeting Conor.

Maybe it was because he hadn't left something for Conor to find that would ruin everything . . .

I tried to calm my racing heart as I placed the clothes back into the bag and attempted to recreate the same haphazard lump they'd been in before.

Once I had his bag zipped back up, I hurried away from it, from the ring and the notes that felt tainted and evil, and out of the room.

Only to enter into a tension-filled room full of doubting stares.

Twenty-Seven

Conor

"Nice," Diggs said as I jogged over to where they were all huddled around the kitchen table, running his hand over his hair. "I dig it."

"We have a problem," Kieran said irritably.

I cut a look at Jess. "I figured."

"A your-new-girlfriend-is-lying kind of problem," Einstein added without looking away from her laptop.

I slowed in my last steps toward them, doubt for both Sutton and what they were saying swirling through me. I made my way over to a chair and gripped the top of it, needing to grasp something. "Listening."

"Phoenix had files from the Tennessee Gentlemen's attorneys in the black folder," Einstein began.

I nodded, already knowing this.

There was a long list on their payroll of attorneys who helped with legal matters . . . and with hiding information.

"I found something in one of those files that didn't match what Sutton had told us, and then Kieran and Jess finally found all the real blueprints tonight."

We'd been waiting on the blueprints. The *twins* had been waiting on them.

I had a feeling I didn't want to know what they'd found.

Einstein turned her laptop and pushed it across the table toward me. On the screen were blueprints of a small house.

"Okay." The word slowly rolled off my tongue. "What does this have to do with Sutton?"

Everyone just stared at me, waiting, until Kieran finally spoke up. "That's below her house."

"Guesthouse, to be exact," Einstein corrected.

"And we didn't see any indication that there was an underground bunker when we checked it last week," Kieran continued, irritation seeping from him.

"That means we might have been right on top of him," Jess said softly. When I glanced at her, she looked nearly as torn as I felt.

"Sutton was in the picture when this structure was built," Kieran continued. "Hard to believe she didn't know about a bunker this size under her guesthouse."

"What's more," Maverick said, grabbing the laptop and pulling it toward him, "is they're on every property of the core families."

"Her parents'?"

He shot me a look, eyebrows raised in confirmation.

"Shit." I dragged a hand over my face as he continued.

"Looks like as time went on, they've gotten bigger. Went from the size of a mini bomb shelter to a bunker the size of the suites you were staying in."

"She might not have known," I said, knowing the argument was weak at best.

"And that's why you won't be asking questions tonight," Kieran said.

"There's so much she hasn't known," I reasoned. "That *we* informed her of."

"If you weren't fucking her, you wouldn't be defending her," he growled, each word was as sharp as one of his blades.

I'd barely taken a step before Jess slammed her hands against my chest, trying to keep me in place. "Conor, no."

The instant I moved her aside, Kieran was in front of me, a cold mercilessness in his eyes that I knew he couldn't help. "Don't touch my wife."

"She was in my way." The words were pure grit as I seethed, "Get your knife away from my ribs."

The temperature in the room seemed to drop a few degrees as he stared at me. I wasn't sure anyone was breathing or moving as they waited.

As soon as I felt the retreat, I laid into him. "You don't want me to ask questions? Fine. But don't talk to me like what I'm doing completely clouds my sense of reason. Of course I'm defending her. Doesn't mean I don't see what you see. Doesn't mean I don't see the case. Considering what happened when you and Jess started—"

I shoved him back when he lunged at me.

Surprise slowly wove through my veins when I realized he wasn't going to try again and that he didn't have a blade in his hand.

"You're a fucking hypocrite. Both of you," I bit out, stepping back to shoot a glare at Einstein. "Talking to me like I don't know what I'm doing and like I'm messing everything up because of it. When both of you have been in my exact damn place."

"Jessica and I were different," Kieran said.

"No." My head shook slowly. "No, she was different for you. She was *it* for you. I found that, and all any of you have done is beat me down for it."

"Don't lump me in with these killjoys," Diggs huffed.

"Shut up, Diggs."

"Conor, she has been withholding information," Einstein said, her usual knowing tone absent. "She's lied to us."

"I understand," I said at the same time Maverick whispered, "That's enough."

Einstein slowly looked in his direction when he shut the laptop. "Who are you talking to?"

"You," he said gently. "Conor's right. He's never once held back from telling the rest of us when he thought Sutton was lying or holding back. He has still tried to get information from her. He's doing his job. Why the hell am I the only one sticking up for him?"

"Dude." Diggs smacked Maverick's shoulder and then raised his hand as if to remind everyone of his neutral stance.

"It's because we know and because it's you," Jess said, reaching out to touch my arm. When a warning rumble came from Kieran, she sighed and shot him a look. "Get over yourself."

But even as she said the words, she went to go stand in front of him.

Once Jess was leaning against Kieran, she continued. "Conor, you protect everyone, and you're the one we go to when something in our lives goes wrong and needs to be fixed. Due to that, we're all extremely protective of you. And with Sutton? It's hard because of who she is and the situation she's involved in. Yes, it's hypocritical. Einstein's the queen of withholding information."

"Excuse me," Einstein said, sitting back to send her a glare, but Jess kept talking.

"And you're right, a lot of bad things happened when Kieran and I started out, and we remember them vividly. But he knows what it's like to be lied to and betrayed because of what I did to him. So, it's hard for us not to step in when we see similarities."

"You're saying Sutton's spying on me to get us all killed."

"No." Her shoulders and expression fell, and old guilt and regret flashed through her eyes. "I'm saying what all of us want more than anything is for you to find someone, and if that's Sutton, great." She pressed a hand to her chest. "I really do like her, but this is a very delicate situation, and we've been through those. They are filled with pain and heartbreak and come at a cost. None of us want to see you go through that."

I looked from her to Kieran to the three sitting at the table.

All wore matching expressions of guilt and worry . . . Diggs not included.

"Delicate. That's one way to describe this." I nodded and sucked in a breath through my teeth. "There's already so much I'm going through just letting myself go there with her. That *we're* going through just trying to navigate what we're doing. So, I appreciate it, but I don't need your worry when it comes disguised as tearing me down and shutting me up."

I focused on Kieran. "I need you to remember everything you told me about those first weeks with Jess. Remember what it was like to fall for her while still doubting everything she did." When he dipped his head in understanding, I gestured toward the room I'd left Sutton in. "Know that I *don't* doubt everything Sutton says. I don't need to. She's a horrible liar. I haven't forgotten the conversations she's avoided or the shit she's said that hasn't added up, but those things don't make or break our case or trust with her, and they don't matter when my biggest priority is keeping those girls safe."

I swallowed thickly, never losing Kieran's hard stare. "Now remember that, even with that doubt, you defended her to the death."

The room was utterly silent.

There was no reason to continue, they understood.

I folded my arms over my chest. "I'm done."

"She still needs to be questioned about what we found," Einstein said a minute later.

"I never said she didn't."

Just then, Sutton rounded the corner into the kitchen and stumbled to a stop.

"Uh, I can—" Her chest jerked, and it was then I realized that she looked as if all the color had been leached from her. "I can go."

I reached for her, mouth opened to ask what had happen, when Kieran said, "We need to talk to you."

She looked from me to Kieran, nodding subtly as she walked forward.

I pulled her close and dipped my head to search her panicked eyes. "What happened?"

"Nothing."

"Sutton."

"I saw the notes and my ring," she whispered after a brief hesitation. "I thought they would be gone or—I don't know. Not out in the open."

I hissed a curse and ran my fingers down her arm. "We need to keep them, but I'll make sure you don't see them again."

Her head moved in quick jerks, pausing when I pressed my mouth to her forehead.

I wanted to tell her I was sorry for what was coming.

I wanted to tell her to prepare herself.

But I just pulled out a chair for her and then took a few steps back once she was seated.

My eyelids slipped shut when Einstein instantly asked, "Where's Zachary?"

Twenty-Eight

Conor

Immediate.
   Straight to the point.
No bullshit.
Full of accusation and suspicion.

When I opened my eyes again, Sutton was staring at Einstein in blatant shock. "I don't know."

"Where's he hiding?" Kieran asked in a voice so low it made all the tiny hairs on Sutton's arm stand on end, but still, she kept her back straight.

"*I don't know*," she repeated.

"Sutton," he began again, but stopped when a sharp, defeated laugh left her.

"I have told you—God, so many times." She gave me a helpless look before directing her attention back to Kieran. "I have told you what I know. *Where* I know of. If Zachary isn't in any of those places, then I don't know where he is.

How many times are we going to do this before you believe me?"

"You could only think of friends or relatives' houses," Einstein said. "It's weird to be with him for so long and not know exactly where he would go, or at least not have an idea."

"It's probably also weird not to know what he wanted for birthdays or Christmases, but I didn't. Whatever he wanted, he bought himself and had delivered to his office." She pressed a hand to the table. "There's nothing I can think of that can help you. I thought I knew him, but I've realized recently that I don't, maybe he never wanted me to. I know what he likes to eat, but that's because he had to be in control of our menu. And I don't see how that's relevant or helpful."

"It isn't," Kieran said, his tone void of emotion. "The place you told us about at the lake . . ."

Sutton moved her head in something resembling a nod. "His parents' place."

"It's your family's."

"Okay, fine. My family's place," she said irritably. "But I've never thought of it as mine, and seeing as I was never legally married into their family, I don't know why you of all people would consider it as such."

"No," he said roughly, sharply. "Yours."

Her body straightened and stiffened as she slowly began to understand what Kieran meant. "My—*mine*? As in my parents'?" She didn't wait for anyone to answer. She pushed back against her chair, her head firmly shaking. "No . . . no, it's my in-law's. I'd never even been there before Zachary and I were engaged."

"It definitely belongs to your parents," Einstein said

dryly. "And your grandparents before that. Not that Zachary's there anyway, but if you'd like to change any of the other answers you've given us, now's the time."

"That isn't—I would've known," she cried out. "I would've gone there sometime in the twenty years before I was engaged to him."

"Now's the time to tell us everything," Einstein repeated. "For example, hidden places you previously, conveniently forgot about."

"*What?*" It was a pained breath that I felt in my chest. "Anywhere that I know of, I have already told you about. Countless times."

When she looked to me for help, the sting and hurt in her eyes made me want to tear out my heart.

She had to know this was necessary.

She had to know how damn difficult watching her be questioned was.

Had to know that my hands were tied because of what she meant to me.

I stepped over to Jess and lowered my voice so it wouldn't carry, "She was blindsided by that. She doesn't know where he is."

"I know," she whispered. "I've seen her deflect and lie, and it's obvious when she does."

Jess touched Kieran's arm and gave him a look that had him stepping toward us with a sigh.

"Don't say it," he said roughly. "She still has to explain the blueprints, and I don't see how she can."

"Then ask, but stop interrogating her," I hissed. "She's going to shut down if you keep pushing her."

"Someone has to if we're ever gonna get the truth." His voice was tense, and his eyes were cold with warning.

I was done with it.

With the constant reminders that he didn't trust her, that he didn't trust me to do my job.

"You're pushing *me* to a limit that we won't come back from," I said in a grave tone.

His jaw twitched under the pressure he was putting on it. With a sharp nod, he said, "You'll thank me one day."

I shoved past him when he started for the table and snatched the laptop away from Maverick.

Opening it, I dropped into the chair next to Sutton and tried to calm myself so I wouldn't snap at her when I spoke.

"The twins have been waiting for blueprints of houses and businesses before going back out," I said, answering her earlier question. "They like to know exactly what they're walking in on. All entrances and exits, secret or not. But every place owned by the Tennessee Gentlemen has falsified blueprints on record. Easy enough to notice when all the floor plans on record are identical to each other. When Jess came by earlier, she confirmed they didn't match the places she and Kieran had already visited."

Sutton's eyebrows had pulled together as I spoke, but even through her confusion, I could see the exhaustion.

As though she were trying to prepare herself for another blow and wasn't able to.

"Okay, so what does this mean?" she asked.

"Were you around when your house was built?"

"Of course. I helped design it. Everything about it, I chose. That's my dream house."

Shit.

I could feel a wall of anger and suspicion slam into me from the people near me.

From the full-body shiver that moved through Sutton, she felt it too.

I turned the laptop so the screen was facing her, showing the blueprint for the bunker.

She blinked quickly and then leaned forward, her eyes searching and studying.

Almost immediately, she asked, "What is this?"

"I need you to tell us that."

Her eyes met mine from over the laptop before falling to the screen again. "I don't . . . I don't know." She shifted back, pushing the computer away as she did. "I have no idea."

No evading.

No lying.

Only genuine uncertainty.

Before she was able to settle against the chair, I slid the computer back to her. "Look again."

A discouraged sigh left her as she leaned forward.

Nearly a minute later, she reeled back. "That's my address." She reached for the laptop and pulled it to the edge of the table so it was directly in front of her. "That's my address at the top there."

Her eyes bounced around the screen quicker than before. Her brows pulled low as if she were trying to make sense of what she was seeing.

"I've never seen this. That isn't my house. It isn't even the guesthouse—that isn't how it's designed. Is this the—" She looked around at everyone when Maverick took the laptop from her so he could glance at the screen. "Is that one of the fake blueprints?"

"No," Maverick said simply and pointed to the screen.

"This number here? That's how many inches below ground it is."

A startled laugh left Sutton before she seemed to understand he wasn't joking. "What?"

"That is a bunker," I answered.

Sutton slowly shifted her head to look at me as if in a daze. "We don't . . . no."

"How often were you around when your house was being built?"

"All the time. Every few days," she whispered, her stare drifting. "They couldn't keep me away." Clearing her throat, she shook her head firmly. "No. No, I would've known. I was there constantly. The construction crew even had a personalized hard hat made for me because I was always there. It's in Lexi's room."

I wanted to beg her to stop talking.

Every time she opened her mouth, it only made this worse for her.

But even still, I could see the resolve and sincerity in her eyes, and I wondered if anyone else could.

"I would know if there was a . . . a bunker under my house."

"Guesthouse," Einstein corrected.

"Guesthouse. What does it matter? I would—" Sutton's mouth fell open, and her eyes widened. For long moments, she just sat there with a distant look. "Oh my God."

"What?" I asked, not caring that my tone held a hint of hope.

"I was mad," she breathed. "I was *so* mad at Zachary because he told the crew not to allow me on the property in the last few days before our wedding. He said he had a surprise for me, and I was upset because they were doing inside details, and I had been waiting for that time." She gestured to the screen, shaking her head as she did. "He'd told me long before that we couldn't have the guesthouse, said we couldn't afford it. When we came home from our honeymoon, they were building the guesthouse. That was my surprise."

I sat back and shot Kieran a glare.

"How long were you on your honeymoon?" Einstein asked, pulling the laptop back toward her.

"Ten days. I wasn't at the house for four or five days before that."

"Enough time to at least build the foundation of the bunker and get it covered," Maverick murmured.

"Yep," Einstein said, already submersed in her work.

I dragged Sutton's chair to mine and grabbed the back of her neck, pulling her closer until her forehead was pressed to mine.

"I'm sorry." It was soft and low and begged forgiveness for so many things I couldn't get into right then.

Her tongue darted out to wet her lips, and like before, that wounded look flashed through her eyes. "I don't know where he is, Conor."

The way she spoke said it all.

The fact that I'd been standing there while she was questioned hurt her the most.

As I'd known it would—as I'd known it *had*.

"*I* know that." I shifted forward until my mouth was at her ear. "We're still working a case, Sutton. You're everything to me, but that doesn't mean I can stop doing my job."

She sagged against me and let her head fall to my shoulder. Her hand raced up my chest until it was clinging to my neck, holding me in place.

"Okay?"

She nodded, and her nails lightly trailed against my skin in response.

"All right, fucking finally," Diggs said with a hard clap. "Let's go huntin'."

I pressed a kiss to Sutton's jaw as I leaned back but kept ahold of one of her hands.

"We need to decide where to go and when," Maverick said. "Which houses should we for sure hit?"

"All of them," Diggs said with a scoff.

"The younger ones first," Kieran said softly. "Then their parents'. I have a feeling if they're anywhere, they're in Aaron Thornton's bunker."

Sutton started. "Wait, he has one too?"

"Every core family does," I said, carefully watching her expression out of instinct. "Including your parents."

Emotion after emotion slammed into her.

After a minute, she shook her head slowly, sadly. "One of these times, I'll stop being surprised."

I tightened my grip on her hand and looked to Kieran. "Thornton hasn't been involved at all. Is that why?"

He gave a confirming grunt before kicking Maverick's chair. "After what they came up with on our soil, we have to be expecting something worse here."

Maverick looked from Einstein to Kieran. "If we're going with that mindset, why wouldn't he hide from us in plain sight?"

"All right," Kieran reluctantly conceded. "Larson, Vaughn, then Thornton and Woods. If they aren't there, we'll sweep the rest tomorrow night, starting with their parents and Sutton's."

"Agreed. When do we leave?"

"In a few hours. If they aren't there, I want enough time to move through all four houses before sunrise. Do what you have to do to prepare."

"Hell yes, go team," Diggs called out, already pumped, bouncing in his seat as he studied the blueprints.

Maverick's stare flashed to me.

His jaw ticked.

"Nothing happens to Einstein."

Before I could respond, Kieran said, "Jessica isn't going either."

An amused breath left Jess. "Funny, it almost sounded like you said I wasn't going."

"You aren't." Low, direct, final.

She sucked in a breath so quickly it sounded like a hiss. "You can't stop me."

He got in her face and growled, "I'll chain you to the wall if you try."

Jess's reaction was instant. Eyes widened. Mouth curled into a sensual grin. Chest hitched with uneven breaths.

The air around us shifted.

"Jesus Christ," I groaned at the same time Einstein said, "And here we go again."

I looked away just as Kieran pulled her against him and slammed his mouth onto hers.

Sutton blinked quickly before she was able to force her stare away.

"Always completely inappropriate," Einstein said, her voice raised. "People are around you."

"I don't understand what just happened," Sutton whispered.

"It's Kieran and Jess," I said as if that was all the explanation that was needed.

"Okay, I'm not going," Jess said once she and Kieran broke apart, her face flushed and smile lazy.

"I can tell you're really torn up about that," Einstein said sarcastically.

A low, wild laugh built in Jess's throat. "I have a feeling I'm gonna get over it."

Einstein mock-gagged. "Gross."

Diggs was the only one trying not to laugh.

"Now that Sutton's probably scarred"—I stood, bringing her with me—"I'm taking her to bed before it can get worse."

Diggs slammed a hand on the table. "Dude, you aren't coming with us?"

I raked a hand through my hair.

I wanted to.

This was what I lived for.

And this fight was mine just as much as it was theirs.

But I'd been given a job, and I'd promised Sutton and Lexi I wouldn't let anything happen to them.

I glanced to Kieran, but there was nothing in his expression that gave any indication of what he thought. He was waiting for what I would say next, and there was a very strong possibility that anything I said would be the wrong thing.

So, I forced a smile and led Sutton out of the kitchen and through the suite.

After stopping to make sure Lexi was still asleep, we continued to her room.

"You want to go," she said as I closed the door behind us.

I wanted to deny it, but the lie caught on my tongue as I took a seat on the bed. She followed, letting me wrap my arms around her hips and pull her close so she was standing between my legs.

"I could see it as soon as they started talking about it," she whispered, her fingers moving in light, teasing trails over my shoulders and up my neck to play with my hair.

"I'm needed here," I said, finally voicing the words I'd been pushing down. "You, Lex . . . Einstein. Jess can handle herself." I tried to laugh, but it fell flat. "I wouldn't be able to live with myself if something happened to you because I left."

"You want to go," she said again, making me think that somehow she understood.

But she couldn't.

I watched her for a while, telling myself to deny it. Trying to memorize the supportive look in her eyes. I knew the second I told her the truth or lied that would change. Because with the truth came my disturbing reason.

A weighted breath dragged from my lungs, and I lowered my head to press it to her stomach. "Yes. I have this deep-rooted need to go. To be the one who finds him."

I tightened my grip on her, pleading with my touch for her to understand.

Not to look at me like I was a monster.

"After what he did to Einstein, we all have a claim in this kill. With what he did to you? I want to drag mine out. Make it slow. Painful. To make sure he knows exactly why it's happening."

Other than her even breaths, she was still, and the

room was silent for the next minute, but then she lifted my head.

Her lips parted as she slowly lowered her mouth to mine.

Those first brushes were soft, tentative, but when her tongue teased mine, it lit a fire, consuming me.

In this girl and this kiss . . .

She crawled onto my lap, but as soon as she was seated, I turned us. Easing her onto the bed and lowering myself between her legs.

"Your mind scares me," she breathed against the kiss, arching against me and trying to get closer. "But I know you."

Her head fell back with a soft moan when I ground my hardened cock against her.

"I know you would do anything to keep us safe." She whimpered when I captured her bottom lip between my teeth. Her eyelids fluttered, heavy and slow as her eyes filled with desire. "Even this."

"Always."

Then her hands were gripping my hair and her mouth was on mine, the kiss hard and fast and broken by our rough breaths and when she removed my shirt.

I lifted hers as I moved down her body, tracing her subtle curves with my hands and focusing on her breasts with my lips and tongue and teeth.

Every hitched breath and moan had me straining harder and harder as I removed our clothes until she was stretched out on the bed.

Wet.

Bare.

Perfect.

I slanted my mouth over hers and trailed my hand between her legs, teasing her until she was writhing in frustration.

I swallowed her moan when I dipped two fingers into her heat, loving the way she trembled around me. As if just that touch was nearly enough to set her off.

I moved my fingers slowly, pulling them in and out and teasing her clit before pushing back inside and fucking her until she was shaking.

Only to repeat the same path over and over again until she was begging for a release.

The next time I pulled them out, I trailed them down, down, down until I hit that tight hole.

Sutton moved. Tensing and twisting away and shoving me back.

"*What*—what are you doing?"

I stilled, trying to take in her reaction and worrying I had triggered something when all I could see was her and everything I wanted to make her feel. "Touching you."

"Not, no." Her head shook tightly. "That isn't—that is not normal. People don't do that."

My brows lifted, and a slow, wicked smile crossed my face. "Is that right?"

Her chest's movements grew more pronounced as her stare bounced over my face.

A shiver rolled through her body when I teased her clit with barely there brushes, and soon, she was lowering herself back onto the bed and reaching for me.

I passed my mouth across hers and waited until she was kissing me before dipping my fingers inside her again.

"Never claimed to be normal." My tone was rough with

my need to claim her. "Let me show you what happens when you take someone the likes of me to bed."

Her hazel eyes were wide with apprehension, but there was so much trust there.

Mine.

This girl was fucking mine.

"Don't think," I whispered as I trailed my fingers down again. "Just feel."

A ragged breath ripped from her when I pressed a finger in slowly, just enough to tease, before easing back out.

Again.

And again.

Then next time I pushed in, her eyes rolled back and a whimper raked up her throat.

And, fuck, if I didn't almost abandon my slow exploration right then to bury myself inside her.

I pushed deeper and deeper and then slipped two fingers into her warmth, fucking her slowly until she was trembling and gripping the bed.

As soon as I pressed my thumb to her clit, she fell apart.

Her mouth opened on a muted cry.

Her body stretched tight before crashing down with a violent shudder.

Each aftershock that rolled through her body had her gripping my fingers tighter and tighter as I pushed her through.

Her movements were both relaxed and frantic as she reached for the button on my jeans, jerking and tugging until they were on the floor and she had my cock in her hand, guiding me to her.

I wanted to go slow. I wanted to take my time.

But *slow* was going to have to come later.

I needed her too badly to restrain myself.

I slammed in, groaning when she cried out and shook around me.

Each movement was harder than the last, and I knew this was going to be over before it began.

Curling my arm under her back, I lifted her from the bed and set her on my lap, savoring each breathless moan and whimper.

Our kiss matched my movements.

Hard.

Fast.

Filled with passion and sensual bites and teasing tongues.

Trailing my hand down her back, I played with the crease of her ass. My lips curved into a smile when, instead of shying away, she gasped and arched against my hand.

Fuck.

I pressed a finger into that tight hole and almost came right then because she was gripping me so damn tight, vibrating in a way I knew meant she was close.

She held on to me as I fucked her, breathing pleas for more and begging me not to stop. And that vibrating grew and grew and grew, driving me out of my damn mind in the best way until she shattered.

Head pressed to my shoulder and nails digging into my back.

My name on her tongue in a breathless moan I would never forget.

Forcing me into my own release.

I held her tight as we came down, my heart beating so damn loudly it was all I could hear.

Mine, mine, mine.

Lowering her to the bed with our bodies still joined, I shifted so my forearms were on either side of her head and slowly began moving inside her.

An exhausted laugh worked up her throat. "What are you doing?"

I bent to nip at her lips. "Taking my time."

Twenty-Nine

Zachary

I stared straight ahead, chest rising and falling in harsh jerks as I listened to sounds I could pick out of a crowd.

Sounds no other man should ever hear.

My blood boiled as betrayal and denial burned deep and fast.

I pulled my gun from my waistband.

The feel of the metal in my palm only served to make the sounds louder and louder until they were ringing in my head and bouncing off my skull.

"The fuck is this?"

No sooner had I opened my mouth than had the nerds flinched and hurried to mute the bugs they'd been listening in on.

My eyelids slowly shut when Garret walked into the room. "What's going on here?"

I didn't respond, just forced open my eyes and snapped, "Have a spine and face me."

The three nerds stopped whispering to each other long enough for them to turn, one at a time.

And each one went pale when they saw the gun I had aimed at them.

"I was just—we were just doing our jobs," the one on the right said. "I'm sorry, Mr. Larson, I don't—"

"Tell me what the hell you were listening to, and think very carefully before you answer."

"There's news. Uh, we heard things," the one in the middle said, taking deep, gulping breaths as he did. "Things you might want to know." Another disgusting breath, as if he'd just come up from under water. "But what you heard isn't what you think it is."

"And what do I think it is?"

"Th-th-there are couples in the room your wife has transferred to." He almost choked on his next breath.

Jesus.

"It was one of them."

I lowered the gun and let an easy smile cross my face. "That right?"

The disgusting one nodded, but the other two just stared.

Not that I needed any of them to confirm what I'd heard.

I lifted a shoulder. "Never know what you'll catch on those things, I guess."

He laughed.

Even his laugh was revolting.

I took a step forward, keeping my smile in place. "If you

think I don't know what my wife sounds like when she's being fucked, you're sadly mistaken."

Before he had a chance to absorb my words, I lifted my gun and pulled the trigger.

Looking to the other two, I demanded, "Tell me what I was hearing."

They both started yelling over each other, stumbling over their words, trying to get them out before the other.

Sutton.

My Sutton.

Having sex with one of those goddamn ARCK people.

"And it—" The one on the right coughed, as if he were choking over his words, and it was then I realized I had my gun aimed right at him.

"Keep talking or I shoot."

"Well, I-I-I don't think it was the first time. Earlier—"

"Yeah, earlier," the other said loudly, "on a different bug . . . but it was far away. Still them."

That denial and betrayal built until it was suffocating me.

"I want everything we have on this guy, and I want him brought to me. Dead."

The remaining nerds looked at each other, hissing something I couldn't hear because I was so consumed by the need to keep shooting until everyone around me stopped breathing.

"Uh, well, he did say he was coming. To kill you." This from the ever helpful one on the right. "We were waiting on more information before we brought it to your attention."

A real smile crossed my face. "Good. If he finds me, then I'll have what I want."

I turned to leave, only to come face to face with a smirking Garret.

"Looks like it is that world," he said. "And there aren't just worries of her being unfaithful, she's moved right on from you. Funny how that turned out."

"I'm holding a gun and have wanted nothing more than to kill you for eight years. If you want to keep breathing, don't test me."

"Kill me because *you* stole *my* girl?" That smirk widened as he took a step, bringing us closer. "Or is it that I've had a taste of her and you can't stand knowing that?" An amused huff left him when I pressed the gun to his stomach. Before he turned to leave, he looked pointedly at the setup behind me. "I'm going to love reminding you that I'm not the only one."

Dead.

At my feet.

I could see it, and I fucking craved it.

"One of these days, I'm going to conveniently forget that I'm not allowed to pull the trigger." The words were a low warning wrapped in a tremor of excitement.

A soft, mocking laugh echoed down the hall in response.

thirty

Conor

Sutton and I stilled when there was a hard knock on the door, but I'd told her when I had her again, I was keeping her in bed for the entire night.

I planned to hold true to that.

I teased her lips with a slow kiss and then continued in my lazy movements.

A minute later, there was another knock, harder than before. "Conor."

Kieran.

I bit back a growl and yelled, "Not the time."

"Five seconds before I open the door."

I didn't have to wonder if he meant it.

Kieran usually didn't knock at all.

I bit out a curse and snapped, "Hold on." I looked to Sutton, an apology on the tip of my tongue.

"I'm not going anywhere," she assured me before I could speak.

I dropped my head into the crook of her neck, breathing her in and passing a kiss across her collarbone. "Thank you."

I climbed off the bed and shrugged into my jeans, every step emphasizing that this was the last thing I wanted to be doing.

It felt wrong.

So damn wrong.

Pulling away from her and leaving.

I wanted to go back and wrap her in my arms. I wanted to hold her and worship her and take my goddamn time with her.

But that was the nature of my life, and Kieran wouldn't be pulling me from this room if it weren't important.

I glanced over my shoulder to make sure Sutton had covered herself before opening the door and pushing through, shutting it firmly behind me as I did.

"I fucking hate you," I said through gritted teeth.

"Are you coming, or not?"

I stared at him blankly. "That better not be the reason you're at my door right now."

When I reached for the handle, he slammed a knife into the door and held tight, preventing me from turning.

"These aren't our houses, you can't do shit like that here."

His expression told me he didn't give a fuck.

Then again, I shouldn't have expected him to.

Kieran was raised to speak in blades and blood and lethal expressions.

"I need you with me," he said in a gruff tone. "This is big, I can feel it."

"Is that why you're making Jess sit out?"

He wavered before demanding, "Yes or no."

"You know where I want to be," I finally responded in a low tone. "What I don't know is where you'll let me be, *Boss*."

"Don't ever fucking call me that."

"Then stop acting like that's what you are."

His eyes shifted to the door before he ripped his blade free. "Not doing this here."

When he took a step away, I reached for the handle.

The shock and disbelief that ripped across his face floored me.

I wasn't sure I could've ever done anything to put that look on Kieran's face, and the part of me that loved him and owed him my life felt bad that I *could*, no matter what shit we were going through.

"You're gonna have to give me a minute."

He responded by folding his arms over his chest, letting me know he wasn't leaving.

I stalked back into the room, already headed for the bathroom to clean up, and found Sutton in there starting the shower.

Her face lit up when she saw me. "I didn't think he was going to let you back so soon."

"He isn't."

And damn him because that light in her eyes dimmed.

I pressed a slow, lingering kiss to her swollen lips. "I'm going tonight."

Her sigh told me she both expected and dreaded those words. "I know."

"If you don't want me to, I need to know now."

"That isn't my place," she said with a half-hearted smile. "Even if it were, I don't know that I'd stop you. It's just something I don't understand, and it scares me and worries me."

"I know." I curled my arms around her, holding her tightly, because there was nothing I could say to ease her worries. "I need to get ready, but you should try to get some sleep while I'm gone."

A disbelieving laugh left her as she pushed against my stomach. "That isn't likely."

"Try. I'll see you in the morning."

She nodded, the movement quick but faint as she pulled away from me.

She waited just outside the shower as I cleaned up, and then as I was leaving the bathroom she said, "Please."

I gripped the doorframe and turned, looking at her questioningly.

"Please keep yourself safe and come back so you'll see me in the morning."

I closed the distance between us in a few steps and pulled her against me. Slanting my mouth over hers and pouring everything I had into that kiss.

My strength.

My peace.

My heart.

"So far gone," I whispered against her lips. With one last feather-soft kiss, I forced myself to let her go and walked away.

I was still shrugging into my shirt as I opened the door to an irritated Kieran.

"That was more than a minute."

"Fuck off. I'd get a knife thrown at me if I ever tried to pull you from a room with Jess."

He didn't respond, just walked away, knowing I would follow.

He ignored the curious stares and Jess's questions as we moved through the suite, and he didn't stop moving until we were in the room I was staying in.

As soon as I shut the door behind me, he rounded on me.

"You think I'm treating you like a goddamn boss?"

"Not think. *Know*." I slowly advanced toward him, sneering as I did. "I've taken orders from you most of my life, so it isn't as if I don't know exactly what it looks like."

"I'm trying to protect you. I'm trying to make you see what you're refusing to. I'm trying to stop you before you get so deep that it fucking ruins you," he said, each word a soft threat.

The equivalent of yelling for Kieran.

I stopped as disbelief filled me. "Sutton? This is about *Sutton*?" A sharp, aggravated laugh burst from me. "I thought we were done with this."

"We can't when—"

"No, actually, we *are* done with this." I stepped back, hand raised in silent protest. "You're assholes. All of you."

"I don't trust her, and you're so blinded by her that you won't see this case for what it is."

"You gave me the green light," I nearly yelled. "Did you forget that?"

"A mistake," he snapped. "I could see where your head already was, and I knew trying to stop you would only make it worse. Then she continued lying and evading, and more evidence turned up that went against everything she *had* told us."

"Evidence that she had no idea about." I gestured to the door behind me. "Were you not in the same room with us?"

"I heard every damn word. I watched every expression. I've *been* watching and listening." Kieran stepped forward, his voice dropping lower. "Her husband could manipulate Dare, Conor. People who manipulate lie detectors still can't get past Dare . . . but Zachary could. She could be playing everyone."

"Jesus, I—" I let out a groan of frustration and rubbed at my jaw. "She is the worst liar I've ever seen. We would know."

"You sure about that?" He rocked back on his heels and crossed his arms over his chest, frustration taking over his features. "Dare, Einstein, *me*. Nothing has ever gotten past any of us . . . no one, no gang, no anything. These people have. There's something so damn wrong with this entire case that I can fucking taste it."

"With the case, yeah, but not her."

"Especially her," he fired back.

"Jesus." The word was a breath. Maybe a laugh. I wasn't sure.

"If you weren't fucking her, you would see it."

"Careful," I said on a low growl.

"I see what she does to you. She enters a room, and you lose your damn head. She could be playing the biggest game of them all, and you wouldn't know." He ran his hands over his head, a huff of frustration leaving him. "I can't stop you. I know I can't. Just tell me you aren't being stupid. That you won't get yourself in a situation neither of you can come back from."

My brows pulled low in confusion, but before I could shoot back any of the things on my mind, I grasped what he was saying.

I watched his expression fall as mine turned to stone.

"Conor . . . fucking *think*, man. You can't knock up a girl you just met. You can't knock up someone you don't know anything about—someone who could be pulling us into a trap."

"I hear you," I snapped before he could continue. "Jesus, I hear you."

Not that there was anything I could do to change the last few hours or how fucking reckless we had been.

I took a step back, trying to gather my thoughts and wrap my head around everything.

I'd been careless.

I was never careless.

But the last thing I thought I'd need on a case was a condom.

The last thing on my mind when I had Sutton in my arms was stopping. I was too consumed by us and the overwhelming need for her to think about anything else but making her feel good. Making her mine. Cherishing her and worshipping her for every minute that I had with her.

But I knew . . . I *knew* this bullshit with Kieran was only happening because it was Sutton. He had never cared what I'd done in my personal life. Never asked, never interfered, until this case.

"After everything we've been through together . . . everything *I* went through to stay alive those first years in Holloway." Kieran's brows pulled tight in confusion, but I continued. "I've never asked you for anything. I am asking you to just be happy for me."

He watched me for a minute before shrugging, the motion seeming to weigh him down. "I can't. I promised Beck I would take care of you, and you aren't thinking clearly."

Disappointment snaked through my chest and leaked through my tone. "Don't do me any favors because of him. He's gone."

"I'm protecting the only brother I have left," he ground out. "You're my responsibility, and I can't watch you go down a path that is going to destroy you."

"That's rich coming from you," I seethed. "I watched your relationship with Lily fall apart. I saw what it did to both of you. I heard every detail of your twisted relationship with Jess, including the betrayal that almost got all of us killed. I never said a damn word about any of it because I knew what they both meant to you. Instead, I protected the girls you loved because you asked me to and I trusted you to know what you were doing. Trust me to know what I'm doing."

"Sutton isn't Jessica. What happened between us—" Kieran's eyes slowly shut. When they opened, they were colder than before. "Worst thing I've been through other than watching the people I love die. But from the beginning, I could see Jessica's struggle. Knew something was coming—clear as fucking day. Sutton's struggling with what we're telling her, *not* with what she's keeping from us. She's going to annihilate you, and you can't see it."

"Then let her." My chest moved with exaggerated jerks. "She could destroy me, and I would let her. Do you understand now what she means?"

A haunting kind of pain flashed across his face. "Better than you realize," he said with a forced swallow. "That's the only reason I haven't taken the information we need."

Shards of ice pushed into my veins.

I didn't have to wonder what Kieran meant.

Kieran gained information one way, and one way only.

"You wouldn't."

"Everyone has a breaking point, and we need answers," he said unapologetically. "No one has ever been able to hide from me, and *two* people are. Not only that but he also knows where she is. Right now, Sutton is our only way to find Zachary."

I closed the distance between us, my words soft and lethal and filled with promise. "If one of your blades touches her skin, I won't hesitate to kill you."

"That limit . . ." His eyes narrowed into slits. "Getting real fucking close. And she's pushing us closer."

"No. That one is all you."

Thirty-One

Sutton

I pulled the short, satin robe over my arms as I left the room, unable to stand pacing in there any longer. I was so filled with nervous energy, I hadn't been able to stay sitting on the bed, let alone lie down on it.

When I made it into the main room, I bent to check on Lexi, and was so thankful for the busy day she'd had.

If they hadn't worn her out so much, she wouldn't have been able to sleep through any of this.

Leaving her in the fort that expanded across multiple rooms, I slipped into the kitchen and stopped short.

Everyone was in there, multiple conversations going at once, both whispered and almost shouted, and there were guns *everywhere*.

Diggs passed in front of me, smiling wide as he took a bite of a muffin. "Hey, Baby Mama," he said, his words muffled and distorted.

"Uh . . ."

Before I could begin to get my brain working again, Conor was in front of me, hands cradling my face as he walked me backward out of the kitchen.

As soon as we were out of sight from everyone else, he pressed a quick kiss to my mouth before asking, "What are you doing out here?"

I stared toward the kitchen but pointed behind me. "I couldn't, uh, I couldn't stay. There. I had to get out." I finally met his stare and said, "That's a lot of guns."

"Yeah, we aren't taking them all. Just deciding who's taking what."

"Oh."

That hadn't been what I was wondering when I saw them.

I wasn't sure why any person, or group of people, needed that many at all.

Then again, I was sure I would have been shocked if someone told me the number of weapons Zachary's family or my family had.

"We're about to leave, do you think you can sleep?"

A shiver of fear crept up my spine. "There's no way."

The corner of his mouth tipped up, but it looked sad. "Jess and Einstein will be out here. Einstein needs to be on the cameras while we're gone, and Jess is watching over everyone. You can stay with them, but I think Lexi should be moved to the room."

"Why?"

"Because if she wakes up before we come back, I don't want her to see everything in the kitchen." He hesitated for a second before adding, "And if someone comes, I want her far from the door."

"Okay, yeah. Yeah, you're right."

I started to turn, only to stop when Conor said, "I'll get her."

I followed behind at a distance, watching as he carefully, gently scooped Lexi off the bed and held her close to his chest as he carried her to the bedroom.

Everything inside me swirled into chaos.

My heart. The wings in my stomach. My world.

I was sure I would remember this picture for the rest of my life.

This tattooed giant of a man.

Our avenging angel holding my daughter as if she were the most precious thing in his world.

When she was safely tucked into bed, he pulled me against his side and led me out of the room.

In that moment, it could have been just another night. One in which he hadn't just obliterated my heart, only to piece it back together in the most beautiful way. As though he hadn't just made me fall impossibly harder for him.

When we reached the edge of the kitchen, he wrapped his arms around me. "I'll be back soon," he said, his words saturated with promise.

"Morning?"

"Morning. First thing I'm doing is coming for the kiss I'm not taking now." Then he slipped away from me and headed back into the kitchen.

It was all I could do to stand there and watch and not beg him to stay, because something about this felt wrong. There was a twisting in my gut that was so much more than worry.

It was dark and ominous and foreboding.

As if I were watching them prepare to walk into a trap, and my mind was screaming at me to stop them.

I flinched when Jess bumped my shoulder.

"You get used to it."

"What?" I asked, looking into her knowing eyes.

"That feeling." She tapped the hand that was gripping my stomach, and I dropped it to my side.

"It feels wrong," I admitted on a breath.

"And you get used to it," she said just as softly.

"How many times have you watched them prepare like this?"

She snorted. "Never. Kieran also doesn't leave without me. But even when I'm with him, there is always a point in which we have to separate, because we both have our talents and do them best alone. Watching him slip into the shadows always has that unease tearing at me until he's by my side again."

I wanted to tell her this was more than unease, but I also hadn't ever experienced anything like this.

It was entirely possible that I felt this way simply because this was all so new.

Because I'd never felt this strongly about anyone before.

Because I had only recently found out what Zachary was capable of . . . or maybe it was because I didn't know what he was capable of at all.

"Why aren't you going this time?"

Jess's sure stare faltered but never left where Kieran was standing, watching the other three guys arm themselves with guns and rifles. "I can do this in my sleep. I've already been in those houses and your guesthouse. I can get in and out of those bunkers better than any of them. He's just being unnecessarily protective."

"It's because he loves you."

"I know." She finally looked to me and gave me a quick, forced smile. "But I've done this for most of my life. Since Beck died, Kieran and I haven't done any type of job apart. To have him sit me out hurts and makes me feel restrained—valid reasoning or not." She loosed a stuttered laugh. "I don't know why I'm dumping this on you."

"It's okay," I said. "It's taking my mind off that feeling."

Her next laugh was fuller, but it ended abruptly when Kieran said, "Absolutely not."

We both looked in his direction to see the twins staring at Kieran and Conor with disappointment.

"What the hell, man?"

I was fairly certain that was Diggs. It was harder to tell them apart when they were both dressed in dark shirts and jeans and wearing matching expressions.

Usually Maverick and Einstein were by each other's sides and Diggs was eating.

"No way in hell am I putting that thing on," Kieran said darkly.

"So harsh. Where's the love?" Definitely Diggs.

Maverick slowly tied a black bandana around his head so it was resting just below his eyes, and Diggs followed the action.

I might've laughed if it hadn't transformed both of them entirely, if the charge in the air hadn't shifted to suffocating.

The twins were at least a head shorter than Conor, but they were still tall and broad. But they'd always looked so normal . . . until then.

Both had rifles strapped to their backs and shoulder

holsters sporting two guns. With the bandanas, they actually looked terrifying. Maverick looked like the assassin Conor claimed him to be.

"Looking at my nightmare," Conor murmured, and Kieran grunted in agreement.

"Embrace it," Maverick said.

"Fuck no," Conor and Kieran said at the same time.

"I don't understand," I whispered to Jess.

"I'm not, uh . . ." She hesitated for a moment and then gestured between the four. "There's history between them that goes back a lot of years."

"The rivalry?"

She nodded. "The bandanas were something every Borello member wore for generations. Probably not an easy thing for Kieran and Conor to see, considering what it represented whenever they *had* seen it."

She pushed out a sigh and walked toward Maverick, snatching the bandana he was holding and grabbing another off the table.

Walking up to Kieran, she gave him a pointed look and started wrapping the bandana around his wrist as she spoke to the entire kitchen. "You guys are supposed to be headed out on a job right now, not standing around arguing over pieces of fabric."

Kieran's jaw was clenched tight when she finished knotting it and moved over to do the same to Conor.

"I know a lot of bad memories are tied to these, and I can't claim to understand the feelings that come with that, but Kieran works a certain way, you work a certain way, and this is *their* certain way."

She shifted back to look at Kieran but gestured to the

twins. "You told me the symbol tattooed on them meant a rebellion. Considering that symbol is now on you and Conor, that links you to them. And that's all they're doing with the bandanas—linking. Binding. One front. No more Holloway. No more Borello. Just a rebellion. Something *you* started years ago when you asked for Dare's help."

Kieran reached for her, but he stilled and shot Diggs a glare when he said, "Damn straight. There's our love."

"All right, we need to move," Kieran said resolutely. "Einstein."

"I'm ready when you are," she said from wherever she was hiding in the kitchen, her voice excited and edgy. "Not a soul in the hall, stairwell, or side exit."

"Parking lot?"

She choked on a laugh. "Yeah, have fun with that."

Maverick bit out a curse and tugged on his bandana until it was hanging around his neck and then grabbed the rifle from his back and placed it into the empty weapons bag. Conor's rifle followed, but Diggs stood there stubbornly until Maverick punched him.

"You don't know they will see me," he argued even as he started putting his rifle and guns in the bag. "I'm ninja fast."

"Kieran's the only one who could get out unseen, and he's the only one whose weapons can't be seen," Einstein said matter-of-factly. "Nice try."

Conor grabbed the bag and came for me, stare locked on my own.

When he reached me, he didn't say a word. Didn't hold me. Didn't try to kiss me.

Just pressed his palm to my cheek and studied me, his

bright blue eyes saying more than we could in that moment.

More than we *should*.

He was coming back.

He was worried about me, worried he was making a mistake by leaving.

He would do anything for me.

He was falling in love with me.

And that . . . that shouldn't have been possible. Except I had a feeling I had already fallen.

Improbable, illogical, unreasonable, and more real than anything I'd ever felt.

My soul shook with the truth of our unspoken words as he released me and headed for the door, Diggs trailing behind with a sly grin.

Maverick watched where Einstein was sitting as long as possible before looking straight ahead, a fierce sort of determination on his face.

Then there was Kieran, holding Jess's face close and whispering to her in a way that was so gentle and pure that it made me feel as if I were some kind of interloper.

Before I could look away, he released her, the action looking as if it physically caused him pain.

A second passed before he nodded to himself, ground out Einstein's name, and then went to meet up with the others, slanting a cold, menacing glare my way as he passed.

"You have ten minutes. That's three times as long as it should take you to get to the car and leave," Einstein called out. "Starting . . . now."

I didn't watch them go.

I wasn't sure I could.

Because that feeling Jess said I would get used to? It was back and worse than before.

Dark.

Ominous.

Foreboding.

thirty-two

Conor

I shouldered the bag as we slipped out into the night, headed for the car, and stuck close to Kieran's side. "You gonna tell me why Jess is sitting this—*the fuck?*"

Kieran had stumbled as soon as Jess's name left me, bringing me up short.

He was stealth and precision and always sure of every move he made. For him to make any kind of misstep, literal or otherwise, was so alarming I just stood there staring at him as he slowly continued toward the car.

When I caught up to him, he started in a jog.

But it was different.

Distracted.

Every couple of steps, he shook his head as though he were trying to clear it.

I grabbed his shoulder, bringing us both to a stop. "Kieran."

He smacked my arm away. "We don't have time for this."

I tossed Maverick the bag when the twins turned to see what we were doing. "Get the car."

"We have a job," Kieran said in a commanding tone. "Let me focus on that."

"You can't focus on shit right now. Go back to the room." I pushed him in the direction of the door we'd just left and started toward the car, but he was right next to me.

Keeping step without ever looking like he was doing anything more than walking in a daze.

"Jessica is late."

"She isn't com—oh. Oh . . ." So much from tonight made sense with those three words.

His aggravation and lashing out and what he'd said.

Not that it excused any of it.

I wanted to comment on it so damn bad, but I just cleared my throat and said, "I took care of Lily for years. That doesn't mean she's pregnant."

He cut me a hard look at the reminder of life with Lily, but it quickly fell away, and he raked his hands over his face. "Late, late. Over a month. She's known and only told me today because she fucking passed out right in front of me."

"Shit."

"Said we were about to move on this case when she realized, and then Einstein was taken, and we all came here. She thought I'd keep her from everything if I knew."

"She wasn't wrong."

What would've earned me a frustrated look before earned me nothing more than an agonized groan. "I should've known. She's been saying she hasn't felt right.

But this isn't what we—we don't want this. She never wanted a baby. I can't be a dad."

"And why not? Your kid would be a badass."

He slowly lifted his eyes, looking at me as if I were insane. "You know me. You know what I'm like and what I'm capable of."

"Yeah, and I've seen you around Lily's kid and Jess's nephew. You're fine. You're in control. You also aren't gonna start training your kid to be an assassin from the time they can walk."

Kieran's head didn't stop shaking the entire time I spoke. Slow, wide movements. "What's inside me is dark and disgusting. I couldn't live with myself if I passed that on."

"That side of you was engrained in you by your dad and Mickey, every day, until they molded you into their perfect weapon. It isn't genetic." I forced out a laugh. "Jesus, does Jess know this is how you feel?" I started for the car again and pushed him toward the building when he came with me. "Your head isn't in the right place. Go back."

"I need this to think—to get my mind off everything."

"Fuck, man. I don't blame her for not telling you before." I placed myself directly in his path, stopping him. "You find out your wife might be pregnant, and the first thing you do is pull her off the case and panic over turning your possible-future kid into an assassin."

Kieran suddenly had the tip of a knife between his fingers so the hilt was aimed behind me. "Get in the car."

"The hell?" Diggs yelled. "We have to go."

Kieran didn't respond, only narrowed his eyes.

"Did you even ask Jess what she wants?" I asked.

"You're saying that, if your wife were pregnant, you wouldn't pull her off a case like this?" he shot back.

What the hell was wrong with me that the first thought to enter my mind was Sutton and how I would never have her anywhere near a case like this.

"Of course I would," I said. "Only, I wouldn't pull her in front of everyone the way you did."

"It was the only way to keep her there," he said after a few seconds. "To make sure everyone knew she was off." He slid the knife into its sheath and rocked to the side as if he were about to start for the car, but then he stopped. "I didn't have to ask. She told me. Freaked out, saying she didn't want a child to ever deal with her crazy."

"She isn't crazy."

"I know that," he whispered. "She doesn't. Started saying she couldn't be pregnant. She's worried that, if she is, it will hurt Einstein. Fuck, I couldn't tell if she was more afraid of that or of it actually being real."

I stared at him, unable to comprehend what he was saying. When I spoke, the word was barely audible. "What?"

Kieran dragged his hands over his face again and again before he stilled.

When his eyes met mine, they were cold and distant.

"The hell did that mean?"

His head moved in a sharp jerk of denial, and he tried to step around me.

I shot out a hand to stop him, but he dodged it.

"Kieran, what the fuck?"

He stalked toward the car, leaving me there.

Motionless.

Dumbfounded.

Anxious.

Halfway there, he turned, hands folded behind his neck.

Indecision played on his face for a minute before he said, "Einstein was pregnant with twins. Last year."

Jesus Christ, everything with Einstein was still too raw not to hurt when I thought about her in that way.

Not to pierce my chest when I pictured her with anyone.

Pictured her fucking pregnant.

"Why didn't I know?"

"No one knew," he said solemnly. "Maverick included."

My gaze shifted to the car the twins were waiting at, still too far to hear our conversation. "Why do *you*?"

"Because she called Jessica for help when she lost them."

My eyelids slowly shut as a deep ache radiated within my chest.

For the girl I had loved.

For the pain she'd always tried to hide and failed to conceal.

Even for Maverick, because I knew, without a doubt, everything that had happened between them had to do with that.

"That was why she spiraled last year," he said, confirming my thoughts. "That was why she left Maverick. He found out right before she was taken."

"Why didn't you tell me?"

"It wasn't supposed to be my story to tell you," he said with a heavy sigh.

I nodded, but I couldn't make sense of any of the emotions spiraling through me.

"Look, I know the two of you are having issues, or

whatever," Maverick said as he stormed toward us, frustration leaking through every word. "But we should've been gone within three minutes. We're now closing in on the ten Einstein bought us. Either you're coming or Diggs and I are going alone."

"We're coming," Kieran muttered and then turned to lead the way.

The drive was short, but it felt like it took hours with the tensions in the car.

Between Kieran and me.

Kieran's panic.

My pain.

And all of us preparing for what we were about to do.

Diggs was trying to ease it, but I didn't hear a word he said.

By the time we'd parked just off the Larson's property, we were all on edge in the worst of ways.

We quickly dug into the bag, checking the guns and arming ourselves, no one speaking as we did.

Kieran just stood by, slowly pulling knives out of his pockets.

"Remember the blueprint?" he asked the twins.

Diggs snorted. "Like I could forget."

"Yes," Maverick murmured.

"Remember everything they did to Einstein," Kieran said gravely. "Remember the way they slowly tortured her. The way she looked when we found her. Remember that we almost lost her because of these bastards." His eyes darted to me before shifting to the blades in his hand. "Remember what he did to Sutton."

I knew he didn't believe a word Sutton had told us.

But I didn't care.

He'd said that to get my head straight, which I was thankful for.

Because the clusterfuck of energy that had been surrounding us had turned cold and dark and cruel, and I knew we were all right where we were supposed to be.

I softly closed the trunk of the car and then gripped my rifle.

Maverick looked to Diggs as he pulled the bandana over his face. "You alive?"

Diggs's wide smile was the last thing I saw before he set his bandana in place. "Fuck yes, I'm alive."

"Keep it that way."

I looked from them to Kieran, who was staring at the twins in annoyance. With a sigh, he started toward the property. "Let's show a cartel what happens when they hurt one of our own."

The rest of us followed, quickly and quietly cutting across the Larson's land and straight for the guesthouse.

I knew it ate at Kieran to be working in a group. Not to be able to go where he felt called.

Could see it in the way he twitched and hissed curses under his breath.

But this had been the plan for every stop.

Jess and Kieran had cleared the places we were hitting last week, so we knew what to expect. Even though we knew where the bunker entrances were this time, it didn't mean we were going straight in.

There were multiple points of entry at every location, including the guesthouse we were approaching, and we planned to use them on the off chance anyone had caught on and was expecting us.

The twins would go in through the back, and Kieran and I would go through the front.

Halfway through the backyard, Maverick and Diggs branched away to go around the house. Rifles pressed to their shoulders. Eyes to their scopes.

Ten feet later, Kieran slammed a hand into my shoulder, stopping me.

He was still, head tilted low but eyes moving everywhere, hearing something that I couldn't beyond the night sounds.

I glanced through the night vision scope mounted onto my rifle and slowly turned, looking for something that shouldn't be there.

Kieran hissed a curse and took off for the left side of the house a split second before gunfire erupted.

A cry of pain ripped through the night, somehow overpowering everything else.

Because I knew in my gut that cry had come from one of the twins.

I charged after Kieran, rifle up and ready, finger resting next to the trigger, and stumbled upon one of the twins shooting at the tree line on the edge of the property.

A bullet zipped past my ear, and I shifted, catching where the moonlight reflected off something in the bushes. I fired two rounds as another roar sounded from beside me.

"Where's Kieran?" I yelled, still looking for signs of anyone else.

"The fuck should I know?"

I risked a glance at Maverick, and caught sight of two people rounding the corner of the house, guns drawn.

"*Down.*"

Maverick dropped without hesitation, already letting off another burst toward the tree line.

I lit into the first as they fired at Maverick and me and was aiming for the second when he staggered back.

Before he could fall, a man as silent as the night slipped up beside him, ripping a knife through his throat.

I rushed toward Kieran, tapping Maverick's back as I went. "You good?"

"Fucking bastards, where's Diggs?"

I didn't answer; I just kept running.

Kieran grabbed me by the collar, trying to force me to the other side of the house. "Get Diggs and go."

"What?"

"Get Diggs and get the fuck out of here."

I looked wildly around, trying to find the twin in question, when Maverick came up beside us, rifle still raised, searching the area.

"There were three over there," he said, his breaths uneven. "My arm."

My eyes darted over him and caught on the dark liquid dripping down his upper left arm.

"Three on the other and two at the back," Kieran said as I quickly unwound the bandana from my wrist and tied it tightly just below Maverick's shoulder, above the wound. "You need to get your brother."

Maverick lowered his rifle and snapped his attention to us. He studied Kieran for a moment, trying to hear the underlying message before racing to the side of the house Diggs had gone to.

"Diggs is bad off," Kieran said. "Get him to the car. I'll be there soon."

"Fuck that, I'm staying with you."

He shoved me back, trying to get me to go to where the twins were. "Three, three, and *two*? That doesn't make sense. Someone's still out there. I still need to check the bunker. You aren't coming with me."

"You aren't going alone."

He gripped my head and pulled me close, his voice harsh. "I'm not fucking burying you too. *Go.*"

Maverick yelled my name just as I was about to argue.

"Go," Kieran repeated in a lethal tone. "They won't see me coming."

I warred with myself until my name was called again and then took off for the twins.

Diggs was on the ground choking out curses, and Maverick was trying to calm him. Both had their bandanas off and were pressing them to Diggs's right side. Neither watching their surroundings for any potential threats.

I went to my knees beside Diggs, searching the area through my scope before looking at him.

"Fucking assholes waited until I passed them before they started shooting. Fucking pussies. And why is my goddamn stomach growling?"

Each sentence was broken with hisses of pain and wheezes. His voice was strained. Even in the dark, I could see his shirt was drenched with blood. His hands and right arm were covered.

And it was all too similar.

Beck.

Lying on the grass, soaked with his blood.

Choking and trying to crack jokes until the very end.

I wouldn't let this happen to them.

I gripped his right hand. "You got feeling?"

"Fuck, man. Yeah. Don't have to Hulk me."

Maverick laughed, but it sounded tortured.

I reached for the bottom of his shirt. "Gonna see what we're dealing with. All right?"

I wasn't sure who hissed louder.

Diggs from the pain or Maverick as he took in the amount of blood flowing from his brother's side and back. So much that I couldn't tell how many times he'd been shot or where.

From the helpless sort of panic on Maverick's face, he knew what I was thinking.

But I wasn't losing anyone tonight.

"Well, you were definitely shot," I said tonelessly and tried not to wince when Diggs started laughing, only to cry out in pain. "I've seen worse, you're just enjoying the attention."

A pained, amused breath left him. "'Bout time I got some love."

"Yeah, we'll see if you still think that after this." I swallowed thickly and pressed the tips of my fingers to his chest and side. "Sorry, man," I muttered before I roughly raked my fingers over his torso.

Diggs arched and yelled curses through gritted teeth as I dragged my fingers over him again and again, looking for gunshot wounds and counting them as I found them.

Chest . . . clear.

Right side . . . one, two . . . three.

Back . . . *fuck*.

His back was riddled with tiny holes and jagged pieces.

I glanced at the shot-up wall of the guesthouse a foot away from us and was thankful that, from the looks of it, they'd missed Diggs more than they hit him.

"Shit ton of shrapnel in his back," I whispered to Maverick and then said, "Diggs, left side."

"No," he gritted out. "No, fuck you."

"Yeah, I figured." I rolled him onto his back, trying to ignore the way he cried out, and showed Maverick where to put pressure against his right side. Once he had the bandanas in place and was pressing down, I said, "Last time, Diggs."

Before he could object, I raked my fingers down the left side of his chest and torso, and about thanked God out loud when I didn't find anything.

I shifted my hands under Diggs and took over where Maverick was pressing down. "Get the rifles. Diggs, we're moving."

Diggs strained and tried not to react to each slight bump and jostle as I hurried to the car, and I tried not to think of how much blood was dripping between my fingers and down my arms.

How little time we had.

What I had to do to save someone's brother when I'd never had a chance to save mine.

"Kieran has bandages in the trunk," I said as we neared the car.

Maverick ran ahead to trade out the rifles for what I needed, and once I was there, I gently lowered Diggs until his feet were touching the ground and he was leaning against the car.

"Need you to stand. I'll work fast."

"Know how to sta—*shit*." He roared when I lifted off his shirt. When I took mine off immediately after, he gave me a weak, wary look. "I don't love you that much."

Despite it all, a laugh forced itself from my chest as I

pressed my shirt tightly against his side. "Sure you do, Diggs." I nodded to Maverick when he rounded the car. "Get a bandage ready."

I pushed as hard as I could, trying to ignore the pained sounds Diggs was making. When Maverick was ready, I took the large bandage from his hold and quickly put it over one of the gunshot wounds.

Over and over until all three were covered.

I'd just finished with the last one when Kieran appeared beside me.

Chest heaving, knives covered in blood and still in hand.

"Diggs?"

I didn't answer.

I didn't want to when both brothers could hear me.

I just gave him a look that told him all he needed to know.

With a sharp nod, he rushed to get in and start the car while I lowered Diggs onto the backseat where Maverick waited, and then headed for the passenger seat.

"Go," I said as soon as I was in.

"There was a guy in the guesthouse," Kieran started as he tore onto the street. "Said groups of nine men were called to *nine* houses tonight. Didn't know who gave the orders or where anyone was."

"Nine houses—*shit*," I muttered. "The four houses from Zachary and Sutton's generation, and all their parents'..."

"That's what I'm thinking. The bunker was empty, but this was on the inside of the door." He reached into his pocket and pulled out a balled-up piece of paper that was smeared with blood.

I opened it, rage building and burning inside me as soon as I read the typed words.

> LET'S PLAY A GAME.
> WHICH OF YOU WILL DIE FIRST?
> WHICH OF YOU WILL DIE LAST?
> I WON'T REST UNTIL EVERY LAST ONE OF YOU IS BURIED IN THE GROUND—DEAD OR ALIVE.

"I'm going to kill him," I seethed. "Slowly."

"You won't get the chance if I see him first," Kieran murmured.

Diggs tried to choke out something but ended up hissing in pain.

"He's mine," Maverick growled. "Einstein. My brother. He's mine."

I looked in the back to where Maverick was holding Diggs slightly up and putting pressure on his side and then whispered to Kieran, "He needs blood."

He mouthed a curse and then accelerated.

"Maverick, what's Diggs's blood type?"

"O positive."

I shifted to look at him, hating that I had put that hopeless look on his face but knowing this was necessary. "You the same?"

He nodded, the movement quick but solemn.

"Buncha vampires," Diggs wheezed.

"Damn right," I said with a forced smile as I looked straight ahead.

I swallowed past the knot in my throat and tried to tell myself it wasn't as bad as I remembered . . . but I could still feel those holes in his side. Diggs's blood was coating my hands all the way to my wrists.

"It won't be enough," I murmured to Kieran. "Shit, I don't think I even have anything to start an IV or take Maverick's blood."

"You have your kit?" he asked.

"In my bag, but I think I only packed what I'd need to fix someone up."

"There's a hospital a couple of miles past the resort," he said as he raced down the freeway. "Focus on what you have to do. I'll take care of the rest."

"Diggs?" Panic filled Maverick's voice and seeped into the car. "*Diggs!*"

I turned in the seat, leaning over to grip Diggs's limp arm.

Maverick held him tighter, mumbling curses and pleas under his breath as I searched for a pulse.

"Faint but fast." Grabbing my phone, I shoved it against Kieran's arm and demanded, "Call the girls. Tell them to be ready."

Thirty-Three

Sutton

"So, what's the deal with the fort?" Jess asked from where she was sprawled out on the sofa bed with Einstein.

"The twins have always done it," Einstein murmured. She took a break from staring at her computer to look at the massive fort, a smile tugging at her mouth before she went back to dutifully watching the screens. "This is nothing. Next time they build one at the Borello house, you'll have to come see it. They put lights in the sheets, pull all the mattresses into the room, and basically empty the fridge and pantry. It's magic."

I waved a hand in the air, gesturing to the massive two-room, two-floor fort. "This is nothing?"

"It just isn't the same. Not as extravagant."

A sharp, disbelieving laugh burst from me. I couldn't

imagine anything more extravagant than what the guys had spent all day creating.

"I'll be there," Jess said wistfully. "Just give me a few days at home in bed with my man first, and then I'll be there."

Einstein pretended to gag. "You guys are disgusting. You know that, right?"

A wry smile slowly stretched across Jess's face. "You try living out of a car with Maverick for over a week and then tell me you don't jump at any opportunity to be all over him."

"It has nothing to do with your living conditions," Einstein argued. "You're all over each other all the time."

Jess lifted her hands in surrender, her smile never fading.

"You guys are living out of a car?" I asked cautiously.

"Only while we're here." She must have read the guilt on my face, because she hurried to say, "Don't worry. It isn't the first time we've lived out of a car during a job. Sometimes it's easier that way."

I blinked slowly, trying to figure out how that could be easier. It sounded awful. "Why? There are so many hotels around here, I'm sure at least one of them has to have a vacant room." I sucked in a quick breath. "Or are you trying not to draw the attention of law enforcement because we were already using rooms?"

Einstein looked up, her brow scrunched together. After a quick, shared glance with an even more confused Jess, she said, "Uh . . . right, I'm not sure either of us know what you meant by that."

"No, I'm sorry. I'm not trying to be rude," I said on a

rush. "Please don't think I'm not thankful for everything you've done for Lexi and me, because I am."

"Yeah, I'm not offended . . . yet," Einstein said slowly and then shot me a look as if she were trying to figure out if she *should* be. "I literally don't know what you meant. And I never don't know what people mean. What attention of law enforcement?"

I glanced at Jess before meeting Einstein's curious, calculating stare again. "I just meant, well, all the rooms that we've been in, Conor said they were under different names and cards. If you've been stealing cards and identities . . ."

I realized how wrong I was when both girls shared a look and then burst into laughter.

"That's what you've thought this entire time?" Jess asked, wiping moisture from under her eyes.

"Names and cards that are linked to our bank accounts. We have different ones set up under false names for this very reason," Einstein explained.

"But these . . ." I looked around the suite we were in. I knew exactly what kind of world I had grown up in. What types of houses I'd lived in my entire life. That didn't mean I couldn't appreciate and marvel at the beauty and grandeur of the place where I was staying. Even the lesser suites we had been in had been extravagant. "These aren't cheap. I know that for a fact."

"Right," Einstein said. "That is why I put this one under a card that's linked to one of Diggs's accounts. Since he'd just rack up the bill with room service anyway."

"Cost the same as the room," Jess mumbled.

"Close enough." Einstein slowly studied me. "Sorry to

be the one to tell you this, but you aren't the only one with money, Princess."

I started at the snide comment. "What? I don't—I just didn't know."

"You thought we stole identities and credit cards to secure rooms. I can guess where your thoughts went from there."

"I didn't—" I pressed my lips firmly together and dropped my head into my hands.

Trying to explain myself would only make this worse.

Nothing I said was well-received, especially with Einstein and Kieran.

Every answer I gave was twisted or taken with a heavy dose of doubt.

There was never any winning with them.

"I'm sorry," I said as I lifted my head.

Einstein had already turned back to her computer and didn't bother to acknowledge me.

Then again, I wasn't sure if I blamed her.

My husband had lured her into a game I knew well, only hers had such a different ending from mine. If the roles had been reversed, I wasn't sure which would win out . . . my empathy and understanding because we'd been through similar things or my bitterness and resentment that she'd put me in the situation to begin with.

It was clear which one had won out in Einstein.

I stood, needing to move, needing to get out of the room I no longer felt welcome in, but I hadn't made it more than a step before Einstein spoke.

"Just because we live differently from you, it doesn't mean we're all that different."

I stopped to watch her as she slowly lowered the top of

her laptop and straightened her back and set her glare on me.

"We've lived through and done things you haven't seen or realized existed even though they were all around you. You were born with a silver spoon in your mouth, which was paid for by the same dark deeds that funded our bank accounts for years. We might not live the extravagant life you're used to, but that's because we prefer to be unsuspecting. Doesn't mean each one of us isn't currently worth more than your piece-of-shit 'husband' or his friends."

My eyelids slowly shut as words I'd said to Conor last week tore through my mind.

"Excuse me for having money and using it. I'll try not to flash it in front of the likes of you again."

"Of course you are," I mumbled.

"But living the way we do is how we're able to do *this*. It's how, when women and children like you and Lexi, need help . . . we're able to give them money to help them start over instead of charging them a fee."

"I'm sorry for what I said and how it came across," I said after a moment. "I took what Conor said about the rooms the wrong way—*clearly*—and for that, I am sorry." I pressed a hand to my chest in a futile attempt to settle my racing heart. "But I don't care how much money any of you have. I wouldn't care if all of you were broke."

I took a few steps back, my shoulders sagging as I did.

"I just . . . God, it doesn't even matter. Nothing I say will make this better. Nothing will change your mind about me."

"Sutton," Jess called out when I started walking away, but her voice wasn't what stopped me.

It was the ringing of a phone.

I turned, my heart stopping painfully before kicking up, faster than before.

"About time we got an update," Einstein said with a relieved sigh, opening her computer again.

Jess barely took the time to glance at her phone and mumble Conor's name before answering. "Hey—Kieran?" Her entire body stilled for tense, torturous seconds. "What happened?"

My hand shot out, grabbing the edge of the chair when it felt like I would fall.

She whispered short questions into the phone as her expression started to fall. Seconds later, she threw the phone at Einstein. "Talk to him," she demanded as she scrambled from the bed. As soon as her feet touched the floor, she was running for the kitchen, yelling for me as she did.

When I made it into the kitchen, she was loading the remaining guns into her arms, already snapping orders at me.

"Help me get these into this room. We need to clear off the table."

"What happened?"

"Someone was shot. Bad."

Dread and fear froze me in place until she yelled my name again, and then I was moving. Running guns and cans of ammo into Conor's room until the kitchen was cleared. By the time I made it back in there from the last load, Jess was climbing the stairs and trying to tear down the sheets from the fort.

Einstein was already off the phone, her fingers flying over the keys on the laptop.

"Did he tell you?" Jess asked, her voice tense as she finally got ahold of a sheet and started pulling.

"No," Einstein ground out. "Move faster."

I caught the sheets as Jess dropped them and hurried to untie and unclip them as she rushed back downstairs, bundled them up, and ran them to the kitchen.

"Sutton," she called over her shoulder. "Conor's duffle. There's a black bag in there, we need it."

I didn't think. I just dropped the sheets where I stood and ran, tripping and sliding over even more as I did.

When I made it back out, Jess had the kitchen table covered with a couple of the sheets and was folding more into a pile on one of the chairs.

"Find something to hold warm water," she said distractedly. "Get all the towels you can find."

I turned in a quick circle, my mind unable to figure out which way to go first, when I caught sight of a large, decorative bowl.

I ran for it, dumped the contents onto the floor, and hurried over to the sink to fill it.

I'd just placed the bowl on a chair next to the table when Einstein called out, "They're here."

Jess and I both froze, looking to Einstein and then the door.

"Jess, get to the door."

She placed the remaining bundle of sheets in the corner and gripped my arm as she passed. "Towels."

"Damn it." It felt like I was running through water as I went from room to room, collecting all the clean towels we had. My mind was so frazzled that I didn't even stop to see if all the commotion, which felt *so* big and *so* loud to me, had woken Lexi.

No sooner had I come back with the last armful of towels than I heard Jess's horrified, "Oh God."

I nearly fell to my knees right then.

My chest constricted and felt heavy.

I couldn't catch my breath.

When Conor came running through the suite, I couldn't even focus on the relief that poured through me at seeing him. He was there, shirtless and covered in blood and carrying one of the twins' limp body.

The massive, open space of the suite suddenly felt too small, and it continued to close in around me as I watched Conor put the body on the sheet-covered table and immediately reached for one of the bandages already on his side.

Blood.

There was so much blood.

The other twin started pacing back and forth beside them, forcing his blood-stained hands through his hair.

Einstein was there, scanning the body on the table while reaching blindly for the other twin. He pulled her close and buried his head into her shoulder—*Maverick*.

Diggs.

Diggs was lying limp on the table.

It was Diggs's blood dripping onto the floor.

Diggs's chest that was struggling to rise and fall.

Jess demanded to know where Kieran was as she set up beside Conor, tool in one hand and a towel in the other.

I just watched in horror, unable to comprehend how this could be real . . . unable to get past who was behind this.

Zachary did this. Zachary did this. Zachary did this . . .

This isn't real. This isn't real. This isn't real . . .

"I need more light," Conor ground out. "Someone get a phone."

I stupidly looked down at my hands, as if one would appear there, and then glanced over to the sofa bed where the girls had been.

I didn't remember running over there, or if I'd even ran. All I remembered was looking over and seeing the phone, and suddenly, it was in my hand and I was next to Conor with the flashlight on.

Jess stumbled into me before righting herself, muttering something that sounded like an apology, but I couldn't respond. I could hardly pull my stare away from all the blood long enough to glance at her.

"Pulse?" Conor asked as he wiped at one of the wounds, only for more blood to trickle out.

"Weak, but there," Einstein answered.

Conor didn't respond. He just kept working, cleaning off Diggs's body and moving to the next bandage. All the while, muttering things about breaks and exit wounds.

Jess swayed toward me before falling toward the table, and I nearly dropped the phone in my attempt to catch her.

"Are you okay?" I asked, my tone at once worried for her and still shocked by the situation we were in the middle of.

"I'm fine," she whispered, her words slurring slightly. "I'm fine."

"Get her out of here," Conor demanded, both gentle and full of authority.

"I said I'm fine."

He shot her a meaningful look. "And I know you aren't. Go lie down."

I glanced to Jess in time to see the worry and fear that

flashed through her eyes before she could push her way around the table.

I watched her go, trying to figure out what Conor knew, when my eyes caught on Maverick's shirt.

The bandana tied high up on his arm, the wetness on his sleeve, and the blood that trailed down past it.

"You were shot?"

He and Einstein both looked to me before they realized that I was talking to Maverick. Then Einstein was stepping away and looking at him. Maverick just stared at me blankly before nodding, as if his grief and his worry for his brother had begun shifting into shock and dread and making it hard for him to comprehend that he was wounded too.

"Arm," Einstein said, looking to Conor, whose fingers were on the edge of Diggs's third original bandage.

Conor whispered a curse. "I forgot. Let me see."

"I'm fine," Maverick said automatically.

"I don't fucking care who is fine right now," Conor snapped. "Show me."

Maverick pulled up his sleeve, revealing a gunshot wound on the outside of his bicep with a trail of blood coming from it. "It was a ricochet. Saw it hit the walkway right before I felt it."

"Can you feel the bullet still in there?" Conor asked as he went back to Diggs.

"I don't know," he said slowly, bending his arm as he did. "Yeah . . . yeah. It isn't deep."

Conor blew out a slow breath, but he never stopped working. "Maverick, sit next to me. Einstein, clean the wound."

"No. Fuck no," Maverick ground out. "I'm fine, take care of my brother."

"The hell do you think I'm doing?" Conor asked. "Kieran should be back any minute. If you want to help your brother, then that wound needs to be closed. Sit the fuck down."

Maverick untied the bandana from around his shoulder and pulled his shirt off as he sat, wincing slightly when Einstein cleaned the area as Conor told her to.

Then Conor pointed a bloodied hand to a package in front of me. "Tear that open and have it ready."

"Damn you," Maverick said through clenched teeth as soon as I had the package in hand.

"Use it before?" Conor asked, a hint of a laugh in his voice.

"Yes, and I'll mean anything I say to you."

At that, Conor did laugh.

Without any warning, he set down the surgical tool he was using with Diggs, grabbed a clean one, and turned to Maverick.

A second later, the bullet was out and he had the cloth I'd taken from the package in hand . . . and then Maverick let out a long string of curses as Conor began shoving the cloth into the bullet wound.

Once he was sure it was secure, he nodded to Einstein. "Wrap the rest of that around his arm. Tight."

Conor was bent back over Diggs less than a minute after he'd left him. And for a moment, I felt like I might need to join Jess.

This isn't real. This isn't real. This isn't real.

I was trapped in a disturbing dream, and I was more than ready to wake up.

With a mumbled curse, Conor began covering the last wound.

"Can't you use those cloths on Diggs?" I asked.

"No." He grabbed Diggs's wrist to check his pulse, but he looked to Maverick. "I'm gonna try to get what I can from his back."

A grim look stole across Maverick. "The bleeding from the gunshots?"

"Nearly stopped."

"That we can see," Maverick said after a minute.

Conor didn't respond as he rolled Diggs onto his side, but from the heaviness that passed through the kitchen, what Maverick was saying was a possibility.

Maverick sat forward to watch as Conor pulled pieces of metal and other unknown chunks from Diggs's back, worry and panic and grief etched across his face. "What broke?"

"Lower rib."

His eyes darted to Conor before resting on Diggs again. "Stop the bullet?"

"Yeah."

Maverick nodded without seeming to realize he was doing so, and after a while, mumbled, "Good."

"Why is that good?" I asked before I could begin to stop myself.

I hadn't been sure I was following their conversation, but I couldn't figure out how anything about this situation was good.

Before anyone could answer, Kieran appeared in the kitchen, arms weighed down with bags. "Saline, pain meds, and antibiotics," he said gruffly.

"I needed stuff for an IV," Conor said as he met Kieran where he was dropping everything on the counter.

"You're welcome," Kieran said distractedly. "Jessica?"

"Almost fainted. Made her go lie down." Conor's hands were busy ripping packages open, but his words dripped with hidden meaning.

Kieran was out of the kitchen before Conor finished explaining.

"Einstein, clean a spot on both twins arms," Conor tossed her a box of what looked like alcohol wipes and then ripped needles from their tubes and pieced them together with others.

"What are you doing?" Einstein asked as she turned to Maverick. "What is he doing?"

"Diggs needs blood," Maverick said gravely, easing Diggs onto his back again as he did.

"Are you insane?" Einstein yelled at the same time I asked, "Is that safe?"

"No, it isn't," Einstein answered for the guys. "It's dangerous in a hospital, but in a kitchen? It's fucking insane."

"So, you do know what hospitals are then?" I said lamely. "Because I've been wondering why we aren't at one."

"There's no way you've done this before. Have you even put in an IV before?" Einstein asked as Conor took over rubbing the alcohol wipe over the crease of Maverick's arm.

"Been a few years," Conor murmured as he moved back to Diggs and felt around on his arm. "But I watched Sofia do yours a couple weeks ago. Probably like riding a bike."

"Conor—"

"Do something useful," he snapped. "Find out which of those meds I can give Diggs, and how much. Find out how much saline I should give him."

Einstein looked like she wanted to continue arguing.

She also looked like she was about to cry.

"Dangerous," Conor said softly. "Got it. We know the risks. But he *will* die if we don't do anything."

Her eyelids slowly shut, and her face creased with pain before she jogged back to the living room to grab her laptop.

She was back with fingers flying before Conor finished getting the IV into Diggs's vein.

He attached an IV line, but at the other end where it would have connected to a bag there was another needle.

Conor stopped in front of Maverick and blew out a steadying breath. "You ready?"

Maverick's face was made of stone when he nodded.

Conor sat in the chair he'd been in earlier and said, "Need you to stand. We need the gravity."

I wasn't sure anyone took a breath until Conor was finished and blood began flowing through the line to Diggs.

Conor sank back into the chair and raked his hands through his hair, sighing heavily as he did before he stood and went for the counter.

With one look at me, I hurried to follow.

"I need you to find something we can set up next to Diggs that will hold the saline."

"Of course," I said quickly, already looking for anything that resembled the poles they used in hospitals.

And once again, I wondered why they hadn't taken Diggs to one.

My eyes caught on the chandelier over the table, and then I hurried through the kitchen toward Conor's room.

Kieran and Jess were sitting on the bed, huddled close together and whispering. Once again, making me feel as if I had just interloped on something I should never have witnessed.

I had the immediate urge to hurry from the room without looking back, but I needed what was inside it.

"I'm sorry. I just . . ."

I backed up out of instinct when Kieran got off the bed with one easy step and began stalking toward me with a vicious sneer and murderous intent in his eyes.

My body felt like dead weight when I noticed the blade hanging from his fingers.

I turned to run at the same instant Jess yelled, "Kieran, no!"

I hadn't gotten to the doorway before he grabbed me by the back of my neck and turned me, slamming me against the wall and pressing the knife to my throat.

"Give me one good reason I shouldn't bleed you dry right here."

Dark. Cruel. Chilling.

I couldn't speak.

I couldn't feel the beating of my heart.

All I saw was the monstrous look in his eyes, so unlike anything I'd ever even seen from Zachary.

All I felt was the cold metal against my throat.

All I knew was this last moment, which seemed to stretch on and pass in the blink of an eye. It was as if it were mocking me by letting me steep in the horrific knowledge that I was about to die.

A harsh cry ripped from me, and I stumbled forward when Kieran suddenly disappeared.

I looked around wildly as the world and the room came back into view in time to see Conor slam Kieran into the opposite wall.

"I fucking warned you," Conor roared as he swung at him. Kieran dodged it, and Conor swung again. It didn't matter how fast Conor's fist was—Kieran was faster.

It was as if the assassin were already in Conor's head, anticipating every move.

Instead of another swing, Conor charged him, sending them both to the ground.

When they landed, Conor had Kieran's collar in his grasp and his other fist raised, inches from Kieran's face.

Kieran had a knife to Conor's stomach.

A horrified scream sounded in the room. After a moment, I realized it had come from me.

Jess was trying to pull me away, but I was frozen in place, staring at the two men on the floor who were seconds away from doing something they would never be able to take back.

Kieran looked like death personified. And Conor . . . shirtless, and covered in tattoos and blood . . . had never looked more like my avenging angel.

It was brutal and disturbing and mesmerizing.

"He hurt you?" Conor called out, never looking away from Kieran. "*Sutton*."

"No," I said quickly, numbly.

"Limit reached. Crossed," Conor said, shoving off Kieran as he did. "We're done."

"She knew," Kieran said in an even tone as he stood. "She knew where we were going tonight. She *knew*, and there was an ambush waiting for us at every spot. There was a note at the first."

"I said we're done. Get the fuck out."

"There's a Kennedy trait," Kieran said, low and disappointed. "Choosing women over family."

He left before Conor could respond, and with a dumbfounded, apologetic look, Jess followed.

I didn't realize I was crying until Conor was standing in front of me and brushing his thumbs across my cheeks.

"You okay?"

My head moved in a slow nod before furiously shaking. Then a sob wrenched from my chest, unable to contain it any longer.

The day.

The night.

The judgment and suspicion. The horror and blood.

All of it.

Conor wrapped me up tight, trying to calm me, but I pressed my hands to his chest and pushed him away.

I forced my stare to the floor so I wouldn't have to see his hurt and weakly lifted an arm in the direction of the closet. "I was coming for a hanger. Put it upside down on a couple of the chandelier branches."

"Sutton—"

"For Diggs."

"Talk to me." He reached for me, but I took a step away.

"You should go to him. Really."

I could feel the pain radiating from him as it echoed in my own chest.

But I couldn't do this.

Not right then.

"This is what happens," he said thickly. "This is my life. People get hurt. People die. Now you understand."

Once he'd grabbed a hanger from the closet and left, I waited until I was sure I wasn't going to break down before leaving the room.

I kept my head down as I passed through the kitchen,

ignoring the way the soft whispers faded to nothing as I did.

When I was in the safety of my own room, I released a stuttered breath and hurried to clap my hands over my mouth before the shattered sob broke free.

I needed to go clean up.

I was sure I hadn't touched anything, but I felt as if I'd been covered in Diggs's blood just from being surrounded by it.

But my body felt so worn out. So weak.

Threatening to crash from the highs and lows of the day.

My eyes caught on the clock, which read just after three in the morning.

The guys had barely left an hour and a half ago.

And it had already been the longest day of my life.

I crawled onto the bed next to Lexi and sank onto a pillow, burying my face in it when another tear slipped free.

I'm fine.

I'm fine.

I had to be . . .

Or else I wouldn't be able to get through what I knew needed to come next.

Thirty-Four

Zachary

"Call them off," I said through clenched teeth as I jerked my chin sharply to the side. "All of them."

"The people you just brought in," Garret said in a dull tone. "All eighty-one of them." A harsh laugh worked from his chest as he gestured to one of the bodies being carried into my house by the nerds. "Shit, excuse me, I meant seventy-two."

I moved into his personal space and sucked in a hissing breath. "I gave you an order. I won't ask—*Woods*," I snapped when he finally answered my call.

"The fuck do you need?" Jason growled. "The last goddamn thing I want to hear is my phone continuously ringing in time with this bitch's moans."

There was a shock of outrage and disgust in the background, but he just murmured for the woman to shut up.

"Garret's calling off the men," I said on a rush.

"They just got here—"

"The next son of a bitch who questions me gets a bullet between their eyes," I shouted.

I took deep, staggering breaths.

Trying to calm myself.

Trying to find control and maintain it.

But all I could hear were Sutton's moans.

Hear her saying another man's name.

My thoughts were consumed by the knowledge that another man had touched my wife. Fucked her. Tasted her.

And she'd allowed it.

The urge to kill someone had only grown and grown until I could practically taste the bitter metal coating my tongue. Until I could feel the thick liquid dripping from the tips of my fingers.

My chin jerked, and I roughed a hand through my hair.

Grasping at the strands. Tearing.

Fucking twitching. Unable to stay still.

"He's calling off the men," I said again, this time slower, calmer . . . darker. "The nine here are all dead."

Jason let out a low whistle. "Fuck."

My nostrils flared, and my heart pounded in time with the voices clawing at my brain and the chanting in my simmering blood.

A fucked-up symphony of Sutton's whimpers and a dark, greedy, hungry voice, begging for a kill.

And another . . .

And another and another until the sounds of people begging for their lives and the sight of the light leaving their eyes replaced everything else.

I swallowed the sour taste crawling up my throat and narrowed my eyes on Garret as I seethed into the phone, "I need a favor."

Thirty-Five

Conor

"Get some sleep," Maverick all but grunted the words from where he sat next to Diggs.

An amused huff left me. "You're one to talk. You almost pulled a Jess in the kitchen."

He'd nearly faceplanted right onto Diggs.

When I'd caught him and gotten him into a chair, he'd been white as a ghost and covered in a cool sweat. And determined to keep giving more blood.

I'd had to hold him down while Einstein took the needle from his arm, the entire time he fought, saying it wasn't enough.

I'd known he was probably right, but it wasn't going to do us any good if Maverick ended up laid out next to his brother.

We'd moved Diggs into the bedroom soon after.

Since then, it had been a waiting game.

I'd already taken out the clotting cloth and re-bandaged Maverick's gunshot wound. Then I'd gotten the rest of what I could out of Diggs's back before cleaning and bandaging it. The bleeding had stopped, he was hooked up to an IV, and Einstein had hacked hospital records in an attempt to figure out what to give him.

There was nothing more that could be done, I knew that.

At least, there was nothing more *I* could do for him.

Not knowing if it was enough was making me doubt everything I *had* done until it felt like I'd go crazy thinking through it all.

"Seriously, go," Maverick said. "You look like you belong in a bad horror movie."

I glanced down at my body. My hands and forearms had been cleaned, but everywhere else was splattered and stained a dirty rust color.

"Yeah . . . yeah, probably not a way Lexi should see me." The corner of my mouth tugged into a grimace, and when I looked up, Maverick was watching me carefully.

"Things haven't added up with this case," he began, his tone wary. "A lot of things, actually."

I breathed out a curse.

I wasn't ready for this fight again.

"But, I don't know, man. I saw the way she looked when you showed up after the ring and notes had been delivered. I saw how blindsided she was when we told her about the bunkers. That looked so real."

"It *was* real."

He lifted a shoulder. "If what you want is to be with Sutton, then be with Sutton. You deserve to be happy, the same as the rest of us. I don't know you as well as Avery does, but I've seen what you've done for every member of my family over the past year or so, including what you did for Diggs tonight. You never hesitate, and you work selflessly. So, if you trust Sutton, that's all I need to know."

He was the last person I ever thought would take up my side.

I gripped the back of my neck as the last week I'd spent with Sutton tore through my mind in flashes and conversations and fights. Ending with Kieran leaving and Sutton pushing me away, refusing to even look at me.

I forced a smile. "I'm not sure it's that simple. Even if everyone else wasn't constantly fighting me about her or digging into her with their doubts, she saw every bad part of our world in one night."

"If you planned to stay with her, a night like tonight was bound to happen sooner or later."

"I would have preferred later. At least then, we wouldn't have had everything else surrounding it."

Zachary leaving her notes. Us just having worked through what we were doing. The interrogation. Kieran attacking her or him and me coming to blows right in front of her.

"I can't speak for Kieran—" He hesitated and then gave a soft laugh. "Shit, I can't even really speak for Avery. But I think, to Avery, you're *hers*."

I glanced to where Einstein was curled up in a ball, sleeping in the chair directly next to Maverick's.

"And fuck, man, that bothered me for so long. I thought something was there or that I was going to lose her to you when all that shit went down between us. I didn't get why she is so damn protective over you until recently. But she had horrible parents and lost her sister. So, she chooses her family, and she chose you from about the minute she met you."

If he'd known I'd chosen her too, only in an entirely different way, he wouldn't be having this conversation with me.

"She met up with all of us after going into ARCK that first day to tell us that she was working with the enemy and we needed to get over it," he said with a smirk. "And said, 'There's this huge, brick wall of a guy, and he has the best smile in the world, and I've decided he's ours now. I'll inform him later.'"

A sharp laugh left me, but Maverick gave me a weak glare.

"I hated you from that moment."

"Yeah, I had an idea."

Maverick was silent for a while as he watched Einstein. When he spoke, his voice was somber. "She missed the threat before, and it almost cost her life. Now, she can see it. Whether the threat is Sutton doesn't matter to Avery; it's linked to her just the same. I think, because of the link, Avery's convinced the threat is coming for you."

"Don't talk about me like you know what I'm thinking," Einstein mumbled without opening her eyes.

Maverick reached for her, grabbing her knee. "I'm right though."

"Don't be smug either. These are my things." A smile broke across her face when Maverick squeezed her knee, but her eyes still remained shut.

I took a step back and was about to say I was leaving when I felt Kieran slip into the room.

From the way Maverick's eyes darted behind me, I knew I was right.

"Problem," he said in way of greeting.

I slanted him a cold, hard look when he came up beside me, but he just stood there, staring at me as he always did. As if our fight from hours before had never happened.

"They're gone."

My heart and my stomach immediately dropped.

Ice-cold fear and pain encompassed me.

I looked to the open bedroom door, as if I could see across the suite to where Sutton was supposed to be, and took a step in that direction.

Kieran went to stop me, but I slammed my palm into his chest, forcing him back.

"Not the girls," he bit out.

I'd made it another two steps before his words registered, but even then, I continued staring at the doorway, torn between checking on them and finding out exactly who he was talking about.

All I could see was the way Sutton had pushed me away.

How she wouldn't let me hold her.

Wouldn't look at me.

I dragged a hand through my hair and turned. "Then who," I demanded through clenched teeth.

"I went to the other eight houses."

If Einstein hadn't been awake before, Maverick's and my reactions would have done the job.

"Alone?"

"Have you lost your goddamn mind?"

"I would've had it handled. I already knew how many people would be there and how they would more than likely set up," Kieran said evenly. "But there was no one stationed there."

"Then the guy you caught was lying," I said. "Would it be so hard to believe *he* was?"

At that, Kieran's eyes narrowed into slits. "There were signs of people recently being at each place. Tracks in mulch, fresh cigarette butts, stuff like that. The bunkers were empty. All of them."

"Damn it." I threaded my fingers together on top of my head and loosed a slow sigh as our biggest lead slipped away. "Notes?"

"Only at the Larson's. They knew that was where we were going first."

I shook my head, refusing to respond to the meaning in his words. "I'm going to bed." Looking to Maverick, I said, "There's nothing else we can do for him right now. Sleep."

He nodded, worry and exhaustion weighing heavily on him. "Thank you. For everything."

I didn't respond. I didn't know how to when I wasn't sure it was enough. I just grabbed my bag and left the room, knowing Kieran was right behind me and hating that he was.

Once we were in the kitchen, Kieran reached for my shoulder and said, "We need to talk."

I shoved him away, rounding on him. "I told you to fucking leave."

He studied me with that cold lethalness. "I don't leave my family."

"What if this all goes differently?" When he didn't respond, I continued. "What if you're wrong? What if Sutton hasn't been playing us and she's telling us the truth? And you and Einstein thinking she's behind this is all still part of Zachary's fucked-up game to get us to turn on each other." I stepped toward him and lowered my voice. "And then I *keep* them. That's the third option you didn't give me, but it's the option I want to take."

The muscles in his jaw strained, and his head shifted in a faint rejection.

"What happens then? Because the reason for keeping them with me is so I don't lose my family. But what's the fucking point of staying around any of you if she'll always be treated this way and we've all shattered ties in an irreversible kind of way?"

"When she breaks you, I'll be here," he said simply.

"If she doesn't?"

His shoulders moved in a ghost of a shrug. "I told you, I don't leave family."

"So, if one day, she and Lexi become my family . . ."

His expression was stone. No hint of any emotion or thought behind that razor-sharp stare.

"Think about what it would be like for you if I *hated* Jess. If I *attacked* her the way you attacked Sutton tonight. If you couldn't trust *me* to be in the same room with her. Would you still be standing there, calling me family and saying you wouldn't turn your back on me?" I leaned close and seethed, "If you forgot . . . we killed every man who ever hurt her."

I didn't expect a response, and I didn't wait around for one.

Thirty-Six

Sutton

My eyes opened when the door to the bathroom shut.

My chest pitched when the shower turned on, and I rolled over, looking for the time. It had only been two hours since I'd come in here.

Then again, with all that had gone down in less than that, I knew anything could have happened in that time.

Especially to Diggs.

My chest ached for the ridiculous man who, in the span of a few minutes, had somehow become my daughter's best friend. Who'd spent an entire day entertaining her and spoiling her.

Everything had been so perfect when Lexi had gone to sleep.

Then everything had gone to hell.

Lexi's little world was going to be rocked when she woke, and I already hated it for her.

I slipped out of bed, my body and my heart and my mind torn.

Stopping in front of the bathroom door, I placed my palms and forehead against the wood, almost as if I could feel Conor on the other side.

I knew what needed to be done.

I just didn't know how I was supposed to make it through.

For the majority of my adult life, I'd pretended the horrible things weren't happening. Told myself it was what I wanted to make it through and face another day with an unscathed façade.

This?

There was no pretended it wasn't happening. That Conor's family wasn't falling apart around him because of me.

Leaving was the last thing in the world either of us wanted.

But it was what he needed.

I reached for the handle and quickly slipped into the steam-filled bathroom, locking the door behind me.

Conor never looked up from where he stood in the shower, hands pressed to the wall, head hanging low, spray beating down on his skin and washing away the blood that had been staining him.

My avenging angel.

Defeated.

Drained.

Beautiful.

I stripped, leaving my clothes next to his, and stepped into the shower.

Body shaking.

Soul reaching.

Heart aching.

My movements were unsure as I wrapped my arms around him, laced my hands together against his chest, and pressed my body close to his, trying to soak up some of his grief.

He gripped my hands in one of his, a shudder rolling through his back when I laid my head there.

For long minutes, we stayed that way, without ever saying a word.

I started pulling away when he loosened his grip on my hands, only for Conor to reverse our positions.

Slowly, effortlessly.

His large, tattooed hands trailed up my body and tilted my head back so he could search my eyes. The pain and understanding there shattered my already slowly breaking heart.

Tears filled my eyes and eventually spilled over, and then his mouth was on mine, taking my breath and the shattered pieces of my heart in a soft, haunting kiss.

Then he was turning us, and I was in his arms as he pressed me against the cool shower wall, ignoring the way I tried to arch away from it and closer to his warm body.

His mouth was against mine.

My legs wrapped around his narrow hips, as if we'd done this thousands of times.

Our bodies fit together as though we were made for each other.

And then he was filling me. Stretching me. Taking me and making me his in the most exquisite way.

In a way that would stay with me forever.

It was rough and filled with his pain and mine.

It was frenzied and passionate.

It was beautiful.

He curled his hand under my jaw, tilting my head back as his mouth and teeth left an excruciatingly hot trail across my neck. When his mouth found mine again, his hand slid to my cheek, cradling and adoring.

Gentle. Powerful. All Conor.

His forehead rolled against my own, his bright eyes locking with mine as he passed his thumb over my lips.

"Sutton, I love you."

He captured my mouth before the shock of hearing those words had even registered.

Tears slipped faster down my cheeks as I tried to hold on to him.

This moment.

After.

It was as if Conor knew I was saying goodbye, and with each touch, each brush of his lips, he was pleading with me to stay.

He held me tight through my release and pushed through to his own.

With each thrust, I heard his confession in my head.

With each thrust, my own responded.

I love you.

I love you.

I love you.

Goodbye.

When it was over, he slowly lowered me to the shower floor, never fully letting me go.

And I could feel it, his fear of what would happen when he did.

I stayed in his arms, letting him wash me and take care of me before I turned to do the same for him. Trying to prolong this moment when I knew it wouldn't last.

Scrambling for time I no longer had.

I sagged against his body when he wrapped a towel around me, allowing myself a few more seconds in his arms to say everything I couldn't.

Thank you.

You're perfect.

You have the kindest heart of anyone I've ever met.

I will always love you.

I traced one of the swirling patterns on his chest before pressing a kiss there and pulling away.

He didn't say anything, but the air felt thick and hard to breathe as I left the bathroom.

I hurried over to my and Lexi's bags, frantically shoving clothes and necessities into the smallest one as I slipped into a clean set of pajamas.

By the time Conor came into the bedroom, I was in bed, facing Lexi. Eyes shut. Destroyed heart racing.

I held my breath when he leaned over me to grab a pillow, lips brushing softly across my shoulder as he did.

And then I prayed.

That he wouldn't set up post in front of the door.

That he would fall asleep quickly.

That he would understand what I was about to do was for him.

I forced the pent-up breath to release slowly when he laid down beside the bed, thankful for that small victory.

I focused on the sounds of his breaths, waiting for when they would even out and deepen.

When they finally did, I began counting them.

After the one hundredth one, I crawled over Lexi, wincing at even the slightest sound, and pulled her to the side of the bed with me, rolling her toward me once my feet were on the floor.

I softly rubbed her back, waiting for when she would wake up, and quietly whispered her name into her ear.

As soon as she stirred, I leaned back so I was in front of her face and held a finger to my lips.

Her tired eyes immediately widened and she nodded.

I curled my arms around her body and lifted her from the bed, pressing my mouth to her ear. "We have to be silent."

I felt her nod before she wrapped herself tighter around me, and then I started toward the small bag I'd packed.

Each step there sounded too loud to my ears, and once I had the strap slung over my shoulder, my footfalls turned into the banging of a bass drum.

The click of the bedroom door was piercing.

But Conor's breathing didn't change.

Once we were out in the hall, my steps came faster and faster until I was rushing through the living room, gripping Lexi tighter to me as I did.

I was a few steps—just seconds—from the door when he appeared from the shadows, directly in front of it.

A startled cry clawed up my throat as I came to an abrupt halt, turning so Lexi was as far from him as I could get her.

"Please." The word was soft and weak and trembled leaving my tongue. "Please, just let us go."

"Can't do that," Kieran said, pure threat and challenge.

"Why? Why wouldn't you *want* that? Do you see what happens when I'm around you?"

"And what—"

"Don't you dare come near my daughter," I seethed, taking a giant step back when he moved forward.

Kieran moved back to his original position as if that had always been his intention, hands raised to show they were empty, piercing eyes shifting to catch my every move.

"Momma," Lexi whispered into my ear.

I tightened my grip on her, my body tensed and prepared for any number of things.

To drop the bag barely clinging to my shoulder.

To turn and run.

To let go of Lexi and fight a man I knew I had no chance of beating.

"Momma, he's sad."

I placed a hand to the back of Lexi's head, prompting her to put it down.

There wasn't anything about Kieran that looked sad.

Everything about him screamed he was ready to end a life.

"What happens when you leave?" he finally asked. "The way I see it, there aren't many reasons for you to want to."

I was about to point out all that had happened just over the course of the night, but he continued.

"You're leaving to get out because Zachary has a team coming for us."

"What? No," I whispered.

"You're leaving to reunite with Zachary and tell him exactly what he needs to know."

My head was shaking slowly. It felt light, too light. "No."

"You know that your leaving will cause even more of a rift within my family, and that's what you want. That'll make it easier to pick us off since they didn't actually succeed in killing anyone last night."

"No," I cried out and quickly lowered Lexi's feet to the floor, pressing her head close to my stomach and covering her ear. "I don't want this, why can't you see that? I don't want what happened last night. I didn't *know* it was going to happen. And I don't—" A pained breath climbed up my throat.

Slow.

Choking.

"God, the last thing I want is what's happening between you and Conor. It's breaking my heart for him and for you, and I don't even like you. But I know how much he loves you, and to see . . ." I reached for my chest before grabbing Lexi again. "He can't lose you."

Kieran's jaw ticked, and for the first time since he'd appeared in front of us, his stare fell to the floor.

"You were right, there are things I haven't told you." When his eyes flashed to mine and hardened, I hurried to continue. "But it won't help you find Zachary. It never would've helped or changed anything. It was nothing but lies on top of lies told to me that I had to figure out on my own. That I had to come to the horrifying realization of, only to bear that shame and regret."

"You don't know what could help us," he ground out.

"That was why we asked for *everything*. You should have told us."

"You're probably right, but it was too late long ago, and it wouldn't change things now," I whispered sadly. "I didn't know about the houses or the bunkers. I haven't known anything that you've told me. And before you accuse me again, no, I haven't told Zachary or anyone else anything that you've done or planned. If I never see or hear from him again, I will consider myself lucky. But I know this is all happening because I'm here with you. You and Conor fighting." My jaw trembled as I mouthed *Diggs* so Lexi wouldn't hear. "I can't imagine that it will stop as long as I'm here, and I can't be the reason anyone else gets hurt. I can't be the reason Conor loses his family. So, let us go."

"Sutton . . ."

My eyelids slowly shut. My face crumpled with a grief so consuming I had to reach out and grip at the wall to ground myself.

Lexi gasped. *"Mr. Conor!"*

She slipped from my hold, and it was all I could do not to fall to the floor right then.

"Mr. Conor, Mr. Conor, look at your beard, it's all different now. And you got a haircut. I like it a lot."

With each excited and adoring word, I felt the shattered pieces of my heart dying. With his low response, I felt my soul reaching out, begging for him.

"Please let us go," I whispered so low only Kieran would hear.

"You love him," was his only response.

My chest pitched with a silent sob. "I can't ruin his life."

"Do you love him?"

"Please—"

"I can't let you leave," he said, his tone soft but final, and then he stepped back to stand against the door the way Conor always did.

My shoulders sagged, and the bag finally slipped from my arm.

I fumbled to catch the strap before the bag could hit the floor, only to set it down.

With a steadying breath, I lifted my chin and turned to face the stare I could feel piercing my back.

It was worse than I ever could've imagined.

Conor was crouched low in nothing but a pair of sleep pants, holding Lexi to him as she chatted animatedly at his side, but his eyes and the hard set of his jaw said it all.

Grief.

Betrayal.

Loss.

Confusion.

Anger.

The tears I'd held back slipped free.

He whispered something to Lexi and stood, breaking our eye contact with a shake of his head as his long strides carried him across the room and toward the kitchen.

As soon as he passed my line of sight, I stumbled back against the wall and sank to the floor, a muted sob breaking free.

Lexi curled up next to me, prying my hands away from my face, studying me intently. "You don't have to be sad, Momma. Mr. Conor said we don't have to leave. So, don't be sad. We can stay with him instead of going back to the bad house."

I pulled her into my arms and rested my head against

the wall, remembering that Kieran was standing just feet away from us almost as an afterthought.

"It isn't that simple, sweet girl," I murmured.

"But you said we wouldn't go back to the bad house. Remember, you said?"

"We won't. Not ever," I assured her. "Why don't you tell me what you want for breakfast."

That perked her up. "Breakfast! Where's my Diggs?"

My heart.

I wasn't going to make it through this day.

I situated her on the floor and straightened myself, taking calming breaths and wondering how I was supposed to do this.

By the time I looked into her excited eyes, all I knew was that I didn't want to.

"You know how Diggs likes to have fun and play a lot?"

"Yeah!" Lexi's eyes brightened, and her smile widened so big I thought she might actually have the capability to heal me.

Slowly.

One shattered piece at a time.

"Well, he was playing last night, and he got hurt really bad."

Her mouth slowly fell into an *O* shape. "Did you kiss it to make it all better?"

The corners of my mouth tipped up before falling again. "No, that only works on you because you're my baby."

She rolled her eyes. "I'm not a baby."

"Of course not." I ran a hand over her hair. "He can't play today or even tomorrow. He might not even be able to talk to you today because he needs a lot of rest. Do you understand?"

She made a face like she was thinking really hard and then asked, "If I say hi, can he hear me?"

"I'm sure of it."

"If I eat breakfast for him, will it help him get better real fast?"

"I think that sounds like something he would definitely approve of." I reached for the bag and then searched for Lexi's toothbrush for a few moments before realizing I hadn't even packed anything from the bathroom. "Can you take this back to our room for me? Brush your teeth and change while you're in there, and then we'll go say hi to Diggs."

Once she was hurrying toward the bedroom, bag dragging behind her, Kieran asked, "You sure she should see him?"

"Don't underestimate her, she's braver than women twice my age."

"If there's anything I've learned in my life, it is not to underestimate women."

I shot him a cold look. "Just don't trust them."

He held my stare before his eyes took on a faraway look. "Only when there's a reason not to," he said after a minute. "I pulled a knife on Jessica the first few times I met her. Wanted to kill her."

"And she married you?"

The corner of his mouth tipped up. "She pulled a few on me too. Even stole one of mine once to do it. I fell in love with her at the exact minute I decided to kill her . . ."

"One of those clearly won out, and I have a feeling this won't go in my favor, considering you won't be falling in love with me."

"I'm saying don't take it personally. I was raised and trained to trust only myself and to eliminate every threat."

"How can I not when you continue to remind me that I *am* a threat to you?"

A cold, cruel look stole across his face. "If I were sure about that, you would've been dead long ago. I wouldn't have stopped when I had a knife to your throat last night. You wouldn't have seen me coming."

So, I had to wait for him to decide if I was.

Wonderful.

I stood, trying not to let him see any of the emotions coursing through me even though he had just been witness to my breakdown.

Before I stepped away, I whispered, "You should've let us go."

Thirty-Seven

Sutton

I joined Lexi in the room and took my time changing and brushing my teeth even though she was bouncing up and down, eager to see *her* Diggs.

There was no keeping her from him. She would ask and ask until she went searching for him on her own. I knew that just as surely as I knew there was no avoiding Conor.

To put it off for even a few more minutes was both fortifying and meaningless.

Because as soon as we stepped into the bedroom where they'd moved Diggs, and Conor turned that hurt stare on me, my walls crumbled and my soul cried out.

I kept a firm hold on Lexi's shoulders when she tried to dart toward the bed. The closer we got, the more anxious she became.

When we reached the side of the bed, I bent to whisper,

"Remember he's really hurt, so don't touch him. Try to stay quiet so you don't wake Maverick and Einstein, okay?"

She nodded, not saying a word, and then slipped out of my hold.

I moved to grab for her but stopped when she simply leaned on the bed and whispered, "Diggs. Diggs, are you sleeping? Momma told me you got hurt. I don't like when I get hurt, but I still act brave because I know it makes my momma sad. Just so you know, I'm sad you're hurt, but I'll act real brave for you."

I placed a hand over my mouth, trying to stifle the choking noise in my throat.

My brave, sweet girl.

It would wreck her if she knew her father was behind this.

"And I'll eat all the food for you," she continued. "And I'll tell you all the stories until you're all better. And then we can play superheroes again." She wriggled slightly closer. "Diggs . . . did you know your fort is gone? It's okay, though, we can make it again it later."

Movement off to the side caught my eye, and I glanced over in time to see Conor leaving the room, hands laced behind his neck and head hanging.

I stepped toward him instinctively and then forced myself to face the bed, knowing his hurt and anger were warranted.

I'd expected them.

I just hadn't expected to be here to witness them.

Maverick stirred and then opened his eyes, shifting quickly in the chair when he noticed us there.

"I'm sorry," I said quickly, keeping my voice low. "She wanted to see him."

"It's fine," he whispered as he looked to Einstein and Diggs and then stood.

When he stretched out his injured arm, a hiss escaped his lungs and his face creased with pain as he lowered it back to his side.

"Bad?" I asked when he came to stand near me.

"Definitely hurts now that the adrenaline and everything are gone."

"Do you need something for the pain?"

"Took something a couple of hours ago, I'll be fine. Not the first time I've been shot." The look on my face made him laugh. "It happened in our line of work. Except for the girls, everyone has been shot or stabbed at least once."

"Conor?"

"I wouldn't know about him or Kieran. Wouldn't surprise me since they have the scars. Conor knows how to take care of them, though, and that was what mattered last night."

"Yeah." I looked to Diggs and worried my bottom lip before asking, "No one answered me about the hospital. Why didn't you take him there?"

Maverick gave me a look that silently asked me how I hadn't put it together. "Police are contacted if you go to the hospital with stab or gunshot wounds. Police can't be involved in our lives—ever. Things happen, we take care of it. Our old boss, his mom has always taken care of us, no matter what happened. She took care of Einstein after—" He swallowed thickly, his eyes focused on where she was still asleep in the chair.

"What Zachary did," I finished on a whisper.

He offered me a forced smile. "That was all I kept thinking last night. Sofia wasn't here, I didn't know how

Diggs was going to survive something I was sure didn't have good odds even in a hospital. And then Conor pulled through, rigging a transfusion like it was just another day."

"He did it all like he's done it so many times before," I said, a cold chill running over my skin as the truth of that statement settled inside me.

"Probably didn't have a choice but to learn. Sofia was forced to learn, picking up things as she went because someone had to do it. Her role has always been to take care of the gang, no matter what that meant. Why Conor was pushed into it . . ." He looked around the room and then gestured toward the doorway with his chin. "You'll have to ask him when he wakes up."

I didn't tell him that Conor was already awake.

I didn't want to have to explain what had happened in the last half hour.

"So, what now?"

"We wait," he answered grimly. "It's only been a few hours, but he isn't clammy anymore. Checked about thirty or so minutes ago, there are no signs of internal bleeding, not that we can know for sure."

"You said it was *good* that his rib broke. I don't understand."

"It isn't that it's good. It could've splintered and punctured something. But a bullet can go in one side of your body and bounce around in there on its way to the other side. This one hit his rib and shattered right there."

Lexi came hurrying over to me, avoiding Maverick's stare and pressing close to the side of me that was farthest from him.

I grabbed her hand in mine and squeezed tight. "We

need to order breakfast. Lexi wants to eat all the food for Diggs so he'll feel better."

He let out an amused huff. "If anything will do it, that'll be it."

"Can we order you and Einstein something?"

"Anything would be good at this point. Coffee too. Please."

I nodded in acknowledgement as we turned to go and said, "I'm really sorry, Maverick."

His stare was on the bed as he dipped his head in response.

Once we slipped from the room, I took Lexi into the living room and turned the television on low to keep her occupied and away from Diggs's room before going in search of the suite's phone.

After ordering enough food and coffee to feed a small army, I slowly looked around the kitchen.

Where the blood and blood-soaked sheets had been hours before, there was just a kitchen.

It was as if nothing had ever happened.

I couldn't wrap my mind around it all. Couldn't believe that it was real even though I'd been standing right there when it happened. Even though we'd just come from Diggs's room.

I shook the memories from my mind and started back to where I'd left Lexi, slowing when I heard hushed whispers.

Nothing I could understand, all of which sounded heated.

Near the door to the suite, Conor, Jess, and Kieran were standing in a circle talking quietly.

As soon as Kieran spotted me, he stopped speaking,

and then Jess glanced at me with a sad smile. Conor was the last to look my way, and once he did, I wished he hadn't.

I was sure that, by the time this was all over, I wouldn't have a heart left because of what this was doing to me.

Because of that hurt I'd put there.

I cleared my throat and gestured behind me. "I, uh, ordered food and coffee for everyone."

Jess was the one to speak. "Thank you."

"Are you okay?" I asked as I started to step away.

Her head tilted to the side, her eyes shifted to Conor.

"From when you nearly fainted," I prompted.

"Oh." A breathless laugh left her. "I was just tired."

I nodded, sure she was lying but positive it wasn't my place to ask anything else.

I didn't feel like I belonged there at all anymore.

Maybe that was what Kieran wanted. For me to suffer and feel wholly unwelcome and unwanted before he allowed me to leave.

As soon as I began walking away, I heard Conor stalking toward me.

Loud, sure, angry.

I stopped, knowing that he was only going to catch up to me in a step or two anyway, and tried to prepare myself for the onslaught that was sure to come.

He grabbed my arm and hauled me against the wall, the action purely Conor in all his gentle strength. Then he dropped his forearms to the wall so I was caged in and lowered his head so his captivating eyes were directly in front of mine.

All rippling muscle and strength.

Fury and pain.

"Why?" It was a demand, and it was filled with a soul-deep ache.

"Conor . . ."

"*Why?*"

"It needed to be done, you know that."

"You leaving?" he said with a harsh laugh. "No. I don't fucking know that."

"I'm ruining everything by being here, by being near you," I explained. "What happened to Diggs wouldn't have happened if they weren't here. What's going on between you and Kieran wouldn't be if it weren't for me. I cannot be the reason for any more pain in your life, Conor."

"You think losing you wouldn't destroy me?" he asked roughly. "You think taking Lexi wouldn't tear out my heart?"

"If we stay, it will only get worse. If I stay and you lose Kieran, you will resent me. I won't do that to you."

"You can't tell me what would happen or what I would think."

"I've never had this, Conor," I whispered, begging him to understand. "I've never had what you all have together. But if I did and someone came and tried to ruin it or steal it from me, I would hate them. And don't tell me I'm wrong either. I can already see it in the way Kieran and Einstein look at me and talk to me. One day, it will make you hate me too."

He leaned forward a fraction so that his nose trailed against mine. "You're wrong."

It was all anger and loathing, and then he was pushing away from the wall and folding his arms across his chest.

"We're right back to having one outcome. One that *you've* decided on. And I can't fucking keep you."

The grief in his last words nearly swallowed me whole.

"I thought you were pulling away," he continued. "I thought Diggs and Kieran and everything from last night scared you, and you were thinking about bailing on *us*. But I thought you would have changed your mind when we woke up or—fuck, that I'd at least have a chance to change it. I didn't know I was going to wake up to an empty room and find you at the door with Lexi and a goddamn bag."

He left without another word, and I knew it was for the best because I was so damn close to breaking.

To telling him that I loved him.

That the only outcome I wanted was one where we were together.

I'd known the minute I saw Conor's fist raised and Kieran's knife pressed to Conor's stomach that this was what I needed to do for Conor—for all of them. I couldn't go back on that.

I finally made my way over to where Lexi was on the sofa bed, lying on her stomach with her feet in the air, smiling at whatever show she was watching as though she didn't have a care in the world.

And I was glad for it.

I wanted her to be happy and carefree.

I didn't want her weighed down with what was happening.

I sat beside her and gripped one of her tiny hands in mine.

"I love you, Momma."

My mouth twitched into a grin. "I love you too, sweet girl. Why don't you tell me about the house from your dreams again?"

I listened to her recount all the details of her house

until a knock on the suite's door sent a shock of fear through me and had me scrambling to sitting.

Lexi rolled to her side to look up at me. "Were your dreams really scary, or only a little scary?"

"I wasn't dreaming," I said on a strained breath as I glanced toward the door. "I wasn't asleep."

Lexi had been telling me about the really, *really* big white and pink flowers out front just before the knock sounded.

I was positive.

But Kieran, Conor, and a hotel staff member were bringing in trays of food and coffee into the kitchen where Maverick and Einstein were sitting, working, and the show on the television wasn't what had been playing when I'd sat next to Lexi.

Assuring me I had, in fact, fallen asleep.

In that moment, I felt like I'd made a crucial mistake in allowing myself to.

Because something about the entire scene felt wrong. Thick, inky tendrils of fear were snaking through my body.

It was a fear I knew.

It was paralyzing and suffocating, and it always, *always* came when I was running out of time before Zachary decided he was done letting me hide.

All I could do was sit there and watch in dread, unable to catch my breath.

Lexi reached for my hand and whispered, "You feel it too?"

"What?" The word came out on a breath, and though I tried to look at her, I couldn't take my eyes off the kitchen area.

"Someone's coming."

I struggled to pull her closer to my side, my movements slow and heavy.

Run.

Run, we need to run.

I slid one of my legs off the sofa bed, looking from the group in the kitchen to the suite door, which was propped open by the door guard.

"Lex—"

"Momma, his smile."

Her words sent fingers as cold as death down my spine, and I shifted my stare back to the hotel worker just as he slanted his head in our direction.

And then he smiled.

Slow.

Knowing.

Cruel . . . so damn cruel.

Conor's name was on the tip of my tongue.

My constricted lungs prepared to scream.

My arm tensed protectively around Lexi, shielding her from whatever might happen, ready to flee with her.

But I never got a chance . . .

Within a second, Kieran turned, arm swinging toward the man as though he were going to backhand him—only to miss. Then a river of blood started streaming from the man's throat, and he began choking and swaying.

Kieran grabbed the man's hair, keeping him still, and spoke words too low for me to hear.

But I'd seen that look.

I'd been on the receiving end of it.

It was harsh and terrifying and made a person feel as if they were staring Death in the face.

For some reason, I couldn't process that the man *was*.

That I was watching a man die.

But I couldn't look away.

Even after Kieran stopped speaking.

Even after he let the man fall to the floor.

Even when Conor began searching the man.

He's dead. There's a dead man on the floor. He's dead.

Why can't I look away?

I jumped and sucked in a sharp breath when Jess appeared beside me, her hand on my shoulder.

"It's okay," she said before I'd even calmed.

"He's coming."

Her head shook as understanding filled her features. "You should take Lexi to another room."

"I can—you don't understand. He's coming." My voice trembled with fear as old memories haunted me.

"You're going to be fine."

"I can feel it." In my head, it was as if I'd screamed the words, when, in reality, they were nothing more than a strangled, whispered claim.

I saw the moment her thoughts changed.

When she stopped thinking I was only rattled over what had just happened and truly believed—*knew*—that Zachary was coming.

Her eyes trailed toward the kitchen before she shifted her head that way. "We won't let anything happen to you," she said softly and then turned and made her way over to Kieran.

For the first time, I wasn't comforted by Jess's words.

It wasn't that I didn't think they would try, it was that I was understanding more and more that Zachary would never let me just walk away. And regardless of their presence, he could still get to me.

The ring.

The notes.

This man.

I realized then not one of them had shown any form of surprise. No one had been shocked or even moved when Kieran turned and slit the staff member's throat.

Jess had been near Lexi and me . . . waiting.

They'd known he was someone bad all along.

I was still dissecting that realization when Jess turned and gestured to where Lexi was—head buried in the bed. "Get her in another room."

Numbly, I did as she said, gripping Lexi's hand and keeping her head turned away as I tugged her across the bed, halting as that familiar ice-cold terror gripped me.

Conor was standing over the body, chest rising and falling heavily, eyes on the stack of papers in his hands.

On the back of the page there were big, bold words.

LET'S
PLAY
A
GAME.

Oh God.

Once Lexi's feet were on the floor, Conor lifted his head.

The look on his face made me want to tear out the remains of my heart.

There wasn't anger or betrayal or pain . . . he was

staring at me as if I was nothing and meant nothing to him.

Just *nothing*.

At least with the hurt, there was still the emotion that reminded me it had been real while it lasted.

He slammed the papers against Kieran's chest, blinked slowly once . . . then twice as he shook his head and walked away.

And I couldn't move.

I wanted to go after him.

I knew I needed to get Lexi away, that we needed to get away from the room where Kieran had just killed someone.

Yet, I couldn't move as I watched Kieran flip from one page to the next. Because I knew—I somehow *knew*—those papers had everything to do with me.

Just as I knew this game was meant for *me*.

I could practically hear Zachary calling my name down the halls of our home in that chilling, monstrous voice.

Could hear him slamming his hand against the wall, letting me know he was coming closer.

"*Maverick*." Conor's yell sent everyone except for Kieran into action.

Maverick and Einstein nearly fell out of their chairs trying to get out of them, and then they were running in the direction Conor had gone—to Diggs's room.

I rocked forward on instinct—partly because I wanted to know what had happened and partly because it was an automatic response to Conor's voice.

Jess started that way before hesitating and looking to Kieran and then us. But even in her hesitation, her feet continued in small steps toward the room the others had disappeared into, as if she were being pulled in three directions.

Diggs's room.

Staying with her husband.

Or coming back to us.

And Lexi? Lexi was pulling on my hand, tugging me away from it all, softly whispering my name. The terror and alarm in that soft voice fueled my own.

I dropped in front of her when Jess started jogging toward Diggs's room and hurried to whisper, "Go to our room and shut the door and hide. Don't come out for anything, understand?"

"But, Momma, I feel it." Pure fear filled her eyes. "Someone's coming. You have to hide too. You have to get Mr. Conor and hide."

"I will," I assured her. "But please go, and remember not to come out until I tell you to."

She threw her arms around my neck, squeezing me tightly for a few moments before taking off for our bedroom.

As soon as she took off, I stood and found Kieran closing in on me.

Eyes cold.

Face unreadable.

"Tell me just how deep this went."

I blinked quickly, trying to understand. "I don't know what you mean."

"This plan of yours." He flipped open the papers but didn't look at them. "You thought we dealt in human trafficking?"

It felt like someone knocked my legs out from under me.

"That we were going to take you and your daughter and sell you off?"

My chest pitched as I struggled to suck in oxygen.

The room spun.

"You were communicating with us . . . why?" It was a demand, pure, simple, and filled with grit. "To keep us distracted while your husband moved in?"

"No," I breathed. "I didn't know."

"To bring the rest of us here and into his fucked-up game?"

"It wasn't—I didn't know," I cried out.

He flung the papers at me, letting them scatter and fall where they may around my feet.

Emails.

Dozens upon dozens of emails from Zachary to me, beginning after he'd moved Lexi and me into a motel.

Him telling me when to email Einstein and what to say in them, word for word.

Coaching me on what to say if Einstein forced me into another call.

How to make it convincing, to make sure ARCK would believe my story because they were smart in their *game*.

Telling me they would know if I was playing them, that they wouldn't fall into the trap. And we needed to catch the people who had stolen and sold Vero.

How the FBI agents would watch over us. How we would be safe. That he would never let the ARCK people get anywhere near me.

Me. Never Lexi.

Zachary never mentioned her other than to order me to tell Einstein about her.

And not one of my responses was there that I could see.

Where I'd demanded to know why he'd taken us to a motel and had ordered the agents not to let us leave.

Where I'd screamed at him for getting Lexi involved—for putting us up as bait when that had never been part of the plan. Where I'd begged and *begged* to know if they were closer to finding Vero. That I was afraid for our lives and couldn't sleep. Where I'd sobbed to him because I was terrified each email I sent the ARCK people to come *save* us brought them closer to coming to *steal* us.

All things he'd never acknowledged anyway.

One of the pages near my feet was the last email I received a handful of days before Conor broke into my hotel room. At the bottom of the page, in Zachary's perfectly masculine scrawl, was a handwritten note that changed everything.

> She knows her place and plays her part well.

My head shook wildly as my throat grew thick with grief and regret. "I didn't know, I didn't *know*," I cried out. "He told me you kidnapped and sold Vero. He said they were going to get her back—I didn't know. I didn't know he was near all of you in North Carolina! I thought they were looking for her. I was supposed to get some or all of you here so you could be arrested—that was all I knew."

"We needed to know everything," he said firmly, bringing up our conversation from earlier. "You should have told us this from the beginning."

"All I knew were lies, it wouldn't have changed

anything," I yelled. "I thought Conor was coming to take us, and then my world was rocked and rocked and rocked, and I went from not knowing what to believe to realizing my entire life was a lie. Everything Zachary had told me was a lie, and everything I had done inadvertently helped him get Einstein. How was I supposed to tell you that? How was I supposed to tell you that I had tricked you into coming here when it ended up being a blessing because it was the only way I could've ever gotten away from Zachary?"

Those cold eyes stayed narrowed on me before he simply said, "You say it."

A disbelieving laugh tumbled from my mouth. "None of you trusted me anyway. If I had said that, I—God, I can't begin to imagine what would've happened."

He shrugged as he folded his arms across his chest and then glanced to the empty kitchen. "It would've looked something like this."

With that, he turned and started toward Diggs's room.

"Kieran, someone is coming," I called out before he could get far.

"Is that something you know?" he asked without turning around, his tone all challenge.

"I have this feeling—I *know* this feeling."

I wasn't sure what I expected when he looked at me, but it wasn't the hardened understanding. "Guilt. Abandonment. Regret. Yeah, we've all felt that at some point." He nodded to the body lying a few feet from him. "Someone did come, if you forgot."

"That isn't—*no*. Tell Conor," I begged when he stalked away, hurrying to follow when he didn't stop. "Tell Conor that Lexi can feel it."

If there were any chance of Conor believing anything, it would be Lexi's intuition.

I stood there just outside the kitchen, wavering over what to do and where to go.

I wanted to continue following Kieran.

I wanted to go to Conor myself—God, what I wanted was to go back before I'd ever hurt him and do everything differently.

But I couldn't do any of that. Not only was I sure I wasn't welcome in that room but I also didn't want to be any farther from Lexi than I was at that moment.

Because that feeling Kieran so carelessly brushed aside was growing stronger and stronger. Just as the need to take Lexi and run far from here was.

My chest rose and fell in short, sharp bursts.

My lungs weren't pulling in the oxygen I needed.

My body felt like it was made of lead, and my legs felt boneless.

I rocked toward the room once again and swayed in my indecision, knowing with every ounce of me that if we didn't get out then, we wouldn't get out at all.

I turned, my movements weighed down by that crippling, consuming fear, and I stumbled into arms I knew well.

A hand slammed over my mouth, digging hard into my cheeks and twisting me so my back was resting against him.

Something pierced my neck, and I cried out, the sound muffled and muted by his hand.

I struggled, my mind racing, trying to grab ahold of anything Conor had taught me.

Lips met my ear. "Let's play a game."

Thirty-Eight

Conor

"Do you feel sick?" Einstein asked. "Can you tell us exactly where you hurt?"

Diggs slanted a glare at her before letting his eyelids drift shut. "Hungry as fuck."

"Okay, well you can't eat right now," she said in that matter-of-fact tone of hers, but her lips were curling into a smile again.

They had been ever since I'd called her and Maverick in there.

Diggs took quick, shallow breaths for a while before saying, "What's the point of being laid up if I'm not getting laid?"

"I think he's fine," Maverick said with a roll of his eyes.

Diggs's mouth twitched, but the action looked weak and forced. "I meant fed."

"When more time has passed," Einstein assured him. "When we have a better idea of what's happening."

A pained grunt escaped him. "If you weren't gonna feed me when I woke up, you shoulda let me die."

"Keep talking, I'm gonna start wondering why we didn't," Maverick said, the words all tease.

Diggs's eyelids suddenly popped open, only to shut almost entirely again. "Shit. Just realized we weren't home." He searched the room before resting his head against the pillow with a heaved breath. "Where are Baby Mini and Baby Mama?"

The storm of emotions that ripped through me at the mention of Sutton could have brought me to my knees.

Everything thundering and clashing so powerfully that I couldn't pinpoint one to focus on before another one took over.

And all of it fucking hurt.

I looked up when I felt eyes on me and realized everyone but Kieran was watching me expectantly.

Jess was staring at me with a somber expression as Kieran whispered to her, which he had been doing since he'd come into the room a couple minutes before.

"I don't know where they are," I finally said.

"She's probably with Lexi in their room," Jess said, clearing her throat and shifting away from Kieran.

"That's good," Diggs mumbled. "Keep Baby Mini away from this mess."

Maverick huffed. "Man, she's already been in to talk to you like the bravest little rebel there ever was."

A startled laugh left Diggs and swiftly turned into a hiss.

I exhaled slowly when Kieran came to stand next to me. "This what you wanted?"

"For you? Fuck, you think I wanted you to be in pain?" He settled against the wall next to me, arms folded over his chest. "For the case? Yeah. It's what I wanted."

Despite the pain and anger and betrayal, a shock of fear went through me, and it was only made worse by the fact that he'd been the last one through the door.

I stayed unmoving, staring at the twins and Einstein talking, when I asked, "What did you do?"

"Nothing."

"What are you going to do?"

"After everything this morning, would you still try to stop me?"

"With my last breath." My response was immediate and sure. I would do anything to protect Sutton. Always.

"Nothing," Kieran answered after a while. "I know what she was hiding now. She admitted this morning there were things she hadn't told us—said she *hadn't* because it wouldn't have changed anything. She was right. By the time she found out the truth about her husband, it wouldn't have changed anything. Doesn't mean she shouldn't have told us."

"Not that I know why the hell the two of you were talking in the first place, but you said that as if all the shit in those emails didn't matter. Like the emails shouldn't be your one reason not to trust her."

"Never said they don't matter. I said she told me what I needed to know."

"And you believe her . . . now. After everything."

"She told me at her breaking point." He pushed from

the wall and sent me a slow, cold look when I slammed a hand onto his chest, keeping him in place.

"You said you didn't do anything."

"I didn't." He shoved my hand away and turned so he was facing me. "*You* are her breaking point. Seeing you in pain. Seeing the way she hurt you. That was what it took for her to start talking."

I shoved down the hope that sparked in my chest before it could build.

It didn't make a difference.

It didn't change that I'd found her trying to leave an hour after I'd told her I loved her. It didn't change that she'd been in on this with Zachary, screwing us over and putting us at risk.

Kieran nodded toward the doorway and started that way. "We have a body to get rid of."

I dragged my hands through my hair as I pushed from the wall. "Let's do this fast, I need sleep. I only got about twenty minutes earlier."

I grabbed the pile of sheets leftover from the night before and followed Kieran into the kitchen.

The man on the floor had set off Einstein's facial recognition, which could have been explained or possibly dismissed had he worked at the hotel.

He didn't.

It was careless compared to everything else we'd seen from the Tennessee Gentlemen, but maybe that was part of their game.

Give us something easy to make us feel like we had a win, only to hit again once we started to let our guard down.

I set all but one of the sheets onto the table and glanced

at the resort's camera feed on Einstein's laptop, not that I knew what I was looking for. "This isn't going to be easy in the middle of the morning at a resort," I said as I turned back to the body, my eyes catching on the uneaten food.

Sutton was the one who ordered it all.

Breakfast was Lexi's favorite. She wouldn't have missed it—especially after promising Diggs to eat for him.

"We'll just get the body prepped and put away and then get rid of it tonight."

"Where are Sutton and Lexi?"

"Sutton sent Lexi to their room to hide." He snatched the sheet from me and started unfolding it. "Sutton was upset, said it felt like someone was coming."

I looked in the direction of girls' room.

My heart kicked up in pace.

"Sounded like bullshit to keep us around her after what had just happened," he continued. "Wanted me to tell you that Lexi could feel it."

"Why didn't you?"

Kieran stopped what he was doing to glance at me, eyebrows lifted in confusion. When he registered my growing alarm, his brow lowered and drew together.

I took a step forward and looked around for anything out of place, trying to decide if the pressure on my chest was from the day and what Kieran had just told me or a threat I couldn't see.

"Been around enough people who have fucked up," Kieran murmured, already slipping blades out of his pockets. "Sounded like she was reaching because she knew she had." His head tilted, listening for something I couldn't hear.

His eyes met mine for a brief second as he passed me,

his head moving in brief dismissal. Even still, the blades stayed in his hands as he rounded the corner out of the kitchen without making a sound.

I didn't wait for him to confirm there was nothing.

Once was enough.

I charged across the suite, looking for any sign of the girls who'd stolen my heart.

"The door's shut," Kieran called out when I was halfway there.

I slowed, barely giving him a glance, but I stopped completely when I found him in front of the main door to the suite.

"Did you close this?" he asked, his tone slow and careful and not at all Kieran.

"No."

"It was left propped open when the food was being delivered. I meant to have Jessica close it."

Meant to.

Before everything had gone to hell with a stack of printed-out emails.

Shit.

I ran for the girls' room, yelling for Sutton as I did. My stomach dropped when I threw open their door and found the bedroom empty.

"*Sutton.*" I hurried through the room, only pausing long enough to see she wasn't in the bathroom before running out.

Kieran was coming down the stairs as I did.

Another faint shake of his head, and I stumbled.

I shot a hand out to the railing to catch myself and dragged in short, thin breaths.

"You left them alone," I sneered. "You left her alone

when she'd already tried to leave today. When she fucking *told you* someone was coming. You should've known they were going to run."

"It hasn't been long. She couldn't have gotten far . . ."

I looked at him when his words slowed and trailed off and then turned to follow his line of sight into the girls' bedroom.

He stepped forward and pointed toward the bed, knife still pressed flat to his palm, ready to use. "That's the bag she had when they were leaving."

Sutton's name scraped up my throat in a whisper of denial at the same moment Kieran slipped past me and darted across the suite, yelling for Einstein.

I walked slowly into the room, searching everything.

Every bag.

Every piece of clothing.

The way the bed looked.

It was all so normal, nothing looked out of place or missing.

Except for them.

I shoved Kieran's arm away when he grabbed my shoulder.

"Einstein's reviewing the camera feed. We'll know what happened soon."

"You shouldn't have left her alone," I ground out, my voice an agonized growl. "They shouldn't have been alone." My head snapped up, and I turned in a tight circle. *"Lexi."*

"We'll find—"

I shot a hand out toward him, silently telling him to stop talking, and continued turning in a circle, stare falling on every part of the room.

"You said she sent Lexi to hide. *Hide*, right?"

He gave a confirming grunt.

"Then she's hiding," I said softly. "Lexi, can you come out?"

No response.

But I felt it in my soul that she was somewhere in there, hiding because her mom told her to.

"Lex, it's really important that you come out. Kieran's with me, but he'll leave if you want him to."

Nothing.

"Leave."

Kieran blew out a slow breath before backing out of the room.

"Lexi, please."

Please be here.

Please come out.

Please be okay.

A few seconds later, shuffling sounded in the bathroom, and then she appeared in the doorway.

A strangled breath punched from my lungs.

Relief filled me, intense and profound.

I dropped to my knees when she ran at me, tears streaking her cheeks, and caught her in my arms.

"Momma was supposed to hide. She was supposed to get you and hide. And I don't think she's hiding," she cried. "It was like in my dreams. My bad dreams. Someone was coming, and I could feel it, and it was scary. And I don't feel it anymore."

Shit.

Shit, shit, shit.

I'd known.

As soon as Kieran had pointed out the bag, I'd known.

Lexi saw things other people didn't. Felt things others

couldn't. And everything she was saying only confirmed the horrifying reality I was already living in.

"You trust me, Lex?"

She nodded against my shoulder, another sob escaping her.

"I will bring your mom back to you. I will not stop until you're together, understand?"

She leaned away, her face scrunched in an attempt to keep from crying. "Promise, promise?"

"Promise, promise."

She wiped hastily at her face before throwing her arms around my neck again. "I'm trying to be brave for Momma, but I still cried."

"Bravest girl I know," I whispered and squeezed her tighter, holding her for a few moments. When I released her, I waited until she was looking at me before I spoke. "I'm probably going to leave you here with some of my friends when I go get your mom—Einstein at least. You gonna be okay with that?"

Lexi's stare fell to the floor, unease bled from her. "Will my Diggs be here?"

"Hell yeah, and he'll need you to keep him company because he's awake."

She tried to fight a smile, but it still crept across her lips. With a sigh and a roll of her eyes, she said, "I guess I can do that."

I flicked her forehead. "Don't roll your eyes."

Her eyes watered all over again and then she was launching herself at me. "Mr. Conor . . . you're my favorite."

Fuck.

I tightened my hold on her.

We needed to go.

We needed to act fast.

But this moment with Lexi meant the goddamn world to me. I would've stopped time for this hug and to hear those words. "You're my favorite too, Lex."

I looked up when Kieran entered the doorway, a fierce and determined look in his eyes that I knew well.

"Maverick and I are ready," he murmured. "We need to move now."

I nodded and set Lexi back on her feet. "Remember what I said, okay? I need you to go see Diggs, but you can't forget he's hurt. Be gentle. I'll be back soon."

As soon as she was running from the room, I stood and hurried for my bag. "What happened?"

"Einstein's in the traffic system, checking the cameras to see where they went."

They not *she*.

My jaw clenched, and my hands curled into fists before I continued arming myself. "What. Happened?"

"Zachary," he said after a moment. "Walked in and right back out with her."

My body was trembling, and my breathing was rough. "That son of a bitch came to us. He was in here, and none of us even noticed. None of us were protecting her."

"He had to have known," Kieran said, his tone taking on that lethal warning I'd known most of my life. "We'll get her back, and he will pay for everything."

I was already stalking toward the door as I finished loading my last gun. "Slowly. I want him to pay slowly."

Thirty-Nine

Sutton

Thud.

My heavy eyelids blinked open.

The room spun around me and my stomach clenched uneasily.

Thud.

A weak groan slid up my throat. It was an effort to press my hands to the bed and an even bigger one to try to push my heavy body up, a feat that was almost too much for my muscles.

Oh God, what is that smell?

Something was poking at my brain.

Trying to force me to remember.

To see.

To run.

Telling me that something wasn't right.

Thud.

What the hell was that sound? Why did my entire body react to it?

My chest pitched.

My lungs ached from holding my breath.

A chill raced down my spine.

I know that sound. I know that sound. I know that sound...

I managed to drag my legs off the bed and bend to rest my arms on my thighs, already exhausted from the little movements I'd made. I tugged absentmindedly at the expensive material resting on my thighs.

What am I wearing?

I tried to look down, to look at myself, but found my attention being pulled to the bedside table instead.

Fear crashed over me like a tidal wave, dragging me under its weight and rolling me in its current and paralyzing my ability to draw a deep breath.

It was a picture of Lexi and me from last fall. I'd taken her to a pumpkin patch to get away from Zachary. I'd been in such a rush to get us out of the house that she had looked unkempt and mismatched and so completely imperfect that she'd been so utterly *perfect*.

It was my favorite.

Zachary hated it.

My heart raced harder and harder with each new thing my eyes landed upon.

The lamp Zachary thought was too big.

The painting he always said didn't match the room.

The nightstand he didn't like the stain of.

They were mine—they were *all* mine.

I'd spent time picking them out when we'd built our house.

I nearly fell when I pushed to my feet, my legs still not working how I needed them to.

My bed, my room, my cocktail dress covering my body—mine, mine, mine.

Thud.

I jolted away from the sound and the wall, crashing against the bed.

Zachary.

There.

Directly on the opposite side of the wall.

I gripped my head, trying to force the spinning to stop, and flinched when another thud sounded in the same place.

He wasn't moving.

He was playing with me.

God, that smell.

It was making my stomach clench and churn and had bile rising in my throat.

I turned, trying to think of where to go and what to do, and my scream tore through the room.

On the opposite side of the bed, the word *"WHORE"* was written in dirty rust-colored letters that ran in a vertical line from the pillow to the footboard.

On the wall opposite me, lined up and piled three high, were nine bodies.

The men were all pale in an unnatural way.

Glazed, clouded eyes were open wide and staring at the ceiling or in my direction.

Dark, dried blood spilled from wounds and was smeared against notes pinned to the wall they were up against.

Let's play a game.
Let's play a game.
Let's play a game.

Different sized papers and fonts, over and over until the last.

The paper on the bottommost corner had one word: SUTTON.

Written in that same dirty rust color that stained the bed.

Blood.

It was written in blood.

I dropped to my knees, my empty stomach heaving, vainly trying to reject anything.

Thud.

I wasn't sure if I whimpered or cried out . . . if I was more disturbed or afraid.

It was as if that single sound—one, lone strike of knuckles against drywall—drove away everything I thought I knew and only left one truth: this wasn't like our other games.

"Sutton."

My body convulsed at that evil, sadistic tone.

I tried to push to my feet, but my body refused to cooperate, betraying me when I needed it most.

Thud.

I crawled to the bed and pulled myself up, trying to breathe through my mouth and look anywhere but at the bodies and eyes and blood as I thought of where to go. Thought of a weapon.

Run.

Hide.

Make him come to me.

I made my way to the bathroom, my progress slow . . . so pathetically slow that I wanted to scream but swallowed it back. Finally, my toes touched the cold tiles, and I all but lunged for the vanity, searching wildly through my drawers for something, anything I could use as a weapon. There was nothing.

The closet . . .

I twisted, almost tripped over my own feet, and scrambled to the double doors.

When I yanked the doors open, I *did* fall.

A horrified scream *did* rip from my lungs.

Time seemed to move in slow motion as I crawled backward, trying to get away from what was in front of me.

Denial filled me as quickly as my grief washed it away.

I didn't realize I was screaming Garret's name until the world seemed to catch up with alarming clarity.

"*Garret!*"

I cried out in pain and hatred and sorrow when I was yanked from the floor by my hair.

"Nice touch, if you ask me," Zachary said with a soft, dark laugh.

I twisted in his hold and swung for him as something pierced my neck. I staggered away, only to be pulled back into his arms.

"I always loved you in this dress." His words ended on a roar when I reached for his face and dragged my nails down it with all the remaining strength I had.

"*You fucking bitch!*"

His hold disappeared.

My body felt like dead weight.

My veins filled with fire and ice.

I couldn't figure out when I'd fallen to the floor or how to get up.

Couldn't figure out how to make my limbs move the way I needed them to.

How to get away from Zachary's enraged face as it dominated my field of vision.

How to escape the drip, drip, drip, of his blood as it fell from his chin.

"Try to stay awake, you're going to enjoy every minute of this."

He gripped my jaw and shoved my head to the side so I was staring at where Garret hung in my closet.

Staring at a nightmare.

My vision blurred, making it look like he was swinging and coming closer all at once.

"He never stopped wanting you. Wanting what was mine. How fucking poetic that they'll find him here, unable to continue living without you." Zachary trailed his nose up the side of my neck, breathing me in. "That is what happens to people who touch what belongs to me. If you think I don't know about you letting that piece of shit fuck you, you're wrong. I'm going to enjoy killing him."

Tears clouded my vision and quickly fell as he grabbed my legs and began dragging me toward the bedroom.

I needed to turn.

To roll over.

To stop him from taking me wherever he was.

But my body was so heavy and warm that all I could manage was a weak, mumbled cry of frustration as I tried to fight.

"We had a plan. We had a goal in mind," he growled once he had me on the bed. He dragged his hand over his face, smearing the blood there and making it look as if he were wearing a mask. "That plan was never for you to actually leave me. That plan was never to make me look like an idiot. That plan was never to have you forget your place and spread your legs like a goddamn whore."

He forced my legs apart and shoved his hand against the apex of my thighs, forcing the tears to come faster.

"The minute you forgot who you belonged to was the minute all *my* plans changed." With his free hand, he roughly shoved my dress up, bunching it around my hips. "I was coming for you. I was going to save you. I have given you the fucking world, and *this is how you repay me?*"

My lips moved in a useless attempt to yell at him, to beg him to stop.

His hand closed around my throat before raking down my chest. The clawed movement both hurt and, somehow, felt like nothing at all. As if it wasn't happening to *my* body. "Your mouth really was only good for one thing, and it wasn't talking."

Disappear, disappear . . . please, God, let me disappear.

"I'm going to make you remember who you belong to. I'm going to make you regret ever tasting someone else's name. Make you wish you could scream mine. Wish you could come crawling back to me like a bitch. Then, when you're still unable to move, unable to speak, I'm going to bury you alive. When that bastard comes for you, and we both know he will, I'm going to watch him find you before I take his life."

A sob stuck in my throat, and I struggled to breathe around it.

I struggled to do *anything*, but my body had stopped responding to me.

My vision darkened, and my eyelids grew heavy.

Too heavy.

I needed to stay awake. I needed to move. I needed to fight.

He bent and pressed his mouth to mine in a long, slow kiss, biting at my lips in a way that made me feel disgusting and unclean.

"Let's play a game," he whispered, his voice distorted and distant. "How long before I accidentally kill you?"

Forty

Conor

He'd taken her back to their goddamn house.

For Sutton, I knew it was a mind game.

For us, it felt like a setup. It was too simple. We'd been searching for him, monitoring this house and other Tennessee Gentlemen houses, and there hadn't been a sign of him.

Yet, that was where he'd led us.

Every step felt as if it could be the last.

Every door opened in their house held the potential for there to be a trap on the other side.

With each cleared room, the possibility grew even higher, and the tension and unease surrounding Maverick, Kieran, and me grew with it.

When we reached the room that had Zachary's subdued voice coming from it, Maverick and I waited by the doorway while Kieran swiftly and silently cleared the rest of the rooms on the floor.

I looked to Maverick, who was on the opposite side of the doorframe from me, his head angled as he listened intently, and mouthed, *Can you see her?*

He glanced through the crack in the door, shaking his head as he did. Pressing his hand to the wood, he searched every part of the crack for any sign he was about to set something off before slowly nudging the door wider.

The dark look that passed over Maverick's face was answer enough, but he still mouthed, *She's there.*

"I'm going to make you remember who you belong to," Zachary seethed. "I'm going to make you regret ever tasting someone else's name. Make you wish you could scream mine. Wish you could come crawling back to me like a bitch."

I rocked forward, body tense and blood boiling, but Kieran appeared beside me and stopped me.

"Clear," he murmured.

Maverick checked the door once again before moving to my side. "Sutton's on the bed, Zachary's leaning over her."

Kieran released a slow breath before that cold, murderous look filled his eyes. He grabbed another blade . . . and then another, gripping three in his left hand and loosely holding one in his right. "Conor, get Sutton. Maverick, look for threats. Leave Zachary for—"

Maverick pressed a hand against Kieran's chest and ignored the dark warning that bled from him. "He's mine."

Kieran pushed Maverick's hand aside. "Look for threats," he repeated slowly. "I'll get Zachary away from Sutton."

He didn't wait for confirmation or another argument

before he slipped past Maverick and settled against the other side of the threshold, pressing against the door. Eyes searching and head tilted as he listened, waiting for the other shoe to drop the way we had since we'd pulled up to this house.

When the door was open enough for Kieran to slip through, Zachary's voice filtered into the hall. "Let's play a game. How long before I accidentally kill you?"

A cold, vicious smile tugged at Kieran's mouth. "Good question."

Before the words finished leaving his lips, he threw a knife and then another, stalking into the room as he did. Maverick and I were on his heels, guns up as we cut in different directions.

Zachary's agonized roar filled the space and made my heart pound.

I'd been waiting for this moment.

For that sound.

I rushed for Sutton, my stare darting between her and the pile of bodies across the room as I did.

Each glance in her direction grew longer and longer because something wasn't right. She wasn't moving. She wasn't looking at me or anyone. She wasn't doing anything.

Kieran gripped one of the hilts sticking out of Zachary's back and used it to force the man away from Sutton and deeper into the room.

The sick bastard was laughing manically, as if he wasn't about to die.

I holstered my gun, panic swirling through my body and forming a vice around my chest when I reached the bed.

There was blood smeared across Sutton's face and neck and down her chest.

I grabbed her wrist and curled my other hand around her cheek, turning her head toward me, and nearly thanked God aloud when her eyelids opened, slow and heavy.

"Sutton?" Fear laced my voice when her eyes shut and her head rocked against the pillow. I gripped her wrist tighter, silently pleading with my touch alone for that pulse to stay steady. "Come on, Sutton, wake up."

I quickly ran my hands over her, searching for injuries, and stilled when I saw the tiny trickle of blood on the side of her neck, separate from the smearing. The puncture that it came from.

"Fuck."

"*You!*"

I looked up at Zachary's voice.

He was staring directly at me from across the room. Face streaked with blood, making him look crazed.

Kieran was in front of him, arms hanging loosely at his sides, knives at the ready.

Maverick had a gun trained on him, his rifle slung behind his back.

"I'll fucking kill you for touching what belongs to me," Zachary sneered. Everything was said with a hint of that laughter. Everything was coated in pain and broken up with choppy breaths.

"What did you do to her?" I demanded, my body torn between helping Sutton and going after the man I'd fantasized about killing.

He smiled. The action slow and pained. "She's mine. Mine to fuck. Mine to command. Mine to decide when she's no longer needed."

"The hell did you do to her?" I roared.

Another manic laugh, this one low and taunting.

"Every time you touched her, I was there, in the back of her mind," he raged. "I'll always be there. She knows her place. She knows who she belongs to." The smile slipped from his bloodied face. "And that isn't you."

He tried to charge toward the bed, but had only made it a step when a gunshot tore through the room.

Zachary fell to the floor, yelling incoherently as he reached for his knee, where blood was rapidly staining the fabric of his pants.

"That was for Sutton," Maverick seethed. He stepped forward and shot him in the shoulder. "That was for my brother."

My body tensed as my blood roared, raging for me to take my claim in this kill but knowing Maverick needed this. Needed this retribution for Einstein, and I had to let him have it.

Sutton was my priority.

I could feel her racing heart.

And I knew getting her away from this was more important than any stake I wanted to claim.

I pulled her limp body into my arms and held her close. "You're gonna be okay."

Maverick's voice was savage when he growled, "And this is for my girl."

I tucked Sutton's head into the crook of my neck and hurried for the door as shots rang out, one after another as Maverick emptied his magazine into the man. As I reached the top of the steps, I heard the echoing click of his gun, and pulled Sutton impossibly closer as I rushed down the stairs and pushed through the front doors.

And came to a jarring stop.

There were two men leaning against Kieran's car.

One holding a shotgun.

The other loosely holding a handgun in front of him.

If I hadn't spent so much time researching them, I wouldn't have known the first was Aaron Thornton and the second was Jason Woods.

That left Garret Vaughn somewhere, still unaccounted for.

And since I'd have to drop Sutton to reach for any of my guns, I knew I didn't have a chance in hell at beating them to the trigger.

"Imagine our surprise when we come looking for one man but found a different one stealing yet another one of our women," Jason called out, all mocking contempt.

"When the women ask for help to get away, I don't consider that stealing," I shot back, making sure my voice was loud enough for Kieran and Maverick to hear, but not so loud it would give me away to the men in front of me.

"Things are done a certain way," Jason shouted. "That isn't for you to step in and fuck up. *Vero* wasn't yours to decide what to do with."

"Drugging your wives to keep them with you is that certain way?" I let my gaze dart around, looking for the last member of their generation, then narrowed my glare on them when Aaron laughed. "What did Zachary give her?"

He shrugged. "Wouldn't know."

Jason smiled, slow and knowing, and glanced to Aaron. "Depends on which time you're asking about."

My teeth clenched. My grip on Sutton tightened. "Let's start with now and work back."

He racked the slide on his gun. "It's just a little something to keep her obedient and submissive until she remembers her place. If she's out cold, he might've given her a tad too much."

"I'll fucking kill you."

"I'm not the one who said it," Jason said, armed hand raised. "From the gunshots we heard, I'm guessing you already killed the man you want dead. Makes our job easier since there are rules we're supposed to follow—even if Zachary already broke them."

"Rules," I stated dully when Aaron lifted the shotgun so it was aimed at me. Inside, my mind was racing, trying to figure out how fast I could grab one of my guns and shoot.

How to lessen any of the impact on Sutton.

"Remaining unknown, for one. Considering you're here . . ." Jason said thoughtfully.

"No TenGen on TenGen murders," Aaron added. "He was too jealous for that . . . and a little too crazy, as I'm sure you noticed."

"The torture and fatal games tipped me off."

"With your little hacker friend?" Aaron laughed. "Those were my idea."

"Oh." Jason drew out the word and then sucked in a sharp breath through his teeth. "Looks like that made you angry. I'll make you a deal, give us Sutton, and we'll pretend nothing ever happened. And by nothing, I mean what Thornton said."

"You've lost your goddamn mind if you think I'm letting her go," I ground out.

But both men had guns aimed at Sutton and me, and I had a sinking feeling they wouldn't hesitate to shoot her just to prevent me from leaving with her.

"No, you're mistaking us for Larson," Jason continued.

"We're the normal ones. But I will tell you it can very quickly get worse for you and all the friends you brought to Tennessee if you don't hand her over. As I said, things are done a certain way, and the girl in your arms is TenGen property. Ours to deal with . . ." His mouth stretched into a wry grin. "However we see fit."

"Try to take her," I said, my tone pure challenge. "I'll kill you with my bare hands."

Aaron racked the shotgun. "With pleasure."

A quick burst of fire shattered the morning air, coming from above me.

I turned, shielding Sutton from the repercussions of that spray, but no return fire ever came.

"Garret Vaughn," I said to Kieran as he stalked out of the house. "He has to be here somewhere."

"Upstairs. Dead." He continued toward the men and bent over their bodies, slitting their throats for good measure.

When he was straightening, he paused for all of a second before turning and storming toward the house again, wrath and the promise of death pouring from him.

"I'm gonna kill him." I was about to ask who when he pointed straight ahead, blood-covered blade in hand, and bit out, "You shot my car."

"I might've grazed it," Maverick admitted as he jogged outside.

"You shot my fucking car."

"We don't have time for this," I snapped. "We need to get Sutton back to the hotel. I don't know what Zachary gave her."

Kieran was murmuring threats as I hurried to the car, and he still looked as if he were contemplating how he was going to kill Maverick when he slid into the driver's seat.

When Maverick finally got into the car, he turned in the seat and gave me an annoyed look. "I grazed the trunk."

"I don't care."

He nodded, his eyes quickly darting over Sutton's still body. "That her blood or Zachary's?"

"After seeing his face, I'm thinking most of it is his."

I hated that there was any on her at all. I wanted to wash it away. I wanted to go back and make sure she'd never been alone so I could've prevented this from happening at all.

But I was so fucking proud of her.

"Think he made her drink something?"

My head slanted negatively. "Injection. *Two*," I added, thinking about the spot I'd seen on the opposite side of her neck when getting in the car. "Must have been how he got her out of the suite without us hearing anything."

Something haunting flashed across his face, and I knew he was thinking about Einstein—how Zachary had drugged her over and over again before he'd ever tried to kill her. He cleared his throat and reached back to grip my shoulder. "If he liked games, then he liked patterns. He wasn't drugging her to kill her. She'll be okay."

I nodded, only because I needed it to be true, and held her closer. "I'm sorry I wasn't there," I whispered softly against the crown of her head. "I'm sorry I left you alone. I'm sorry I let him near you when I swore I never would."

I brought my hand up to cradle her face and passed my thumb across her full mouth.

"You should know, Lexi is safe. She's keeping Diggs company and waiting for you to come back, being brave for you. When you wake up, you can tell her that she'll never have to be afraid of Zachary or his bad-man's smile again."

I studied her face as unspoken words gathered on my tongue, begging to be said.

Words I couldn't give voice to.

Not in that moment, maybe not ever again.

You should know that I still love you.

I will always love you.

Forty-One

Conor

"You'd think they like staring at their money or some shit," Maverick muttered.

I huffed, letting my stare drift along the walls of the Tennessee Gentlemen's meeting room.

The walls were covered in frames, and each frame held fifty thousand dollars' worth of thousand dollar bills. The bills looked to be in perfect condition, as if the Tennessee Gentlemen started hoarding them long before they'd gone out of circulation.

I'd thought Mickey's penchant for displaying his wealth was bad when he was alive, but these assholes put him to shame.

After making another pass around the room with my eyes alone, I focused on the wide doors, ready for what came next to begin.

Ready to close out this goddamn case.

By the time we'd gotten back to the resort that morning, Einstein had news for us.

Zachary and two other men had arrived at the resort a few hours after we'd made it back from the guesthouse ambush in the early hours of the morning.

Zachary had walked into the hotel, took an elevator up to our floor, and entered a room across the hall and two down from ours. From the way he had smiled at cameras as he went, he'd known two things: at least one of us had been badly injured—if not worse—and the person we had watching the camera feeds was too distracted to monitor the footage.

Cocky son of a bitch.

The only plus for us was Zachary had left those other men in the room when he'd grabbed Sutton.

Men Kieran and Maverick went to "talk" to while I'd waited for Sutton to wake.

It hadn't taken much for the two men to spill everything from the first meeting with Garret and Zachary to hacking ARCK's servers. They told them about going with Zachary, Jason, Garret, and Aaron to North Carolina to help set up Einstein's "game" and how they hid out with Garret and Zachary in the Larson's bunker until they realized we were coming for them.

Zachary was there for obvious reasons, but Garret was there because Zachary didn't trust him not to go after Sutton. And because the men were Garret's employees and he had provided the bugs and tracking devices.

Zachary had planted a few of those bugs in Sutton's and my clothes when they had been sent out to be cleaned. They had also implanted a tracking device in her diamond-encrusted heels before she'd ever been moved to the first motel.

Heels Zachary knew she wouldn't go anywhere without because they were her favorite.

Those goddamn shoes.

They had also figured we would be monitoring Tennessee Gentlemen security footage, so they'd had the same two days playing over and over again, that way we would never know when people were coming or going from houses or businesses.

Like when Zachary moved from his bunker.

Or when the ambushes were set up at the nine houses.

Zachary, Garret, and his employees had waited out the entire thing from a house across the street. The men we'd killed in the ambush? They were the ones stacked like grotesque logs in the master bedroom.

All the men could tell Kieran and Maverick was they'd been ordered to wait outside afterward and that Garret and Zachary had been arguing about Sutton.

When Zachary had come out of the house nearly an hour later, he was alone and freshly showered.

We'd seen the master bedroom, we knew what he'd done.

In exchange for letting the two men go with their lives, Kieran and Maverick demanded they figure out a way to set up a meeting with the rest of the core Tennessee Gentlemen tonight.

They had.

Then Kieran had slit their throats.

After all, Aaron's idea or not, Einstein's game had only been possible because of them.

Voices echoed down the hallway leading to the Tennessee Gentlemen's meeting hall.

I thumbed the safety on my gun off before setting it onto the table and pulling the bandana up over the lower half of my face.

Maverick followed.

Just before the door opened, we settled back in our seats and waited.

I had to give the men credit—there were hesitations and missteps, but each held his head high and continued stiffly into the room, watching us carefully.

Then again, they must have known we were in town if nearly half of them had nine men guarding their houses from us less than twenty-four hours before.

Once the men were in and standing behind the chairs of the large table, situated so they were facing us, I said, "Clearly, we aren't any of your sons, and they won't be joining us." A rumble moved through the room, so I waited, allowing it to calm on its own before I continued. "It's pretty clear what you think of your women, which is why we're involved at all. See, we help women who need it, and a few of your sons weren't . . . appreciative of our help. They decided to act against us, kidnapping one of our own and leaving her for dead." I locked eyes with Sutton's dad, my jaw clenching. "And when one of your daughters was being raped and drugged and told it was normal, we were, once again, attacked for trying to help her."

The fact that not one of them seemed shocked or infuriated only fueled my own rage.

"To put it simply, we don't take well to being attacked. Bodies pile up when we are, and they aren't ours. We were told you do things a certain way, so we left you your sons' bodies for you to deal with."

At that, accusations and denials flew across the room and at me.

When the roar grew louder and the men started crowding closer, Maverick and I reached for our guns.

The room fell silent immediately.

Another similarity in our old lives and how the Tennessee Gentlemen ran their cartel: meetings were weapon free.

It was smarter that way.

Tensions and tempers flared all too easily.

Except, we weren't a part of the Tennessee Gentlemen, so we didn't have to play by their rules.

"Here's how it's going to be," I began. "You're no longer unknowns—hell, I'm not sure you ever really were, but that isn't my fucking problem to work out for you. Leave us alone, and we'll do the same. Come after any one of us ever again, we won't stop until every last one of you is in the ground—and trust that we know every person connected to the Tennessee Gentlemen by blood and marriage and payoff. And the guy next to you? You'll never see him coming."

A low laugh came from Maverick when sounds of surprise and shock went through the men when they noticed Kieran standing in the middle of them. Still as stone, arms folded over his chest, multiple blades resting against his arm and side.

Looking every inch the notorious assassin he was.

The men closest to where he stood began jumping away, pushing each other to get farther.

I set my gun onto the table and sat back in the chair.

"We'll give you three minutes to leave. If anyone is left lingering, it will be considered an invitation for open war on your already crumbling empire." I paused to glance at the watch that wasn't on my wrist, and said, "Beginning now."

"This is our hall," one of the men yelled in animosity.

Maverick lifted his phone. "Two minutes and fifty-five seconds. Two minutes and fifty-two seconds. Two—"

A few of the men took off running before the rest began scrambling and shoving each other away to get out the door.

Kieran stalked toward us, looking more irritated than lethal. "Someone pissed themselves."

Maverick didn't try to conceal his laugh as he stood and slipped his phone into his pocket. He'd never even turned it on.

"This fucking day." He sighed and tugged his bandana down. "Let's go. I want a normal night with Einstein. All the other bullshit can be dealt with tomorrow."

I followed them through the back door and to where Maverick's car waited.

A normal night sounded like fucking heaven after the last ten days.

But my normal had shifted, only to be ripped away.

She was safe, and she was *there*, but Sutton and I had never felt further apart.

And everything about that was wrong.

Forty-Two

Sutton

Lexi bounced around next to the couch, a plea already in her eyes before her mouth ever opened. "Can I eat with my Diggs? Please, please, *please*."

"You have to be gentle." It had only been a few days since he'd been hurt, which was something she kept forgetting.

She squealed excitedly before racing off toward his room.

"Gentle, Alexis," I called out, watching her closely as she continued running.

Ever since I'd woken in the resort suite, she had been splitting her time between Diggs and me. Even though she hadn't known any details of what had happened with Zachary, I knew she could sense the severity of it. She stayed close to my side, as if she knew I needed her near. She would be there for hours, but then, as if a switch were flipped, she'd get all amped up and begin bouncing around, saying Diggs needed company.

Her Diggs.

The man whose personality couldn't be slowed down, even by some bullets and shrapnel. But as much as he wanted to pretend he was fine, they could slow *him* down.

He was the reason we were still here.

This suite held memories I wanted to flee from, but he wasn't able to be moved yet. So, here we stayed.

The only difference from before was the atmosphere.

It was calmer. The heavy tension and arguments were missing, not that I was sad to see them go. Kieran had even made Lexi laugh. Granted, he'd been playing with knives . . .

I blinked quickly when Einstein sat at the opposite end of the couch, set her tablet on her lap, and said, "We need to talk."

That was one of the only things that had stayed mostly unchanged.

The tension was gone, but that was only because she hardly spoke to me.

When she did, it was clear her distrust had been replaced with dislike, and she was only speaking to me because she had to.

"Okay . . ."

"Do you have a preference in names, or can I get creative?"

The wicked smirk tugging at her mouth told me that, even if I'd known what she was talking about, I wouldn't want to let her get creative.

"What do you mean preference in names?"

She shot me a look from under her eyelashes before

setting her attention on her tablet again. "Despite Zachary no longer existing and a handful of the cartel being scared for the moment, they might decide they want vengeance later. Relocation is still the best option for you. So, name changes for you and Lexi. I'm getting all the paperwork and IDs ready so I can create everything as soon as I get home. Then we'll get the two of you on your way."

In a few sentences, she'd torn away the future I'd started to see. Taken even the possibility of it and crushed it.

I glanced to the side, to the spot against the wall Conor had claimed as his post.

Always nearby, interacting with everyone and polite to me but not the same Conor.

There was a sadness that hung around him that made me ache, and it bled from him as he processed what Einstein was asking me.

He looked ready to object, but then his mouth formed a firm line and his expression went void of emotion.

I wanted to beg him to say he didn't want me to go.

I wanted to go back and do everything differently. Tell him from the beginning about the plan to get Vero back. Not attempt to leave, even though I still knew in my soul it was what was best for him. Not break his heart . . .

Then it would still be Conor and me. Then the plan would still be the three of us together at the end of this.

Not Lexi and me with different names in an unknown location without him.

"I don't know." My lips parted as I tried to come up with names, but the only thoughts in my mind were of Conor.

How he had inserted himself into our lives so quickly

and had shown me what it truly meant to be loved and cherished and adored.

How he'd shown me that it was okay to be myself and drop the mask my mother forced me to wear.

How wrong a life without him would be.

"I'm sorry, I can't do this," I whispered, my voice thick.

"So, I'm allowed creative liberties," Einstein said excitedly.

"No, I don't want this," I snapped. "This isn't how—" I looked to Conor, choking back the rest of the words.

This isn't how this is supposed to end.

He was staring at me, but all I could see were flashes of him.

When he broke into the motel room that first morning.

That smirk on his face when he watched me fail during our training sessions.

The way he looked when I irritated him.

The fierce possessiveness when he made me his own.

The devastation on his face when he realized I was trying to leave with Lexi, and the *nothingness* that preceded the days of civil, but withdrawn smiles.

"Do whatever you want," I finally said as I pushed from the couch. "It doesn't matter."

I walked to my bedroom, unable to be near them any longer, and didn't realize until she started speaking that the door had shut on a delay.

"Doesn't look or sound like it doesn't matter."

My body tensed at Jess's unexpected arrival, but I continued toward the bed.

"What I want doesn't matter," I replied lamely.

For long moments, I lay there staring at the ceiling, but

then Jess climbed onto the bed and sat with her legs crossed so she could look at me.

"Okay, I'm no Einstein, so I might get confused if we keep going in this direction." She grabbed a small section of my hair and began braiding it, her eyes focused on that as she said, "I *will* tell you that Kieran and I were under the impression you and Lexi would be coming to North Carolina . . . for good."

A pang hit my chest, and I fought the urge to rub it. "Yeah, I think you missed some things."

"I haven't missed a thing except you deciding to still be relocated."

I didn't say that I didn't want to.

I didn't say that what I wanted more than anything was to be where Conor was—no matter the location.

I just lay there, trying to accept the hand I had dealt.

"It's for the best," I said minutes later. "Everything kept tearing us apart. The situation, our personalities, his friends, my secrets. Constant push and pull, fighting and clashing back together, like a brutal storm. But all storms die, so it was inevitable we would too."

"Is that really what you believe?"

"It's what I'm trying to convince myself of," I breathed. "It will make this easier if I do."

"I'll say this and then let you be alone," she said carefully. "Kieran told me why you were leaving the other morning. He also told Conor. I get it, I do. I'm pretty sure it's a female thing. The mob raises a special kind of breed. They are fierce and loyal, but they don't work the way we do. *Conor* doesn't work that way. It doesn't matter what you or Kieran say, he doesn't see you leaving as something that would benefit him, he sees it as you running from him and your relationship."

I drove my fingers into my hair and fought back the knot of emotion in my throat. "After everything we went through to get to the point we were at, he had to know that wasn't what I was doing."

Her head shook faintly. "Men like Conor will fight and fight and fight for you because he knows he can protect you and that he is who's best for you. Damn everything else. They won't walk away unless they've been betrayed. And then, despite whatever they feel, they'll keep a distance to protect themselves." She leaned closer and gave me a knowing look. "But if you don't fight for them, they'll *stay* away. Trust me, Sutton. I'm married to one."

She twisted on the bed and slid off it, looking graceful and sultry in a way only Jess could pull off, and then she walked away.

When she opened the door, she turned to glance at me, eyebrow raised in question and challenge.

Her mouth twitched into a grin when I climbed from the bed and started in her direction, my steps coming faster and faster until I was rushing through the suite to where Conor was talking with Kieran and Einstein.

Conor turned when I neared him, but I didn't stop or slow or think. I just jumped into his arms and crushed my mouth to his.

All I could comprehend was that I needed him. That I hadn't lost him yet, but the possibility could become a reality at any moment.

He caught me as if he'd been doing it his entire life. After a brief hesitation, his lips responded to mine, moving and searing and branding in a kiss to erase all others. And then he was moving, taking long, fast strides through the suite until we were back in the room and he was lowering me to the bed.

"Wait." I wove my fingers through his hair, holding him away. "This isn't how I should be doing this. I wanted to talk to you, but then I was running because I had this overwhelming fear that the next second would be the one I lost you, and I can't lose you."

His eyes searched mine as his thumb brushed across my cheek. "Nothing's coming for us. We're safe."

My head moved in a faint shake as I laid myself bare. "You shatter my defenses and encourage me to be who I truly am instead of an acceptable version you want to create and hinder. You call me out and push me harder and test my limits. You stole my heart when I least expected to fall in love—Conor, *that* is what I can't lose."

"I'm right here." He slanted his mouth over mine, capturing my lips in a soul-shaking kind of kiss while effortlessly rolling us so I was on top of him. One of his hands pushed on my back, pressing us closer together. His other hand cradled my face gently, guiding and deepening the kiss.

"I'm sorry," I breathed when the kiss slowed. "I'm sorry for Diggs and for Einstein. I'm sorry for hurting you. I'm sorry for everything I kept from you. I'm sorry for trying to leave . . . I thought it was for the best." I sat back and pressed a hand to my chest when my voice came out strained. "People were getting hurt, and your relationships with your family were stressed and breaking because of me."

"They're family, Sutton," he said deliberately. "We're going to fight. They'll be there no matter what we go through. But I can't stop you from taking yourself from me. I can't hold on to you if you've already decided to walk."

"It was the last thing I wanted," I admitted. "I was only able to because I knew it was best for you."

"That isn't how this works," he said immediately, confirming what Jess said earlier. "You need a minute before you're ready to argue with me? *That's* when you walk away, but not out the door—especially with Lexi and a bag. That's a hard limit for me."

I curled in on myself, pressing my forehead to his chest as his emotions from that morning flashed through my mind. "I'm so sorry."

His large hand made lazy passes up and down my spine. When he spoke, his voice was gentle but firm. "You walk out, it means you're done with me or you can't handle my life anymore. Understand?"

I nodded slowly and let him lift my head so he could search my eyes. "How do we get past this?"

"You tell me what you want," he said easily, as if it were as simple as that.

"I want you."

His bright eyes darkened with hope and desire and need, but I wasn't done.

"I want to be wherever you are. Be loved and protected by you, pushed and encouraged by you. I don't want to change my name because you have this way of saying it that makes my entire body come alive. I want Lexi to know that I love you. I just—"

Conor sat up, capturing my mouth with his and swallowing my surprised whimper.

His hands gripped and tugged, pulling me closer.

"Say it," he begged, nipping teasingly at my bottom lip.

The corners of my mouth twitched up. "I love you."

A laugh climbed up my throat and got lost in our next kiss.

"I love you. I love you," I whispered against his lips.

He pulled slightly back, his stare bouncing over my face before resting on my eyes. "Nothing could make me stop loving you."

I rested my forehead on his and lightly dragged my fingers through his beard. "Even after everything?"

"If your judgmental attitude didn't push me away, I don't think anything could."

I dropped my head into the crook of his neck as a full laugh broke free. When I faced him again, his eyes were light and dancing.

"I just want a life with you," I whispered. Fearlessly. Boldly. Without reservation.

"I can do that."

Our next kiss began slow and quickly built.

Consuming.

Pushing and pulling.

Fighting and clashing.

A beautiful storm that had no ending.

Epilogue

Conor
TWO YEARS LATER

As soon as we set foot inside the Borello house, Lexi tore off after Diggs, bright laugh echoing through the halls as she chased him.

Sutton twisted so she was in front of me, walking backward in the direction of the room we occupied during the times everyone stayed here. A mischievous grin tugged at her full mouth.

"How long do you think we have?"

"In this place?" Where a dozen other people—including kids—already were, or would be soon?

But, Jesus, for this girl, I would find a way to give us forever.

I dipped down to steal a slow kiss. "Let's go."

She pushed up onto her toes when I started pulling away, making the moment linger a little while longer before gripping my hand in both of hers and heading to our room.

I pulled her close to my chest as we neared the door, teasing her neck with faint kisses and whispering things I planned to do to her, only for it all to stop when we rounded the doorway and found the room missing something crucial.

Sutton's fingers paused in my hair before her arm fell heavily. "Where's the bed?"

"Fucking Diggs." I released her and stalked through the house, shouting for the twin I was about to kill.

I found him in the kitchen, tossing stuff from the refrigerator to Lexi, who sat on the island, giggling the entire time.

"We're making monster sandwiches, Dad!"

For that brief second, my irritation fell away.

Everything had the first time she'd called me that, and everything continued to.

I hooked an arm around her and pulled her toward me to kiss the top of her head. "Not too big, Lex. There's gonna be a lot of food tonight."

"They have to be the biggest," she said with a roll of her eyes. "They're called monsters."

I flicked her forehead. "Don't do that."

She gestured to Diggs. "It's what he did when he said it."

I shot him a glare that promised pain for so much more than this conversation.

He shrugged, arms weighed down with ingredients. "Dude, it's true."

"Our bed is gone," I said through clenched teeth. "Not just the mattress, the entire thing."

He scoffed. "What do you think I am, an amateur?" He dropped the contents in his arms to the island, then straightened with a satisfied smirk. "I learned long ago with Lily that once the baby bump starts popping out, beds get moved. Never made that mistake with one of the girls during their times of need since. No one misses sleepovers for anything."

I dragged my hands over my face, groaning as I did. "I'm sure I'll be thankful for that later. At the moment, I fucking hate you."

Lexi flicked the side of my head. "Don't say hate, it isn't nice."

Diggs held up a fist toward her, but he never stopped looking at me. "Damn straight. All about the love in this house."

My eyes narrowed as I pushed away from the island. "Lexi, normal size."

"Biggest ever," Diggs whispered.

"I heard that," I called out but kept walking.

Ever since I'd come back from Tennessee with Sutton and Lexi right by my side, the three of us had *sleepovers* in the main Borello house once a month, without fail.

At first, we'd all pitched in, giving Diggs the forts he'd given everyone else for years. Once he was back to getting around the way he used to, he'd gone back to setting them up with Maverick.

When the twins worked together, there was no stopping them. They went all out every time.

Lexi loved it, and it had ensured Sutton got to know everyone, and them her. We were all together constantly, whether at the ARCK office or getting together to eat, but Sutton had quickly fallen into a routine of just watching everyone during those times. It wasn't until the first sleepover that she started opening up to people other than Jess and Kieran.

Not that I blamed her since Dare's first words to Sutton had been, "So, you're why we almost lost Einstein."

Then Einstein showed up at our house in the middle of the night a couple of months after our return, sobbing, and went straight for Sutton, pushing me out of the room as she did.

When I'd called Maverick to figure out what was going on, he'd said, "It's Einstein, man. Bad shit happens, she pushes it aside and lets it consume her until she deals. She's dealing."

Those two had been inseparable since.

Somehow, the friendship worked with Sutton's attitude and Einstein's harsh way of talking to everyone.

They were even due three weeks apart.

More rebels to add to our growing family.

Kieran and Jess had just found out they were expecting a second, and I hoped this one was a girl as wild as her mom. Because their first had been the calmest, most controlled kid from the day he was born.

Barely cried and studied you with sharp, knowing eyes. When he started crawling, he would appear beside you. Once he started walking, it only got worse.

Little shit was just like his dad.

And Kieran fucking loved it.

As for *my* family . . . we'd bought a bigger house since I was no longer living alone and then had gotten everything they needed to go through life again.

Birth certificates, social security cards, IDs, background

stories. Only their last name was different, and six months later, we changed it again to mine.

And there wasn't one damn thing about our marriage that wasn't real.

Sutton was mine—she always would be.

Just as Lexi was officially my daughter. We'd done that legally, not through Einstein's creations.

Lexi was in school and dance and had an attitude that rivaled her mom's, and Sutton was working at the salon in town. Every night, she walked into the ARCK office, exhausted and with the biggest damn smile on her face. And every night, that smile reminded me that this was the life Beck had always wanted for us.

It was why he and Kieran had worked so hard to pull us from Holloway.

So, we could have this.

Work we were good at and passionate about.

Kids running around instead of being hidden away on the backs of properties. Our women living their own lives, pregnant, and not having the constant threats to them or our unborn children hanging over their heads.

I just wished he'd been around to enjoy it.

As soon as I made it to the bedroom, every frustration disappeared.

I stopped in the doorway, hand gripping the frame, and just took Sutton in.

Sitting cross-legged on the couch, scrolling through a list of names on her phone I knew she'd already been through a thousand times.

Smooth skin and curves that fit perfectly against me on display.

She'd changed into one of her satin robes and left it

open, revealing nothing more than her lace bra and underwear, and the most perfect bump in the world.

When voices echoed through the house, I stepped into the room, shutting the door behind me and twisting the lock. "You're beautiful."

She set her phone down and lifted her head, her bottom lip caught between her teeth. Blush crept up her cheeks as she leaned back against the arm of the couch, the sight a perfect contradiction. All shy looks while begging me to look, to come closer.

I pulled my shirt over my head as I closed the distance between us, dropping it onto the floor a moment before I placed my hands on either side of her. I bent to press a kiss to her stomach, then captured her mouth for a lingering, unhurried kiss.

"Bed?"

"Diggs took it for the fort." I passed my lips across hers once more, trailing my knuckles against her five-month bump as I did. "Because of this."

A hum of acknowledgement sounded in her throat. "Thoughtful."

"Not right now."

Her fingers dragged through my beard, gripping and pulling my face back to hers.

Her lips brushed against mine when she whispered, "We have a perfectly good chaise right here."

I gripped the sides of her underwear and started pulling them down. "For everything I wanted to do to you, I need that bed."

"But think of what a man the likes of you could do to me right here."

"The likes of me?" The question was pure tease. I

nipped at her bottom lip and reminded her, "You married the likes of me."

"It was the beard," she said breathlessly as I stretched her legs out and finished removing her underwear.

A rumble of a laugh sounded in my chest. "That right?"

"And the tattoos."

I parted her legs and trailed the tips of my fingers up her thigh, savoring every part of her reaction when I touched where she was ready for me.

Her soft gasp. How she arched away from the couch. The way her eyelids fluttered shut only to open again, revealing eyes filled with lust and need and love.

She pulled me closer, her lips brushing mine with each breath.

Teasing.

Pleading.

Driving me crazy and making my blood pound its claim with each beat of my heart.

Mine, mine, mine.

Just before she took control of the kiss, she whispered, "It was you."

The End

Look for more *Rebel* novels from Molly McAdams!
Lyric
Lock

Coming Soon . . .
The Brewed Series

From New York Times bestselling author, Molly McAdams, comes a new, captivating series! Each stand-alone focuses on one of the Dixon boys—the hottest bachelors around. What everyone doesn't see is the strain threatening to destroy their family and their parents' dream permanently. Based in a small, country town, the Brewed series is filled with tension, excitement, and passion—feuds will transform to romances, and chances will be given again in true McAdams fashion.

Made in the USA
Middletown, DE
02 June 2019